Shadows of Seduction

THE BOTTOM LINE

PT 2

Kenisha "MIAMI TIP" MYREE

THANK YOU

First, I'd like to thank God for this opportunity to create and share my stories! Secondly, I'd like to thank everyone who has supported me thus far and patiently waited all this time for part 2 of my baby: "THE BOTTOM LINE!" It's because of each and every one of you that I can live out my dream as an author and I truly appreciate that. Lastly, I'd like to thank my family and friends who understood when I had to lock in. Those of you who didn't take it personal when I couldn't attend certain functions. Those who kept pushing me even though they didn't understand the vision. Trust me, it's all a masterpiece coming together and I am most grateful that I get to share it with you all piece by piece.

THANK YOU!

Kenisha "MIAMI TIP" MYREE

ISBN: 979-8-9908945-0-1

TABLE OF CONTENTS

1

01

BIA

"Bianca, get your ass down here now and clean these dishes."

Dad was always having me do something. It was like damn, why can't you do it? I hated it when it was only him and me while Mom had to work at night. She usually left at 8 p.m., came home at 8 a.m., and then he would leave for work at 7 a.m. The entire time Mom was gone, Dad called me for every damn thing. I never understood why he was so hard on me. When Mom was home, he was a lot nicer and less needy.

One night, Dad called me downstairs to massage his feet.

"I know you may think I'm hard on you but I'm molding you into the perfect wife. The perfect wife caters to her man's every need. Therefore, I ask you to do everything so that you're already used to it and not like your mama!"

I didn't know what the hell he was talking about. I didn't even have a boyfriend yet. Mom always made it known to worry about books now, and boys later. So, I don't know why the hell Dad would think I needed training for a husband.

"Your funny looking ass better be ready to cater to your man cuz that deer in headlights look you got may not cut it."

He would always remind me that I was funny looking. I despised it when he compared me to an animal. Mom would always say I had the biggest, most beautiful eyes, yet it was hard for me to believe her.

"Mom, why do you have to work so much?" I whined to her one morning when she came home. "I hate when it's just me and Dad. He always makes me do all the work while he watches TV or talks on the phone."

I was always truthful with her about some of the things that happened when she was gone.

"Baby, give me two more months and I promise you I will have you out of this house and it will be me and you."

I never told her what Dad's plan was with me because I knew it wasn't right and my mom would go crazy. I trusted what she said. Two months and we would be gone.

That's exactly what happened. We were out of that house, away from my dad. Mom cleared all our stuff out of the house and we left one day while Dad was at work. I didn't know why we were leaving but I didn't care. What I can say is, I never saw or heard him disrespect Mom. They barely talked and when they did, it ended in an argument.

Most of the time, Mom would avoid him altogether. Maybe he was taking his frustrations out on me. On her days off, we went to Aunt Kathy's house and stayed until Dad had to work the next morning. One night, I overheard Mom and Auntie talking.

"I'm so glad you decided to finally leave that controlling motherfucker. I can't stand him. Always wanting things his way and complaining when they're not. Meanwhile, he ain't even the damn breadwinner. Then has the nerve to put his hands on you! Now, I couldn't believe you stayed all those times. But whatever, you left now and that's all that matters. Got your daughter out of that hellhole!"

By the time I was nineteen, I was ready to be on my own. I had a little job at a local sneaker store. I saved every dollar I had. It was quite easy, being that I still lived with Mom, and she didn't let me pay any bills. I tried to help but she didn't want it.

Every chance she got; she would preach. "Focus on your schooling to get yourself in a position where you will never settle or need a man."

Once I moved out on my own, I had to damn near slave for bills. I was starting to realize living with Mom was the better option. However, her new boyfriend consumed a lot of her attention. Therefore, I had to work damn near fifty hours a week to pay bills. Adulting was not what I thought it was gonna be. Lacking a life outside of work was truly depressing.

One night I said, "Fuck it, I'm going out!"

I googled a couple of places in my area, and I was intrigued by the name "PUSSY CATS," an adult entertainment venue. I wanted to see what it was about. I got cute for the night and headed out.

Outside the club was slammed with cars and anxious patrons. I couldn't believe it. When I finally got to the front of the line, the security told me, "No females allowed without a male escort."

What type of shit is this? I thought to myself. That's when a guy stepped up in front of his friends and said, "She with me."

I quickly looked up and saw this dark chocolate man. He was okay looking and dressed pretty decently, so I didn't mind. He even paid my way.

"What's your name?" he asked when we got inside. Apparently, he was buying bottles, so they led us to a section.

"Bianca but everyone calls me Bia."

He smiled. He was actually cute.

Now this was my first time in a strip club, but I couldn't let it be known. I was really amazed at all the shit going on. There was a plethora of fine ass naked women everywhere. The stage had two performers on it doing some acrobatic ass shit, which was making men and women alike throw hell of dollar bills at them.

One performer caught my eye. From what the DJ announced, her name was Dream. Boy, was she a dream! Her body was perfectly shaped. Her hair and makeup were flawless. Although she had a regular hot pink two-piece bikini on, it was the way she moved seductively with confidence around the stage that had everyone in a gaze. I admired that she could command such attention. I think everyone felt like me, like we were the only ones in that room getting her attention. She was gorgeous. I noticed how she didn't even get naked like the others, and she still got paid. When she was done, she had a garbage bag full of money. I wanted in!

The guy who got me in, Jefe was his name, ended up being real cool. His friends as well. They ordered liquor and we began vibing, having a good time. Next thing I knew, Jefe was pulling out stacks of money from a bookbag he had.

First, this man didn't even look like he had that amount of money. Like he wasn't dirty or nothing; he was real simple in oversized jeans and a white tee. Nonetheless, he ended up giving the waitress twenty thousand for ones. I'd never seen twenty thousand dollars. So, to sit there and watch him get twenty thousand in ones for strippers helped me make up my mind. I was applying for a job at PUSSY CATS the next day!

Now my body wasn't like Dream's body, but I wasn't that far off. I had a little baby fat. Nothing major though. If I worked hard enough, I could save up to get my body like Dream's.

Jefe had a couple girls dance for me and his friends, and he gave me two thousand in ones to throw. I so desperately wanted to put the money in my purse, but I didn't want to seem like I wasn't used to nothing. After a while, I couldn't stomach it anymore. Those girls were getting paid to be fine and have fun. There I was not knowing how I was gonna pay for my Burger King on lunch break tomorrow. I had to go home.

Jefe expressed his dislike of me leaving. "Damn shorty, you not having fun?"

I told him I was, and I thanked him, but I let him know I had to work the next day. We exchanged info and I left.

Once I got home, I couldn't sleep thinking about "PUSSY CATS." There was no way it was that easy to make money out there. The next day I didn't go clock in at my job. I was going to get hired at PUSSY CATS, then I was going to take my last little bit of savings and buy what was needed to start.

I was hired on the spot. Although I was a nervous wreck, it went pretty well. They made me do an audition where a lady they called the "House Mom" and two male managers watched my non-dancing ass twist around the pole. I had no idea what I was doing, so I tried to imitate everything I remembered Dream doing.

The first song I was fully clothed, the second song they wanted my top off, and the third song completely naked. Thankfully, I was an avid kitty waxer, so I was fine. However, to bare my full asshole in front of these people was nerve wrecking. Apparently, I didn't do too bad because when I was finished all I was asked by the house mom was, "You getting your hair done, right?"

I assured her I was, filled out some paperwork, then left. I took a trip downtown where most of the stripper stores were. I copped a few outfits

I thought were cute and some shoes. Then I went to get my hair done. Due to my budget, I had to get a ten-inch bob. I went home and practiced anxiously in the mirror until it was time to "go to work."

My first few nights at PUSSY CATS went fairly well. All I did was watch the other strippers until I could maneuver on my own. Beginning to work in a strip club, you kind of gotta figure shit out on your own because nobody is taking time away from THEIR money to teach YOU how to get money. Unless you get lucky and find a partner. I didn't have that, so I had to watch and catch on quickly.

I quickly learned to charge the customers ten dollars a song and twenty dollars for lap dances. Then it was a hundred dollars to go in the back plus fifty dollars a song. I already knew I wasn't going in the back... ever! I didn't like how the girls or the customers who went in or came out of there looked. A bunch of tricks and hoes. I wanted to dance, get my money, and go home. Nothing extra.

I was making decent money for the first few months. Hell, it was way more than I was making working a job. So, I was able to do a little more and had a little more time to spend with my mom. I would give her like a few hundred dollars once a month and help out with what I could. Mom and her boyfriend were doing pretty well. I was happy that she was happy and that's all that mattered.

Eventually, I told Mom what I was doing.

"You like that?" she asked quizzically.

I told her all about the life, how I actually did like doing it, and the benefits it came with.

"I want to get my breasts done," I revealed to her.

I explained how it wasn't because damn near every other stripper had their breasts done. It was to help boost my self-confidence. Yes, I liked my natural breasts, but they weren't as perky as I would have liked them to be.

Mom gave me her approval and within a few weeks, I was walking around with my two big new pretty homegirls. My confidence rose and you could see it in the way I walked, especially at work. Therefore, the money started coming in a little more. I was no longer shy or scared to walk up to a nigga afraid he would tell me no.

One night it was kind of slow and in walked Jefe and his crew. Now we had been texting here and there, but not enough for me to be sure he remembered my face or anything. So, I gave them a few to get settled and then I walked over to say hi. He did a once-over, grabbed my hand, and made me do a three-sixty spin.

"I don't remember you being this fine the last time I saw you. Why you ain't tell me you dance?" he asked.

"Honestly, after the time we came here when we met, that's when I decided to start dancing the next day," I admitted.

We had a small convo and he ended up drinking and getting ones. Before the night was over, I had made five thousand dollars from Jefe. Not such a slow night after all.

Before he left, he made me promise we would be in touch more this time around. I would text him from time to time only for him to sometimes respond a day later. After a couple of times of that, I figured he must have a girlfriend or something, so I left it alone. He would text if he wanted to keep in touch.

Eventually, I ended up meeting this guy at work who had come in a couple times and made a movie on me. I'm talking 'bout thunderstorms of money, on just me. He was a dope guy, but he was fat. I think his swag overrode all the flaws. He wasn't an ordinary fat guy; he was a boss in every sense of the word. We started going out and getting to know each other. It was going better than I thought it would.

Turns out he was a scammer; that's what funded his lavish lifestyle. Fatboy, that was his name, had top of the line everything. Clothes, cars, jewels; you name it. Everything we did was next level shit. Restaurants were nothing but five stars. Clubs were nothing but top tier and the pull up game was strong. So, me, him and his entourage was always hopping out nothing but the finest looking the flyest. It wasn't long before everyone knew we had a thing.

I really started catching feelings for Fatboy. However, soon I started seeing that everything wasn't really what it seemed. After asking many times why we never went to his house, I soon found out he was living with his mama in the hood. That didn't sit well with me. Like how was he dressing designer down, driving foreigns, and sleeping at his mom's house? Coming in the club throwing thousands but his affairs weren't in order? It all rubbed me the wrong way, but we were still talking because I needed them coins!

Nevertheless, I put it in my brain to fall back from Fatboy and no longer let my feelings get deeper. After a while our situationship started to die out. When he would come into the clubs, he no longer made me his priority and he would be dancing other girls. What blew my mind was how happily he was throwing away all that money and how he made it his business to be the center of attention, but he was living with his mom damn near in poverty. Not real poverty but the way he was living did not match the persona he put on in the clubs. Like he really thought he was making me mad or jealous when, in all actuality, I was disgusted.

"Bianca, this won't last forever. You need to have a plan in motion," Mom preached to me.

She was constantly preaching to me, and I loved it. She was right, and I assured her that I was going to make sure I put my money and time to good use.

One night, I randomly got a call from Jefe inviting me out to dinner. He told me he was picking me up at nine and that it was a surprise where we were going. I had nothing else to do, so I accepted the invitation. I wanted to make sure I was fine as hell. Thankfully my hair was already done so I only had to get my makeup done. I settled on this yellow knee-length dress. It was giving TROPHY!

I expected him to pull up in something nice but not a Lamborghini truck. Oh Lord, here we go again. Another nigga putting on while his mama barely got gates around her house and the AC hardly working. At this point in my mind all I was thinking was, *I'm tired of these cappin' ass niggas. Since I'm dressed, I can't turn back now. Might as well go get this free food and hookah and bring my ass back home, then block this nigga.*

I got in and we had small talk on the way to the restaurant. Shortly after, we pulled up to an upscale rooftop called "QUEEN." I had heard about it but had never been.

It was killing me, so I had to ask. "Is this a rental?" I blurted out as we walked away from the valet and into the restaurant.

To my surprise Jefe laughed at me. It was a laugh that made me feel stupid for asking.

"Yea, you used to a lot of other niggas but I ain't them. That's ONE of my cars, girl," he answered while continuing to laugh.

Once inside, he ordered a bottle of wine that we sipped slowly. When the wine started hitting, the conversation started flowing more effortlessly. We asked each other the normal questions: age, where you from, what you do, what you do in your spare time, etc. He was younger than he gave off. He was twenty-five and into real estate investment. He had one child that lived with its mother in another state.

He also revealed that he had a long-time, live-in girlfriend. It wasn't a reveal since I already kind of felt it. I was glad he didn't hold that info back. I wasn't tripping being that I didn't know where this was headed. We enjoyed the rest of our night and ended it after the restaurant because he had to get up early.

Before I got out of the car, he let me know he wanted to see me again ASAP. I really enjoyed his company that night. He was the total opposite of what I expected.

Over the next few months, we kept in touch by calling or texting each other. Since he had a girlfriend, I really was following his lead.

In the meantime, I was working and stacking my money so that Mom and I could make some major moves. What the moves were? I didn't know but if and when we decided, I wanted to be ready.

One day, I was shopping in the mall and distracted by my phone. I ran into this guy. When I looked up, I looked into one of the most handsome faces I had ever seen.

"Excuse me," I said softly.

"Na, excuse me, cutie," he responded. I was blushing, and I was kind of embarrassed. "Damn bay, them cheeks are redder than a rose! Glad to know I got that effect on you, but I hope you can see how red my cheeks are because of you!"

He stole my heart right then. We exchanged info, and then I continued my day.

It had been a few days, and I couldn't stop thinking about Anton. *Why hasn't he called me yet?* was all I could think as each day went past with no call or text. Finally, after about a week, I got a text from him. He asked what I was doing.

"On my way to work and you?" I responded.

I never missed a chance to let a nigga know I was going to work. How they answered that determined to what capacity I was going to deal with them. It may sound harsh, but let's be real: time is money.

The conversation ended with him saying he was coming to see me at my job. Anton entered "PUSSY CATS" while I was onstage. Out of the corner of my eye, I watched him settle into a space at the bar. Once I got off stage, I went to freshen up and then made my way to Anton.

"What's up, baby? You looked good on that stage. I ain't know you had it in ya," he said.

We started vibing over a couple of shots. After a while, he put a stack of money in my lap.

"I know you're at work, and I respect the hustle, so this is for your time. Just wanted to see your pretty face. I'm about to head out. Hit me up when you leave."

And with that, he hugged me, then left. I thought it was a stack of ones in my lap, and to be honest, if it was, I probably would have never reached out to Anton again. However, it was a thick pile of twenties that ended up being twenty-five hundred. I was happy I could call it a night and take my ass home.

I texted Anton on the way home, and he asked to take me to breakfast. Why not? I had nothing to do, so I met him. This man gave me butterflies with how fine he was, and he was just the right amount of hood. After breakfast, I wanted Anton for breakfast, and I let him know that. So, we ended up at a hotel. That night, I fucked the shit out of Anton. The chemistry and everything was on point, so the sex was an extra bonus.

It had been a few months, and Anton and I were still going strong. Come to find out, he sold weed, so he made his own schedule. That allowed us a lot of time together. Soon we decided to move in together, which for me was perfect because I was tired of being an independent woman.

It wasn't long before I started seeing another side of Anton. He became even more attached. He wanted me home more often than not. It was like he wanted a wife, one who sat at home, cooked, and cleaned. So, that's what I started doing. While he was out busting moves during the day, I was holding the house down. Every now and then he wanted to show me off, so we would go out. I would get crazy drunk, come home, and fuck the shit out of him. Our sex was crazy. This nigga usually had me folded up in all types of positions.

That's exactly why I started going through his phone. Nigga wasn't about to have me not working, sitting in the house, and him out doing his thang. I really didn't see anything I couldn't overlook. What was a priority for me was keeping my man and keeping him happy. So, when I did go through his phone and saw him talking to a girl named "Tweety," I went above and beyond to make sure he never thought about no damn "Tweety."

One time he went out of town, and I was home bored. I decided to go to work. It had been a minute since I was on the top side. It was a Thursday so, I wasn't expecting much. I was sitting at the bar drinking when Jefe's ass walked in. I hadn't really been in touch with him since I met Anton.

"What's up stranger?" he asked from behind me.

"You're the only stranger in this conversation," I replied.

He laughed it off and greeted me with a tight hug. "I came here just to see this pretty face."

He could have fooled the hell out of me, and I told him that.

"I've been busy working. I had a few properties to get rid of and things of that nature, but I'm free now."

"So, because you're free, I'm supposed to up and be free?"

What was he thinking?

"I was thinking that," he blurted out.

The nerve of this nigga. I let him know I was seeing someone now and I couldn't sit around waiting on him. It was almost as if he didn't hear what I said because he had no reaction to it. Like he didn't care at all.

"How is you and your girlfriend?" I asked, to stir the pot a little. I got no answer.

He asked me if I wanted a drink, to which I said yes. We started drinking, and he told me to dance for him. He didn't throw any ones. This time he paid me in a bunch of tens and fives at the end. I didn't even question it; I was happy for the money.

"Can I see you tonight?" he asked.

The way I was feeling, I wouldn't have minded.

"I can't. I live with my man," I told him.

"I didn't ask you who you live with. I asked if I could see you?"

He never took his eyes off mine. I really wanted to see him. I had to figure out how I was gonna do this.

"I mean, I can see you, but I can't stay with you."

And with that, we agreed to meet at a hotel on Hollywood Beach.

I showered as soon as I got in. Next thing I knew, Jefe was in the shower washing me up. The way we were kissing so passionately you would have thought we were a newlywed couple.

When the shower was done, we made our way to the bed. Jefe pulled my towel off me, threw me back, spread my legs, then went to work on my pussy. I had no choice but to grab his head and give him everything he wanted.

When he finished, I returned the favor and gave him the sloppiest blow job ever, before he bent me over and stuffed his raw hard dick inside of me. Given his size and his overall appearance I didn't think the sex was gonna be good but when I say it was great, that would be an understatement.

"Damn, baby, I been missing out on this good shit all this time," he said as we were both catching our breaths.

I don't know if it was because of the good sex or what, but I was feeling a little different about Jefe. Soon as a text came through my phone from Anton, I was back to reality. What the hell was I thinking! He had a girl, and I had a man.

"I gotta go. I guess you will hit me up in the next six months as usual."

I was being sarcastic. He assured me he would reach out to me sooner. I got home just in time to lay in bed for Anton's FaceTime.

I was shocked that this time around Jefe was kind of keeping his word. He was texting or calling me a couple times a week. I was doing a good job of balancing him and Anton. Me and Anton's relationship was good; we had no problems. However, every time I went through his phone, here and there, there was another girl he was talking to. I never let him know I knew. I kept the house in order and had my thing with Jefe brewing. I didn't want to risk saying anything to Anton that would cause him to go through my phone and put me on pins and needles. Or worse, he might get annoyed and leave me.

As long as he was home when he was supposed to be, and nothing was in my face, I wasn't tripping. However, when he came home from his trip, I noticed he was acting differently. He would go outside more often for phone calls and started to come home later after nights out with the "homies." I brought it to his attention, and he blew up out of nowhere.

"What are you trying to accuse me of? If that's what you're fucking doing, be a grown woman and say that shit! That's your fucking problem, you're too immature and you ain't got shit going on. You think being pretty is enough, huh? You won't ever find a nigga willing to take you in like I do!" he yelled before storming out of the house.

He didn't return for two days. I called him a million times with no answer. I cried and slept the entire two days waiting for a response. I was also throwing up, I guess from anxiety.

Not too long after, Jefe ended up randomly texting me that he wanted to see me. Since my nigga was ignoring me, I went to see Jefe. We started our night in a white strip club drinking and having a good time. I could tell that he missed me because he couldn't keep his hands off me.

"Man, I'm tired of sharing you. When are you leaving that nigga?" he asked.

If I didn't know better, I would have thought he knew what was going on with me and Anton. "Sharing me? Hell, I'm sharing you!" I yelled out.

"You're not sharing me. What I got going on is situated. We're not on that. I need you to be mine," he said.

It would have been perfect if he didn't have a girl, but what did I look like sitting at home waiting on a nigga to be done with his girlfriend? But then again, that's what I'm doing now in a sense, except I was the girlfriend getting cheated on.

"I'm used to having shit my way, and all this waiting until you're free or when your nigga's gone, I can't do. I can take care of you and all your needs. I don't need no nigga's help."

Jefe knew what to say 'cause my heart was damn sure melting, and that night we made love to each other. He devoured every part of my body, and I loved it! To my surprise, we didn't wake up until checkout time. That wasn't normal, but I didn't question it. I knew my man was somewhere doing him, and I didn't know where Jefe's girl was, nor was it my business. I was enjoying my time with him.

When we finished eating breakfast, he walked me to the valet. "Look it's something about you I don't know what it is, but I didn't stick around this long for nothing. I fuck with you, and I want you to know I want you. So, make it happen," he confessed.

I could tell he meant business. Before he left, he dropped a stack of hundred-dollar-bills in my lap. "Go shopping, I want you extra fly next time I see you."

My ride home was confusing. However, it was back to reality. I began to call Anton. I had to have called at least twenty times. We were now going on day four of no call, no show.

I understood he was mad, but come on now, respect is due to a dog. I began to worry. This was in no way normal. I called his father and asked about Anton, and to my surprise, he hadn't heard from him either. I couldn't tell if his dad was telling the truth or not, but nonetheless, this was scaring me. Something told me to check the jail system. I searched the Tri County area, and nothing pertaining to anything new with Anton came up.

Later that night, I shockingly got a collect call from a detention center. It was Anton. I knew it had to be something like this. He was mad, but to leave home with no contact was extreme. Sad to say, I was relieved to have this call from him. At least I knew it wasn't him caught up with someone else or him trying to leave me.

Come to find out, Anton was busting a move and got caught. He was saying if I hadn't gotten him so mad, he would have been able to think straight. But because his mind wasn't right, he made a move he shouldn't have made. I apologized to him, although there was stuff in his phone indicating he was cheating on me. I told him that whatever we needed to do to get him out, we would.

I later found out Anton was convicted of trafficking and some more crazy drug charges. The bad part about this was that he was already out on bond for something similar. On his first court date, the judge denied bond. So, we were now in the process of retaining a lawyer.

Every lawyer wanted fifty thousand or more. I hadn't been working much, so whatever money I did have usually went to my mom. Therefore, at the present moment, I had nothing to help with. Anton had some money in a shoebox, and it was a little over fifty thousand, which meant he was gonna have to take every dollar he had and pay for the lawyer.

I noticed during this time I was throwing up more and feeling nauseous on most days. At first, I figured it was stress, but then I went to a doctor and found out I was pregnant. Four months to be exact. The timing was not good for me, but there was no way I was getting an abortion. I waited a couple of weeks, at least until we picked and retained a lawyer, to share the baby news with Anton.

"What? You sure that's my baby? I know your ass probably out there messing around with niggas and shit."

His response really threw me for a loop.

First off, yes, I did have sex with Jefe; however, there was no way it was his because I was four months pregnant. I would have had to already be pregnant, which meant it was for sure Anton's. There was no way Anton knew about Jefe, so his accusations made me angry. I couldn't even take it. So, I decided to remove myself from Anton's life and go ahead and start my journey to being a mother on my own.

All I needed was Mom's support, and I had that. I changed my number and moved all my stuff back to her house. During this time, I had to fall back from Jefe. I didn't want to tell him I was pregnant, nor did I want to have another man's penis in my belly with my baby. I avoided him at all costs. I also went the rest of my pregnancy without talking to Anton. There was no way for him to reach me either. I was happy that way, and my pregnancy was a smooth one. I welcomed my son, Romero, with my mom. He was a healthy, happy, bouncy baby. This was a love I never thought imaginable. I spent the first few months at my mom's house, but it started feeling overcrowded. My baby and I needed our own space.

Soon, I moved us out and into a one-bedroom apartment. I started school to become an architect. I knew this was the best way to get some insight behind it in hopes that my mom and I could invest. This was a long-time passion of mine. I was doing great. However, being on my own and being able to save to invest would mean I had to go back to work. We decided Mom would watch Romero at night while I started back working at Pussy Cats. Although I started back dancing, I vowed not to give up on getting my bachelor's in architecture. I assumed it wouldn't be long before I saw Jefe, and my intuition proved me right.

He walked in one night with his entourage. I was kind of hiding behind customers at the bar; I didn't want him to see me yet. I waited until he got settled in his section to make my way over, but I was interrupted by the DJ calling me on stage. I made my way to the top side and tried not to look Jefe's way, but I could feel his eyes piercing into my soul. Now I had butterflies and couldn't focus on my dance moves.

By the time my last song came, I saw Jefe throwing wads of dollar bills on my stage set. I made eye contact with him, and he motioned for me to come to his side of the stage.

"You gone act like you don't see me?" He smiled.

I giggled like a schoolgirl. It was unreal, the effect he had on me. Of course, once I dropped my money to the back, I went over to his section.

"Why you playing with me? Where you been? I've been calling you, no answer. I even came here a few times, and you weren't here. What's up with you?" he asked.

I admitted to him that I had gotten pregnant and had a baby; that's why I fell back. He was surprised but he realized there was nothing he could do.

"Shit, I don't know where the baby came out from, but look, it's time for you to stop playing. I still want you."

Honestly, at that point, I was like fuck his main girlfriend, she was gone have to share. Clearly our feelings for each other were not changing. Shit, if he was willing to play step daddy in exchange for me playing side bitch, then we were all good in my book.

Jefe and I had started becoming serious. Like real serious this time. He asked me what I wanted to do, and I let him know my plans to finish architecture school and my plans to build and invest. He was excited about that.

"You actually do have a plan. If you didn't, I was gonna second guess this shit," he admitted one night over dinner.

Every day I saw Jefe, it was like I got butterflies in my stomach, even after all that time. That night, after some drinks at dinner, we went to this lounge that was popping on the weekends. Jefe had all his jewelry on, looking fly as hell. Of course, I was dressed to impress. Body and face never declining. We both decided to take a piece of ecstasy and that shit kicked in fast. Our bottle was brought over by this fine-ass waitress, and her ass kept flirting with me. I could tell Jefe was intrigued, so I was flirting back. Had her ass taking shots with us and all.

Next thing I knew, I was getting my pussy ate in the penthouse of a hotel, while MY man was fucking her from the back. Sent her on her way right after we were done.

"Thanks for last night, baby. That was amazing," he said.

That was the first of many threesomes we had. I mean, shit, if his main girl wasn't gonna do it, I might as well. Plus, I really enjoyed watching my man take another girl to pound town. Every so often, we would enjoy an evening out and luck up on a threesome. We spent the next year getting closer. So close, I damn near forgot he had a main girlfriend until one day she contacted me through my email.

"Hey lil girl, I know you FUCKING my man." That's what the email read.

I don't know why, but my anxiety was high. Like who the fuck was she calling a little girl? However, I quickly remembered my loyalty was to him, not her. I didn't respond, and I let him know what happened.

"Yeah, don't answer her. She's catching wind of what we got going on because of my schedule and her popping up when I'm over here with you sometimes."

Jefe and I were getting more serious by the day. Our chemistry was unmatched. He spent enough time with me that no one would have thought I wasn't the main girlfriend. However, those nights he did have to go home, I couldn't help but wonder why he wouldn't leave her.

"Nigga, we fucking raw. You eating my pussy and in my bed at least four days out of the week. Why can't you leave her?" I yelled throughout many arguments, and his response was always the same. "I need some time."

As frustrating as things were, there was nothing I could do. I accepted him and his baggage from day one. Jefe started picking up most of my bills so I wouldn't have to work, but I figured since it didn't look like he was going to take me seriously and make me his only woman, I might as well start fending for myself again. I started working more and making myself less available for him. I started spending more time with my mom and my son. It wasn't long before he noticed or got wind of my drunk nights at work.

"You wanna be a hoe, don't you? I don't understand. I told your ass to focus on the architectural shit you got going, and I'll take care of the rest. How the fuck do you want me prancing around with a stripper? You know who I am? You know who my main bitch is? She would laugh if she knew this shit!"

This was the first time he reminded me I was not number one, and I didn't know how to take it. Honestly, my feelings were hurt. I could tell at that moment he knew he fucked up.

"Look, Bia, my bad, man. I apologize for that. You know how much I love you and wouldn't do nothing to hurt you. It's frustrating, man. I'm putting all this effort into you leveling up and you ain't getting it. You're stuck on what I got going on with her, which is understandable, but how do you expect me to leave an accomplished woman for someone who keeps running back to the strip club? You ain't even tryna find another way to make money until you finish school."

This was a lot for me because it was a bitter truth I had to face. Yeah, I was young, yeah, I was cute, but what did I have to offer besides pussy? His girl helped him create an empire, and although he wasn't completely satisfied with her, it was evident he wasn't leaving unless it was worth it. I took everything he was saying, and I started trying to find other ways to make money without going back to the club. I came up with opening a storefront that sold clothes for dancers. Since I was popular in that world, I knew what was missing, not to mention all the girls would support. I mentioned this idea to Jefe, and to my surprise, he liked it. He agreed to help me in any way possible to make things happen.

A couple months later, "Tease Me" storefront was opened, and business was booming. Jefe was also taking the time out to show me the ropes in the credit world and making the money for my business work for me without my own capital. Overall, things were going well.

One day, I was out food shopping when this woman walked up and stood in front of my shopping cart. She was extremely well dressed and beautiful. I smelled her before she even got close. I knew exactly who she was before she opened her mouth.

"Hello, my name is Sheree. You may not know me, but I'm the one who emailed you. Jefe's longtime girlfriend. I saw you push past me, and I knew it was God because only He knows I've been waiting for this moment. So, what exactly is it that you and Kendrick got going on?"

I couldn't believe she was brave enough to basically run up on me, asking about OUR man. I decided to play it cool but ruffle some feathers.

"Oh, I know who you are, Mrs. Sheree. Me and Kendrick are really good friends; nothing more, nothing less. I prefer not to mess with men with girlfriends, and being that you two are going through it, I decided to wait my turn. So, despite what it may look like, he is all yours. Now excuse me, I have to get back to my shopping," I said so nonchalantly.

I could see hate in her eyes. Thank God I still looked halfway decent to go food shopping. She didn't budge; instead, she decided to continue on.

"Oh yeah, that's nice. I mean, he did tell me you were nothing but a stripper that wasn't worth shit. So, I probably should have had more faith in my man, knowing that I would never stoop that low."

And with that, she stepped aside to let me push past her. Instead, I pushed my ass right into her face, and we were eye to eye.

"Ain't no way he could have told you I was simply some stripper when we sleep together damn near every night in my bed. Sometimes in his. The one I'm sure you've been in, at that nice plush house of his. You know the one with the king-size bed and the leather lounge chair in the corner. As a matter of fact, if you look under the bed on the left side, there are some handcuffs we be using. I'll let y'all figure that out though. Now, excuse me."

I strutted right past that bitch. I can't even lie; I was fuming on the inside. *Like, how could this nigga talk about me like I ain't shit? Like, he ain't 'round here doing all this shit for me just for a little pussy? And who the hell she thought she was, running up on me like that? Something ain't hitting in paradise if her nigga was checking for me the way he was.*

I got home and tried contacting Jefe to no avail. Over the next few days, I must have called Jefe fifty thousand times. He wasn't answering me. I was sick to my stomach. There was no way this nigga was deading me for that senior citizen. The only thing that kept me going those days without communication with Jefe was my son. One midafternoon, I got a call from a strange number. I wasn't gonna answer, but something said answer.

"Hello?" I answered, annoyed.

Then his voice was in my ear. "Baby!" I squealed.

"Man, don't baby me. Why the fuck did you do that shit,? I thought me and you were better than that?" he yelled into my ear.

What the fuck did this nigga mean, what I did? "First of all, nigga, why the fuck are you over there telling that bitch I'm nothing but a stripper? I'm not just a stripper when you're over here eating my ass, am I?" I yelled back into the phone.

"You see, man, you don't get it. You're steady rushing me to try and choose or say it's only gonna be you when you can't even see how dumb and gullible you are. You gave her everything she was searching for. You fell right into her trap."

I couldn't believe this nigga was blaming me. "Nigga, you over there talking about me to her, downplaying our situation, but you calling me gullible? Fuck you talking about, nigga, I'm defending myself. How the fuck does she know I'm a stripper? I didn't even know she knew who I was."

There was a long silence over the phone before he answered.

"Man, I never told her shit. Just like I don't tell you shit about her. Y'all over here being private investigators and shit. Y'all know it's because of y'all digging and searching. She found that out on her own and used that against you. And of course, it took nothing for you to turn on me.

"Look, I never told you this because I didn't feel like I had to. I thought you were a rider and a G, but I thought wrong. Man, me and this lady have been together for almost ten years. She helped turn me into a corporate nigga and helped me build my empire. The ways I was able to help build your brand was off her back and everything she taught me.

"Hell, me and this lady have multiple businesses that I invested in, in her name. House in her name, my cars in her name. Now, while I have love for her, I fell out of love a couple years ago and she knows that.

"Yes, she's beautiful. Yes, she's got a lot to offer. Yes, she showed me a lot. But that's just it. She works and works and works, forgetting about a nigga. That's where you caught me at; you had time. You showed me appreciation. You were also willing to listen and learn, outside of the fact your fine ass was mad fun and willing to fuck hoes with me. It was a win-win.

"You needed the right nigga to guide you and you were gonna be perfect. But I need a strong woman. A woman who won't be so easy to break, a woman who ain't easily swayed by whatever the fuck I got going on.

"Now, juggling both of y'all has been stressful as fuck, to say the least, but I was never fully complete with one of you. Where she lacked in fun and outgoing shit, you had it. Where you lacked in maturity and business, she had it. So, I admit a nigga was stuck.

"But now that this happened, she's threatening to take everything away from me. And you know what? I ain't putting up no fight. Before I put a woman in a position to threaten me again, I'll start all over.

"With that being said, man, I gotta let both y'all go. This shit's gonna hurt, but I gotta do what's best for me. I bought you that house you wanted because I was proud of the work you were putting in. I put your keys in an envelope in the mailbox with all the paperwork. Enjoy, lil mama."

I couldn't hear the dial tone over my sobs. I tried calling back a million times, but Jefe never answered.

It had been a while, and I hadn't seen or heard from Jefe. My baby daddy got out of jail and all. We agreed to coparent, although he was trying to get back with me. I don't know what made him think that was gonna happen after what I went through with him.

To say the least, things had been working well with the coparenting. I was still on course, working towards my architect degree, and that was also going well. My storefront was doing good, so I didn't have to dance as much.

One random night, I went to work and in walked Jefe. Just my luck! He had lost weight; he was dressed fly as hell. He looked so good; I couldn't believe my eyes. What were the chances? I was kind of embarrassed but then again, I had every reason to be proud of myself. So, fuck him and what anyone else thought about it. I decided not to approach him, given the way things had ended between us.

Now what I can say is that if he had paid attention to someone else, I think I would have been distraught. I still had feelings for him, but I was still hurt from the way he did me. However, over time, I am now understanding sometimes people gotta do things for their mental sanity. That was the excuse I fed myself to get over the way I was handed the short end of the stick in the situation. I also understand that some people come into your life to show you some things, whether good or bad. It's all lessons to help you in that moment. Not everyone is meant to stay in your life.

What I also realized is that regardless of how good you are to any man, they will value you as much as you value yourself. If you put up with certain things from jump, then that's how they will view you forever. I would check Jefe's girl's social media posts from time to time and I knew they were still together. Shit, they actually got married. She posted their fly ass wedding, and she would always post a new gift of some expensive ass diamonds or a purse. Hell, even luxury cars and more houses. I'm talking about big gifts that she wanted to show off. I couldn't even get mad or jealous because what is it having a man that can shower you with gifts but is not truly happy and will and has cheated on you plenty of times?

As for me, I appreciate everything Jefe helped me accomplish and I realize that thankfully, I'm still young and I'm a young boss on the way to greatness. Regardless of how my daddy tried to instill in me that I must stick by a man through anything, I now knew there had to be boundaries. I also knew my value. I'm not okay with sharing a man. I believe in true love and marriage and moving with intent and purpose.

With that being said, when Jefe called me over that night, I had to let him know.

"I came here for you," he said, while sipping his drink.

"That's funny because let social media tell it, you and your WIFE in a happy, loving household complete with gifts and a lot of love," I responded to him.

He pondered for a second. "I'm not completely happy," he admitted.

I already knew this. "I feel sorry for you, Jefe. The truth is you hurt me. For months I couldn't understand but, over time, I tried to make sense of it all and what I came up with is that I'm too much for you. Even though you tried to down talk me by saying I was immature, I was young. I was a woman still trying to find her way.

"Yes, I may have been immature, but I would have done anything for you. If you couldn't see that and it didn't amount to nothing in your book, that's cool. I thank you for everything but I gotta choose me. I wish you and your wife all the best and I pray I don't find myself in the same position as her. Feeling like I'm doing everything in my power to keep my man happy while the entire time his heart is somewhere else. You're selfish and I refuse to give you a second chance to play me the way you are playing her, and her emotions," I said softly before I downed the rest of my drink and walked off.

Some of these niggas look at strippers as women with no emotions. They try to play strippers like they ain't worth shit. Whole time they have a wife or a main girlfriend and a full relationship with a stripper on the side. As women, we cannot let a man devalue us in this game. Know your worth! It ain't always about the money. Sometimes having your dignity is THE BOTTOM LINE.

02

DESTINY

"Girl, your drunk ass ain't driving. We calling you a uber."

That was how most of my nights went after work. As long as Ibeen doing this shit, I didn't know why they always felt the need not to let me drive. That was my thought process during the fight for my keys, but the next day I was always thankful! I danced at a club called Mascara's in South Miami. The hottest club in Miami. Everyone you could think of passed through there.

I had been through damn near every phase of strip clubs in Miami. If it was poppin', I was there. First it was Diamonds; I ran it up in that shit. Then it was KOD aka King of Diamonds; I ran it up in that shit. Then it was QOD aka Queen of Diamonds; I ran it up in that shit. Then it was G5; I ran it up in that shit. Then it was the Office; I ran it up in that shit.

All those clubs were "Black" clubs, if you will. Some were high end, and some were hood. Nonetheless, I was dat bitch in all of them! I was different from all the other girls because I was a wild one. I had a lot of energy and I used it to climb up and down and flip off the poles. I was the show! I'm not sure how it all happened, though. Like being the most popular dancer and all that shit.

I grew up in a single-family home. Just me, my mom and my brother, Isaiah. My dad was a coward, so he wasn't there. Growing up I played a lot of sports. My mom didn't force me; it was what I wanted to do. As long as my brother and I were being active, she was okay.

As a teenager I got involved with a local dance group. I fell in love almost immediately. I went to school in a predominantly white school, so it was pretty much clean choreography. I ran away from home one time, which I did frequently, and came across these kids practicing at a park in a known hood on the other side of the tracks from where I lived. Being a light skin black girl in a white school was hard for me. It was like I wasn't one hundred percent accepted in either group. Black kids or white kids.

However, coming from the struggle, I was more comfortable with my black friends. The only thing that kept me from clicking with them all the way was that in the area where we lived, if you were black, that meant your parents had money. Obviously, if you were white in that neighborhood, you would be rich. My family wasn't either. My mom hustled and busted her ass so we didn't have to go back to the hood we had come from. So, I grew up not being totally accepted.

Therefore, I started running away every time my mom made me mad. It was a reason to take my frustration out on something or someone. One time, I ended up meeting a guy who was ten years older than me, so it was easy to run away to his house. His house was in the hood. I loved it. When he would be running the streets, I would walk to the park to practice with the new dance team I found. I liked their style more because it was more hip hop, and more booty shaking. Not to mention, I was accepted all the way! That was a good feeling. I could be myself. I didn't have to lie about why I didn't have the new Jordans, because guess what? Most likely none of us had them. This dance group by the name of High Voltage introduced me to the spotlight. Our group gained popularity because of our dance routines.

Our group was a boy and girl group. Now, some of our routines were a little raunchy but it was a way of life in South Florida. Over the time I danced with them, I began to get better and better. I got to the point where I was able to do solos. Only the good dancers had solos. That was where I became comfortable being onstage in front of a crowd all alone.

As time moved on, my mom and I went through a lot of ups and downs, but she was always there to support me. Every show we had she was there. Anything I needed she was there. I really loved dancing. I loved the attention. My dance group was popular, so we got extra attention. Our dance moves got better and better. I really knew how to dance when it was all said and done. It was never my goal to be a stripper, let alone the most popular one. My mom was going through hard times and I felt I needed to help. I didn't know how I was gonna do it, but I was determined to help my little family.

"Why don't you strip like me?" one of my homegirls asked.

I was completely shocked and damn near didn't know what stripping was. "Strip? What you mean?" I wanted to know more.

"I mean, think about it. We spend days getting dressed when we bored, to walk to the corner store and all the boys go crazy. Hell, that's how you met your man. And we still do it to this day. Just to get they numbers and see what we can get out of them. Imagine doing the same shit. Getting cute to go on a stage, be sexy and get paid for it? I be making like seven hundred dollars and shit when I go. We cute and young. You should try it."

It sounded good and all, but I don't know how Sam, my boyfriend, would take that. However, it wasn't like he was giving me extra money.

He would give me money for my hair and phone bill but that was about it. I guess he felt like because I stayed at his house when I left my mom's house, that was good enough.

Truth is though, it got to a point where my mom stopped chasing after me when I ran away. I think she got tired, plus she had my brother and was trying to keep herself afloat. Whenever I would go back home, I could see the stress on her face, and I could see the extra stress I was giving her. I felt bad every time I went home to see her struggling. I couldn't bear to watch it. I wanted to help. But working at McDonalds was not going to cut it. My little brother was getting older and he was starting to get into his dressing and his appearance. I didn't want him to feel how I felt in middle school. Something had to give.

One night I went to hang out at the little hole in the wall strip club my homegirl was working at and I must say it was a whole new world for me. See, my friend, Chyna, the one who introduced me to the club, she was fine even at sixteen. Plump titties, small waist, and plump booty. So, she kind of fit in with the more developed older dancers. On the other hand, I was just athletic. All I had was muscles. But I was cute, and I knew it.

I watched Chyna move from customer to customer and hit the stage here and there for the entire night. At the time, I couldn't tell if she was a rookie or not but thinking back on it, she ain't know how to dance a lick. The only other thing she had going for her, besides her youth, was her mouthpiece. Hell, in this game if you got that, you good.

Chyna explained to me how she bought a fake ID. She finessed some pimp man in the city where she was from; convinced him that she was gonna give him her money when she danced every night. So, he gave her the five hundred dollars to go to some guy and get the ID made. Of course, the guy who made the IDs liked her and they kept in touch. She explained I was gonna have to go Key West by myself and meet with him to get the ID done.

"I ain't gone lie, this nigga crazy looking but in a sexy way. I don't know how to describe it. Nigga got a slash across his face, but he got some nice ass teeth. He gone flirt with you, but baby, remember why you there."

We said in unison, "To get the ID."

I didn't know how the hell I was gonna get to Key West, but I had to get there. I was scared but wasn't no turning back now. I decided not to tell my boyfriend what I was gonna do. Hell, he wasn't looking out enough; there was no need for him to know. I left his house, and I knew he would think I went back home. In actuality, I went to stay with Chyna at her apartment she shared with her grandma in the city of Overtown, in an area they called the Slums.

Chyna's mom left her with her grandma for the streets at an early age and she never knew who her dad was. So, it was only her and her grandma, who was getting sicker by the day. That's why Chyna started hitting the streets to make quick cash so young. Chyna was tough. A sweetheart but tough. We had our street smarts and toughness in common. For a couple days I stayed with Chyna and her grandma in their small, cluttered apartment, trying to come up with a way to get to Key West.

One night Chyna came home from work and woke me up. "Bitch, I told this grown ass man I been talking to that you needed to get home to Key West tomorrow and that I needed a ride to drop you off. So, he gone pick us up tomorrow and imma ride wit' him to drop you off but I'm leaving to come back with him."

She saw fear and confusion on my face.

"Bitch, you know I can't be in that area too long since I finessed that pimp and I don't know the ID man like that so I don't want to be there long enough for him to call the pimp nigga on me. Look, you been here three days, no ride. Now I got you one, you just gotta get back."

I didn't even have a plan to get there. How the hell I was 'posed to get back? I thought for a few minutes. "I'll take the bus back."

She quickly glimpsed at me.

"I mean, what else I'm supposed to do? I need this ID. It's the bus or the train. By the time this nigga picks us up tomorrow, I'll know what imma do."

She shrugged her shoulders and started counting her dollar bills out of a garbage bag.

The ride to the Keys was long and boring. Her "guy friend" picked us up in a damn Chevy on 24s with bright ass orange candy paint. This nigga looked like he was our dad. Kept rubbing his hand up and down Chyna's leg. If it wasn't for the weed, I would have been very annoyed.

That morning, I woke up and walked to the store to get a bus pass and to look at the schedules. Lucky for me, there were only two buses I needed to take to get back home but it was gonna take like two and a half hours. I needed that ID, though.

When we got close, Chyna made the man pull over and we got out of the car to chat really quick.

"Listen, he gonna flirt. He may even want to fuck. Here is the five hundred so you can show him you cash ready and he know you mean business. Keep your eyes on the prize. I know the process to make the ID is about three hours. So, you should be able to catch the last bus home. When you get to our side, get to a pay phone and call me. Okay? It's right up this block, two houses before you see the beach, a little blue raggedy house with a Jamaican flag on it. Be safe. You got this. Your whole life gonna change for the better once you get this ID."

I listened to her intently, watched her get back in the car and they pulled off. I walked to the house she told me about and knocked on the door. The weird looking man answered the door.

"Hey, I'm Chyna's friend."

He looked outside the door both ways. "Where Chyna de?"

Guessing he was asking where she was, I replied, "She couldn't make it, so I came alone."

Now Chyna made me put on these lil ass shorts and a wife beater. So, my shape was visible and my hair was in a neat bun. When we got inside the dark, hot ass house, with blankets covering every window, I sat on the couch closest to the door.

"Wa ya name?"

I told him my name and he asked a couple more questions before he asked my age.

"Sixteen, so I need my ID to say I'm eighteen."

He licked his tongue slowly across his lips as he stared at me. I had to look away.

"Sixteen, aye? Come, let me see ya."

He motioned for me to walk to him.

With my eyes on the prize, I walked over to him, slow and sexy. I leaned in front of him, put my eyes to his eyes, and whispered, "I got your cash."

Then I leaned up, crossed my arms and looked down on him.

He picked up a Guinness, unbothered, and damn near downed the rest of the bottle. "What if me na wan cash?"

Being that Chyna had already put me up on game, I was one step ahead and I was ready. "What if that's all I got?"

I rubbed my hand across the scar on his face, sat down on his lap, and made sure my lil ass was on his penis. "See, I know you see this young ass and you want to ram your dick all in it but this pussy here worth more than that five hundred you want me to pay you for your ID."

I was about to play this shit all the way out. I had no idea about the turnout, but I wanted to get the ID and get the fuck back to the slums.

He pressed play on a little radio he had by him and some reggae tunes started to play. He offered me a Guinness, which I declined. He started directing my hips in circular motions on him.

"Chyna said it's a process to make this ID, so I'd like to get started."

He sucked his teeth and then grabbed another Guinness. He made me get up and stand in front of a white backdrop. He took three close-up pictures.

"Dance fa me na. Make me see ya likkle hips wine."

I looked at him like he was dumb. The face he gave back made me snap back into game mode. I turned around, bent over and looked at him from between my legs while moving my ass from left to right.

"You want this, daddy, don't you?"

He licked his lips, then sucked his fingers.

"Start the ID, then we can talk."

I watched him walk into the kitchen and start the process of making the fake ID. I stood where I was and acted like I was enjoying the music and dancing. I knew he was watching me from the side of his eyes.

Once he walked back over to me with his camera as he was rolling a joint, he said, "Get naked."

I was stuck. I didn't want to get naked. I didn't move. He circled around me slowly, rolling his joint, looking me up and down.

"Get naked." This time he said it more aggressively. "Make me see dem pretty titties."

I stepped in front of him, looked him in his eyes, and started to slowly wind my ass on his penis. I looked back at him and licked my lips. "Let me give you a lap dance first. So, you can enjoy while we smoke this blunt."

I wanted to stall him as much of the three hours that I could. "You want me to get you another Guinness?" I asked as he sat down while he finished rolling up. The more he drank, the better for me. I grabbed one for me also. I needed to loosen up to navigate this situation.

We started smoking and talking for about an hour. He told me a little about his life. Little did he know, I could have cared less. I was there for one thing only. I didn't even try to figure out if he was lying or not because it's like, who the hell was I? I didn't know that damn man from nowhere. Plus, he was a pervert. However, that hour went smoothly while he smoked and talked. Two hours to go.

He walked over to his ID maker station and checked on the ID. "Coming along good."

All I could think was Amen! I had to figure out what my plan to stall for the next two hours was gonna be.

He sat back down but now he sat on this lil raggedy ass couch closer to me. He rubbed his hand across my leg and stared at me. "Me wan fuck." He didn't blink an eye.

Scared was not the word. Maybe something like traumatized was the word. I had to toughen up and finish the game out until the end. I was in the third quarter at that point. I put my game face back on.

"I told you, you ain't fucking me for no five-hundred-dollar ID. And I brought the cash, so I don't want it for free."

He quickly jumped up and paced the small, lightly lit room. "*Hmmmm!*" He was rubbing his chin and the scar looked like it protruded more the madder he got.

He started asking me questions about myself. Like about my family, how many siblings I had, what school I went to, if I had a boyfriend and some more shit. I lied about every damn answer. I never even knew I could lie that much or that good.

Another thirty minutes passed. He sat near me again. This time he aggressively pulled on my shirt and said, "Get naked."

Play time was over. I didn't even want to test the guy with that look on his face. I stood up and slowly started taking my clothes off as he started to roll another blunt. He began staring at me once I was completely naked.

"Bend ova pon de couch. Me wan see ya likkle pum pum."

I was hoping that would be all. He turned the music louder and I did as I was told. He started smoking. I could tell from the smell and fumes in the air. I was as still as a mannequin.

He crept up behind me and I damn near jumped out the house, how scared I was. I wanted to go home to my mommy and my brother at that point. Why did I let Chyna leave?

He interrupted my train of thought by walking over to check on the ID. I followed him that time because I wanted to see with my own damn eyes what it looked like and how much longer I had to endure this mess.

The ID looked almost done. I could see part of my picture on it. Thank God. If I could only figure something out to hold off another hour. Think fast! I got it! I would make him drink another Guinness because his half ugly ass was already kind of twisted. Then I would act like I wanted to drink one with him. I would have to make him cum some way without having to have sex and then he would fall asleep. Then, I could get my ID and dip.

He started to undress himself and my plan disappeared.

"Lay down," he demanded.

Oh my God! I did as I was told.

"Daddy, why you rushing to get this pussy? Get me and you another Guinness."

He side-eyed me but he went and retrieved the bottles. I sat up to drink mine and he sat damn near right on top of me. He finished his quickly and then started eyeing my pussy. I felt so disgusted. But I put my game face on. I spit on my hand like I'd watched on pornos and I started playing with his penis. He immediately fell back and relaxed. If I could simply do a hand job and make him cum, I would never put myself in another situation like this again. Lord Please!

Sure enough, within two minutes, that weirdo came and it leaked down my hand. I was so disgusted, but I couldn't let it show. He told me to bring him a paper towel. I walked into the kitchen past the ID station in hopes of catching a glimpse while washing my hands. Almost done, yes! I washed my hands and returned to him with a paper towel.

He threw the paper on the floor, put his penis up, and mumbled, "You will be done in a few."

Miraculously, he knocked out. I sat quietly for thirty minutes until I mustered up the balls to creep to the ID station and get my shit. Now, I didn't know how to tell when all was said and done but it had been enough time and I should've been done.

So, I quickly grabbed it out of the water and threw it in my pocket. I looked at the weirdo and the loud snores let me know he was still knocked out as I made a dash for the door. I ran all the way to where the bus stop was. It wasn't a short distance, but I would be damned if that man tried to come get that five hundred from me.

While on the bus I studied the ID. It looked official to me. I couldn't wait to get to Chyna for her to check it out. I called her from a pay phone once I got off. So, she could meet me halfway, like she asked. Nobody wanted to be walking the streets of Overtown at night alone, especially not a young female. I went over every detail of what happened without noticing I was crying.

"It's okay. I know it's a hard pill to swallow but look at the bright side. You'll probably never see that man again. You on the way to making the most money you ever seen in your life. You can finally help your family out. You're not alone and it was worse for me. I actually had to fuck him because he put that fear in my heart. You're strong. Put it all behind you."

Just like that, I went to work. It felt so good being able to help my mama out. My mom was skeptical at first about what I was doing to be able to help. Well, it wasn't like I never helped before but not like I was now.

I would go visit them and before leaving, I would leave her the rent money in an envelope on the table. For a while she didn't question me until her curiosity got the best of her.

"What are you doing out there? I mean, you coming in all dressed. Nice hair and nails nice. Buying your brother everything he wants. Hell, paying damn near all our bills. Something ain't right?"

She sat me down one day as I was rushing out. I was prepared for that question. It took longer than I expected. I was about to be eighteen years old and with how I had been in the streets, you would have thought I could tell the truth. However, my mama still put that fear in my heart as if I was three years old.

"Mama, I work at McDonalds. I save my checks and plus, my boyfriend helps me out here and there."

I lied straight through my teeth. She wanted to believe me, but she knew better. I think that was one of the only times she felt some things were better left unsaid. With my mom and brother tucked away in Coral Springs with the white folks, it was easy to hide what I had going on.

Within a couple years of dancing, Chyna and I had gotten our own apartment in Pembroke Pines. Pembroke was a city that sat between Miami and Fort Lauderdale. Not too far from Miami, not too far from my family. Chyna and I were slowly climbing the exotic entertainment ladder. Things were coming together for us. We were finally able to help our families and better our situations with no worries.

Chyna and I were two peas in a pod. Two young hungry hustlers coming for everything that was ours! As my name started getting bigger in the game that meant more notoriety. More notoriety meant more money. I was the fans favorite and rightfully so. Besides my stage presence and my young tender body, my personality was what got everyone. I was the life of the party.

Chyna was lit in her own way. She was a pothead though; you know smokers tend to move slower and party differently. On the other hand, I had started drinking Grey Goose. I loved it! To think I went like the first six months without drinking, I should have kept it like that.

My first night drinking, a customer offered me a shot. Rather he demanded I take three shots, or he wouldn't spend any money on me. I looked at the eight racks he had on the bar, then said, "Let's do it."

I took the three shots back-to-back. No chaser, no ice, no nothing. I wanted to throw up and I think he suspected that before he offered me a Red Bull. I chugged it down and the cold drink soothed my throat. I loved the courage the liquor gave me. Not only did I make four out of the eight thousand from him, but I was mingling with customers in a way I never had. In return they were throwing money at me.

I went onstage and killed my set that night. It was like all my problems went away and I could enjoy myself with no worries. The feeling was awesome. That night, if a customer didn't offer me a shot, I was ordering them myself. By the end of the night, I had a total of twelve shots. You can imagine how much I was stumbling. I couldn't even make it to my car before throwing up all over the dressing room bathroom.

"Bitch, how much did you fucking drink?" Chyna yelled as she held my weave behind my head while I hurled over the toilet. Thank God, Chyna and I were sharing a car, so she drove me home.

The next day I woke up feeling like shit. It was unexplainable. My head was pounding nonstop. My throat was dry as hell. I was on and off the toilet all damn day and I had no energy. I thought I was coming down with a weird cold or something.

"You got a hangover, dumb ass. That's what happens when you drink too much. Not to mention, you a rookie. What the hell possessed you to drink like that?" Chyna asked while standing at the doorway of my room.

"Man, you know that man that used to always dance Dream and spend like 10K? He came in there and I so happened to be standing next to him. He told me to dance, then ordered eight thousand. Then he says, 'You want this money, you gotta take three shots.'

"Bitch, I wasn't about to let them eight thousand walk away from me. So, I drank them. Then when I was done with him and moving around, other people offered me shots and I ordered my own. I loved the way I was feeling. No care in the world. Hell, I was damn near walking up to customers like, 'This is a stick up! Give me all your money!' And they would."

Chyna and I shared a laugh. She explained to me the way I was feeling was normal for people who drank too much the night before. She told me her grandma said to take a BC powder and ginger ale. I did that and went back to sleep. I didn't know how long it would last but I wanted it to be over.

Later that night, I woke up refreshed. Back to normal and back to work. Once I got to work, I wasn't really feeling the vibe like that, so I started drinking. After three drinks, I began to relax and feel happy. I guess I was turning into my alter ego. Once again, I made more money than I could imagine. The liquor had me telling lies like the time I was tryna get my damn ID from that weird Jamaican guy. By the time the weekend was over, I had made twelve thousand dollars, so I went to bring my mom five thousand.

"Where are you getting this money?" my mom demanded to know.

Now she had been questioning me for quite some time, but it was never like that. I finally had to tell the truth. "I dance, Mom."

She looked at me with a confused expression.

"I strip."

Mom broke down crying.

"Mom, it's not that bad. I do it for us. Mom, to help you. To help Isaiah. I hate to see you stressed and struggling."

She cried loud and hard. After a while she stopped and intently looked at me. "Get out. You are a disgrace. You have been running the streets and going against my rules since you were a little girl. Not once did you ever apologize, and you think this stripper money can replace all those nights I sat up crying wondering where you were? All those hot ass days I went from tree to tree, house to house, handing out missing flyers? GET OUT and do not come back here."

I noticed my brother peering at me from the hallway. He began to cry as I walked out the front door.

Granted, I wasn't the perfect daughter. However, I'd been going through a lot emotionally since I was a kid, trying to be accepted. My mom worked too hard and too much to realize it. I don't think I had a lot of emotional support from my little family. I was forced to mature fast, so I didn't get swallowed up in the streets. I got my hustle from my mom, so why couldn't she understand why I was doing what I was doing? I only wanted to help.

It felt good leaving money in an envelope for her. It felt good relieving stress off her shoulders for once. I simply couldn't grasp why I was being shooed away. But fuck it. I went back to work. Every day I worked, no days off. Even if I made two thousand dollars, I went to work the next day like I made nothing. I couldn't sit at home thinking about my mom and my brother and not being able to talk to them. Working was my escape.

One of my coworkers saw the stress all over my face. "Girl, you seem stressed. Have a drink."

That drink led to five and it damn sure made my whole life better for the time being. The hard part was waking up the next day because I was feeling like shit.

"Girl, you didn't drink no Pedialyte or take any BC powder?" the house mom asked me upon my arrival to work.

They were not used to me not showing up to work for days straight at a time. I got back fully rejuvenated, ready to turn up once again. It was like turning up became a way of life. From the way it made me feel the first time I took shots; I couldn't believe it. I mean, when I drank, I made more money than the times I didn't drink. Plus, drinking helped me forget everything.

Besides work, my family was all that consumed me. It was hard. I even tried reaching out to my mom and she was still being stubborn. I was able to get on a quick call with my brother, only to hear how sad he was from not seeing me. That was killing me the most. I put all my energy into work. If I got too messed up from a hangover, I would sleep it off and return to work.

Chyna and I started becoming even more popular amongst the athletes and celebrities that passed through. That made all the local dope boys and scammers want us even more. Boy, did we have our way with them! We made sure to keep our bodies and style up to par. So, every time we stepped out to party, them niggas knew this was the big leagues.

Hell, most the time them niggas knew they had to pay us to take off work and hang out. So, it was a win-win for everybody. We got paid while making them look good. Possibly with a happy ending. Yea, I mean fucking!

I even had this big fat Spanish customer. His name was Hanky, and he was rich. But boy, was Hanky ugly. He would come into the club and spend at least 20K every time. He made his way around the club, messing with a few girls. I thought it was disgusting. He would tip me here and there when I got onstage and I would say thank you, but that was the gist of our relationship... Until one slow night.

He had come there with some friends after another club. There weren't many girls working so the familiar faces were me and Chyna. He had us dance for his crew. Of course, he got ten thousand singles. So, you know me and Chyna was hype. We started helping them drink their liquor and having fun. All I know is in the midst of all the turning up and money throwing I looked to my left and fat ass Hanky was staring at me.

He waved for me to come to him. I had to down two shots before I walked over. "Sup, sweetie, you over there looking sexy," he damn near whispered in my ear.

Now, I was tipsy but If I had to take one for the team, I had to get drunk. QUICK!. I made him order a bottle of champagne for me and Chyna. I started grinding on him extra seductively. He couldn't control himself. I felt his little ass penis, rock hard, poking me in my butt. It disgusted me. He wanted to sit off to the side and have a conversation. I downed the rest of the bottle.

When we sat down, he was rubbing his hand across my thigh and it gave me flashbacks of the Jamaican guy. Just like in that ID situation I kept my eyes on the prize and put my game face on.

"Damn, Daddy, all this time you come in here and you don't pay me no mind."

He began explaining how he felt like the girls used him for his money so he didn't like getting close to anyone anymore. What I wanted to say was "DUH!" but I kept my cool.

"Yea, I don't know why girls do that. I guess it be the broke ones. Cuz a bitch like me, if I don't like you, I DON'T LIKE YOU."

He ate it up! I'm not gonna lie, though. The more we talked, the more I saw how cool and smart he was. Turned out he had a nursing home business.

Soon came the question I knew was coming but I dreaded. "You coming home with me?"

A part of me was still disgusted but I guess the liquid courage kicked in. "I mean, I can, but I got bills to pay tomorrow."

I knew that big, fat, ugly nigga didn't think I was going home with him for free.

"I got you. Go get dressed."

Chyna and I picked up our money and went to the back. We talked about Hanky and how I didn't want to go. "Bitch, you know he good for it every time he come out. You better close your eyes and think of somebody else. Cuz when you wake up you know he gone bless you."

I went home with Hanky that night. We fucked. It was the weirdest shit ever. His thang was so little he couldn't even keep it in. The good part was it lasted five minutes. I was so grateful for that part that I even rubbed his big ass belly until we fell asleep.

The next morning, when I woke up, besides the hangover I had, I was disgusted. Thankfully, he had somewhere to be and left me two thousand dollars. I got the hell up out of there.

Hanky texted me all day every day and I had to play along. I would see him once a week and he would pay me well. It made my anxiety run up whenever that time came. I would get drunk as hell before I went to see him. I couldn't stop because, at that point, Hanky was paying for my Benz I was about to get.

One night I went to see him and he wanted me to suck his penis. I damn near threw up when he tried pushing my head down there.

Besides his thang being small, he was uncircumcised. I thought about all the bills I had and how much money I could put up for my mom and brother. I pulled that skin back and went to work.

With Hanky taking care of me for those weekly appointments, I started working less. It was like why work hard when I get an allowance, per say. Chyna and I started hanging out more, frequenting clubs on the beach and popping our own bottles. All the promoters respected us. All the niggas wanted us. I was addicted to being a local celebrity. It was easy. Get drunk and bring the vibes.

I finally got my Benz I had been plotting on. Now, I no longer had to ride with Chyna or Uber everywhere. Chyna and I were doing better. Once I got my car, I had to pull up everywhere VIP. So, we were outside damn near every night. Slowly, I was starting to realize my money was running low. One, because I was starting not to see Hanky that much. I got what I needed out of that situation. No need to keep pretending. I put up with enough of Mr. Hanky and his shenanigans. I was able to put twenty thousand down on my car. However, due to my credit, my monthly payments were fifteen hundred a month. Another bill. Time to slow down on the partying and get back to work.

I was in hustle mode for a couple of months. Not that I wasn't ALWAYS in hustle mode, but for me that meant back to working every single night. I had to stack up and I was. One night I was drunk as hell.

"You need to get a hold of yourself, Destiny? You been in here drunk every night. Tonight, I can't let you leave in the state you're in," the house mom said to me.

In a drunken rage, I went off. Damn near tore up the whole dressing room. I was throwing stuff from the counter to the floor and cursing the house mom out. It took Chyna and security to calm me down. Once I knew I couldn't win the battle I fell asleep half-naked right on the counter in the dressing room.

When I finally woke up, it was only me and the house mom. She was cleaning up the dressing room. “Oh, you’re up,” she said once she saw my disheveled head popping up.

All I could do was grunt, with the way my head was spinning. She walked closer to me and started rubbing my back as I looked at her through the mirror.

“Now, I been working with you since you started. I’ve been seeing you transition and evolve. For the most part, it has been for the better. You recently started drinking and you have been drunk since you started. Getting into unnecessary trouble and confrontations. That’s not like you. Then you drive and I don’t see how people, even the ones you call friends, let you drive like that. I get scared to death for you every time you leave in that condition. You need to slow down before you end up in destruction. I’m only saying this because I care. That’s why I didn’t let you leave tonight and why you will be taking an Uber home right now. You can’t be letting these hating hoes see you like that. They pull out they cameras and shit, instead of making sure you straight. You need to tighten up; shit ain’t a good look.”

My head was spinning too much for all that. I did hear everything she was saying but it was like I was having too much fun at work. I couldn’t help that everyone offered me drinks, shots, and or bottles! I slowly explained this to her through my throbbing headache.

“You can say no sometimes. You are in control. Don’t lose control in this game. It’s hard to stay focused, but it's either that or, God forbid, something worse,” she shot back.

I didn’t have time for that shit. I got up, got my shit together, and asked for the Uber. It made no sense fighting for my keys. Besides, I didn't have the energy anyway. Just like there were good nights, there were bad nights. But it seemed like the bad nights came when I already had a lot of shit going on. Like all my bills and misfortunes hit at once. I had a very slow month. I didn't think anything of it because I had had a six-month winning streak. But then all my bills hit. My rent was thirty-five hundred, my car note fifteen hundred, and I gave my family two thousand a month. Not to mention my designer clothes and nights out. I was averaging about 10K a month and that was merely to live comfortably. That meant I had to make 20K a month to keep up. So, when those slow nights hit, they HIT!! The liquor was the only thing helping me make money because if I was sober, I would look at all the customers like they were crazy and they would look at me looking crazy.

One slow night during a slow month an old ugly Mexican man came in by the name of Pedro. Pedro was short and shaped weird like an ant with skinny legs and a pot belly. He always wore his sombrero and cowboy boots. Pedro would drink Patron and get FUCKED up. You hear me? But when he was fucked up, he spent some money. One night I had no choice but to go talk to his ass. He was the only one who could give me money that night.

"Sup, papi," I said as I walked up to his drunk ass.

He looked at me all crazy before smiling and quickly pulling me into him. He smelt horrible. I had to hold my breath every time he spoke. One time he spoke, a big blob of spit hit my face. I was disgusted. He offered me drinks and I had to order plenty to even be able to let him continue touching me. He would rub me with his big, wrinkled hands and dirty ass fingernails. I hated dirty fingernails.

By the end of the night, I was drunk as hell and Pedro's boss demeanor was sexy to me. He was so demanding and whatever he wanted, no matter the cost, he got it. Pedro wanted me to go home with him. I let him know I had to be taken care of and he had no problem. I knew he wouldn't; that's why I told him four thousand dollars. Although I was intoxicated, there wasn't no way I was getting in the car with or being stuck somewhere with Pedro's drunk ass. I was leaving right after we were done. I gave him my number and told him to text me.

The house mom tried to take my keys but tonight was not the night for that. It had been too damn slow in the club for that shit. I told her I was going home with the customer and I needed the money, but I was not getting in the car with him. I did a good job convincing her I was sober. I got in my car and left to meet Pedro.

On the ride there I was lit. I had the music blasting my favorite songs and was having a good ole car karaoke. I called Chyna and talked shit with her for a while. We talked about the night, and I let her know who I was going home with. I liked to let her know my whereabouts and who I was with in case my ass turned up missing. It was a dangerous game we played, leaving with those men. Never knew what beef they had, who was following them, or who was waiting to rob their asses after seeing them spend all that money in the club. Guess it was a roll of the dice, trying to get that money. In the midst of me hanging up with Chyna, I guess the light turned red. I must have missed it because next thing I knew, I was waking up in the hospital.

I woke up to Chyna at my bedside with my mom and brother. Looking at my mom, I wished I was still in a coma. When I opened my eyes, it took a second to realize it was reality. My mom was crying tears of joy.

"Oh, thank God, my baby is awake!" was all she kept yelling.

I looked over to see my brother watching from the corner, slightly smiling. Everyone explained to me what happened, and I couldn't believe it. I went into shock after realizing I was handcuffed to the bed.

"Take these off! Why are they on me, Mom? Take them off!" I was pulling and yanking my arm. Yelling and screaming to be let loose.

A nurse ran in, followed by a policeman. I was totally confused.

“Mom, what's going on?” I pleaded for an answer.

Mom burst out crying again.

The officer stepped up. “You were involved in an accident due to you drinking and driving. No one else was hurt. You’re the only one who suffered any damages. Thank God, your charges would have been worse than a DUI and reckless driving. Once the hospital releases you, you will then be transferred to the main jail.”

I couldn’t believe my ears. Chyna and my mom neglected to tell me the entire story. I didn’t know how to feel except grateful to be alive.

I was discharged and transported straight to jail. I could not believe that shit. I was denied bond. I had to sit in there for three weeks until my court date. While sitting in jail I had a lot of time to reflect on my life and my lifestyle. Believe it or not, as much fun as dancing may sound, the game comes with a lot. Like some of these men I wouldn’t ever give a time of day to, had I lived a normal life. It wasn’t like I woke up and said let me be a stripper. I wanted to help my family and the cash came quickly. I fell in love with what the game could do for me, but I didn’t know how deep the dark side was.

I felt like if I could come up with some kind of goal or something, I could take myself out. The problem remained trying to do it sober, especially after that accident. I went to court and the judge sentenced me to two years’ probation with AA classes. This meant if I got into any kind of trouble I would be going to jail.

I got out and, of course, went straight to Mom’s house. She was stressed behind everything we were going through, and the accident didn’t make it any better. I needed a hug from her. Of course, we had to sit down and talk things out. I’m happy it all worked out for the best. It was the separation from my family that made me feel like I needed the liquor.

My relationship with my mom got better and I was finally happy I got to be back in my brother's life. I still had to help my family and keep up with my lifestyle so I still worked as much as I could. Although I put a plan into place for my family and me, we needed a lot of money to start.

So, I was right back hustling like crazy. This lifestyle started out a little shaky for me and I never would have imagined being blessed the way that I have been. All I wanted to do was help my family and I got way more than I asked for. I may have lost myself along the way and made some dumb decisions, but that's life. You live and you learn.

After I was released and went back to work, I tried the whole not drinking thing and let's say it didn't last too long. There was no way I could be this fun party girl and act like I cared about these niggas and their problems without drinking. I had to try to at least control it and, for the most part, I was doing good. I really put myself on a schedule. If that's what I could call it.

Usually, I started drinking soon as I got on the floor at work. So, what I came up with was not drinking unless I was drinking with a customer. Then I also came up with no more buying my own liquor. Believe it or not those rules helped to a certain extent. I mean, dancing was my bread and butter. I made and touched more money than I'd ever touched in my life. There was no way I was gonna stop any time before my goals started making me money. Therefore, I had to do what I had to do to turn into this alter ego to keep these niggas spending they bill money on me.

I accepted the fact that I had to drink but I was being more mindful of how much I was drinking. My mom didn't like the idea of me drinking but I needed my family to be straight. That was all that mattered to me. So, while I was there in this dressing room fighting for my keys once again, I knew that meant I made one hell of a bag that night. I shouldn't have been drinking as much, but at least I knew people at my job would make sure I was safe, cuz I had to get that money regardless. Sober or drunk, the money is THE BOTTOM LINE!

Note from author: This dancing game causes a lot of us to use drugs or drink unlimited alcohol. While it may be fun or make it easier to deal with the task at hand - "making money"-it's definitely not smart to lose control and overindulge. I want all dancers to be mindful of how much they are drinking or using drugs. More than anything we need to always be on point. Most importantly, our family and loved ones need us.

03

POOCHIE

"You're going to track practice today, no if, ands, or buts about it," Mom snarled at me.

I really wanted to take a break from sports. My schedule consisted of school, followed by an hour tutoring session, and then practice for whatever sport I was in at the moment. I had been in sports since I was four. If it wasn't soccer, it was karate. If it wasn't karate, it was gymnastics. Now it was track. Mom was adamant about keeping my schedule busy. I pushed myself up to get my things ready for school. I was able to get two days off from track by lying to my mom about not feeling well. I really wanted to sit at home with nothing to do. It wasn't like I didn't like being in extracurricular activities. I actually enjoyed them because it gave me more time to be with my school friends. However, I needed a break sometimes to be a normal eighth grader.

My upbringing was as good as it was gonna be. We lived in the hood my whole childhood. However, my parents knew there was better out there. They made it their goal to have me experience that life. I went to school on the other side of the tracks because they felt it was more opportunity for me to excel in life. It was a predominately white school. My parents were happily married with decent jobs to maintain our little lifestyle. Mom was a little strict. I guess because I was an only child, and they didn't want me to be a statistic. My parents spent whatever little money they had left to fund me in all my sports. School was hell for me. I didn't make many friends because I felt like they couldn't relate. How would they? We came from different worlds. I would get teased a lot because of my extremely fit body. They would say I was shaped like a boy. I had no breasts, a damn eight pack, and a little muscle booty. It made me very insecure then but looking back, I was perfect. I dreaded going to school but, of course, I had no choice because my mother wasn't going for any of my excuses not to attend.

By the end of eighth grade, I was student and athlete of the year. When I got to high school, I was in cheerleading and then track. High school was even more intimidating for me. Some girls had already gone through puberty. So, it was big breasts with cleavage shirts. Short shorts with full butts. Then there was me. A stick in an oversized Nike two-piece. It was like I wasn't hitting puberty at all. Only difference for me was that my period was now here. To keep my mind off my peers I started training harder for gymnastics. So, if I didn't have a game to cheer for or a track meet, I would go to training for gymnastics. Therefore, I had no time to even think about what I didn't look like. I was insecure but to keep myself from going into depression, I kept busy.

I didn't have any "cool" friends. I only really hung out with one girl, Ashleigh. She was in the computer tech program. She wore glasses and plain clothes. She was a tad bit oversized, but Ashleigh was smart as hell. She was a loner like me. We bonded over that. What little free time we had, we spent at Ashleigh's house where we would have our sleepovers because my neighborhood was not where I wanted anyone from my school to pull up. We were comfortable at her house, so comfortable she never even asked about coming to my house. Like me, Ashleigh merely wanted a friend or acceptance. We would talk about everything from our insecurities to our crushes.

After a while, we understood that we weren't accepted by our peers. Ashleigh's parents were rich. They damn near lived in a mansion. She had no brothers and sisters, so when I did sleep over at her house, we pretty much did what we wanted. Ashleigh's mom was usually drunk on the other side of the house and her dad was never home. Now that I think about it, he probably was never home because of the mom. She wasn't a cute wine drunk; she was like a belligerent drunk. I could tell when I was over, Ashleigh would sometimes get embarrassed when her mom came out of nowhere to bother us. We could never understand what the hell she was saying.

What I can say is Ashleigh never got out of line or disrespected her mom. She would choose her words wisely when responding to her and try to calm her down before walking her back to her room. Sometimes it would take a while for her to return because she had to relax her mom so she could lay down and go to sleep.

I was surprised one night when Ashleigh came back crying. "I hate this shit, man. It's like, when is she going to change? She doesn't even care that my whole life and special moments are passing her by."

I felt so bad for my friend. I'd never seen her express her emotions about her mom. I hugged her and gave her a pep talk to let her know everything would be alright.

"As soon as I turn eighteen, I'm out of here. I want nothing to do with them. I don't want any of their money, any of their help, or nothing," she cried out.

I thought she was tripping at that last part. Who doesn't need help from their parents when they are first jumping into the world? One thing I did know was that Ashleigh was going to be super successful, as smart as she was!

It didn't really come as a shock when one day after our graduation Ashleigh called me and said she was leaving her parents' mansion. She was going to live on her own and figure it out. She mentioned that she had a serious conversation with them, and it went in one ear and out the other. She couldn't take it anymore. She wouldn't take it anymore.

I asked her what her plans were and she answered she didn't have any. She was taking her allowance money that she had saved over the years to get an Airbnb and go from there. Of course, I let her know I was here if she needed me. I was happy to have graduated. The day of my graduation made everything my parents put me through, worth it. Now I wasn't like Ashleigh. I was not ready to leave the bird's nest yet. My parents and I were close, and they only wanted what was best for me. My plan was to go to college and get a good job. The typical American dream. That's what would have made my parents proud.

Ashleigh and I remained close. She left her car with her parents so I would drive to go see her and take her to run errands.

"I'm going to dance Norma," she blurted out as we drove to a Walgreens one night.

I damn near stepped on the brakes in the middle of traffic. I couldn't believe what I was hearing. Ashleigh wasn't even the dancer type. Like her look. She was plain. She was still a little overweight. She was shy. She was insecure. Nothing was adding up. What the hell did she mean to dance?

"Like... like... like stripper dance?" I asked.

We both laughed because it took me a few attempts to get it out. I was genuinely appalled.

"I need money and I've hit up a bunch of tech companies about internships, but no one has reached back out.□ I don't want to wait until my money runs out to start making money. I met this girl who does it. She told me I could try it and save money to get my body done. This way I could really make bank until I get a real job," she explained.

"What about college?" I managed to ask through my silence.

"Let's be real, college costs and I have not a single dollar toward it. So, I want to dance and save to get my body done and then save for college. I can't go back to my parents. I have to make this work. I gotta do it."

I couldn't do anything but support my friend. The situation between her and her parents weighed a lot on her. Last thing she needed was me telling her how crazy she was and all the obvious reasons I believed she shouldn't do it.

Ashleigh had the club where she was going and all. She even made me go with her to get her outfits and shoes. This was crazy! She told me she had been practicing dance moves and all. My friend was determined. I knew there was never going to be another chance for trying to talk her out of it.

We walked into the club and honestly, it was something I had never seen before. A whole bunch of naked women in front of gawking men and women alike. It was unreal. The place was shabby, though. Like small and dark. It felt like we were in a little country town but no. This place was right in the middle of our city. The music was blasting, and the liquor was pouring.

Ashleigh met up with the girl she knew and headed to the manager's office. I stayed outside to watch what was going on. The girls were not top notch at all. Nothing I imagined strippers looking like. Some were smaller than me with no ass at all. A couple looked older than my mama. I even saw an extremely plus-sized woman. I was confused. I figured Ashleigh was talking to the manager about getting hired and coming right out. I didn't expect to be waiting over thirty minutes.

An hour later this pretty plush girl walked up to me and after a few minutes, I realized it was Ashleigh. She had on a one-piece black lingerie number. Her makeup was flawless and she even had some little curls in her hair. She had traded her glasses for stripper heels!

"ASHLEIGH?" I yelled out.

We both fell out laughing. I couldn't believe how good my friend looked. Hell, she didn't need any damn surgery. She carried her weight well. For sure, she looked better than what was in this little hole in the wall.

"My name is Poochie!"

She laughed while I was confused.

"Your name is Ashleigh." I was confused as to what the hell she was trying to say.

Once again, she laughed. This time I didn't know what was funny.

"No! When you're a stripper, you need a stripper name! So, my stripper name is Poochie," she exclaimed.

I don't know where she got the name from, but whatever worked for her worked for me. The girl Ashleigh knew was not bad looking. She wasn't grade A but she wasn't bad. She had a mouthpiece on her, though. I watched her work the room and get in every man's ear. The men were older drunks. Some looked like washed-out lawyers. Others were dirty and ugly. She didn't discriminate; she went to each one. Some shook their heads "No" while others let her lead them to a back room. She would return after a few songs and attack her next victim. I must admit it was fun to watch. Soon she came and grabbed Ashleigh, who was standing by me drinking.

"You can't get no money standing here. You gotta go get it."

She pulled Ashleigh with her. I then watched her show Ashleigh how to work the room. It wasn't long before Ashleigh was working the floor on her own. I was really surprised. She was dancing and going in and out the back rooms. This was not the shy, insecure Ashleigh I knew!

This club, not like all the other clubs, opened at six and closed at three. At three-fifteen we were walking out to my car while Ashleigh was giving me the details of her night.

"Girl, all that matters is I made eight hundred dollars!" she yelled with excitement.

Ashleigh was used to seeing that type of money at one time. I wasn't. At least not in one day. Like I would have to save weeks for that. So, my new hustle was taking Ashleigh to work and I would stay there with her to keep her company or hold her money. At the end of the night, depending on what she made, she would give me some money. Her goal was to make five thousand dollars for her surgery.

"First a BBL, then my nose, then my breasts." These were Ashleigh's goals. She was catching me off guard. This was a lot.

"I thought you wanted your body done so you can go to a better club and make more money quicker, then quit for school?"

I wanted to keep my friend on track. I was putting in a lot of time to help her out in between my work shifts.

"Soon, I'll be leaving, and I won't be here to help you. You had a plan. Stay on track and get out. This game is not long term. Ash, you had a plan. Why are you adding all this other stuff that you don't need? You're beautiful the way you are."

Every night Ashleigh went to work, I could feel her shifting. Gone was the quiet, shy, insecure Ashleigh. Now it was the confident, loud Ashleigh. Her attitude changed. The way she dressed changed and the way she acted changed.

"You're letting the money change you, Ash. I don't like it." As her friend I felt compelled to let her know I noticed the difference. "You don't even have a car but you're buying clothes and shit you don't need every day. Who are you trying to keep up with? Those strippers? Ash, you had a plan. What's up?"

Every time I asked, she told me she was sticking to the plan and to mind my business. I couldn't. Sometimes I would leave work and pick Ashleigh up from work. She would get in the car drunk or high off weed. This was new to me.

"This lifestyle is taking over you. I leave for college in two days. I hope you can handle yourself."

I could see she knew the time was here and I was really leaving. She would have no one who even cared a little bit to even try to keep her head on straight.

"Yes, you will no longer have me in your hair, or someone trying to keep you straight. I really want what's best for you. I hope you can keep it together."

It was a bittersweet moment for me. I was super excited about going off to college, but I didn't want to leave my friend who seemed to be falling off track. I had to do what was best for me, though.

Once I made it to college, Ashleigh and I talked here and there.

"This girl told me I can get butt shots first. It's cheaper so I think I'm gonna do that," Ashleigh revealed to me one night over FaceTime.

I thought that was scary. "I don't think you should do that. Like yes, you need a butt, but if you gonna do this surgery stuff, you need to do it right. You can sacrifice another month of working to save up to get the actual BBL."

Ashleigh looked like her mind was made up already. "Well, I booked the appointment for the butt shots during the time you come down for break. You gotta come with me."

I don't know why she would think I was going with her. I was trying to say it as nicely as I could to my friend. It wasn't like she had the best body to simply just add a butt. Hell, in my opinion, she would look like an Oompa Loompa. Big butt, big gut. That was so backwards to me when she could get it done properly and be snatched like a video vixen. I don't know, to each their own, but I let Ashleigh know I wasn't going to take her to do butt shots. She was better off asking one of her stripper friends.

After that talk, Ashleigh hadn't been answering me or calling me. So, when I got in town, I told myself I would drop by her Airbnb before I left. The night before I was leaving, I dropped by. It took her a minute to answer the door. I was about to leave when Ashleigh opened the door.

She looked like she was in great pain. When she saw me, she fell into my arms. I couldn't figure out what was wrong through her crying, but I did notice her butt was bigger through her robe. Really big!

"Oh my God, Ashleigh what's the matter? You're hot as hell!"

I couldn't do anything but hold her and help her inside. Once I sat her on the couch, her face was red as hell, but she was finally able to get a couple words out through short breaths.

"I. Can't. Breathe. Please," she stammered.

I anxiously called the police.

When paramedics arrived, they quickly got her inside and took her to the hospital. I met them there. They wouldn't let me see her when I arrived but they did say her condition had worsened. I couldn't help but beat myself up. I left, knowing she needed me. I could tell she was headed down the wrong path and I should have stayed home from college to help her.

I slept in the hospital, and it wasn't until the next morning I was able to hear anything about her.

"Your friend is lucky to still be living. Apparently, she has gotten some illegal injections into her body that have traveled almost everywhere, including not too far from her heart. That caused a major bacterial infection. That's why her breathing was short. If she didn't get here when she did, her heart would have completely stopped. She'll be staying with us for a couple of days so we can monitor her but as soon as she's out of here, she must get that stuff removed from her body," the doctor explained.

I couldn't believe what I was hearing. I had told Ashleigh not to do that to her body. Now, look.

Ashleigh was released a few days later. Mentally she was in a dark place. I took control. I began doing research on doctors that do silicone removal. I set up a consultation appointment for a couple of days away.

Over the next couple of days Ashleigh was coming around. We were finally able to talk. I asked her how long she had been in pain.

"Man, I can't even describe how bad this pain is. I wouldn't wish this on my worst enemy. It's like my whole butt is hot like fire and hard like cement. It wasn't too long after I got it done when I started feeling the pain. I kept asking the lady if the hardness was normal and she said yes that it was still early. I knew it wasn't supposed to be this hard. I guess I was hoping it would soften."

I told her about the doctor I looked up. I also let her know I set an appointment for two different doctors. I had to go back to school but I would be back for her appointments. The answer she gave me had me in disbelief.

"One of my homegirls from work told me about two doctors in Colombia that I should go to. She said the doctors here are expensive and if I go there, I could get the shots out and they will also do the BBL."

It took me a minute to process this before I responded. "Okay, so is this the same homegirl who told you about the person who did your shots? You know what? It doesn't even matter. I sat here a couple extra days when I'm supposed to be back at school. I've been researching doctors and the best help we can get you. Yet, here you are again, telling me what some girl at work told you to do. You not tired of taking the cheap way out, especially when it comes to your body?

"Yes, Colombia may be cheaper but are they safer? You don't even speak a lick of Spanish so the language barrier will be there. You know what? I've got to go back to school. Let me know what you do."

I cleaned her up a bit and made sure she had everything she needed within arm's reach before I walked out and tended to my own life. At that point, I was thinking Ashleigh had a sickness or something. If it was me, I would never listen to another low budget stripper in my life. I could see if she was maybe getting advice from a girl whose body was perfect. But the girls I had seen at the club Ashleigh worked at were nowhere near perfect.

I went back to college and continued my life. A few months went by. In the beginning I would check on Ashleigh, but I could tell she wasn't interested in talking to me. Probably because I didn't agree with her plan. I ended up getting pregnant. Therefore, I started to slow down on checking on Ashleigh so I could focus on my bundle of joy. I didn't even know if she went to Columbia or not until I went home to bring my baby to visit my family and friends. Once again, I didn't want to leave town without checking on Ashleigh. I packed my baby and went to her Airbnb, but a neighbor let me know she had moved.

"I think she rented an apartment on the other side because I still see her from time to time," the neighbor said.

I drove around to the other side of the complex and I was right on time because I saw a slimmer Ashleigh walking out.

I walked up to her. "Hey, Ashleigh!"

I was super excited to see her. We hugged and it was something about the hug that let me know something was wrong with my friend. I pulled back and looked into her sunken, pale face. I let her know I came to introduce her to my baby. That's when a sparkle went through her eyes. She played with my baby and told us to come upstairs. We sat and talked a little while she played and cooed over my baby.

Not too long after that, her sparkle was once again gone. So, I asked her what had really been up with her.

"I ended up going to Colombia to visit a doctor who *supposedly* specialized in injection removal. I did a consultation over Zoom and he told me he could be of service to me. I flew in and when I walked into the first appointment, it was like a slaughterhouse. Women were lined up, at least thirty, waiting on the doctor. Some already had surgery, some were getting surgery that day, and some were there for consultations. That should have been red flag number one for me.

"But I so desperately wanted my butt fixed. I go in and explain to him, in detail that I wanted the injections out, but I also didn't want a big, unnatural looking butt. I had an area of concern towards the bottom that I wanted to make sure he would be able to shape right.

"He said yes. So, I paid the rest of my money. It was twenty thousand total for butt reconstruction, BBL, and breasts. Surgery was scheduled for the next few days. I spent my time waiting, doing tourist stuff, exploring the country and all. I finally went in for surgery.

"When I woke up, I noticed my stomach wasn't hurting or anything. Now, I had never gotten lipo before, but I know I was supposed to feel some pain or burning or something. My butt was bandaged and in pain, so I figured he did what he had to do there. Also, my breasts felt like a truck was sitting on them. So, I knew he did what he was supposed to do there.

"I mustered up some strength to go look at my body. My breasts and butt were wrapped so I couldn't see but my stomach was not touched. I called for the nurse and asked her why, if that's what I paid for. She had no clue and told me she would get with the doctor.

"Every day for a week straight I asked to see the doctor and finally got to see him. I asked him why lipo wasn't performed and that's what I paid for. He said, 'Oh I did lipo but if you think I didn't, I'll do it again.'"

Ashleigh broke down at that point. I couldn't believe what I was hearing.

"Is that even legal?"□I asked. "In America, you have to wait three months to be put under again."

Ashleigh shook her head and gained her composure before continuing. Thankfully my baby girl had fallen asleep.

"I was so scared because I had no one to call and tell that I was going under again. He had no explanation for me not having lipo, only saying he did it. But I know he didn't because there was no pain and still a gut. I was embarrassed to have spent all that money only to come back home looking botched again.

"So, I went under again a week later. First off, he did my surgery at nine p.m. at night, which was crazy to me but like I said, his office always looked like a slaughterhouse so he was slicing every patient up and trying to get as much money per day as he could. Even if that meant doing surgery at eleven p.m. at night. Anyways, I went in at nine and I was up by ten. Again, no pain, no nothing. I began to cry and within a few minutes I was in a cab going back to my recovery house on my own."

I was appalled at what Ashleigh was saying. She did a lipo surgery under anesthesia and was on her way back to her recovery house within an hour.

She continued her story. "Now, I had lipo marks with no lipo again. At this point, I was ready to go home. My butt he didn't fix exactly how I liked but I could tell he got some of the shots out. So, it looked a little better. And get this! I met a girl crying in the recovery house, saying she went into surgery to get her shots removed but when she woke up, nothing had changed. So, it seems like the doctor was promising services, not doing them, and taking our money.

"I came home frustrated, annoyed, disappointed□and helpless. Like, why me? I've been sitting here dwelling on that. I still need my butt fixed and now I may have to do some real research and find a doctor here that speaks English and understands me and what I need. This shit is draining!"

I sat in silence for a few as I dissected this horror story Ashleigh had revealed to me. I couldn't help but feel sorry for my friend, who only wanted to be accepted in a world she didn't need to be a part of because of emotions stemming from her upbringing.

Like how does a little girl who comes from extremely smart, successful parents succumb to this? You would think a kid like me from the hood with parents with little to no money would have succumbed to that life of fast money.

"When was the last time you talked to your parents?" I asked.

She said she hadn't talked to them in a while. She stopped calling when she realized her mom hadn't changed and her dad still consumed himself with so much work, he didn't have time to care.

"I think that's what needs to be done, Ash. You've been seeking acceptance since we were kids. You wanted to be noticed by your parents for all your hard work and good grades in school. All the accolades you achieved and not one single praise from your parents. I feel like you carried that into your adult life. Now you're looking for acceptance in a world you have no business in.

"You're beautiful, you were beautiful before all this. You're hella smart, Ash. You still have time to take over the world being authentically you! It's time to face your parents and address your trauma or pain with them. Besides, Your mom needs your help. It's worth a try, Ash."

I had to give it to her as real as possible without causing any damage. I think I did a good job because Ashleigh agreed with me.

We spent the rest of our time bonding and playing with my daughter. I made sure before I left Ashleigh was going to meet with her parents and talk about everything so that they could move forward. She promised she would.

On the ride back to my parents' house I couldn't help but think about how different our upbringings were. How stereotypically, I shouldn't be where I was and headed where I was in life. I wasn't born with a silver spoon like Ashleigh. She had all the resources and funds to do whatever she wanted. I realized the difference was that my parents' whole purpose was giving me a better life. So, they instilled morals in me, they encouraged me, and they praised me on everything I achieved. They were at every game, every tournament, supporting me my entire life.

Although they had no money, they filled that void with much love and support. Unlike Ashleigh, whose parents had only money to throw at her in the form of support. Now, my best friend was out there looking for all the wrong things in all the wrong places. I get it, she wanted to show them she could do it without them and that she didn't need their support. Truth was though, she needed their support the most at that point. She needed her parents to care about what she was doing. She also needed them to call and encourage her to go to college and instill in her that she could be the next Elon Musk or the biggest tech female ever.

What parents instill in us as children goes a long way. Sticks with us our entire lives. I wanted my friend to mend things with her parents and get back to her true self. Distractions come in all forms, no matter what side of the track you are from. All money ain't good money and that's THE BOTTOM LINE.

04

NYA

"Meet me upstairs," Lonnie said as he walked past me while I was dancing for a customer.

Now Mr. Lonnie—as I liked to call him—was the guy who ran the club where I worked. The club was called Scarlett's. Mr. Lonnie had recently started running it and I must say, he was doing his thang. I wasn't a vet in the game, but I wasn't a rookie either. For me it was all a fantasy, but in real life, if that makes sense. Not sure how I ended up being a stripper. Well yes, I do.

Since I was a little girl, I only remember having the finer things in life. My mom was a single mother but my little sister and I were well taken care of. She kept us all looking pretty at all times. Mom was a looker. Caramel-colored, tall, and slender with a face card out of this world. She used it all to her advantage every chance she got!

We spent Sundays getting our hair and nails done. Every single week! I don't think we ever missed an appointment. At least I don't remember missing one.

Mom would lecture us when we complained about spending the day at the salon. "It's important to take care of yourself. When you feel your best, you will attract the best from the universe."

It never failed that one of the guys from the barber shop next door would flirt with my mom and she would make them pay for our services. Every week! I watched her work those men so gracefully, it was like having front row seats to watching the art of seduction.

Of course, it became second nature to me. It started for me as early as high school. I didn't have a crush on a guy. Never! They all wanted me, and I loved the attention. I had them buy my lunch to be able to sit with me. I even had them purchase me the colorful pens I loved. When I got to my junior year, the high school boys weren't my thang anymore. I wanted more. I deserved more. I wouldn't even give them any attention and they soon labeled me as bougie. That was fine with me.□

My third period teacher was named Mr. Peters. Mr. Peters was a fine ass white man! He pulled up to the school in a nice BMW and he always dressed and smelled good. He was so sexy to me. He was soft spoken and had great patience with his students. I would sometimes find some questions to ask him or make up a problem, to stay after for some one-on-one attention from him.

One time during class he gave us back graded tests, which I just knew I passed mine. When my paper landed on my desk with a D, I couldn't believe my eyes. For the rest of the class, I was livid so I remained quiet. I was an honor roll student; there was no way I could get a D. I was going to wait until class was over to see what the hell Mr. Peters was thinking.

When the bell rang and everyone else ran out of class, I walked over to Mr. Peters, who was reading something at his desk. Today, I happened to have on my best push-up bra with a low-cut shirt. I looked cute as hell with a mini jean skirt and my hair pulled back in a ponytail. I quietly pulled up a seat and sat down.

"Mr. Peters, why did I get a D on my test? I did everything correctly. So, what's the problem?" I demanded to know.

He was startled when he heard my voice. He looked at me intently before responding. "Now, Miss Nya, I had specific rules. That part of the test was supposed to be done on the first day. You didn't finish that part until the third day, which leads me to believe maybe you had time to google or cheat for the answers. I can't have that."

I can't lie, I knew I was supposed to finish the first day, but the first part took me longer than I expected. I explained this to him. I leaned closer to Mr. Peters.

"Mr. Peters, do I look like I cheat? I would never cheat on you," I whispered while moving closer so he could get a whiff of my Dolce and Gabbana perfume.

I know he saw my titties perking up at him, too. He nervously looked at me and I could have sworn I saw sweat beads forming around his forehead.

"I did not cheat so what imma need you to do." I laid back slowly, spreading my legs a little and giving him a view of my bald vagina.

Mr. Peters didn't know what to do with himself. See, I knew by the way he looked at me sometimes that this would be easy.□ If I didn't know any better, I would've thought he had given me a bad grade on purpose, for that moment right there.

"Change that grade to an A like I deserve. Don't I deserve an A, Mr. Peters?" I asked, staring into his eyes.

"Uh... um... uh... can you close your legs please, Miss Nya?" he stammered.

I smirked while doing as I was told. "I like being told what to do!"

I quickly jumped up. "Change that grade, Mr. Peters. I can't make honor roll with a D. Thanks!"

I walked out of the classroom, leaving Mr. Peters confused and mesmerized at the same damn time! Of course, my grade was changed. That was the first time I could understand what Mom was doing to those men. It was so easy to manipulate them and get them to do what you want, as long as you had a pussy!□

Me graduating was extremely important to Mom. She did everything she could to give my sis and I every opportunity she didn't have. Graduating was one of them. My mom was the loudest one in the room when I was walking across that stage.

Not too long after I graduated, we found out Mom had colon cancer. Come to find out she had known for a while but kept it from us to "protect" us. It was hard on me because how had I been so consumed with my little high school life that I was not paying attention to my mother? Now that I knew, it was like the signs were there. She was frail and often had dry coughs. She was also moving slower by the day. Mom was my everything. I idolized her. She was my rock. I vowed to do everything in my power to care for her and my sister.□

After a while, things were starting to get difficult. Mom could no longer work. Her hair was now falling out due to chemo. Nevertheless, through all her pain, she was still flawlessly beautiful as ever. I had to tend to her night and day and keep a close watch on my sister.

Thankfully, she had a good amount of money saved up, but with medicine and doctor visits, that was surely to diminish. I needed a plan, and I needed one fast. Everything was beginning to take a toll on me.

One night I decided to step out with one of my close friends to a local strip club. It was a white club. My friend, Petunia, said she liked the white clubs because one, they were cheaper, and two, the white men loved black girls.

Now, I had never been to any strip club or a white club. Walking in the place was incredible. It was like I could smell the money. It was big and dark, with bright lights strobing around with loud techno music playing.

“Girl, one thing about these white clubs is that the liquor is real!” Petunia shouted over the music.

I didn’t know what the hell she meant. I was not much of a drinker.

She continued to explain. “When you go to the black clubs, they ass cut the liquor like these dope dealers cut coke!□ They put cheap liquor in top shelf liquor bottles and sell it. So, you don’t get as drunk as quickly. It takes damn near ten drinks to get drunk, whereas you come to the white clubs, one drink and you are tipsy!”

At that moment I had just finished my first drink and I did feel a little wavy. We were mingling around the bar, eating, drinking, and vibing.

“At any given moment, one of these sugar daddies is going to come and want to mingle with us. That’s when we put everything we ordered on their tab or make them pay for our tab,” Petunia yelled over the music.

Shit, she ain’t have to tell me twice. I was with it. Hell, I was raised that way.

Sure enough, like clockwork, Adam came over to us. “Would you gorgeous ladies like a drink?” his old ass asked while staring into my damn eyes. He wouldn’t take them off me.

I quickly did a once over to see what he had going on. Adam had on some Walmart looking shoes and clothes. I couldn’t do that. First, he was old.

Petunia nudged me to snap me out of my daze. “You not gonna answer Adam’s question Nya?”

I had to ask him to repeat the question.

“Would you mind if I join you?” he repeated.

I told him sure and nodded at the empty seat next to us. We had a couple rounds and kicked shit with Adam. After a while he got up and went to the bathroom. I took that time to express my dismay to Petunia.

“Girl, he may be old, and he may have on Walmart clothes, but his watch costs 60k and his glasses are the latest Gucci. Yes, they both are plain but you gotta know what’s going on out here to know what’s what with these white men. You used to flashy niggas who don’t have a dime to they name. It’s another ball game with these white men. Shit, you heard Adam, he owns his own software company. He is loaded! He clearly wants you. You better not miss out on your blessings, wanting a nigga with a diamond chain who sleeps on his momma couch!” she schooled me.

Right then Adam walked back up, said he had to run to his office, and he wanted to see me again soon. So, we exchanged numbers. The waitress came with his bill and Petunia had her put our tab on his bill. He didn’t say anything.

“See, Mr. Adam is a winner,” she stated on the ride home.□

□I liked that strip club, so I started frequenting it more often with Petunia. She put me up on a lot of game. She taught me about watches and designer things. She taught me how to talk to “Sugar Daddies.” It was easy.

I had met a couple that I added to my roster with Adam. But nothing too crazy, just phone conversations. It ended up being Adam as my top payer. He would want to talk to me on the phone about his problems and then he would send me a few hundred to my Cash App.

That's how it started when one day he said he wanted to spend time with me.

"Bitch, tell him your mom is sick and you need a nurse to care for her while you're gone and it's gone be a thousand dollars! You probably won't even have to fuck his old ass. He only wants some attention. So, rub him and smile that big pretty smile of yours for him," Petunia exclaimed.

I did exactly what she said and sure enough, Adam had no problem paying. We started meeting up maybe once a month. We would frequent high end restaurants and smoke bars because he smoked cigars. I would listen to whatever he wanted to talk about and act like I cared. I had to let his old ass run his hands all over me and kiss my neck. It was creepy but the money was good, so I had to fake it! During that time, Mom seemed to be needing more medicine and doctor visits and my sister needed more and more things.

One day Petunia and I were lounging around the house talking with my mom, trying to bring her spirits up. When she fell asleep, we came up with a plan to work at the white club.

"Man, my hat goes off to you, Nya. You are a strong woman. I don't know how I would have the strength to watch my mother like this. I commend you, friend, but I know you need more money and more help. The money is at that club. Why don't we go dance?" Petunia suggested.

I had never really thought about that nor was I immediately on board but fuck it. I had nothing to lose.

The next night we went and got hired at the club. It was easy. We were both pretty and had slim body figures, so I didn't see them turning us away. Petunia and I were nervous as hell. Yes, we came to that club to hang out here and there but we had never worked here. We headed straight to the bar to get tipsy.

"Ya'll not gonna make no money sitting at the bar getting drunk. This is a white club. Look at all of them lonely, insecure white men sitting out there. You gotta go cheer them up and get the money out of them," the bartender, Beth, yelled to us.

Petunia and I were stuck for a minute but then she got up and tugged me to follow her.

From then we started working the floor. We went up to a couple customers and kicked shit for a few. Once we realized they weren't spending money we moved on to the next. After a few weeks, we had a system. We would walk up to them. Petunia would sit in their lap and rub their heads while I rubbed their legs and whispered questions and sweet nothings in their ears. Our goal was to get these men to the private room so we could get a lump sum and pay by the hour.

Just to go in the back rooms was eight hundred dollars and then a hundred dollars an hour... per girl. So, you had to already come into the club with some money to play. Sometimes going in the back consisted of watching white men do some weird shit. Some of them wanted you to watch them snort coke the whole time or lend them a boob or an ass cheek for them to snort coke off of. Some of the customers snorted so much coke they didn't want to have any sex. They just wanted company. We provided that. Other customers wanted us to spank them with their belts and shit, while some wanted to vent about their problems.

Through it all, Petunia and I got drunk. We had customers that wanted to have sex, of course, but I wasn't able to do that yet. Neither was Petunia. So, we would work our set without having sex. Shit, they just wanted to cum anyway so if we could make it happen without giving up some pussy, why not? One of us would give the hand jobs and the other would purr or whisper in their ears. Sometimes we would rub our knees on their dicks, and because the white men were so horny and usually came fast just off their penis being touched, it would be easy. Sometimes we would make them think we were having sex with them, but we were really using our hands. Like I would straddle them from the front and grind slowly while Petunia pulled out lube from her boot and snuck some on my hand. Then I would reach behind myself and under my butt to their penis, then jack it slow while Petunia moaned in their ear. It worked every time!

Nine times out of ten those white men's dicks were so small they wouldn't notice the difference! See the catch was if they were looking to cum it was an additional one thousand dollars. Petunia and I would bust down everything. It was a cool system, and we were making money. It helped me out a lot.

We started devoting our weekends and maybe one day during the week to the club. I barely had time to see Adam. He would call frequently to try and get some time in but between having a hangover, being tired and spending time with my mom, it was almost impossible.

"Bitch, Adam is a good ass trick. You better make time for him," Petunia said over the phone.

She was right. Hell, I needed every dollar. My mom's health was deteriorating so I needed to have all my money saved for me and my little sister. Eventually, I gave in and started seeing Adam more. We were now going out once a week and every day he was calling to chat.

Therefore, off Adam alone, I was bringing in at least two thousand a week. This was a lot for a young girl like me, who never had a job. I was starting to like him. Besides being very rich, he was very smart and very business minded. He started sharing more about his upbringing and his background.

He basically came from nothing, worked like a slave, and built an empire for his family. He was divorced once and had two kids from that marriage. He also cared for his mom who lived on Sunny Isles Beach in Miami. His whole purpose was to build generational wealth. I found that attractive.

Weirdly, I started looking forward to seeing him. If he skipped a week, I whined and complained, and he would send more money. Since the places we visited were full of other wealthy people, I told Petunia we had to visit on our own so she could snag herself a few tricks.□

□We showed up at the cigar bar one night dressed in our finest. I scoped the scene to make sure Adam wasn't there and we sat at the bar to drink while waiting on our first victim. As anticipated, it wasn't long before one of the horny ass white men came up to us.

Petunia and I instantly started our system. She was talking and rubbing on Bill, that was his name, while I engaged with the biggest smile on my face. Bill was a fat ass hillbilly who was mesmerized by Petunia's dark skin. He kept complimenting her. We kept drinking and taking shots with Bill. He mentioned he was married before he suggested we go to the casino with him. Of course, Petunia jumped right into the money.

"You gonna pay us for our time, big daddy?" she asked, never taking her eyes off him. She promised a great night.

We soon found out what his version of a great night was. He agreed to five hundred a piece for us and he gave five hundred upfront with a promise to pay the rest later. We followed him straight to the high rollers room where, of course, it was like heaven for me and Petunia. Nothing but rich white men everywhere.

All eyes were on us when we walked in with Bill. He sat at a blackjack table and put twenty thousand down to play. Before he started, he gave us two thousand and told us to go gamble and come back. Chile, we pocketed that money and spent an hour walking around the casino checking everything and everyone out. It was safe to say the men we wanted were in the high rollers room, so we went back.

Bill was drunk, losing, and mad at this point. He was ready to go. He told us since he frequented the casino, he got free suites and that he had one for that night.

He invited us up and, to my dismay, Petunia said, "Let's go."

So, I followed suit. The view in the room was breathtaking. There was a patio with a shower on it overlooking the city and all. We ordered a bottle of champagne and started drinking. At one point, Bill went to the bathroom and that's when Petunia pulled out a pill. I didn't know what the pill was for, when she said it was going to knock him out for a little while and we wouldn't have to fuck him. Anything not to fuck him. I was down. She put the pill in his champagne.

When he came out, she gave him the glass and we all toasted. Out of nowhere Bill demanded, "Get naked, nigger."

We weren't sure who he was talking to or why his attitude changed but we slowly did as we were told.

"No, not you." He looked at me. "The black nigger," he said, looking at Petunia.

His robe was open, revealing his sloppy ass stomach hanging over what should have been a penis but it was a nub. We were scared as hell at his new attitude.

He locked the room door and told me to sit in the bathroom where the toilet room was. He had Petunia get into the waterless bathtub.

"Tell me you want to suck my cock, nigger."

He was slurring his words, and I could hear Petunia's sniffles. I began crying to, trying to think of how we could fight the seemingly three-hundred-pound man. Then I remembered the pill in the drink. I prayed it would kick in soon. He kept telling Petunia to say what she wanted him to do to her and I would hear her repeat his demands through her sniffles.

"I want you to fuck this black pussy, baby."

Then I heard what sounded like water drops trickling. It wasn't the faucet or the bathtub. As I listened harder and peeked, it was him pissing on my friend.

She was screaming, "Nooooo, stop please I don't want this."

Hearing her cries made him enraged and it sounded like he was putting his hands on her, so I busted out the toilet room.

"What the fuck are you doing?" I yelled.

He quickly looked at me and started to charge at me. Petunia jumped on his back and started choking him. Then we both attacked him and within, I would say a minute and a half, he went limp. We stood frozen. Had he died? Was he unconscious or was the drug kicking in?

Petunia checked his pulse and breathed a sigh of relief. "He has a pulse. It could be the pill kicked in. He will be asleep for a couple hours and his drunk racist ass probably won't have any memory. This girl at the club told me she slips these pills into her tricks' drinks so she can take more money out of their pockets. In this case we taking the fat bitch's money and that expensive ass watch he has on."

She quickly slipped the watch off his hand, took a quick shower, and before we left, we made sure he still had a pulse. Right before leaving, I took all his clothes.

"Let his fat ass walk through the casino naked," I yelled as we laughed and ran out the door.

We knew it was a possibility Bill wasn't going to be publicly looking for us because then his wife would know how his watch went missing. One thing we knew about the married ones was they never wanted their wives to know about their secret rendezvous.

With our new hatred towards white tricks, we now had a new strategy. We targeted married men with expensive jewelry. We got these men drunk, then created a sexual vibe so that all they wanted was sex. Then they would want to leave with us and book a room expecting sex. That's when we would order drinks or champagne and Petunia would put the pill in their drink. Then we would pretend we were taking a shower together.

In most cases they were high end hotel rooms, so they had bathtubs in the middle of the room or glass showers. Therefore, we would have them watch a girl on girl show until the drug made them pass out. Then we would take cash, if they had any on them, and their jewelry. I made taking all their clothes a thing also. The only thing we never took were their wedding rings, because then they would have to explain to their wives where the hell were the wedding rings. They would wanna file police reports and shit. We didn't have time for that. We hit a couple licks, then sold all the jewelry. Quick come-up.

Mom ended up passing away. It was a really difficult time for my sister and me. She did have an insurance policy set up, but I told Adam she didn't, and he offered to give me the money for the whole bill. He and Petunia were all I had during that vulnerable time for me and my sis. I started falling for him.

After a while we went out to try and help get my mind off things. We ended up going to a concert and having a good time. I got drunk and let loose. It felt good. I made him get a room where I made love to him.

Now Adam's penis was the size of my pointy finger, but chemistry made sex great. This blew my mind. I guess we blew each other's mind because now he was talking about moving me and my sister into his mansion. I wasn't too smitten by that idea.

"I need my own house, Adam," I stated.

I explained that although it had been some time since Mom's passing, I didn't think my sister would be ready to attach to someone else. He understood and told me to look for a house. We would start by visiting each other and work our way towards living together. I explained that I would have to stop dancing so I would need an allowance. Once again, he agreed.

Things were really looking up with Adam holding me down. I went to work one last time and told Petunia my plans to stop. I was gonna hit one more trick with her that night and then it was over. We did that and came up on a rare Patek Philippe. I told her she could keep all the earnings from it.□

□A couple months later, it was Adam's birthday, so his mom and I planned a surprise birthday party. I didn't really know any of his close friends outside of his favorite cousins so that was his mom's department. My job was the event space, decorations, and getting him there. The only people on my invitation list were my sister and, of course, Petunia.

At 9:15 p.m. sharp, I had Adam in our new Rolls Royce heading to the venue. He thought we were going to dinner when we pulled up to this massive event space. From the outside he had no idea what was going on. I told him to be quiet and follow me.

He was completely shocked when we walked into the room and everyone yelled "HAPPY BIRTHDAY!"

I was so happy to see how happy and shocked he was at the gathering of all his loved ones.

"Brice will be here in a few. He got stuck at the office," his mom exclaimed. I had no idea who Brice was, and I think he felt the question in my head.

"Brice is a silent partner in my business. He keeps this business away from his wife. He is my childhood friend. Sometimes he engages in things I don't like but he's still my partner, so I put up with him. Pretty rambunctious dude," Adam explained.

We enjoyed the party in the meantime. Petunia, my sister, and I were mingling with some of his family in the back room when Adam walked in. "LOOK WHO'S HERE, EVERYONE!"

Following behind him was Bill! All I heard was a glass drop. That must have come from a shocked Petunia. The whole crowd looked at her and I quickly turned the attention to Adam. We quickly slipped out while everyone was greeting Brice, or Bill, or whatever the fuck his name was.

We were in the bathroom panicking. Me, for sure, because I couldn't leave, and we didn't know if he remembered us or not. I had to go back in, this was my man, damn near my future husband's party.

"I thought you said they don't remember anything?" I asked her ass. Truth was we both weren't sure.

We had to pull ourselves together when Adam walked in the bathroom. "I been looking for you, babe. Why the hell you locked in the bathroom? I wanna introduce you to my partner I was telling you about." Adam was clearly intoxicated.

Next thing you know an even more intoxicated Brice or Bill walked in. Petunia and I were stunned.

"Baby, this is my partner, Brice. This is my future wife, Nya, and this is her best friend, Petunia."

As Adam introduced us all, Petunia stood wide-eyed with hatred. It was so quiet you could hear a pin drop. After a few seconds that seemed like hours Brice stuck his hand out to us. "Nice to meet you beautiful ladies."

He had broken the ice. Now we knew for sure he didn't remember a thing. As bad as I wanted to kick his fat ass in his stomach, Petunia and I gave each other a quick look, knowing we had to play this off.

"Nice to meet you, Brice. Why don't we get out of this bathroom and go back to the party," Petunia said as she ushered me and the two drunk men out.

Come to find out Brice was worth millions of dollars. He had divorced his wife because she discovered his secret obsession with black women. So, at the time of Adam's party, he was single and ready to mingle. Petunia came up with a plan to seduce him and rock his world, make him marry her, then leave his ass with nothing. He wasn't going to know what hit his ass.

A few years later, they arrived at mine and Adam's beautiful wedding hand-in-hand. You would have thought she truly loved him. Later, when I threw the bouquet back to all the women in attendance, my best friend and I shared a wink when she caught the bouquet and Brice jumped for joy.

"That means you guys are next!" I squealed.

Who would believe we would get in a game so tough and make it out with only a couple of scratches?

Truth is these men will leave scars that last forever but you always gotta be not one but ten steps ahead of their asses. Emotions sometimes become cold in a game where the money is THE BOTTOM LINE.

05

LE'LANI

Looking in the mirror at myself tryna figure out WHERE THE FUCK DID I GO WRONG was a normal, thirty minute part of my day these days. Never in a million years did I ever think that I, Marissa Brown, would be bamboozled by a man the way I was. My story has got to be a one in a million, because I doubt that anyone else is as naive as I am in this world.

"Le'Lani to the top side," the DJ yelled over the music blasting through the speakers at club Infinity.

You see, club Infinity was the spot! All the celebrities and socialites came to this spot. It had a reputation of being one of the safest clubs around and the ambiance was on another level. Nothing but the baddest women and the biggest ballers were in attendance daily, and I was nothing short of every man's fantasy. Standing 5'9" with no heels on, bowlegged, shaped like a Coca Cola bottle and brown-skinned with a red undertone, kind of like a Malcom X color. I demanded attention in every room I walked in, and it was no different whenever I stepped onstage at work.

I moved to West Palm Beach not too long ago. Therefore, I was a fresh face, which meant new pussy in the strip club world. I was already popping and had made a little name for myself in the industry before I got to West Palm Beach, but once I made it my home it was like I was meant to be there. The money kept flowing in consistently. Nonstop! I never thought anything could get better than my hometown. I was single and, for the most part, had my priorities together. You know living good, driving good, dressing nice, bills paid. The usual.

My upbringing was pretty good. Mom was a successful doctor and Dad, well, he was a successful street pharmacist. If you will, a drug dealer. My mother was very attractive and had the brains to match. She was tall with a thin frame and fair skin. Breathtaking. Her confidence and personality only added to her amazing aura. She was perfect.

My dad, on the other hand, was very dark. I'm talking blacker than Wesley Snipes and good looking. The fact that he maintained his prison form made him even more irresistible to the ladies. My dad was very cocky and moved with a lot of caution. He was very laid back and never in a rush. He even talked slowly like he thought about every word before it came out. Some people thought he was a pimp with how much ease and confidence he went through everything in life with.

My parents both loved me to the moon and back. An only child and the first born for both, you can only imagine how spoiled I was. With my mom earning a great living for herself before my dad, she already had the finer things in life; he added to it. So, when it came to me, my mom made sure I had top of the line everything. My dad? The way he catered to me was on another level. I was ten years old being driven to private school and picked up, by Bubbie, my dad's security. Bubbie was one of my dad's childhood friends who he trusted with his life. I grew up with Bubbie by my side whenever my dad couldn't be there.

Now when I say Bubbie watched me like a hawk, he watched me like a hawk! I think growing up like that, I became accustomed to it. It wasn't until I got to maybe middle school that I started realizing it wasn't everyone else's norm. Furthermore, this is when I found out the truth about my dad's profession. My friends started looking at me with their noses turned up. I had no one to sit with during lunch. I also realized a couple of my teachers were treating me extra special.

I would tell my mom and she would say, "In this life you either got IT or you don't and, baby, YOU GOT IT! The people hate you or love you; there is no in between. Don't pay attention to those kids. They are mad they can't live the way you do."

One day this girl who I used to consider a friend started bullying me. She would pull my hair or do stupid things like bump me when she passed me in the hallway.

"What the fuck is your problem, Keki," I yelled out after I had gotten tired of letting her slide.

She looked at me with the most hateful eyes. "Bitch, what the fuck you think you is? A princess? Because you get chauffeured with personal security and wear all the latest clothes to school with a new hairdo every week?"

I couldn't catch her drift. We were once friends. She used to come to my house and we talked every day.

"Well look, bitch, you ain't no princess. Matter of fact, you ain't shit. Your daddy just a drug dealer. That's why you live the way you live. If he go to jail tomorrow, you and your mama will be bums."

When she said that, it was like she pierced my heart. My dad, a drug dealer? Why would she say that! I never in a million years thought my dad was a drug dealer. I mean, drug dealers don't marry doctors and they don't move with as much class as my dad.

"Ma, is it true that daddy is a drug dealer?" I questioned my mom the moment I saw her.

For a few seconds I thought she didn't understand me, so I asked her in Spanish. "Mami, es cierto que papi es un traficante de drogas?"

I guess that was one good thing my drug-dealing father made sure of; I was bilingual.

"Sweetheart, where did you hear this?"

I explained to her what was going on in school and what had happened with my ex-friend Keki.

In so many words, Mom told me to ask my father. I waited for him to get in from "work." I think she had given him a heads up because he came straight to my room and sat down.

"Sweetheart, your mom told me you had a question about what I do."

I looked at him with tears in my eyes. This was the man I looked up to my whole life. The man I looked to for comfort, guidance, and direction. To discover his whole persona was a lie was devastating. I broke down. There was nothing left for me to do or say to the man I adored.

"Baby, look, I was going to tell you when I felt the time was right. I didn't have the luxury of growing up the way you are. I lived in the Liberty City Projects. I watched my mom overdose on heroin and my dad get shipped off to prison for life. I had no guidance and therefore, I had no choice. What I was using as a quick way to get money became my way of life. Just when I thought I could stop, I met your mother. She already had a certain lifestyle that I chose to maintain to keep her. Then when we had plans to invest and do major things, we found out she was pregnant. I had to keep bringing home the bacon. I don't plan on doing this forever but know that I do it for us."

I told him I forgave him to end the situation. But something inside me never did.

After knowing about my dad, going to school to face everyone else who knew before me was hard. I started acting out, skipping school, and smoking weed to ease my nerves. I didn't feel like being humiliated on a day-to-day basis. My relationship with my parents changed. I mean, after all they were both liars my whole life.

By the time I got to high school I was very rebellious, which was far from the normal me that my parents knew. I was skipping school to go smoke weed with my homegirls almost every other day. I would give my parents an attitude even I didn't know I had. I think it was all just resentment of them, making me feel like my whole life was a lie and having to prove to other teenagers that I was normal just like them.

I started declining the chauffeur rides to school from Bubbie. I explained to my parents I was too old for that and if my dad wasn't a drug dealer I probably would be living a normal life and furthermore, if my dad was doing good business, I wouldn't have to be guarded so heavily.

I spoke these words to my mom and dad one night while having a talk over dinner and my dad jumped across the table and slapped me. "Who the hell do you think you're talking to? Do you know what I do to make sure you go to that nice ass school you go to? Do you know what I go through to make sure you're dressed in the finest?"

His face was red and spit was coming out of his mouth. I was scared but gave him an unbothered face, which made him madder, and I knew it.

"GO TO YOUR ROOM AND DON'T COME OUT UNTIL I SAY SO!"

I stomped away from them and up to my room where I plopped myself on my bed, crying my life out. I could never be normal as long as I was in their house under their watch.

So, I left. I packed one of my Louis Vuitton suitcases and left through the back door of our big house. My dad was probably not home, and my mom was probably asleep for work the next morning. I called my friend, Ananda, whose parents also worked a lot and were rarely home. She told me I could come over.

When I got to Ananda's house it was full of teenagers like me. They were out in her pool house smoking weed, listening to music, and talking about our kid problems.

"Guess who's coming over, guys?" Ananda yelled as everyone stopped to wait for her to reveal who was coming over. "AARON is on the way! So, you know we're about to have a real party!"

Hell, I thought we were in a real party already. I couldn't understand what she meant. I asked Barbara, another of the few black girls that attended our school.

"When Aaron comes, the party gets better because he brings booze and coke." She jumped up with excitement.

"Booze and coke?" I had never tried anything but weed so this was scary. I was kind of scared I even left my house.

Everyone explained to me I would be fine, and that coke wasn't all that bad. "Your dad sells it, Le'lani. You should have been trying it," someone yelled out and everyone laughed.

I hated Dad all over again. I mean, if he was selling it, then it shouldn't be a problem if I indulged. That's exactly what I did when Aaron appeared at the party. That was the night my life went left.

A FEW MONTHS LATER

"Bitch, you bet not put that whole bag up yo nose. You ain't pay fo dat." My best friend Shirley did not play about her drugs, especially while working. She had to have that fix every hour or so to get through the night and I ain't gonna lie, I was almost there.

You see, once I started using while I was in school, it became a part of my social life. Then it became more frequent, to the point my parents found out. My mom tried to pacify it. She didn't want to believe that ME, her drug dealer's baby, would start using. Well, I did! My dad wasn't indulging in this situation. To him it was as long as my mom felt like I was using, there was no reason for him to even talk to me.

In other words, he basically disowned me. I had a choice: the good life or drugs. The good life came as a cover up that I still couldn't get over, so I chose drugs.

Aaron became my best friend. He always had that good shit. When I say always, I mean always! So, I really didn't have to look far. It wasn't until Aaron disappeared that I went crazy looking for him. Calling his phone back-to-back, asking all my friends for him. Hell, they were also looking for him. Eventually, word got around that Aaron was locked up. For how long? No one knew. We were sick for a week until I got this bright idea.

I was a pretty girl with a body men couldn't resist, even if I was only in high school. I always heard Bubbie talking about going to pick up money for Dad in Pompano, a city not too far away. I figured that's where the drugs had to be. Everyone knew Pompano wasn't the safest place, so the drugs had to be there, right? Well, me and Ananda were gonna find out.

"Oh my God! Look at those guys on the corner. They look like they'll kill us if we stop."

Ananda and I were two prep kids from a rich area and although I was black, I wasn't used to what we were riding through Pompano witnessing.

"Look, we have to stop or go home empty handed. Don't you want to party right this weekend? You throw the best parties. Everyone's gonna talk shit if we don't get no white."

Truth be told, we were both too scared to stop. Ananda finally pulled over at the next corner store where men with golds, dreads, and pants hanging off their asses were playing dice.

"Let's go in the store. Surely, they will like us. I mean, we're new, we not from 'round here, plus we cute. We go into the store, grab whatever, and figure it out from there. It can't be that hard." Ananda was trying to convince us both.

"Okay, let's do it."

We both got out of the car, walked towards the front door of the store and sure enough, all eyes were on us!

"Aye, lil mama. Aye, lil mama."

I stopped and turned slowly, confidently. My eyes landed on the finest blackest man I had ever seen. He had a low cut, a mouth full of golds, some Dickie shorts and a wife beater on revealing his toned body.

"Our names ain't aye," I snapped back.

The whole group started laughing. I looked back at Ananda, who shrugged her shoulders letting me know I was on my own.

"If I knew your name I would have called your name. What's yo name, lil mama?"

The one I liked walked closer to me and Ananda. I told him my name and we exchanged info before Ananda and I could even walk into the corner store.

Although Ananda and I were on a mission neither one of us could work up the nerve to ask this guy where we could get white. On the way out he tried to tell me bye and that he would call me. Ready to try my luck, I told him to walk me to the car.

"Hey, um, you know anybody who got any white?" I finally asked.

He smiled, showing all his gold teeth. "Today is your lucky day cuz I'm the man. What you need, baby?"

I tried to conceal my excitement as much as possible. "Just an eighth," I said.

He yelled some sort of coded phrase out to one of his homeboys nearby and just like that, we were back on and just like that, my life switched lanes.

The fine boy we met that day at the corner store turned out to be Vonte, who turned out to be my boyfriend, for a while after. Vonte was everything I thought I needed. He was that bad boy I never ever came across at my high school or on my side of town. He was older, a few years older. He was street smart, and I guess you could say a businessman. I mean, selling drugs is a business, right? I should know first-hand that it's a lucrative business.

Only difference with Vonte was that what was done behind the money and materials it could buy wasn't hidden from me, and I liked that. I was in heaven! On the other hand, I felt bad because I failed to mention that I liked to do a little coke. A couple days after we met and were talking on the phone, he asked who the coke was for. I told him it was for my friends.

"Being that I am one of the few black girls in my school they felt I had connects since their plug ran out." As far as I knew he bought that excuse.

Being with Vontae had its ups and downs. He was sweet and considerate. Then he was controlling and manipulative. Vontae learned who my dad was and, as I expected, his goal was to be like my dad. After a while he noticed that I had no relationship with my dad and barely talked to my mother. At this point they had given up on me. I was still bumming at Ananda's house since her parents were never there. However, sometimes I wanted to get away from always having a bunch of teenagers around being loud and ready to get high and party.

When I needed a break from Ananda's house, I would stroll into my house like nothing was wrong and lock myself in my room. My mom would come check on me and apologize for lying to me. However, I could never look at her the same and our conversations would be dry. Being home meant I had rules. When I got tired of the rules or my dad's attitude, I was back bumming on Ananda's couch.

One night I went home, and my mom told me if I wasn't willing to walk the right path according to their rules, don't bother coming back. Who the hell were these damn frauds? Anyway, at this time I was a senior and I had Vonte. I really didn't want to go to Ananda's house, so I called Vonte crying.

"You want me to come get you?" he offered, and I answered yes.

That wasn't a smart move. Vontae came and got me and brought me to his trap house. The trap was a small efficiency type spot in the projects in the middle of Pompano. It was tidy but not homely and not what I was used to, coming from mansions. However, I had no choice, and I was with my man and if this was his way of living that was fine. During the day, it was customers coming to the window all day and more towards the afternoon were the street guys getting their re-ups. I would be there witnessing it all. I got so bored sitting there watching that.

One night I asked Vontae what I could do to help. I mean, I wasn't used to him not paying me attention. When I was home or at Ananda's, I guess he would see me when he had the time. However, now that I asked to stay with him, not thinking it would be a trap house, I could see how busy he really was. So, I wanted to make myself useful since I was barely going to school to be around him.

Vontae taught me how to break the bricks of coke down and bag them up. It was simple. The coke would break down easy if I banged on it with a sturdy object and I had the dime bag zip locks. Then I would push the coke in and close it. Wala, magic! This is what the feigns were coming to the window for day in and day out. The smell was strong as hell and it would bother me, so I started wearing a mask. Vontae loved when I bagged for him because I was so fast. I loved making him happy! Therefore, I loved doing it anytime he wanted me to. We would work all day and have sex all night. As long as the feigns didn't come to the window back-to-back. It was a life I got used to. Freedom away from my parents. Not depending on my friends and being somewhat of a ride or die for my man.

"Bitch, what the fuck I told you about talking to hoe ass Ananda? Dat bitch fucked two of my homeboys for coke. You know you are who you hang around. So what, you a powder head?"

Whenever Vontae saw Ananda called or texted my phone it was a problem. It got to the point I started ignoring one of my few friends and maybe the only person I missed from my real life. True enough, as time went by, it seemed like Ananda started getting on drugs HEAVY. Once she knew I would be at the trap she would act like she was coming to see me, and while I would be excited, eventually she would ask what I could give her.

Vontae knew she was a coke head, so he watched our interactions closely and eventually stopped it. Soon, I got tired of sleeping on the futon at the trap and asked Vontae when we would be able to move into a separate place. I mean, after all in all Jeezy's lyrics, he preached "never serve a nigga where you sleep at."

Vontae's answer surprised me. "You see YOU live here. I sleep here with you, so I can keep an eye on that pussy. Your ass don't do shit but sit here, bag dope up, and let me cum in your pussy. What else you bring to the table to help pay bills if I decided we live together?"

When I say I was hurt, I don't think there was a word for the way I felt. This whole time I'm thinking, I'm helping him by staying home from school and in the trap all day bagging the coke faster than any of his workers. I thought that would make him appreciate me. If I was sleeping, he definitely woke me up. He was right, what did I have to offer?

What also hurt me is me not even knowing he had a whole different place to stay whenever he wanted. He would leave the trap from time to time a couple hours here, a couple hours there, but he always came back and I never questioned him. That's when I figured it out. I was too focused on his world instead of trying to figure out what the hell I wanted to do for myself. I didn't say anything. I kept it in the back of my head and continued how we were moving. Until one day I asked to start going back to school.

"Fuck you want to go to school for? Your ass ain't been worried about school. You want to go be around your hoe ass friends and them lame ass schoolboys."

At this point I was confused and I expressed that to him. If I didn't go to school, I wouldn't graduate and if I didn't graduate, I couldn't bring anything to the table.

"I want to help you. That has always been my focus! Obviously, me staying away from school, sitting here bagging up, is not enough help if I want an actual bed and not a futon."

Vontae stared off into space long enough for me to worry.

"Hello?"

He snapped out of it. "Aiight, cool. That's what you wanna do, Le'lani? I can't stop you. Go ahead."

Returning to school was a breath of fresh air. I was back around kids my age and was able to feel like a kid again. Weird, right? I was confused as to if I wanted to be away from my parents and be grown or be at home and able to be a child. Truth was, I did miss home! My big clean house. Even my parents. The talks my mom and I shared, the hugs my dad and I shared. But they were fake. I was never going home. So, I should make the best of where I'm at! Wandering through the hallways, seeing all my friends, I realized after my fourth hour class I still had yet to see Ananda.

"Oh, she is in rehab. You haven't heard? Wow, you've been gone that long; not even keeping tabs with us," one of Ananda's and my mutual friends said to me.

I was so concerned. Like How? When? What the hell?!

"Yea, she overdosed, and her parents finally came home one night to her not responding."

Everything around me started spinning. Why couldn't I have been around to help her and to make her stop like Vontae made me stop? Well, he didn't really make me stop. I couldn't let him know, which resulted in me slowing down and finally stopping. I wasn't able to get any white and I was too afraid to even think about taking anything from Vonte's supply.

Over time, Ananda got out and got better. She stopped doing drugs. "That overdose scared me shitless!" she said upon her return.

While being back in school, I was able to get ahold of some white from Shirley at times. Since she was the supplier and Ananda wasn't using anymore, I became closer to Shirley. Shirley was coming to school with makeup and new hairdos. Not to mention crazy jewelry, but she was always tired. Something was different about her and I had to ask.

"Shirley, what's going on with you? You dressing flyer. Your makeup stay done. Like you look really good."

Shirley giggled and said, "I just been getting money; that's all."

I was confused. She would give me the drugs and I would take a couple of bumps before heading "home" to Vonte. He couldn't tell. Or so I thought.

One day I was just getting "home" from school, and I walked in the trap only to hear moans of Vonte and a girl. I really had to take it all in. So, I sat down on the little bench that was used as a couch. With tears slowly running down my eyes, I felt betrayed. Again. By another man. After all I did to try to help Vonte. From busting licks to sitting in the trap all day, to bagging up the coke for him. I was putting my whole life on the line for him to do this.

Once he was done, I guess, Vonte and some chick walked out of the room. He stopped dead in his tracks. I looked at the other young girl across from me looking like she was on cloud nine. She was younger than me.

"Yo shorty, see your way out," he told the girl, and she walked out confused.

The betrayal was all I could think of. "If I wasn't good enough, why couldn't you tell me? If I wasn't doing enough, why couldn't you tell me? This is what you do while I'm at school? I'm loyal to you. I would do anything in the world for you and you know that... I gave you my virginity! You're the only man I loved beside my father, and you betray me the way he did?"

Vonte could see that I was hurt and tried to say what he could to make the situation "better," if you will. Truth is, I couldn't take looking at him. Maybe I was young and so naïve that I missed all the signs. Maybe I was too wrapped up in Vonte's world to realize it was all a fairytale. Like who was I kidding? A local, fine ass dope boy, getting money, driving fly, could get whoever he wanted. He could even get the women his age, but his preference was young. And in my case, I guess dumb. I had no idea where I was going but when Vonte left to go "bust a lick," (I didn't believe that anymore) I packed my stuff and left.

"Hey, Shirley, where are you? I really need to talk."

My friend heard the pain in my cries and picked me up from around the block in a heartbeat. She pulled up in a new Chrysler. Although I was going through something, I couldn't help but ask, "Where the hell you got this car?"

She came from a well-off family, but they had like six other kids and really didn't have it to spare money for a car for all of them.

"Girl, I told you I been getting money!" she exclaimed. Right now, wasn't the time for me to dive into that so I began spilling my guts to her about Vonte. "So, you didn't know he was fucking that white sophomore, Kelly?"

Another blow. "We thought you knew and didn't care."

I couldn't believe my ears. I didn't think I could survive any more stabs to my heart. I did so much talking, I didn't realize when Shirley pulled up into a semi "hood" apartment complex in the middle of Lauderhill.

Shirley told me to get out and follow her. We walked into a little apartment. One of those that had the bedroom, kitchen, and bathroom all in one space. But it was hooked up nicely.

"Whose place is this, Shirley?"

Now it was Shirley's turn to spill the beans. She began telling me how her parents pretty much had too much on their plate to pay attention to their middle child. She felt isolated and abandoned. She expressed this to her parents, and they agreed to emancipate her. Pretty much with no questions asked. She had met a girl who told her about stripping. The girl brought her to the club and when Shirley saw the money she was hooked and never looked back.

"I had to buy a fake ID for a few hundred dollars. I didn't even have money" Shirley laughed. She said this girl she had met loaned her the money and it was game over. "I've never seen so much money in my life. It was like this girl, her name is Keisha, was an angel that came right on time. I quickly learned the ropes and got on my A game. That's why you've been seeing the difference in the way I look or the way I dress. Cuz I'm getting money, bitch!

"I'm finally eighteen now and all I wanna do is graduate. Like I have to graduate to shove that in my parents' faces. That's why I don't care if I'm dead ass tired coming to school. I'm gonna graduate!"

I was in total shock about this underground world Shirley was telling me about. But I must admit it sounded kind of fun. "Shirley, I have no money and no place to go."

She quickly looked at me. "Looks like you gonna be on the top side next to me."

I had no idea what the top side was, but I was about to learn and quickly.

Club Infinity was a world of its own. Some shit straight out of a movie. I'm talking about hella money. Plenty of fine men, beautiful black women dressed to impress, or should I say barely dressed! I had never been to a strip club. Shit, just turning eighteen, technically I wasn't supposed to have been to one.

I sat and watched Shirley work the crowd, work the men, and get that money. Of course, before we got there, we both loaded up on some white. Therefore, we both were in another world. Except she was working, and I was watching. Some of the men, I won't lie, I wouldn't let touch me with a twelve-foot stick. However, I watched as Shirley made her way around the room and even sat on some of the not so cute ones. I don't know how she did it. I do know one thing, though. She came home with over a thousand dollars.

"That is a lot of money!" I damn near yelled out once we got inside the apartment.

We both giggled and talked until we came up with the plan that I was to start tomorrow, and we fell asleep.

The next day Shirley loaned me a couple hundred dollars to go shopping with. I bought makeup for Shirley to show me how to do. I also bought dance shoes and clothes that I must say, did my body a lot of justice. Later on, we walked in, and I got hired with no problem because I was Shirley's friend.

"That was easy," I whispered as we left the manager's office.

"That's what happens when you suck good dick."

I was confused. "You sucked the manager's dick?" I blurted out.

"No, baby, that's mediocre, I suck the owner's dick!"

We both fell out laughing. I went to the dressing room and changed into my first outfit.

Shirley had my hair and makeup done to a T! I wasn't a bit nervous. I was ready to show everything I had. It was sorta like school for me. I was always best dressed, I always looked good, and I always got the attention I wanted. So, when I walked out on the floor of the club, it reminded me of how I used to hop out the truck at school when Bubbie dropped me off. My first night I wanted to really take it all in, so I didn't do any white. I didn't feel like being all hyper and bugged eyed. Shirley, on the other hand, was in her zone. I made six hundred dollars my first night and I was amazed.

"You could have made more if you only took a couple bumps. I'm telling you, you ain't never gone be able to entertain all them different men sober. Them dollars don't always come from the cute niggas. Sometimes you gotta sit on a fat, drunk nigga and grind on him until you empty his pockets."

I was so disgusted, and I knew she could tell.

"What? I'm serious. In this game the dollar bills don't have a face. You treat all they asses like kings and run it up. You get in your zone and keep them drunk. Trust me, the drunker or higher they are, the faster the money come out," Shirley explained.

I didn't like the idea of entertaining the ugly or fat ones but I had to do what I had to do.

For six months, things were looking up. It didn't take me long to learn the ropes. Especially learning from someone who hustled like their life depended on it. It wasn't a man, a female, or couple who came through those doors that Shirley and I didn't attack. Of course, now, I got high most of the time to be able to turn into my alter ego "MARISSA," which was the dance name I chose. I had control over it, though. Unlike Shirley, who seemed like she had to have a bump every five minutes. It was almost seeming as if Shirley was hustling to get high. I tried to point it out to her, but she wasn't tryna hear me.

I was able to move out of Shirley's efficiency and into my own one bedroom. I was proud of myself, and I was also mad I couldn't share it with my parents. We were still not speaking. Well, I was not speaking to them. My mom always tried to reach out, however, I wasn't ready yet. I had copped me a new Benz, so you know nobody could tell me nothing. To be honest, I don't think nobody knew I was only eighteen. Shirley was the only person who knew my real age. We were in a whole different world than our high school friends. Most of our friends had graduated and were trying to figure life out. While me and Shirley dropped out and were making thousands a month. Unbelievable to me.

I always wondered what I would have been doing if everything was still all good with my parents. I never thought about what I wanted to do in life. I was so consumed with the fact that my parents lied to me and just started figuring things out as they came along. Now, I'm here. Not doing too bad. Working at the club gave me a certain sex appeal which led to a certain confidence. I looked good and with money I was able to pay the price to live a certain lifestyle.

Slowly but surely, I was moving on up. There was no man or woman I couldn't have. I chose not to deal with them. I knew how to finesse my way with words like Shirley taught me. That's all I really needed. I would make promises that I knew damn well I wasn't keeping.

"Damn, baby, I know this tight ass got some good pussy attached to it," one of my customers said as I was grinding my ass all over his lap in the private room. I was even rubbing my hand up and down his crotch. They all loved that while I purred in their ears.

"Gotta make it feel real. Make them feel like they can have it if they want it." I always kept what Shirley would say in the back of my mind.

Vonte never crossed my mind. Once I started earning my own money, my heart turned to ice. Especially after my parents deceived me. What happened with Vonte hurt, but I didn't think about it. I vowed to be more careful when dealing with people. My parents betrayed me so I wouldn't put anything past nobody ever again! Vontae was not even a thought, until one night he walked his fine ass inside of the club. I was in the back with one of my faithful white customers when Shirley came running back there.

"Lani... Lani..." I heard her tapping the wall and whispering my real name. "Vonte just walked in."

I stopped dead in my tracks. That was the last thing I thought I would hear.

I ended the lap dance, got my money, and walked on the floor. I spotted his purple ass right away but thank God his back was turned. I had time to rush to the dressing room and check myself out. I was panicking but I wanted him to see me. I wanted him to see that I looked good, and I wanted him to know I was doing well. I did a once over in the mirror and I was extremely satisfied with how fine I looked. I sashayed my way onto the floor acting like I didn't know he was there. I walked to the bar so I could be in his view. He spotted me right away and our eyes locked. I shyly smiled at him, ordered my drink, and turned my back. A few minutes later, longer than I expected, Vontae was standing right next to me smelling all good and shit.

"What's up, stranger?" His voice melted my heart.

The convo for me was awkward at first but I managed to pull myself together. He was telling me how he had heard from one of his homeboys that I was working here, and he wanted to apologize to me face-to-face. He said he was young-minded and didn't think it would have an effect on us the way that it did. We were drinking, and after a little while I loosened up. Thankfully, I had slowed down on the white. Because I'll tell you, I wouldn't have made it through that conversation without being paranoid, feeling like Vontae could tell I was high. That would have been embarrassing.

I explained to him that out of all people, I never would have expected him to disrespect me the way he did. I mean, he was one of the few who knew my situation and feelings about my parents. He kicked me while I was down. I told him I was trying to figure myself out while trying to do what I could as a teenager to be there for him.

We ended on a good note. We exchanged numbers and promised to be in touch. The same butterflies I had when I first saw him at the corner store were back.

Vontae was my first love so quickly getting comfortable with him again wasn't a surprise. It was like we had never been apart as long as we were. He definitely bossed up even more and was on top of his game. He hustled so much, but I never knew what he was hustling for. So, I asked. "Babe you're always working and making so much money, what is the plan?"

I think he was shocked at my question. "I do it for my loved ones. I mean, I ain't never had shit and I ain't tryna be like that again. It really ain't no goal but to not go back to that. And to stay out of jail."

Weird as it may seem, I didn't really know what I was hustling for either, besides not having to crawl back to my parents on my hands and knees.

Over the next few months, me and Vontae became closer and closer. The closer we got the less he wanted me to work. Truth be told, I really didn't have to, because we lived lavishly on his bill. We moved in together, which made things a little easier on both of us. Well, maybe it was because I wanted to know his every damn move. Of course, he wanted to know about mine, too. Living together was great. He had his hustling hours and was home at a decent time. I popped into work here and there. Although I didn't go to work that much, I started noticing a change in his attitude when I did go.

"What is it? You wanna be the only one bringing money home?" I asked him one night as he turned his back to me in bed.

"That lil shit you make you can keep that. We don't need it. Yo ass wanna show yo pretty face and pretty pussy to weird niggas. I ain't on that."

Sometimes I was confused as to whether he really wanted to take care of me or was he trying to control me. However, that was my man and really, I ain't' want to be in the club like that no more anyway.

I started slowing down going to the club. Trying to gear up to stopping. I was going to the club maybe once a month because I wanted some extra cash I didn't have to ask for. Soon I finally completely stopped and Vontae became sweeter. He would come home with gifts and I'm talking big designer gifts. Sometimes he even came home with flowers, and I think I liked that the most. He also realized that I was not the girl he would leave in the trap doing nothing. I was a woman now. I was cooking and cleaning and making sure things around the house were in order.

I got word that Shirley was somewhere doing bad on drugs. I made a couple of attempts to help her but to no avail. Another of my close friends bites the dust on drugs, which meant I had no friends. That was my cue to stop and now it was me and my man against the world.

We sat and came up with a plan. We wanted to buy a house and hopefully get into real estate investing from there. We had the money. It took some studying, and I had all the time in the world. Every day that went by, Vontae and I got even closer. It was a fairytale. Sometimes I would even ride with him to go check his trap out or make some runs, keeping his drug dealer partners together. I felt like we were Bonnie and Clyde. Vontae barely wanted me to do anything alone. I felt protected. I felt loved.

When we went out you know I was always dressed to impress. Makeup, hair, nails, all that. Slayed. Like I said before, I was always used to attention. I don't think Vontae liked it too much. It was like he wanted to show me off but got mad if, maybe he walked away from me for a minute, and someone came over tryna holla at me. Or if I went to the bathroom and he saw someone stop me to try and talk. Now I knew none of these niggas in this world was worth my man. I was living the life, and I was taken care of. Furthermore, our sex life was fantastic. It was hard trying to get that across to Vontae after coming home every time we went out.

"Bitch, you trying me wit des po ass niggas?" He would be yelling at the top of his lungs. "Hoe, I take care of you. Fuck you entertaining these niggas fo?"

I couldn't believe the person he would turn into when being mad. There was no calming him down. It's like he put his own stories in his head and believed them. It was frustrating to me, because anyone with eyes could see I only wanted him. This behavior came out of nowhere.

Ninety percent of our relationship, we were in love and doing well. It was only when we were apart that it was a problem. That was hardly ever. If I wanted to go to the mall, he would throw a fit.

Even when I wanted to get my nails done it was a hassle. "Baby, while you're working, I'm gonna go get my nails done."

"What you need your nails done for? Let me see them. They straight. What, you tired of me?" he would say and then I would have to baby him and talk him into letting me go.

It wasn't like I wanted to be away from him. But outside of studying real estate I had to keep myself busy. So, I figured running errands or doing womanly things should not have been a problem. For a long time, I shrugged it off.

After a while, I stopped dressing up. No makeup, no hairdo, and only wearing sweats. That was my everyday attire. He was happy with that. Except when we would see a good-looking woman out and then he would ask why I didn't get dressed anymore. This is when I realized maybe he had a problem. I mentioned it to him.

"What you tryna say, I'm crazy? Bitch, I ain't crazy. You wanna be a slut. These hoes don't got no niggas and that's why they wanna show it all. They want every nigga attention. That's what you want? Tell me that's what you want, bitch," he snarled.

It wasn't even worth the argument at times. I didn't dress up and started to feel insecure.

One day Vontae and I went food shopping. I happened to have thrown on a maxi dress that accentuated my curves. I was being rushed so I threw it on without a thought. When we were leaving, Vontae offered to go get the car while I waited at the entrance. Less than two seconds of him leaving some nigga walked up from behind me.

"Damn, lil mama, you fine. I don't know who you waiting on. I hope it ain't yo man cuz I wouldn't let you out my sight if you was mine."

I knew better than to react or respond with Vontae crazy ass pulling up any minute now. *Scrrrrrrreeeeccccchhh!* was the sound of his car coming to an abrupt but loud stop in front of me.

He jumped out of the car. "Get yo dumb ass in the car now!"

I couldn't believe the way he was speaking to me, let alone speaking to me in front of this man. He started snatching the bags out the cart and putting them in the back seat.

"Aye yo, what you standing there fo? Can I help you, nigga?" Vontae shouted to the guy who stood and stared at Vontae for a few seconds.

"I aint yo bitch so I know you ain't talking to me," the guy said before he began to creep up on Vontae, who quickly changed the subject and jumped in the car.

As soon as he jumped in, he punched me in the face. My head went from the headrest to the glove compartment in seconds. There was a loud ringing in my ear for a few seconds so the sound of him yelling was very far.

"That's why I tell yo dumb ass stop coming outside with them hoe clothes on. You ain't no stripper no more. You tryna go back in the club? I'll send yo ugly ass back."

At this point, this was going too far. All I could feel was blood running down my face. I didn't even entertain that man and there I was being beaten up behind it. Vontae had never put his hands on me. I didn't know how to take that.

When we walked in the house, Vontae's whole face changed. He looked so sad and when he spoke, he spoke in a whisper. "Damn, baby, why you made me do that to you? You know I love you. I love your body. I love your pretty face and everything about you. Why you talking to these niggas? You know it makes me mad."

I know he was trying to justify hitting me. Usually, after he talked down on me like a dog, this was what I got. This time was different. I never imagined a man putting his hands on me. Let alone the man I rode for. I couldn't forgive that. I waited for Vontae to go to sleep before I called Mom. She was happy and shocked to hear from me. The sound of her voice made me break down. I couldn't help it. I needed her through it all. She came to get me. I threw some clothes in a bag and left.

I slept at my parents' house and, of course, I woke up to a million texts and missed calls from Vontae. However, I wasn't ready to talk. I had to take the whole situation in. I slowly walked to the kitchen with memories of me taking the same steps in my childhood. I missed my home. I missed my parents. I missed love.

"Good morning, honey," Mom spoke as I entered the kitchen.

The smell of breakfast really brought me back to my childhood. I noticed Dad wasn't around and that was good. I wasn't ready to talk to him either. I knew Mom was going to have a million questions and she did. I broke everything down to her from the first time I left the house. I explained all my feelings and emotions. She listened intently. We both did a lot of crying. It wasn't easy but it was refreshing.

Mom apologized on behalf of her and my dad. She also explained that Dad knew I was there but decided to stay away as much as possible because he felt like I had no loyalty.

"Family should be able to get through shit regardless of what it is. Blood don't make you family. Loyalty do. She has none. She decided to leave and be on her own. Let her find out shit ain't greener on the other side. Hopefully, she finds a family out there."

She told me that's how he felt. Now that I was grown and taking in everything, I understood. She was adamant about us talking and I told her I agreed to it.

Later that night, Dad came home, and we had an emotional sit down. Unbeknownst to me, he knew I had been dealing with Vontae. He said he had sent several messages to Vontae about taking care of me and nothing happening to me or else. Now that I thought about it, maybe that's why Vontae always got close to hitting me but never did until recently.

Mom and I agreed not to mention that part to Dad until I was ready. So, I didn't during that talk. She expressed how furious she was hearing that, but she knew Dad would take it to a whole other level. Therefore, it was important for us to think it through.

I spent a couple well-needed days at my parents' house before I started to miss my man. We had been talking and trying to get through the situation.

"You didn't tell your dad the mistake I made, did... did... did you?" Vontae stammered out.

I let him know I didn't and that there better not be a next time. He promised it wouldn't. Even though I missed him I still wasn't ready to go back home. I wanted to be free from the controlling ways. I wanted to get dressed. I spent every day getting dressed and spending time with my mom, shopping or going out to eat. I never craved attention from men. I realized at a young age that's what came with being beautiful like my mom. I watched the attention she got everywhere we went since I was a little girl. From my early teenage years, I saw it started happening to me. So, getting dressed up was never for attention; it was a part of who I was. Mom was always a classy woman, who dressed nice and always smelled good. She passed that on to me. I felt free being able to be myself.

During the time staying with my parents, I didn't want them to know I was going broke from all the shopping and outings, so I decided to go dance a couple of nights. I told my parents I was going out with friends to keep them out of my business. Returning to work was a breath of fresh air. The money was flowing like I never left. My daily routine was work and then back to my parents' house.

I would wake up and study my real estate while Mom was at work. My parents were usually home at night so I would mingle with them. Then when the weekend came around, I would sneak off to work. Vontae and I would talk here and there. He would always apologize and tell me how much he missed me and wanted me to come home. I still missed him dearly, but I was enjoying my freedom. I also was not over that last encounter. I'd heard many stories about men who hit women and once it happened, it was bound to be more times. Therefore, I had to really tread lightly with my decision of going back home or not. Especially since my dad would put the nigga in a body bag.

After a while, I started wishing all of it had never happened and I could be home with my man. Everything would be back to normal. I would pass my real estate exam and then we would buy property and live happily ever after. Just like our plan. I mean, I literally had one chapter left and then I could go for my test.

The closer I got to my testing date the more home sick I became. I ended up letting Mom know that I was ready to return home. Of course, she didn't want me to go but I explained to her that Vontae was extremely apologetic, and I doubted that he would do it again, knowing that we would tell Dad. I also reminded her that all relationships go through bad times. We needed to talk through things and work it out. Besides, Vontae really needed me home. I set the appointment to take my real estate test the following week. I would pass my test and return home to my man, ready for our future!

I continued studying and decided to go to work one night. I was overworking to keep busy. I wanted to be up under my man so bad that all these other men, regardless of money, creeped me out. Like I was uninterested in anything they had to say. I was dancing for one of my regulars and he was making it thunderstorm, so I decided to have a couple of drinks with him. That would help me keep the fake conversation going. I was grinding on him extra sexy, again, to keep the money flying. After a little while I looked up and spotted Vontae sitting, with his arms crossed, in a corner staring at me. Like he didn't blink an eye. I told my customer to give me a second and I made my way to Vontae.

"Hi, baby." I quickly reached to hug him.

He gave off a little smile. "You know you naked, right?" he blurted out.

I was so used to dancing naked, I really didn't pay attention before walking up to him. I really should have.

"Yea, baby, I didn't know you were coming in. The guy I'm dancing for, I gotta keep him spending and he likes it when I'm naked."

Vontae started staring back in the direction that I was dancing in. I couldn't really pinpoint if he was mad or not, but there was a weird vibe. "I miss you, girl. Come see me when you get off."

He stood up to leave. I was super ready to jump in the bed with him. The liquor wasn't helping me control my urges for him. I returned to dance for my customer. Luckily, he was drunk as hell and ready to go.

So, I had the floor men sweep my money up and put it in a trash bag. I tipped everyone and I was out! I couldn't drive home fast enough. I knew I had missed my man but not this much.

When I walked inside the house it was dark in every room. I heard calm nature music playing from our bedroom. I followed the sound into the room.

"Baby, where are you? Why is it so dark?" I asked excitedly.

"Get naked." I heard Vontae's voice behind me and I was kind of startled.

"Baby, I need to shower. Cut the lights on. I wanna see you. I miss you so much."

The closet light flicked on, but it was still kind of dark.

"Get naked." His voice changed and I did as I was told.

He wrapped his arms around me from behind and aggressively turned me around to face him. "Suck my dick."

I was taken aback. Suddenly, my excitement was leaving my body. I knelt before him and took his massive penis in my hand. I spat on it first like he liked. Then I went to work. Now sex was something we'd done a million times. Hell, this was the guy who taught me what good sex was. It was always romantic and magical. Something was different about this time. I didn't like it.

"Suck it faster, bitch."

He had his hands gripped on my head, so I had to move with his motion. I was gagging and could barely breathe. He didn't care. He kept pushing. He wasn't moaning or anything. It was straight silence. Finally, he let go.

"Get on the floor, hoe, and bend over."

Something in his voice told me to do exactly as I was told. He rammed his dick into me and started fucking me crazy.

"You like showing this pussy to other niggas, don't you? Answer me, bitch." He was asking me crazy questions that I didn't know how to respond to, or should I say I didn't want to answer wrong.

"You don't want to answer me, huh? I saw how you was looking at that nigga while he was throwing you money. You a hoe. You wanna show your pussy for money?"

He was pulling my hair and choking me. He would let my neck loose every couple of seconds to let me get some air but then he would wrap his hands back around my neck tighter.

"Grip this pussy around my dick harder, bitch. What, you went and fucked that nigga, now your pussy can't get wet? Let me show you how I fuck hoes like you."

He kept ramming his dick into me. I was screaming and crying. I was scared to death. He pulled out of me then kicked me in my stomach. I couldn't believe what was happening as I gasped for air. He pulled me by my hair and started dragging me to the dark living room where he threw me up against the couch. He went into the kitchen, and I heard him rumbling through the drawers. I was trying to get up, but I kept falling. I wanted to make it to my phone.

When he walked back in, I looked up and saw the rage in his eyes. "Didn't I tell you, you was mine?" he asked before pulling a knife from behind his back and stabbing me.

After the first stab, I went into shock. I was going in and out and I could hear him yelling and screaming at me. After a while I came to, when I heard him crying, but I didn't make a sound. I didn't want to move or anything.

I listened as he walked around the house. I could tell he was pacing because his voice would be far, then it would be close. He was talking to himself.

"Why you made me do this to you, baby? Why you make me kill you? Why you had to be a hoe?" He was sniffling as he spoke.

I was in excruciating pain. I had to think of something fast. Meanwhile, I wanted to stay alive. All I could think about were Mom and Dad if I passed away like that.

After what seemed like an eternity there was silence. I didn't know where he was or what was going on. I had to keep playing dead. Then I heard rumbling from what sounded like the bedroom closet. Then I heard rumbling in the dressers. Oh God, I prayed he was leaving. I heard him zip his suitcase before he was walking towards me. He knelt down beside me. I had to hold my breath. All I could do was pray harder at that moment. He was rubbing his hand across my face slowly.

"I love you." Those were the last words he spoke before I heard the door slam.

Finally, I was able to breathe silently. I laid there quiet for a few minutes; in case his crazy ass might walk back inside. By the grace of God, my phone was in my bag that I had left in the living room when I first came in. I had to muster the strength to get there. I slowly slithered my way to the couch. It felt like my whole body was on fire. My shirt was wet with blood.

"Hey, I've been stabbed and I'm bleeding uncontrollably. Please send help." That was all I could say before I lost consciousness.

By God's grace, I had survived! I heard the news once I gained consciousness two weeks after the incident that Vontae had jumped off a bridge and killed himself. The entire ordeal was extremely traumatic for myself and my family.

Months later, after being released from the hospital, I was still trying to get back to even a somewhat normal life. I hated that my parents had to endure it all. Everything was taking a toll on me. I had so many emotions. I spent so long running from my parents because of a mistake they made. I lost so many of my young adult years chasing love or loyalty that I thought I didn't have, when all I had to do was allow my parents to be human. I didn't even try to understand the fact that they were trying to protect me from a life they sacrificed so much for me not to have to be a part of. A life of struggle.

If I hadn't been so stubborn, I would have realized my dad was the true definition of loyalty. He did everything he could to make sure my mom and I never wanted anything. For generations after us, he didn't want anyone to live the way he did growing up. I didn't want to see that, at that moment. It could have all been so simple. I try not to think shoulda coulda woulda. But let me tell you I struggle with it every day. I ran from my parents into the devil. I had mistaken Vontae's possessiveness for love. I had mistaken him being extremely protective over me as caring. I had it fucked up. All the red flags were there but I ignored them.

As I think back on situations in our relationship, that nigga was mentally crazy. But like I said, looking for love I thought I didn't have, I ran into the devil. My daddy taught me all the ways a woman was supposed to be treated. Not just financially but emotionally. He catered to my mom in every way. He catered to me in every way. So, I knew what it was supposed to look like. I guess the gifts and the times Vontae didn't want me out of his sight were not because he loved me but because he was insecure. Why couldn't I see through it? Again, how did I become so naïve?

I wanted to show my parents I could do it without them. It bit me in the ass. I literally ran into hell! I regret it all but I can't beat myself over it because at the end of the day I learned to be a survivor. In a situation where money was the goal, I guess for me the universe had a different route. Being sheltered by my parents was not gonna help me grow the balls I needed to survive in this life and, even worse, in real estate. I passed my test, and I am now a real estate agent and, baby, it's just like the strip club game. Maybe a different game but the outcome is the same. Houses and closings mean money. I may have gotten off track before but from here on out, fuck love and that's THE BOTTOM LINE.

06

YUMMY

As a young girl I was raised in a very strict household. My parents were from the islands, so that means extremely strict. We didn't have a lot. My dad was a taxi driver and my mom stayed home to cook and clean. Therefore, we really lived paycheck to paycheck. One thing I can't deny is the fact that my mom kept us looking good. Meaning hair done, face greased, and clothes ironed stiff. Although we didn't have the new Jordans my mom replaced that with the time and love she put into dressing my siblings and me. We looked forward to getting dressed for school or for any event with Mom. I never realized that we were poor because of the love she poured into us. Mom always made sure we all left the house with our heads held high. Hence, why I always had an "IM DAT BITCH" attitude.

It wasn't until I was in high school that I started realizing I didn't have what the other kids had. I started paying attention to the popular high school designers the other kids wore and wanted hairstyles that the other girls had.

"We can't afford those things," Mom softly explained one day after I expressed my wants to her. "Those things don't define you, Mya. What's more important is how good your heart is, how well you treat others, and the confidence you have wearing what you do have access to."

I was in high school. I didn't want to hear that shit. I couldn't really tell her the reason why I wanted to be like the other girls. Reason being, the other girls had the boys' attention. I wanted that same attention. It always felt like I was on the outside looking in. I was a loner. Very quiet but approachable. I had a couple friends who I was comfortable with and to a certain extent, just like me. Not extremely poor but not rich. We weren't a part of the "most popular" crew, but we were cute girls and dressed decent enough.

We really didn't give a fuck to fit in with the "popular" girls, we only wanted the boys to pay us attention like them. We came up with the idea to try out for the cheerleading team. What better way to get attention from boys and be a part of something that's cool? We tried out, however only Maria and I made it. Our other friend, Nicole, didn't and it tore her apart. We felt bad but there wasn't really anything we could do. We wanted to be a part of the cheerleading team and bad!

Becoming a cheerleader did a lot for me. It made my high school years better. I was a part of something cool. We got to get to know the popular girls because, of course, they made the team. Most importantly the football players liked us and kids around school recognized us.

Being a part of the team boosted my confidence. While being around the other cheerleaders, Maria and I confirmed what we already knew. We didn't like them and didn't need to be accepted by them. We were cordial with them since we had to interact with them every day for practice and the games. However, they were fake, they were extra, and realistically, they were whores. We went to a few outings or parties with them. They would be smoking and drinking and doing all the stuff the boys liked.

Maria and I would smoke a little here and there to look cool. Melissa was the team captain and at one of the parties she was drunk and let a couple of the football players run a train on her.

One thing I can say is that even then I wasn't letting nobody have this little cat with no benefit to me. My mom raised me cleaning my private area thoroughly and treating it like gold. Once the train was ran on Melissa she was known as the school whore. She was a rich and beautiful girl but her reputation was tarnished. What I noticed was that this was a normal procedure for the "COOL" kids. Link up, do drugs and alcohol, then have sex with whoever had a hard penis or legs opened. This is when I realized I didn't even want the boys in my school.

"Girl, you know the quarterback drove Eliza home and she gave him head in the back seat of his car one block away from her house," Maria told me one night while we were on the phone gossiping.

"My mom has been right my whole life. These boys only want what's between our legs or beneath our nose. I'm totally not interested in having any of them popular, rich or not, playing with my cat," I exclaimed.

Right before my high school graduation my whole world changed. I came home to my siblings and dad yelling and crying. My mom had passed. She had complications from a rare disease that I didn't even know she was battling. Like why would they hide that from us. I was beyond hurt. My whole world crumbled around me. It was hard for me to watch my dad have to send my mom away. I had to step in and take charge because he couldn't hold it together. I completely understood but it was imperative my mom had the right homegoing. She was everything to us all.

Her funeral was beautiful and my dad was able to get it together to do a beautiful speech. My mom meant everything to him. After all, they had been together since they were eighteen. That was common for island people; to be together for years and years, even if the relationship wasn't working. Fortunately, for my mom and dad, they had a great marriage and were closer than most. Dad never did anything without Mom's consent or approval and it was the same on her end. It took a toll on me but I had to step up and become the mother figure for my brothers and sisters. My dad still had to work, so someone had to hold the house down.

Everything my mom instilled in me, I kept instilling in my siblings. This only made me want more for us. The hardest thing for me was having to lie to my siblings about our appearance or why we didn't dress like the others. It bothered me a lot because now I felt that every time I begged my mom for more or better clothing she had to lie to me and I feel like it may have hurt her way more than it hurt me. How selfish of me? My parents were doing all that they could and I wanted more. I didn't fault my siblings because they were in the shoes I once was.

Consequently, I started keeping it real with them. "We got everything we need because Daddy works day after day. We don't need to rush to be like other kids. Truth of the matter is they may have way more but they are miserable. We got a dad and each other to love unconditionally and our real friends won't judge us. So, ya'll better walk in that damn school with your head held high and realize you are just as good, if not better, than everybody in that damn building!"

It had been a couple years since my mom's passing. I graduated high school like she wanted. Once I got out, I wasn't sure where my life was headed. I was still taking care of my siblings while Dad worked. I had this little part-time job but it was a lot of work for pennies.

One day I met this guy there and he invited me out. I had a thing for older men; high school boys really disgusted me. At least a grown man had some money or could show me some things. The guy's name turned out to be Antonio. He looked like a rapper with diamond chains and diamond rings on damn near each finger. His haircut was immaculate. He sported a Versace wardrobe and left in a brand new 750 BMW. He was raw!

So, when he stepped to me, I put my confidence on one thousand. "What you tryna do? Cuz I ain't no freak bitch you think you gonna take out and then take home to smash," I blurted out.

He looked like the type who had hella hoes and pussy thrown at him. I wanted him to know right out the gate I wasn't on that.

"Na, I wouldn't try you like that. I really wanna take you out and get to know you." He said it so smoothly I couldn't resist. We set the day and time and exchange contacts.

Antonio put me onto some new shit I definitely didn't imagine. From the beginning, he was paying my cell phone bill and giving me extra cash on top of taking me shopping at Forever 21. Shit, I was used to wearing Old Navy and making it look like something.

Despite his appearance, Antonio worked at the port. He wasn't a rapper or street guy like I thought he was. He was a man with a decent job and good morals. He always let me know he could have any girl he wanted.

"It ain't nothing for me to walk in a strip club, spend a couple racks, and come out with a whole bitch. But I like women with standards; that's why you mine."

Now, I'm not sure why he always felt the need to tell me this but I would always remind him that he could do what he chose and I would still be the same me. I didn't know who the hell this nigga thought he was but I was the right one. Come to find out Antonio was doing exactly that. Going to the strip club, spending racks, and leaving with a whole bitch every time.

I had never left my little job. I wasn't gonna be dependent on nobody to help my family out. Or whenever Antonio got into a bad mood and didn't want to help me, I still wanted to be able to help myself. Some way, somehow, I got pregnant. I didn't want a damn baby;

Lord knows I didn't. I tried everything in my power to talk Tonio into letting me have an abortion to no avail, so there I was adding another mouth to my family to feed.

My daughter was born and we named her Layla. She was beautiful. A mixture of her egotistical daddy and me. In the beginning, Tonio and I were cool. He loved his daughter, so every chance he got he rushed home to be with her.

As she got older, he started going back to his old ways. I couldn't go to my family's house with my baby because it was already cramped as it was. So, I thugged it out with Antonio. I didn't bother him when he was out all night. I knew what he was doing and I didn't need him throwing in my face everything he did for me and Layla every time he got mad. So, I simply let him be.

One night Maria invited me out and I asked him to babysit. He was confused because he wasn't used to me going anywhere, or even having friends. Maria was probably the only person I kept in contact with from high school. I'd been a mom to my siblings my entire high school years so she and I kind of drifted apart. She always made sure to reach out to make sure I was good. I didn't need Antonio's approval. I was going anyway. He knew that and it bothered him.

Maria had us meet up with some dudes. A guy she was involved with and his friend who was an upcoming rapper. His rapper name was Fargo. His real name was Justin. This man was so fire. His mannerisms, his appearance, his aura, EVERYTHING!

We started at a hookah spot that night and then ended up in a local strip club. I had never been to a strip club. I only knew my boyfriend attended frequently.

When I walked in, I could see why my "man" liked it. Nothing but a variety of half-naked, beautiful women. When we walked in with

Fargo, we got VIP treatment. I'm talking front side parking, skipping the line, a table, and bottles in VIP.

The entire night, everyone and they mama made their way over to Fargo to greet him. Strippers even flocked to our section. I ain't never seen nothing like it.

Fargo told me and Maria to choose the girls. We chose extra fine, pretty girls with fat asses. Next thing I knew four thousand-dollar stacks were brought to us. I didn't know what the hell to do. Maria had to teach me how to throw money at strippers.

Liquor was flowing, dollars were throwing, and asses were bouncing. I liked that. The liquor started kicking in more and I started my deep thoughts. This time I felt a light bulb turn on in my head. I could do this. Be a stripper! I was cute, my body was good, I liked to get dressed and I liked money. It all made sense to me.

When it was time to go home Fargo was not trying to pressure me into ending my night with him or anything. He was a complete gentleman. I loved it.

On the ride home, I told Maria my idea. "Bitch, you're crazy!" she screamed. I didn't see the crazy in it. All I saw was the money and how much I could help my family.

I got home that night and, of course, Antonio couldn't take his own medicine. He woke up yelling and screaming and questioning me about why I was getting home at 5 a.m. and asking me where I was.

"Antonio, you do this shit all the time! I go out once and you act like you losing your life!" I shouted back.

He didn't like that. "Bruh, I'm the one who take care of you. You keep that lil job cuz you want to; not cuz you have to. You and our daughter straight. What more you want from me?"

I figured he would somehow throw in what and how much he did.

"Nigga, you knew from the jump I was a package. It was me and my family. Now our daughter is added to that. And to be frank, since you want to throw around what you do for us, YOU REALLY DON'T DO SHIT!

"I work because you don't give me extra money to sit around and I have siblings that need me. Even before our daughter, you weren't doing shit. You pay the bills here cuz this yo shit! Even if I wasn't here, it would be paid. You begged me to be here and you begged for this baby. So, the little that you are doing you are supposed to do!" I retorted back to him, annoyed as hell.

"Man, listen, your siblings ain't my dilemma. So, I don't give a fuck what you say. The point remains, you and my daughter straight."

If looks could kill, he would have dropped dead right then and there. *Like how dare you count my family out? Knowing our struggle, knowing our story? Knowing they are the reason I work the way I do. Knowing they are my whole life?*

I ain't gonna lie. I was hurt at his response but it wasn't unexpected. That was Antonio. But it was time for Antonio to feel me.

The next week I left the baby home with Antonio while I went and got hired at The Mint; the same club I had visited with Fargo and Maria. They hired me that same night. The next day I went to get dance clothes and shoes and prepared to go back to work that evening. Being that I knew Antonio would not be okay with me going out two nights in a row while he was left with the baby, I left the baby with my siblings. There was a possibility of Tonio walking in at any given moment and seeing me, but I didn't care. Fuck his cheap over complaining ass.

"Damn, you look yummy!" the DJ yelled over the music as he licked his dry ass lips while looking at me.

"Yummy. That's my dance name: Yummy," I said to myself as I sashayed away from his creepy ass.

Once I got through the first night, it was over. It wasn't hard for me to learn to dance. I simply relied on my sex appeal. I understood how to be sexier than most and the men loved it.

I started making money and being able to help my family more than ever. That was the best feeling. Dad even minimized his working days. That was helpful because I needed him to oversee my siblings watching Layla.

Word soon got around to Tonio that I was dancing. "Bitch, you only dancing to get my attention. But you a hoe now so them other niggas can run through you. I'm straight. Don't call me for shit," he yelled through the phone and that was the last time we spoke for a while. He literally didn't see Layla for months.

Although I hated the thought of calling, I had to. He was the Baby Daddy, after all. It wasn't fair to leave all responsibilities on me. He never answered or returned calls. I even reached out to some of his friends. Nothing. I was heated. I wanted to ruin his life and I was going to do it. I did what every nigga fears. Started the child support process! I even went and got a good ass lawyer to speed up the process.

Sure enough, not too long after, Tonio tried to reach out to me.

"You ain't wanna talk when I was trying to talk. Have your lawyer talk to my lawyer, fuck boy!"

I didn't know what the hell he thought it was but he was about to learn that day. I went to every court hearing and I wanted every damn victory there was. I made his life a living hell on purpose. I was trying to be the nice guy, but he made it come down to that. He got visitations every other weekend and, thanks to his job, he had to pay twenty-five hundred a month in child support. He hated me. I loved it!

Dancing brought in more money than I imagined. I was able to upgrade my and my family's lifestyle, as well as upgrade my body. Over time, in the club, I felt like I did in high school when I wanted the attention the "popular" girls had. I noticed the girls who made the most money were the girls who did pole tricks and the girls who had the perfect bodies.

I damn sure wasn't getting up on the pole so I focused on my body. I went and got surgery and came out way better than I expected. It was on now. On top of raking in more attention, I was raking in more money.

One night, while at work, Fargo came in. It had been some time since I had last spoken to or seen him. Some things had changed on both ends. He was a big artist, very well-known, and I was a stripper. At first, I felt weird and was scared to walk up to him.

"Bitch, you gone miss that money. You better go speak," my homegirl, Minks said, trying to amp me up.

It worked because next thing I knew I was walking up to Fargo. He was shocked to see me in the rare uniform but, nonetheless, he embraced me. Eventually, he got some ones and had Minks and me dance for him and his crew. We had a good vibe talking and catching up.

"I would love to see you tonight," he whispered in my ear as I gyrated my hips around his penis. I mean, he did spend five grand. So, I didn't think it would be a problem for me to go.

That night I met him at his Biscayne condo. This wasn't a regular condo; it was massive. There was colorful artwork everywhere. The décor was bomb. You could tell he had made it to the big league.

He told me to make myself comfortable so I plopped right on his couch. He rolled a joint and we passed it back and forth over conversation. It was like he was really interested in me and my story. We both talked about our upbringing until the wee hours of the morning.

By the time eleven hit, I was beat and ready to sleep. He showed me to the shower and once I was done, I laid in his bed butt-ass naked. For some reason, we weren't having sex. He climbed in the bed, pulled me close to him, and we cuddled until 8 p.m. that night. I got up to missed calls from my family but it was time to go home and get ready for work all over again.

I checked in and made sure everything was good with them and Layla, then headed to work. Throughout the night, Fargo and I texted consistently. He was in the studio working. At one point I called to hear his voice and heard nothing but females in the background, laughing and talking. I didn't really care. If I really put effort into it, I could have had him. Yes, I did like him, but I wanted him to spend more money on me before he got anything more from me.

Within months, we had become closer; not sexually but mentally. We would have deep conversations and pick each other's brains. He even invited me to his concerts and hosting gigs. We would have a ball.

"Bitch, what is ya'll doing? Cuz at this point ya'll go together," Minks asked.

I giggled at her comment because it was kind of true. It was like we were together but not. I don't know; it was weird. My little sister's eleventh birthday came up and he surprised her and her friends. You don't know how big of a deal that was to a group of preteens. I was the coolest sister ever that day. If I didn't know it before, I knew it that day. Fargo really fucked with me.

One day he told me to pack a vacation bag; we were going away for a couple of days. I didn't ask any questions. I packed and was ready by the time he said he was sending the driver. I really did wonder where we were going but I trusted him and wherever it was, it would be a good time.

The car dropped me to the clear port. I was too amped because I had never been on a jet before. We pulled up to a line of black tracks full of his friends outside of one big ass jet. They loaded our bags and I watched as the guys took pics and clowned before we all loaded the jet.

"I'm happy you came," Fargo said as he sat next to me. "We going to the Bahamas for two days. A quick reset. I thought you might need one with all that hard work you be putting in," he said while staring into my eyes, causing me to blush bad.

"I truly appreciate you thinking of me," I said through my wide smile before he leaned in and kissed me.

The kiss was a shock. Not that we didn't kiss all the time but this was different.

Once we landed in the Bahamas, we had to wait on a group of girls either Fargo or his friends flew in. I was kind of jealous since I assumed that I was the only female tagging along. As soon as we got to the hotel, everyone was ready to turn up. We went to the pool and started drinking. Of course, I took the initiative to turn all the girls up. I didn't want them to think I was acting bougie because I was the one with Fargo. We ended up having a good time, drinking and bullshitting until the sun went down.

By eight p.m., we were wasted. "We going swimming with the pigs tomorrow at 11 a.m. All ya'll asses better be ready," Fargo yelled out as we all split up.

Fargo and I made our way to our suite. Soon as we got in, he started tonguing me down. My pussy started leaking instantly. He stopped abruptly and made his way to the shower. While he was in there, I filled the tub up and added bubbles before I got in. I told him to join me and he did. I straddled him once he got in and the kissing started again. This time, he was pulling my hair while doing so. I could feel his dick rising below me.

He began sucking on my nipples and I could tell he knew what he was doing. I wanted to suck his dick but I didn't want to drown at the same time.

I kissed him all over his face, neck, and chest. My moaning got a little louder and quicker. He knew I wanted him to fuck me so bad. He quickly flipped me around and bent me down into the water, then slid his dick into me. I noticed he didn't put a condom on but I was too drunk and too horny to stop him. Besides, by this time we were comfortable with each other.

Mid-session this nigga lifted my ass up and started eating my pussy from the back. My type of party. He was so gentle with it too. After I came all over his tongue, he slowly put his dick back inside of me. He was slowly stroking me while kissing my back.

After twenty minutes of great fucking, Fargo came. "Shit, I don't think I pulled out quick enough!" he exclaimed.

Shid, I wouldn't mind having his rich ass as a baby daddy. After all, my first one was the wrong choice. Now, I had to go above and beyond to make his life a living hell.

The next morning, we all met up in the lobby of the hotel and headed to feed the pigs. Of course, we had liquor with us so it was another turn up day. The girls they had were having a good time twerking wherever they could and on whoever they could. I had to keep it cute because I didn't want Fargo's homeboys thinking it was a chance for them. Any twerking from me was for the richest nigga in the crew and that was Fargo.

Once we got back to the hotel, I was exhausted. I went to the suite and fell straight to sleep. They kind of had a little party in the living room area so I kindly closed the door to the bedroom and went to sleep.

When I woke up, people were still in our suite smoking, drinking, and kicking shit. I went into the living room and didn't see Fargo. I asked his homeboys where he was and nobody seemed to know.

Although the three rooms on the other wing of the suite were for his homeboys, I casually went into every room and, lo and behold, I spotted Fargo laid in the bed with two girls knocked out. Everyone was half-naked and the room smelled like straight pussy. I knew instantly what had gone down. It would have bothered me if I didn't already know niggas wasn't shit and if Fargo was my nigga. I ain't gonna lie, it stung a little but what the hell could I do. I pulled his legs to wake his ass up.

"What are you doing?" I asked.

He woke up delirious. He looked around to see where he was and put his surroundings together. When he realized it was me who woke him up with those girls lying next to him, he began to apologize.

"Man, you know how this shit is. You one of my close friends. You should know what we on, anyway. We here to relax and have fun. That's what I want you to do," he explained as we walked over bodies and empty liquor bottles to get back to our bedroom suite.

"I mean, I'm confused as to why I didn't see a condom in sight," I responded.

He came up with some excuse about how he threw them away... blah, blah, blah. From then on, if Fargo and I were to ever have sex again, it would be protected.

The remainder of the trip was the same shit: wild, freaky, and fun. All the guys were having their way with the girls and all the girls were happy to be there and willing to do whatever. Therefore, I had to pretend to want to turn up. But really, I was ready to get back to the money.

It had been months since that Bahamas trip and Fargo and I hadn't been speaking as regularly as I was used to. Meanwhile, I had met this trapper nigga from Chicago.

One night, while at work, this man came and threw a stack on me while onstage and told me to see him when I was done. He wasn't the cutest but I could see he was a boss. When I got to him, he told me to dance and threw me like four thousand more dollars. While he was showering me with dollar bills, we were conversing over the unlimited drinks the bartender was bringing us.

His name was Gee and he was down here on some business. He had told me he wanted to fly me to Chicago because he had a flight to catch in the morning. "I'll take care of you; just come."

That was all I needed to hear and with that, the following week I was in Chicago.

Gee picked me up from the airport in his Bentley truck. He took me to a hotel to freshen up and change for dinner. We started at a luxury steak house and then made our way to a club with his homeboys and some of their girlfriends or dates. Everything was top of the line. I could tell I was with "them niggas." Gee was one of the top niggas and I had hit the jackpot. The way he catered to me made my pussy wet. I was going to fuck the shit out of Gee when we got to the room. That's exactly what happened.

Gee's sex was so good and by the time my trip came to an end, we were damn near boyfriend and girlfriend. Following that trip Gee made his way back and forth to Miami and I made my way back and forth to Chicago. Gee was no longer getting me a hotel; I was now going to his mansion on the outskirts of Chicago. There was no denying I had to reel that nigga in.

Every time he came to visit, he spent a check and made sure I was straight. That was the good thing about him not being from where I was because he didn't know anything. Only thing is that when we started making our way around both cities, people started noticing him with me at home and me with him when we were in Chicago. More people started paying attention to us. Of course, all the haters wanted what we had and the females was on his body hard.

One morning, one of my homegirls from the club woke me up with a phone call. "Why Gee was in the club dancing Cotton Candy and spent a check!" she quickly yelled into the phone.

I had to wake up and wipe the crust from my eyes. I couldn't believe what I was hearing. That was my worst damn fear, the nigga getting a hold on one of the other hoes. Cotton Candy wasn't no nothing ass hoe. She was cute and she was lit. So, it was a possibility that she could snatch his ass from me.

I hung up with my homegirl and called Gee. No answer. I called at least fifty times with no answer.

He always stayed at the W when he came down so I made my way over there. I called the hotel from outside in my car and gave them his first and last name to put me through to his room. He was there so I had them call his room repeatedly until the receptionist told me enough.

I politely went inside and finessed some white man to let me up to his floor. I got to his room and banged on the door for thirty minutes before I gave up and went back to my car. If that nigga thought it was gonna be easy getting rid of me, he had another thing coming.

I sat right out front and waited for his departure. A few hours later here comes this nigga walking out with Cotton Candy. I jumped out of my car, immediately going off. I paid her ass no mind because I had to respect the game. But I went crazy on his ass. Jumped right on him and went in his shit.

Security came out and separated us after finally getting my hands to let his dreads loose. I can't lie; it was a ghetto mess but that nigga had to feel me.

After a couple days of me calling with no response, he hit me up. "Yo, you crazy, man. What was all that for? We ain't no item. We was just fucking."

I couldn't have cared less what he had to say. "Nigga, we been fucking for months; not to mention raw. What the hell you mean, why I'm going crazy?" I screamed.

I needed more money or looks out this nigga so I calmed down and told him how much I missed him. He also let me know that crazy shit turned him on and he had me on the first flight to Chicago.

During this time, Layla was growing up and, of course, my main concern was making sure my family had help, so in turn they could help me with Layla. Therefore, all those days going to hang out with Gee was an investment. He always made sure I was straight. We spent a couple days fucking all over the house. You could tell we missed each other. He even came in me during one session.

On my last night there, he told me he had to take care of something and he left me in the house. After a few hours, I started calling and texting him, reminding him of my flight the next day and to check on him. Once I realized he wasn't answering, I didn't think he may be in danger. I was too familiar with his patterns. He was with a bitch. That thought made me furious. Like, nigga you couldn't wait till I left?! Okay. He was gone learn today.

When it was six a.m. and I was still not getting a response, I made up my mind. *Now THIS nigga gotta feel me.* I went into his room, searched it up and down until I found what I wanted. A stash of money he had hidden in his closet. It was over five hundred thousand and I took three hundred fifty of it. I switched my flight to an earlier one and left the house to head back to Miami. *Fuck nigga wanna play. Let's play!*

When I landed in Miami, I had a thousand text messages. When I turned my phone on, it was ringing nonstop.

"Hello." I answered my phone with the calmest voice.

"Hoe, you better bring my bread back!" he yelled through the phone.

"Oh, now you know me?" I questioned, realizing that approach would make him mad.

"Bitch, fuck do I know you! Give me my shit! Don't make me come down to Miami and get my shit!"

I was unbothered. "Guess that's what you gone have to do cuz you ain't getting shit from me. Playing with me like I'm some peon. You know what type of niggas I fuck? Nigga, fuck you!" I yelled back through the phone.

He wasn't gonna fuck with me no more so I had to go out with a bang. Make that nigga think twice 'bout fucking over any female. EVER.

For a couple weeks I did lay low from the clubs since I assumed Gee would be looking for me. I hadn't really been spending time with my daughter or family so I used that time to do so. Layla was really growing up on me and so were my siblings. This would normally make someone want to slow down on their fast life but it motivated me. I had to get it by any means necessary and for me, that was finessing niggas and trapping the right one!

When I started back going to work, sure enough, Minks let me know Gee had been there looking for me. Based on the thousands of text messages and voicemails he had sent, I already knew. I couldn't care less; nigga wasn't getting his money back.

After my little hiatus, getting back to work was exactly what I needed because the money was not stopping. It was like the customers had missed me and it had only been a couple of weeks. I decided to work the slow nights upon my return because Gee wouldn't suspect that I would work slow nights.

On a slow ass Wednesday, this rapper walked in. His name was "Huncho" and he was the biggest rapper out! Ten times bigger than Fargo. When he called me over, I wouldn't say I was shocked. I am a bad bitch, but I was shocked!

When I got to his section, he didn't do anything but smile. "Turn your sexy ass around," he demanded as he twirled me with his hand.

Guess he was impressed because he spent a few thousand on me alone. Before the night was over, we exchanged info.

A couple days later, I got that "wyd" text from a California number and realized it was him. He was in the studio and wanted me to come and chill. I got super cute and pulled up on him. The studio was full of niggas smoking and entertaining whatever groupies they could.

I sat alone in a corner and watched him work. It turned me all the way on. I was offered every drug you could think of but I settled on drinking Casamigos. Huncho would come out of the booth and check on me from time to time, totally ignoring everyone else.

After a few hours, he called me outside the studio. We went on a patio and we talked while he smoked. He asked to see me once he was done. I anticipated that and had shaved my pussy bald.

We met up at the Versace Mansion. I followed him to one of the luxurious rooms. He showered, then I showered. We talked and smoked in bed. He was passing me the joint. I didn't want to seem weird so I was smoking. He was so intellectual, which turned me on even more. He was in the middle of talking when I grabbed his dick and started sucking slowly.

I sucked his dick for all of five minutes before I noticed his shit was not getting hard. This was new for me because anybody I touched, it did not take that long. I tried for five more minutes before I asked what was wrong.

"It ain't you, baby. It's this damn lean, I think. I don't know. This shit don't be happening to me."

I laid down disappointed while he rubbed me to sleep. The next morning, we woke up and I said my goodbyes and got out of there with a promise to hit him up. As soon as I got in the car, I had to hit up Minks. I let her know what had happened.

"You know he got like five kids already, girl, so something somewhere works," she reminded me.

It must have slipped my mind, how many kids he had, and all I could fantasize about was me having one by him. "Do you know what that will do for me on social media? Fuck that, you know how much child support I would get?" I excitedly asked Minks.

"I think the more kids a man has the lower the child support is. I'm not sure though cuz I only got one by one man who has two and he ain't on child support. So, don't quote me but if you doing it for child support, that ain't a good angle."

Chile, I was not trying to hear none of that shit Minks was talking. I was on a mission.

"I MISS YOU, BIG DADDY." I texted Huncho as soon as I hung up with Minks. He quickly responded "LIKEWISE" and that was all I needed. I jumped up to go to this herbal place and bought some fertility pills. If and when we had sex, I was gonna be ready.

Huncho and I frequently kept in touch and soon he was back in Miami wanting to see me again. We met at the Versace mansion again. This time he was ready! To my surprise he went in headfirst with no condom. I thought it was gonna take a couple sessions for this comfortability but there we were. He pulled out though and I was mad. Nonetheless, the sex was okay. He couldn't stay hard long enough. This time was better but I wasn't completely satisfied.

Again, I left with promises to keep in touch. Soon after I left, Fargo randomly hit me up and I drove straight to him and fucked the shit out of him.

"Damn, I don't think I pulled out quick enough," he blurted out after he came.

In my mind, I was mad because I didn't want him as a baby father anymore. I had bigger fish to fry this time around. But then again, I better take what I could get because who knew how many more rich niggas I would come across. I left Fargo completely satisfied after all the pussy and ass he ate. Not to mention he laid that pipe all the way down.

After a couple days, I was feeling an itch in my vagina along with discharge. I never had that problem. EVER. I waited a day to see if it would go away or get worse. It got worse. I went straight to the gynecologist and they told me I had a yeast infection. The doctor prescribed me some pills and sent me on my way.

I called Fargo soon as I walked out and told him. "Well, who you been fucking outside of me 'cause I definitely ain't been fucking, let alone with no condom."

All I could do was think about the Bahamas trip where I didn't see a condom in sight. I really couldn't understand how dumb Fargo thought I was but I didn't even feed into him. I just said okay and hung up. I knew damn well the yeast came from him and not anyone else. I had vowed to fall back from his dirty dick ass. I was still taking the fertility pills and so far they weren't given a chance to work, except for this time.

Time will tell, I guess.

Huncho had hit me up a few days later and told me to meet him in Atlanta. He had a concert he wanted me to attend and when I landed, he had the driver take me to the mall. I went to Phipps Plaza and picked out a cute Louis Vuitton outfit with the shoes and purse to match.

The concert was sold out and the vibe was incredible. I was in the suite with all his homeboys so, of course, it was smoked out. Not to mention everyone had a soda bottle full of lean.

When the concert was over, I met him at his hotel suite. We talked about his concert and a few other unimportant things before he fucked me.

"Girl, I never stopped taking the fertility pills and he came all in this pussy before going to sleep, but Fargo and Gee each pulled out a little too late. Girl, I don't know what imma do if I'm pregnant. I can't wait to announce I'm pregnant because regardless of who it is, they all famous and got money. You know what that would do for this online store I'm working on? I'll turn all the nosey people into dollars," I excitedly explained to Minks.

"Girl, you need to slow down. It's more than just babies out here. Plus having a baby for recognition and not love is a bit weird," Minks responded.

"Who said I'm not having the baby for love? Any child of mine will be loved. Look at Layla! It's just this time it will be rich as well," I said, a little annoyed but matter-of-factly.

"Well, no one even knows you have a child already. You're barely with her. Giving her money instead of time is not direct parenting. I'm saying this as your homegirl. You gotta make better decisions. Make sure you doing it all for the right reasons."

I rolled my eyes as I hung up with her. Whose side was she on anyway?

Two months later, I took a pregnancy test and, sure enough, I was pregnant. Anxiety hit me. I wouldn't know who the baby daddy was and I was hoping it was from Huncho. I couldn't have the baby without knowing. I hit up Fargo and Huncho and then told them the news. They both opted for an abortion in which I told them both I need a hundred thousand for an abortion.

Like you niggas knew you was coming in me but now I was supposed to get rid of my meal ticket? Fuck out of here! All communication stopped with both men and I danced until I started showing. Soon after, my money started running dry, so I hit up Gee. I told him the news and he denied he was the father. Fuck all these niggas! I was gonna go get one of those early paternity tests and whoever was the daddy was gonna either pay up or live a life of hell.

I needed their DNA for the paternity test. I decided to see if I could rekindle with Gee and get his first. He would be the hardest to get around being that he was still mad about his money.

I called him and made myself cry while apologizing for taking his money but reminding him of what he did to me. "WE WERE NOT TOGETHER!" he yelled through the phone.

I kept crying, only now I did it more dramatically. Finally, he calmed down and told me to come to Chicago. I bought my paternity kit with me. When I landed it was like when he saw my baby bump, he softened up. If I wasn't mistaken, he looked like he wanted to tell me to keep it.

"Are you sure it's mine?" he questioned a million times over dinner.

"Of course, it is," I answered every time.

We went to a hotel where he fucked me in every hole and fell asleep like I knew he would. While I slept, I snuck the cotton swab in his mouth slowly and got the DNA I needed. I quietly went into the bathroom and sealed the cotton swab and stashed it in my bag.

Two days later when I got back, I mailed it off. While I was home, I hit Fargo up and told him I wanted to meet up. I was gonna have to fuck him as much as I didn't want to. So, I decided to play a guilt trip on him as well. Soon as I saw him, I broke down and told him how much he hurt my feelings by saying I was fucking other people when I got a yeast infection and that I knew it was from him.

He only responded by saying, "If it was me, I apologize."

Of course, we ended up Fucking. One thing he knew how to do was eat some pussy and I wasn't gonna deny that. Once again, I put his ass to sleep and snuck my paternity kit out and swabbed his mouth. Snuck to the bathroom, sealed it up, and stashed it away in my purse. The next day I mailed it. For this company it took two weeks for results, so I was gonna have to wait a minute for all results.

Gee was heavily invested in the baby. Little did he know I didn't want it to be his. Two weeks passed and I said a prayer before I opened the results. In each envelope each result was negative for both guys, which meant Huncho was the dad. JACKPOT!

I called him right after and reminded him that I was pregnant. Once again, he told me to get an abortion and once again, I told him I needed money to do that. He ignored me so much I had to call a mutual friend of ours to let him know what was going on.

He called Huncho on a three-way and what I heard hurt my stomach. “Fuck that bitch. She knows what she doing. I’ll pay somebody to kill that hoe before I acknowledge her or her baby.”

I could see not wanting me to have the baby but to want to have me killed because of something you did? I was on the way to a voodoo priest. That nigga was gonna feel me one way or another. I was gonna make his life a living hell.

As soon as my baby was born, I filed for child support. That way a paternity test would have to be established. The news hit the blogs everywhere. I gained a lot of followers. But I needed and wanted more money! I paid a top-notch lawyer with money I didn’t really have. But I couldn’t play. I needed to come out on top.

Soon after I had to fire my lawyer and get another one. Slowly but surely my money was running out to the point I was renting out my car for some change. Over the course of a year, Huncho and I went back and forth in court and the judge eventually ruled for thirty-five hundred a month in child support. My baby daddy was a millionaire and all I deserved was thirty-five hundred a month? I was going to appeal that decision.

I guess this was my karma for everything I put these men through. But in the end, it was my family over everything. I needed that fame because fame was gonna bring the money and the money was always THE BOTTOM LINE.

07

DOLCE

I had been dancing for around five years before I began to feel like the shit was taking over me. Initially, I turned to dancing because shit was rough. I needed some money! That was my main motivation.

Most of my family resided in Grenada. The reason for this was that when my mom was younger, she would frequently travel back and forth between Miami and Grenada, working various jobs to save up and invest in real estate there. She met my dad in the States, and when she shared her goals with him, they became their goals.

However, things took a turn when my dad visited Grenada. That trip became a bit scandalous, as my mom cheated on her husband with my dad, resulting in my birth. Although her husband chose to stay with her, he always made me feel like an outsider.

Fed up with my mom's complaints, my dad eventually obtained a travel visa for me and brought me to live with him in the States. It was cool because my dad was a great guy who never disowned me or anything. My mom would often visit, and sometimes she would take me back to Grenada to spend summers with my grandma. During those visits, my mom would showcase the houses she was buying and renovating to sell.

The family home was raw as hell, almost unreal. However, I wasn't allowed to stay there because her husband and my siblings lived there. I could only visit during the day while he was at work, and by nightfall, I would find myself back at my grandma's house. My siblings sometimes stayed with me at grandma's during the summers. My brother and I became inseparable. Separating from him in late summer was always heartbreaking.

Being in the States, my dad led a regular, working life. I'm not sure what happened with the business ventures he and my mom had, but they never flourished. In Miami, my dad had a girlfriend named Camila, who I grew attached to. She became my mother figure, as my dad was always busy working, never missing a day and always on time. He did his best to provide for me, and although it wasn't crazy lavish, I can say that I never lacked anything.

After graduating high school, I went to college out of state. I received an academic scholarship to Albany State University in Albany, Georgia. My dad was incredibly proud, and I was overjoyed to have made him proud. Unfortunately, my college experience began as a struggle. My dad had injured his leg at work, so he couldn't work as much for a while. Camila, who relied on my dad, was a stay-at-home woman, which meant they couldn't financially support a broke college student at that time. It was a real struggle.

I'm not going to lie; I was ready to sell some pussy 'round that bitch. I had always been attractive, and in college, my Miami swag and foreign looks made me stand out. However, let's face it, college boys couldn't offer much either. They were broke too!

I wasn't the type to casually be with guys. It wasn't until I started attending off-campus parties that I began to see what my college city had to offer. It was a small, tight-knit community, and everyone seemed to know each other. I felt like an apple in a world full of oranges.

One day, my dorm mate, Samantha, invited me to a party. Samantha didn't spend a lot of time in our dorm. I figured she had family who lived close by. Samantha was pretty, quiet, and kept to herself. That's why we got along so well. We were the perfect dorm mates. Our room was always clean and peaceful, and we respected each other's space. So, when Samantha invited me to this party, I was surprised. But sitting in my dorm room wasn't helping my state of mind. I agreed to go.

At first, I thought the party was pointless since it seemed to be the same people I went to college with. I felt like I could have stayed in my dorm.

"Girl, calm down. I'm telling you; the big boys are coming. College kids come early because most of us have class or homework. Just chill," Samantha reassured me after I complained for the tenth time within an hour. She handed me a drink, and soon enough, I began to relax.

Samantha didn't lie. By midnight, the college kids were leaving, making way for new faces. The "BIG BOYS" had arrived. That's when Abdul walked in. He was tall, fine, and exuded sexiness. The moment I laid eyes on him, my body tensed up, and I couldn't leave without getting his contact information. It felt like fate because while I was on the dance floor, Abdul found his way behind me. We danced without saying a word for a while.

"The way you stand out in the middle of all these people, I have to know your name, shorty," he whispered in my ear. His voice sent chills down my spine.

The rest of the night, Abdul and I spent ducked off, getting to know each other. He had an accent, but I couldn't quite pinpoint where it was from until he said, "New York."

Eventually, Samantha came looking for me, letting me know it was time to head back to our dorm.

"Oh, so you're a college student here? Why didn't you tell me? You're a good girl; I like that," he said upon learning that I attended college.

With that, we exchanged numbers, and I went to sleep with Abdul on my mind.

The next morning, I woke up to a "Good Morning" text from him. Abdul was cool and all, but I needed to know what he was all about. What kind of money he had because two broke people couldn't do much for each other. Abdul had been the one asking all the questions the previous night, and I was so mesmerized that I forgot to ask him about the things that truly mattered.

Soon enough, I found out that he was twenty-seven, six years older than me. He had moved down to Georgia from New York to escape the fast life and build his empire. He claimed to simply be giving it a try, but since he started doing well in Georgia, he never went back.

Thinking back to the clothes he had on and his overall appearance from the night before, I could tell he was doing good. He told me he was single and lived alone. Another good sign. You gotta have some money in order to pay your bills, right?

Abdul and I became extremely close. We went on dates, even if they were simple meals or whatever little activities we could find in little ole Albany. One night we went to this strip club around the way, a request of Abdul of course. My ass ain't never been to no strip club nor was I too fond of it. I ain't get the point.

I must have had a great time because all I know is I got tipsy as hell and woke up in Abdul's bed. From what I could remember we had one hell of a session that night. That nigga fucked the shit out of me! After that, I always ended up at Abdul's house. More so than not.

I don't know if at that moment I would say we were together, but we had a thing. Abdul became someone, other than my brother, that I could be my complete self with. It wasn't but a few months in, when Abdul started questioning me about what I did besides go to class.

"Well, that's the thing. I kind of don't know what I'm doing, I really just got to a point in life where I don't have the backing of my family like I'm used to," I explained. "I really haven't found my passion. I would get a job but with classes, it's kind of hard and I don't want to fall behind on work."

I was telling the partial truth. I hadn't found my outside passion yet; However, I didn't really need anything in college. Although my dad couldn't take care of me as much as I was expecting, he still sent enough to get by.

"Na, shorty, you too grown to be depending on your pops. I understand you in college, but you can't be waiting for an allowance to eat. You don't want your own money?"

I wasn't sure if this was a lecture or what, but I responded with what I thought was common sense. "Of course, I want my own money, Abdul. That's why I'm in college. I gotta put in work with my books before I can get a job with a good payoff. Why would I work at Walmart like other college kids? That's taking time away from my books for three dollars an hour. I rather do something I'm passionate about or focus on my dreams."

I felt like I was right, but Abdul wasn't buying it. We dropped the conversation when we realized we weren't seeing eye to eye on the topic.

Our relationship began to grow in terms of time; however, we weren't seeing each other as much, and I kind of missed that. Abdul was consistent with his "Good morning" texts and his nighttime calls, but that was it. Abdul said he had a situation where money was slowing down for him, and when those moments happened, he needed to hustle. He had no time for companionship at the moment.

I took the free time for my studies. My brother and I would talk every night about our current situations, and that would help keep my mind off Abdul. My brother was also in school there in Grenada, and he was almost done with it. It seemed like he was having a hard time, like I was, being that his dad did not want to help make his life easier while he was in school. Things his dad did always made me cherish my dad. Here his dad was in a position to help him but wouldn't.

Although my dad was not in a position, he did what he could, and if he were in a position, he wouldn't let me struggle. Those late-night conversations with my brother were very well-needed as far as venting. I wanted to help him badly, but I couldn't, and that bothered me.

One night, later than usual, my phone rang and woke me up out of my sleep. "Hello?" I answered sleepily.

"Man, babe, I'm going through it, and only your voice can make me happy. I hope I didn't wake you," Abdul said in an unhappy tone.

I assured him I wasn't asleep and I was happy I could make him happy. He apologized for not being able to see me as often. He said he was trying to turn his situation around, but it was getting worse by the day. He told me he was down to his last hundred dollars and was now in panic mode.

"Babe, I don't want to go back to Brooklyn empty-handed. I came here with a dream and things were looking up. Now this," he whined. He lectured that's why he was so hard on me about not depending on my dad and getting a job so that I wouldn't get to a point where I was panicking like him. "What are we gonna do, babe?" he asked.

I felt helpless. What could I do? I had nothing.

For a couple of weeks after that, if I thought I wasn't really seeing Abdul before, I definitely wasn't seeing him now. This time around it was different; he wasn't even making sure he called me when he woke up or when he went to sleep like he was before. That put me into a deep depression. I wasn't able to be there for my man or my brother. All I did was go to class, then back to my dorm, in my bed.

This went on for weeks and Samantha noticed. I ended up venting to her a little bit, and she tried to cheer me up, but that ain't work. I grew worried about Abdul, so one night I popped up at his house. I don't know why, but I was surprised that he was there. I was more surprised when I walked in, and he was there damn near having a party with his homeboys. I was even more surprised when I saw Samantha and a couple of other girls there. This didn't seem like the house of someone who was going through tough times. I was confused, so I asked to speak to him privately. I had come there to get an answer on why I was being ignored.

"Look, Lizzy, I'm not in any position to be booed up, and I damn sure ain't in any position to be booed up with someone who can't help me. Not only financially, but you ain't even capable of helping me come up with a plan on how to get out of this hole. I get it, you're a few years younger than me, you're in college, and you don't come from the same world I come from, but I need some bread. I can't be laid up with you and broke. That shit don't sit well with me. So give me my space until I come up with a master plan," he explained.

I felt worse than I did before I came there. The reality of the truth hurts. I really didn't have a plan to help.

"Look Abdul, I apologize for taking the easy way out and only being consumed with my dreams of being a dental assistant and putting my studies before a job. No, I do not come from your world. I come from my dad taking care of me, and I guess I got comfortable with that. I feel like shit not being able to help you or my brother, and all that does is push me to go harder in school so I can get to the end goal quicker. I want to help you; I want to be there for you, so if you need me to, I'll go get a job at Walmart or something," I replied.

It was like I said something to hurt his feelings, the way he looked at me with disgust.

"Walmart? Bitch, you think Walmart money gonna help me? You wanna help me? Go to that strip club and shake yo ass. Yo pussy on that stage the only thing that can help me right now," Abdul blurted out.

He paced the room while I sat in silence.

My mind raced for what must have been five minutes before I responded. "I'll do it," I whispered.

Abdul stopped in his tracks. "Do what?" he asked, then waited for me to answer.

"I'll go dance."

I don't think he believed me. Hell, I don't think I believed me.

He pulled me onto the bed, and we began to come up with the next move. "You gonna make so much money wit yo fine ass. I promise you, baby. You won't have to do it for long, and I'm gonna pay you back every dime."

Although I was nervous about the decision I had made, I had nothing to lose. He sent everyone home, and that night Abdul was the sweetest I had felt from him in a while. The man licked every part of my body before making me scream his name a million times. I couldn't understand the fact that Samantha was there, but I pushed it out of my mind.

The next day I went to class and was called out by the head of the college. This was weird. I grabbed my books and headed to Ms. Sheree's office. When I walked in, she had a concerned look on her face and told me to sit down.

"What happened Ms. Sheree?" I asked.

She took her glasses off. "Well, it seems that you are not an American citizen. I was sure that it was a mistake and tried to fight it because how the hell they telling me you're not a citizen, but you made it to college? COLLEGE!"

Ms. Sheree and I were pretty close. I could tell this was bothering her, and she wanted so badly to help me. The truth was my dad, and I knew this day would come. Shid, we never expected for me to get that far, with a scholarship and all.

Initially, my dad had started the process for me to become a citizen. Over time, being that the process was so deep, with my dad going through financial problems, he stopped. I was waiting to become a dentist and file for my paperwork, or at least some kind of income to help. The shit wasn't cheap.

I think Ms. Sheree was shocked at how emotionless I was. "Ms. Sheree, I apologize. I'm not sure what's wrong or what this means." I tried to play dumb in hopes she wouldn't ask me for more info.

"Look Lizzy, we can't continue to let you go to classes or live here on campus until this is situated. Now, I will try to help you as best I can, but until then, you have to leave this campus," she explained.

It was like my whole world was crashing down on me. I walked out. I had no idea what I was gonna do. I called my dad to explain, and he started crying. We both knew we didn't have the money to fix this. I did not want to go back and cram in my dad's house with him and Camille. So, I called Abdul and told him my situation.

"Come live with me, baby. We both in fucked up situations. You gotta go apply for that club asap; that's the only way we gonna get out of this shit," he pleaded.

Over the next couple of days, I was moving my stuff into Abdul's house. On the first day, Samantha had walked into our dorm while I was packing.

"What's going on? where you going?" she asked, clearly shocked.

"Oh, I have some things that need to be taken care of. Can I ask you a question?"

I think she knew what I was going to ask. Samantha knew about Abdul and me. Hell, I thought I was the one who introduced them, which still wouldn't explain why she was at his house.

"Why didn't you tell me you were going to Abdul's house that night?" I waited for her response.

"Oh, I talk to his homie, Paul, and he invited me to go smoke. I said yea, but I didn't know we were gonna end up at Abdul's house 'til we got there. No biggie."

She looked as if she was confused. It was believable, so I left it alone. She started to help me pack and expressed her dislike of me leaving and how she was gonna dread getting a new dorm mate.

"What if she is messy? What if she talks a lot?!" she blurted out before throwing herself on her bed.

I was gonna miss Samantha too. I was gonna miss dorm life, period. I think that was when it hit me that my future was being put on hold. I had worked my entire life to get there. I had dreamed of walking into my own dentist office millions of times. What once felt so close now felt so far away.

The next day, I finished packing, and Samantha left class early so we could say goodbye. Eventually, Abdul had pulled up to help me take my things to his house. I didn't even unpack because the way he said I was gonna make money, it would be no time before we got a bigger place of our own. Over time, I started realizing credit cards were left around the house that didn't have Abdul's name on them.

"Babe, I was cleaning, and I saw another card that wasn't in your name." It was a statement and a question at the same time, but I was ignored.

I entered the strip club world without any knowledge. Sure, Abdul brought me there to hang out once or twice, but that was it. I was too busy getting drunk. I didn't pay attention to anything outside of the women walking around naked, and I couldn't even understand that. Now I walked in, and I was looking with a fresh pair of eyes, paying attention to all the money being thrown.

Abdul and I must have come on slow nights because the way the money was flying (well money for a small country town) on this Friday night was crazy! We had walked in a little early in order for me to get comfortable. I was nervous as hell. I started to check out the women making the money, not really what you would call fantasy women.

"That's what would separate you from the rest. You gonna make a killing, baby," Abdul assured me.

I was taking it all in and prepping myself to make my way to the manager's office when I saw Samantha walking onto the stage. All those nights she didn't spend at the dorm now made sense. I stopped in my tracks and watched as she made her way seductively around the pole. This girl was a whole damn professional at this shit.

Now I was mad at myself for being so secretive because she could have told me about this shit a long time ago. It was all coming to me, the way she dressed and how she moved. I should have known that no college student was moving the way Samantha was moving without a job. I figured she had family helping, and maybe she stayed at their house on the nights she wasn't in the dorm. I don't know what I thought, but bitch, there we were.

Samantha was on stage now, baring it all. It was like it was nothing to Abdul.

"You see who that is?" I asked Abdul, who was in a trance.

"Yeah, so?" he responded. "Most college girls who got guts and want more come dance here to make some money."

Something told me he knew about it already. Maybe he would see her there when he came without me. Maybe that's how they were so comfortable when I saw her at his house. Because they already knew each other. Nah, couldn't be. Whenever they crossed paths because of me, they barely spoke.

Samantha had just walked off stage when I walked up to her. You could tell she was shocked to see me.

"Hey girl, why you ain't tell me you were a stripper?" I asked playfully.

"So, what now? You gone judge me?" she responded back with a little aggression.

"Hell no, girl. I was thinking if I knew, you could have helped my broke ass a long time ago." I laughed, trying to lighten the mood.

Abdul walked up behind me.

"What's up, Abdul?"

Samantha greeted him dryly. The vibe was weird. So, I said bye and pulled Abdul to follow me to the office.

"Alright, baby, you go in and get hired, I'mma be right here chilling."

With that, I took a deep breath and knocked on the door that was soon opened by a white man. I went in; they asked me some questions like my age, where I was from... blah, blah, blah. I presented my ID, then they told me I could audition the following evening and I would be hired.

I would be lying if I said the word audition didn't make me even more nervous. With the way the girls looked here, outside of Samantha, they needed my ass. When I left the office, I was surprised to see Samantha talking to Abdul. It seemed like they were engaged in a serious conversation before I walked up.

"Nice to see y'all chatting," I said.

Samantha looked away, and Abdul claimed it was small talk while he waited on me. I shared what the manager said about the audition and how I felt about the girls.

"You starting off wrong already. Don't judge a book by its cover. Shit, some of those girls got a mean talk game and probably make more than my pretty behind do shaking ass. The others just suck dick in the back. If you can do one of three: dance, talk well, or suck dick, maybe even all three, then you will be fine," Samantha preached.

When I first started, like I said I was nervous as hell. I didn't even know how to talk to anyone while I was half-naked. One girl noticed me sitting in a corner and said, "Don't worry, once you get that first one, you'll be alright."

And then it happened. Some white man came in and wanted a lap dance in the back room. Bitch, I started sweating at that moment because, first off, the man looked creepy. Secondly, the hall to the back rooms looked creepy.

"What's the matter, sweetheart? I just want one lap dance to make me feel good, and I'll give you six hundred dollars," he said.

That definitely made me get my shit together. "Follow me," I said and led the way to the back room.

He had a firm grip on my ass as I grinded on him. I told myself it was gonna be no more than four minutes, and even that was a little long for one song. Unless a damn Teena Marie song came on or something, and I knew that wasn't happening in there.

Right when the song was about to end, he gripped me a little tighter, which caused me to grind on him with more pressure. Next thing I knew, he was panting like a dog. Just my luck that on my first day of being a stripper, I got a man to bust a nut. It was disgusting, but I now had six hundred dollars in my fanny pack. I could do this, I thought to myself.

From then on out, I was a student of the game, eventually turning into a savage. I can't lie, I was addicted to the money and what I was able to do with it. I was able to send my brother and my dad some funds regularly. That felt good. Above all, Abdul and I were back in a better position. He didn't work, but he helped manage the money I was making.

Not too long after I started, we moved into a two-bedroom. Enough space for both of us. We had also been able to upgrade his Dodge Charger to a Camaro, complete with rims and a top-of-the-line sound system. I got a cute Honda Accord. This was my first car, so I was ecstatic. I really wanted a Benz, but Abdul said it didn't fit my image.

"What, you tryna show off for everybody? Tryna have these niggas on your body? You look just fine in that Accord, and they're good cars," he insisted.

My overall appearance started transforming since I was able to pamper myself more consistently. There was even a makeup artist at work that I was using, and she had me looking bomb every time I worked. My clientele was starting to boom. I had customers who would wait until I was done with another customer for me to dance for them. Life was good. My man and I were happy, and my family was taken care of.

"This job is killing me, man. So many hours, not enough money. The money you send me helps me out, and I appreciate it, sis, but man, I wish I could come to America," my brother complained.

Recently, he had been complaining more than usual because the homecare market over there was oversaturated. I understood that and assured him that soon I might be in a better position to help more. I couldn't right now because I was the only one working. Abdul told me things in his lane still hadn't picked up too much.

"I promise, babe, I'm gonna pay you back. I'll be able to help soon," he would explain.

I was doing my part, but it was damn sure time for some help. Shit, after a while, the club starts to take a toll on you, especially when you were working four nights out of the week. Sure, we were living better than how we started, basically doing what we wanted. VIP everywhere we went. New outfits for every function. Hell, I was gaining a lot of attention. I was turning down men everywhere I went. However, it was all part of the plan.

It was time for maybe some investments or something. I couldn't do it alone. I spent most nights at work wasted. That was the only way, for me at least, to keep the money rolling in. I would see Samantha some nights, and we would speak, but we weren't as close as we were when we shared our dorm room. I was okay with that. I did notice her body was snatched, and she had a new car. I figured life was good for her. I admired how she kept leveling up. More often than not, we even danced together, and I think we both knew we could only trust each other when it came to that club. We didn't have to worry about either one of us stealing money from the pile or one of us being money hungry.

We were the best-looking in the club. Whoever walked through the door and wanted top-tier, they called for us. So, we were cool in that sense. But once the money stopped flying, she went her way, and I went mine.

One night, I was able to leave work early to go home. When I entered, Abdul was asleep at the computer. I noticed he had a stack of credit cards and some notes written down with what seemed like people's social security numbers. He must have felt my presence because suddenly he jumped up.

"Nigga, you doing fraud?" I had to ask. Like, what the hell was going on?

All the times I saw credit cards here and there popped up in my mind. I was so oblivious to what was going on. This nigga had been doing this shit the whole time. Well, then, where was the damn money?

"Baby, look, I can explain. My homie put me on some shit. It's an easy way for me to cash out." He was lying through his teeth, and I let him know that I knew that.

"Abdul, I've been seeing shit around your house since you lived alone. This didn't just start," I yelled. Like, why was he playing on my intelligence?

Furthermore, for him to have been doing it this long, what was he getting out of it? Because I was the one spending the most money.

"Look, I was gonna put you up on what I was doing sooner or later. I had to get a method that works. I think I finally got one," he tried to explain as I listened intently. "I mean, I know I got one. It will make us millionaires in no time. You can forget that club in a heartbeat, and we can get a mansion and live a crazy lavish life. I just need your help."

I heard him, but I was stuck on the part that he needed my help. What the hell was I supposed to do? One thing about it and two things for sure, my ass was scared of jail. He must have sensed my uneasiness.

"Look, babe, you gotta trust me. If we can get some girls to agree to get the money sent to their accounts and when they withdraw it, we give them a cut, we will be good. I'm working on one kink, which is getting info, and hopefully, I get that soon. Once I do, I can help you out, baby."

He stood up to talk to me, and when he did, I noticed he was wearing a big-ass diamond chain I had never seen him with before.

"Where did you get that chain?" I asked, disregarding everything else he said.

"This old... I put it on to motivate me," he answered. Something wasn't right, but I was too tired to investigate. "Think about what I said," he blurted as I walked away.

I called my brother to tell him what was going on. I had to tell someone, and he was the only person I could trust. I was still confused about the whole situation. But when my brother mentioned that he could and would be willing to help, I really didn't know what to think.

"Look, as long as he is paying well, I can help. My patients are in hospice. Most of them are rich, and some of them were rich, and now their kids are rich, and that's how they afford the hospice care. I have access to all information. Their names, addresses, socials, and the info of the family member who is caring for them, along with the credit card on file for payments. I'm tired of struggling, and I'm tired of asking you to look out for me. Let me help. I promise it will be like once or twice, then I'm out. And I won't let anything happen to you," my brother pleaded.

I didn't feel right, so I told him to let me sleep on it. All this was incredible to me. First, my man reveals some shit, now my brother wants in on this whole thing because of money problems. This couldn't be real.

That night, I went ahead and relayed my brother's message to Abdul.

"Babe, that's it, that's the piece to the puzzle I'm missing. We gonna make a killing, I'm telling you! Tell your brother to download Sap Sap. It's an app for gamers. That's how we can communicate through that app because the IP address is undetectable," Abdul explained. "Babe, you in? I'm telling you; I won't lead you wrong. We can make a quick bag, then be straight," he said.

It was gonna be hard for me to say no to helping two of the men I loved. "Yes, I'm down. What do you need me to do?" I replied.

Abdul told me to scope out some girls from the club, preferably not the ones who were established, but rather the ones who looked like they needed some money outside of dancing. So, I went to work on the prowl. I knew exactly who to step to, so right out the gate, I had two girls interested. I noticed Samantha watching me.

"What's with you talking to Goldie and Peaches all of a sudden? That nigga got you recruiting?" her nosey ass asked.

"No, they're actually cool and approachable, unlike some people I know," I quickly responded, then walked off.

Out of all the shit she could have asked me, why would she ask me that? That shit had me thinking, but there was no way she knew what I had going on. Maybe it was just a coincidence.

It wasn't long before Abdul had a whole little operation going. My brother was sending the info via the Sap Sap app. Abdul would take his time to structure everything correctly and get the money wired to one of the girl's accounts. Then the one whose account we used would have to go in and withdraw the money. We had used each girl twice, and now Abdul wanted me to get more girls.

"I don't want to burn their accounts out like that. So, get some new candidates," he explained.

We had made over a hundred thousand in a short time. I wanted to stop. But it was like, the more money we made, the more we spent. Also, the less I had to work. When I complained about stopping, Abdul used those moments to remind me, "You don't like going to the mall whenever you feel like it? You don't like this house you're living in? We even upgraded your car, and none of this came from dancing. You ready to start working again?" he would ask.

I definitely was loving my new life at home more. So, I went to work for one night and found another candidate. I can't lie, Abdul was running it up. My brother was happy and everything was fine. The last girl I got, her name was Smooches, she had a friend named Taylor that she brought in.

One day while Taylor was working, she was stopped outside the bank. We sat in the car watching the police take her in from afar. This made Abdul very nervous. I was trying to keep calm, but the way he was panicking started to scare me. Tears started rolling down my eyes. This made him madder.

"What the fuck you crying for? Stop fucking crying. Don't tell me you gonna fold under pressure. Let me know now so I can get rid of your ass. You crying now, that means you gonna cry if the police come for us. I can't have no pussy on my team," he yelled.

The nerve of him, mad at me when he was the one scared first. Although Taylor only had Abdul's throwaway phone to communicate, we hadn't heard from her. That weekend, I decided to go to work to see if I could see her or get word, and sure enough, she was there. I really wanted to choke her ass out for not reaching out to us, but I calmed down.

I pulled her aside and asked her what happened.

"Girl, it was nothing. They knew the ID was fake, and it sent an alarm through the system, I guess. The teller gave me the cash, and I thought I was good until the door locked as I was walking out. Next thing I knew, the cops were coming. I already knew it was for me. They asked me a bunch of questions; I acted like I ain't speak English. They took me to jail and charged me with aggravated identity theft. So now I gotta get a lawyer," she explained.

I knew aggravated identity theft came with, like, three years in the feds, and the way she was so calm about it was suspect to me. If you're facing fed time for your first offense, you would not be this calm. So, either she didn't know how serious this was, or she was really confident she was gonna beat it.

"Dolce, I need some more money, so I need some more runs, please." She grabbed me before I walked off.

I turned and looked into her eyes. "That's funny, you didn't reach out to us sooner to let us know what was going on. Now you need more money." I let my seriousness sink in.

"I didn't want to reach out until I knew for sure they weren't watching me. That was all," she said, and with that, she walked off.

"I don't know, I don't trust that shit," Abdul said to me when I told him what Taylor said.

"I mean, she did make sense when she said she wanted to make sure they weren't watching her," I replied. "She wouldn't want to chance going into the banks again if she felt like she was being watched. I mean, we don't need the money, so we can take a break, but I think I believe her."

Abdul was in deep thought. We continued on with what we were doing, and Abdul gave Taylor a break. After a while, she sent word through Smooches that she was ready and needed work. Smooches said she had been at work and paying her lawyer, so the least we could do was send her some money or give her work. The truth was we had enough eyes and ears involved already, so to avoid adding new ones into the mix, Abdul sent Taylor back into the banks. We made sure to travel about five hours away and disguise her with wigs and makeup. That way, she couldn't be recognized.

The first run she did when she came back, which was technically her second run, went well. Abdul usually only used them twice before moving on. However, since her first run wasn't a success, he decided to run her a third time.

Now, my brother came across a patient whose family was rich from oil. They were worth billions. "This one, we gotta take her ass to Ohio or some shit. We gotta get the hell away from here to make sure this shit goes smoothly," Abdul said excitedly.

Soon, the three of us jumped on a plane to Ohio. We scoped out the area and found a bank to try. Abdul gave Taylor all the fake credentials with a pep talk and sent her on her way. Usually, a job would take about forty-five minutes, but it was after forty-five minutes and still no sight of Taylor.

Later, Abdul and I headed back to the hotel. As we exited the car, it was like the whole SWAT team had us on the ground with guns and flashlights pointed at us, instructing us to get down. You would have thought we were murderers. In less than five hours of being in Ohio, we were now sitting in a cold-ass jail.

A detective had me sitting in a private room questioning me. "Let me start off by telling you we know everything. We know you and your boyfriend run a wire fraud operation. We also know you are the head of the females. Should I keep going or are you ready to answer these questions?" the detective asked me.

"I don't know what the hell you're talking about, ma'am." I lifted my head for a quick second to respond, then I put my head back down.

After about thirty minutes, she got the picture that I was not talking. I wasn't doing any talking at all. Although I wanted to protect myself and my man, more importantly I needed to keep my brother hidden from it all. How the hell could this happen? I had no time for this shit now! All the shoulda, coulda, wouldas went through my brain. We said we were gonna run it a couple of times, stack up, and then stop. But no, we had to be greedy. We had to keep going.

My brother had made way more than he ever could have anticipated. Enough to get him out of his misery over there in Grenada. Hell he could of even gotten his citizenship and moved here. Abdul and I had more than we ever could have imagined. We should have stopped. The cars, the jewelry, the clothes, the upgraded apartment, and the limitless clubs and parties were not worth all of this.

Soon, my new reality set in. My bond was set at a million dollars. This scared me because why the hell was my bond so high? I knew why. They wanted to keep me in there as long as possible while they still built their case. Luckily, I wasn't the one really doing the dirty work, so I wasn't too worried, but I was nervous.

I had been in the county jail for about five days after my court date when a detective came and called me out of the pod. "Looks like your boyfriend's main girlfriend was apprehended too. Samantha Cower ring a bell? I'm sure you know her, you guys were dorm mates and sister wives," the detective stated.

What the hell was she talking about? Samantha was his main girlfriend, and we were sister wives. Samantha was not even involved in our movement.

"See, Samantha and Abdul have been here before for this same exact thing. Well, not to this level, but fraudulent activities for sure. Seems like she is his, what you would say, um, his ride or die. You were a pawn who fell for their dirty tricks. Now they were counting on your smarts to bring something new to the table, and lo and behold, you brought your brother in on this. Wow, you are something special!" she continued.

I was beginning to feel dizzy and lightheaded. I felt like all the air in my body had been knocked out.

"You reeled your little brother in Grenada in on this scheme for the information he has access to. Then you rounded up some girls at your job, and you sent them on runs. You split the profits with your boyfriend Abdul, who then split his profits with his girlfriend Samantha. Yeah, Abdul is hipping us to everything. He even says how you promised him a million dollars from this last scheme you masterminded. Welp, now your brother is in jail over there, until we figure out what we are doing with him. Abdul and Samantha have been released. You're stuck in here alone, and I doubt your man, excuse me, Samantha's man, will bond you out. So, you can tell us your part, or you and your brother can rot in jail for many years."

She smiled a mischievous smile.

There was no way Abdul was telling these people I masterminded this thing. That was the furthest from the truth as this could be. But how did they know about my brother?

"My brother had nothing to do with this," I stated.

I couldn't even think straight, let alone talk to this lady. I didn't want to put myself in even more trouble, so I told her to get my lawyer.

My whole world was spinning. All I wanted was financial freedom for myself and my family. How the hell did it turn out like this?

Every last one of my choices was running through my mind as I waited for an appointed attorney to walk into the cold-ass room and talk to me. I had nothing but time to think and reflect on how I got there.

Abdul and Samantha actually did prey on me. Being my dorm mate, Samantha knew what I was going through financially. She invited me to that party, knowing Abdul would be there and I would fall for him. She knew he would be able to manipulate me to do things that would benefit them both, and it did. It was why she stayed with new cars or was able to get surgery and new jewelry. Stripping could have paid for it, but the work from the girls Abdul made me lure in sure did add to that.

They had their own operation going, and I fell for the trap. All those times I was feeling like they knew each other, my gut knew it, but my dumb ass was not paying attention. I ignored all the signs over some dick. I thought this nigga really loved me, but come to find out, this was all a part of their plan and obviously something they had been doing.

It was too late to be crying over spilled milk now. My only goal was to keep my brother out of the mix, even if I had to plead guilty. As I waited for my lawyer to show up, I couldn't help but realize I fucked up and got the short end of the stick in the situation. Many of us come from backgrounds where we didn't have much. Therefore, we spend years trying to catch up on what we missed out on, which would probably land some of us in the fast life.

Getting the fast money and living the fast life with no major goal, we are destined for failure. While it damn sure is a nice feeling to get money to provide for yourself and your family, my situation has made me realize that sometimes you gotta have more discipline and control your urges, and that is THE BOTTOM LINE.

08

CASH

Growing up for me was hell. Now that I think about it, my whole life has been hell. I mean, everything was tough from the start. I know that God gives his toughest battles to his strongest soldiers, but I can't understand why I couldn't get a break.

Growing up, both my parents were around; however, my dad was weak. He let my mom control everything. He didn't have a say-so on anything, and I learned this from an early age. My mom was strict. Extremely strict. She didn't let me have too much fun as a child. I didn't get to go outside to play with other kids. I never got to go to sleepovers. I wasn't even allowed to join any extracurricular activities.

Through family members, I had heard my dad wasn't always like this. While in the army, he had to go to war. When he returned, he was not the same tough stand-up guy that he was before the war. No one knows exactly what happened as he never talked about it. All we know is that he came back severely depressed.

We almost lost everything because my mom always depended on him to handle all financial responsibilities. Once she realized there was actually a problem with him, she stepped in and took over everything. The roles had switched.

My dad began seeing doctors and therapists, but after every session, he came home the same. Eventually my family gave up on him. Now my mom, who was used to staying home, had to get a job. However, she had never gotten a degree or had experience in anything. That being the case, she found a job at Walmart.

Over time, my mom was no longer the sweet, gentle lady I once knew. In short, my mom turned into an evil bitch! When I was ten, I was receiving severe beatings and verbal abuse from her. Looking back, I now believe everything was taking a toll on her. She took it all out on me. If I looked at her a certain way, I got a beating. If I sneezed when she didn't want me to sneeze, I got a beating. If I got home one minute late from school, I got a beating.

Throughout my teenage years, it had only gotten worse, and never once did my dad say a word. My mom was careful not to leave marks or bruises visible, but under my clothes, I had nothing but war wounds. I became numb to the pain and accepted the fact that I was a punching bag.

Once I got into high school, naturally, I became curious. I didn't have my first crush until I was in like tenth grade. Any time before that, because of my mom, I damn near thought it was illegal to like boys.

The boy I had a crush on, his name was Mat. He was the school valedictorian. He was polite and very intent and blunt with his words. That's what I liked the most. I could tell he was going to be some kind of politician or something. I would have dreams of him being the President and me being his First Lady.

One day, I had the courage to pass him a note expressing my admiration of him. It wasn't anything flirtatious or sexual. I told him he was a great guy, he was a great speaker, and I wouldn't be surprised if he became the President of the United States.

"Thanks for your kind words. What's your name?" Mat had come to sit next to me during lunch.

I was so nervous. I didn't want him to know I liked him as more than just the President of the United States. My letter did exactly what I wanted it to do. Made him notice me.

We had a great conversation, which led to a great friendship between us. Eventually, things grew to be more. The whole relationship was concealed from my mother. Communication between Mat and me was very minimal outside of school. He couldn't understand why until one day I felt comfortable enough to reveal to him what I had been going through at home.

"If my mom knew about us, she would kill me with her bare hands," I admitted.

By the time Mat and I were seventeen, we had a full-blown relationship. I would sneak out and go to the movies with him or simply go chill with him at his house. One night, I got caught. I was sneaking back into my bedroom through my window at about two a.m. I had not expected to see my mom sitting in the dark waiting for me. So, when I turned on my light and faced her, my heart dropped because I knew this was about to be bad.

My mom beat the hell out of me that night. This wasn't like the beatings she had been giving me all these years; this was horrifying. It was so bad even my dad tried to come and intervene. When she was done, you couldn't recognize who I was. This was it for me. I had had enough.

The next morning, I was at the local police station. When it was all said and done, CPS was involved. Being that I was about to be eighteen, they enlisted me into this shelter for teens. That shelter was where I spent my time until I was eighteen.

When I turned eighteen, legally the shelter didn't have to keep me, but my advisor knew I had nowhere to go. "You have to get a job at least,

Maria. Then we can figure out what's next. It won't be long before they're hounding me to get you out of here. I'll give you a list of places to go to fill out applications."

Mrs. Natalie wanted to help me. I did as I was told and went to every spot on the list she gave me in one day. It was weeks before even one of them called me back. It was the job of cleaning the lanes after customers and the bathrooms at this bowling alley. I didn't care who called back; I was just grateful I was able to get a job.

The next step now was figuring out how I was going to save up for a place to stay. After about two or three paychecks, I knew I would have to get a second job to speed up the process of leaving the shelter. I kept in contact with one girl from the shelter named Melissa. She had left when she was eighteen, and occasionally, we would text. One day, she hit me up randomly. After chatting for a while, she told me she was a server at this lounge. She revealed the money she made and said she owed it to that job that she could sustain in life.

"Yea girl, it's downtown, a small little lounge type vibe, nice crowd on most days, and as long as you're cute, you make good tips," she explained.

I told her I was looking for a second job, and she urged me to come to her job.

"You will most likely quit the bowling alley. Or you can keep both until you save up and move out of the shelter. Then once you get settled, you can focus on the lounge. The money is that good. I'm confident you won't need the bowling alley."

After hearing Melissa's speech, I went down to her job. She introduced me to her manager, and just like that, I was hired. Look at God. I was so happy. You know, I never really let my situations get the best of me because from a young age, I was used to everything being bad.

However, this was a special moment. As I was getting older in the system, I wanted to have my own and be on my own. This job would help me out major.

The shelter was full of new teenagers daily. Fights every day. Girls who suffered from mental illness and had breakdowns every day. It was a lot. I would cry myself to sleep at night, wondering when I was gonna be able to be free from all the mess.

The time was finally here. I showed up to both jobs for four months before I found a room at this lady's house that she was renting out for four hundred dollars a month. It wasn't too bad. It had its own entrance and bathroom, and that was all I really needed. Once I moved in, like Melissa predicted, I wasn't going to need the bowling alley anymore. I ended up quitting.

When I first started at the lounge, I was a bit uncomfortable with the uniforms. We were basically naked.

"You got a nice ass body; you shouldn't be scared to flaunt it." Or "The more body, the more money," the other waitresses would say to me, trying to make me feel comfortable.

It took me about two weeks before I was like, oh yeah, this might work. Once I was able to become a little more confident with myself, it became a little easier. I was working that lounge like I owned it, or so I thought. The money was coming easy the more confidence I had.

Now, this lounge was not your average lounge. It was a lounge with a certain caliber of people who came. Pretty much rich Middle Eastern or white people, and as long as you looked pretty and served them well, you were guaranteed a good tip.

For the most part, everyone loved me. I would get offered to go out on dates, even was invited to fly on jets to other countries. I always declined because I wasn't where I wanted to be financially. I also wasn't confident in dating; my mom ruined that for me.

So, while working at the lounge, I would curve everyone who even flirted with me even a little bit. Honestly, my stoical attitude turned a lot of them on. Of course, I was nice, but I wasn't like the other girls who were extra flirtatious. I wasn't that type.

Melissa had pulled me to the side one day to let me know the managers weren't feeling the way I carried myself at the job. She told me I should probably start looking for another job if I couldn't be more "social" with the customers and get higher liquor sales.

Hell, my liquor sales were good enough for me. What were they talking about? I tried to get more "social," but it was like the people were looking for more than the liquor and food that the place was selling. It began to get a bit uncomfortable between management and me, so I quit.

Now, with no job and an efficiency to pay for every month, I was scared shitless. I had managed to save a little over two thousand dollars, so I would be good for a month or two, which meant I had thirty days to get a job. I had gotten used to the fast tip money from the lounge, Therefore, I wanted to stay in the waitress field.

I went around to all the restaurants and lounges locally to apply. Someone would call me back; I just didn't know when. Either way, I wanted to be ready when one of them did.

The boots I was working in at the previous lounge, although they looked good, were uncomfortable. I decided to go to this local store that sold shoes and accessories for waitresses to get some new ones. I was roaming around the little store when I noticed these girls who came in after me, staring and looking in my direction.

They must have sensed my confusion because one girl blurted out, "Girl, what club do you work at?"

Now I was even more confused. What the hell did she mean by what club I work at?

"Uh, club?" I responded.

"Yeah, girl, 'cause you're cute and you're fine. I know you're a dancer or bottle girl at one of these strip clubs," she said.

I mean, I was flattered by the compliments, but I had to ask, "Why would a dancer be at this store?"

She and the girls looked at each other and giggled. Another one of the girls started speaking. "We are dancers, but we come here for the cute shorts and little accessories. It's clear you're not a dancer. So, what club do you do bottle service at?" she asked.

I didn't even know what a bottle girl was. "A b... b... bottle girl? What is that?" I stammered.

They giggled again.

"Okay, so what do you do? Where do you work?" the first girl asked.

I let them know about the lounge and what I was going through.

"Well, you can come do bottle service at our job. I'm sure it's more money being that it's a strip club, and it's an urban club, so it's the popping place to be. They pretty much wear the same thing you described for your last job. And these guys will be on you because you're cute, but not like the last spot, being that this is a strip club," the first girl explained to me.

I ended up swapping information with her, and I left the waitress store anxious to go check out this strip club.

I couldn't believe the shit when I walked in. It was a whole new world for me. Most of these girls were walking around naked freely. I'm talking busting it open but with extreme seduction. I don't know how to explain it. Then the girls who I assumed were the bottle girls, because they were bringing the bottles out with sparkles and accessories, were damn near finer than the strippers. This was totally next level from the lounge. I won't even mention the bomb-ass DJ. This was definitely where I needed to be.

I remembered the girl said the men might flirt but probably not a lot because their focus was the strippers, and now I could see why, but that's also what made me comfortable. The uniforms were pretty much the same as the lounge, except these were a little more stylish. I felt like body-wise, I fit right in. My body never really consumed me, but I knew I had a nice one, and comparing it to the other bottle girls, it was perfect for the club.

The manager told me to return in two weeks for training. That was kind of disappointing to me, but what could I do? Those two weeks were the longest of my life. My anxiety was through the roof. The day of my first training night, it was like the night before the first day of school. I was too excited. I was so excited and ready to get the money that I was fifteen minutes early to the training.

I was shocked at how many other girls showed up. It was like twelve of us. There was no way they were hiring all those girls. When the manager came in, he explained that only five of us would be chosen, and those who were chosen would get a call back later that night.

Training was simple, basically a tour of the club and showing us how their system was set up. I began to get nervous. I didn't know what the basis was that they would pick the girls from. Like, was it looks? It couldn't have been work ethic; we didn't even get to show any skills. Not that you needed much for bottle service.

I had to calm myself down because I started thinking, what if this is a sign this is not the job for me? Like, what if it did require extra flirting and making promises to the customers like they expected us to do at the lounge?

The manager ended the training with, "We are here to make money, ladies. Making money requires selling tables and selling liquor. However you do it, it's on you. Just be sure to get it done."

Now I was nervous again. I went home and I was hoping they wouldn't call me. At nine p.m., my phone rang, and it was the manager telling me my first day was that weekend. I was not enthused, but I said thank you and I'll be there. The truth was, I wasn't sure I was gonna show up. Surely, I could find an establishment that wasn't so sexually based.

"Yeah, you can go to Longhorn or something, but the money damn sure won't be the same!" Melissa exclaimed after I was venting to her on a phone call.

I had a couple of days to weigh the pros and cons, and it looked like I was showing up to the strip club for my first night at work that weekend.

My first night went well. I had to shadow one of the senior waitresses and pay attention to how she maneuvered. What I realized right off the bat was that I was going to have to hustle if I wanted anything out of that job. I wasn't going to be able to depend on the establishment for money like I did at the lounge.

I watched as Monique, the waitress I was shadowing, finessed every opportunity that came her way. She poured big-ass shots to get rid of the bottles quicker, in hopes that the group she served would want more bottles. That meant more money for her. I also watched her choose dancers to dance, at the customer's request, but she only chose the dancers who agreed to split some money with her.

Monique not only focused on the bottle tables, but she also focused on the people standing on the floor. She would walk up to every person missing a drink and ask if they needed anything. Hell, she walked up to every person with a drink as well. I was happy I was able to shadow Monique for that weekend because the next weekend I was on my own, but I felt ready just because of what I saw from Monique and some tips she gave.

It had been a year and a half since I applied at the club, and it was going well. Over time, I got used to the environment being sexually based, but I understood it was more for the dancers. Here and there, I would get men who flirted or even men who offered money to take me out. However, I knew that came with sex, and I still wasn't ready for any type of relationship like that.

Yes, I was still traumatized from my childhood, but I also knew that men had one thing in mind, and I didn't want to be another number on nobody's list. I kept my legs closed, my heart protected, and did a good job at doing so.

Working at the club helped me upgrade my look and overall personality. I don't know, something about the strip club turns you into a grown woman. I was getting my hair professionally done now. Away with the little girl ponytails. I was getting my makeup done. Hell, I had gotten my makeup done so much, on some nights, I was able to do it myself. I was evolving all around, which I believe helped attract more unwanted attention, but I did like the woman I was becoming.

Eventually, I was able to upgrade to an actual apartment downtown. I had saved up enough to buy a used Honda. I was doing good, and I was happy.

One Friday night, I went into work. It was a normal Friday night, when Mat walked in. What was crazy was how the girls were going crazy over him.

"Oh, girl, Mat is here. Tonight's gonna be a good night," one girl squealed as she ran past me.

I couldn't believe this. Even the bottle girls were fighting to be his server. I was curious as to what the big deal about Mat was, so I asked another server, "Who is he and why is everyone going crazy?"

She looked at me like I couldn't be serious. "Girl, that's Mat. He's a baseball player, and he likes to come here and spend. He usually goes to the private room. But whoever is his server or his dancers for the night are usually well taken care of."

I went and freshened up a bit so that I could be in tip-top shape when he saw me for the first time in years. I scoped out his section, which they had given to this waitress, Daisha. I wanted to make sure he wasn't with a woman. He wasn't. So, I walked to his section. Daisha saw me first.

"I'm the server over here, and I don't need any help, sweetheart," she kind of snarled.

"Oh, it's okay. I know him," I assured her.

I tapped Mat, and when he turned around and screamed my name, her jaw dropped. She was even more dumbfounded when he picked me up and spun me around while hugging me tightly. I was just happy he remembered me.

"Maria, where the hell have you been? How the hell have you been? I mean, you look great!" he yelled with excitement.

I gave him a shorter version of an update on how I got to exactly where we were at that exact moment. It was like we never lost touch. He offered me drinks, and I had a couple, so our conversation was flowing freely. He gave me an update on his life. He was doing really well.

"I just knew you would be in politics," I reminded him. We shared a laugh.

"You know what, you did, and I even thought I would, but baseball became my passion, and I got lucky, I guess," he responded.

I felt like I was taking too much of his time away from the dancers. If looks could kill, I would have been dead from their stares.

"Look, take this." He handed me two thousand dollars in singles. "Let's keep in touch."

When he pulled out his phone, Daisha and the dancers were stunned. I don't know, it could have been jealousy. Whatever it was, they didn't like that he took his phone out to receive my number. I took my time entering it into his phone, so they could gag even more.

Before I walked off, he whispered, "I'm gonna call you tomorrow."

And with that, I left those hoes stunned. I couldn't see the big deal. Like with Daisha, she was mad because she thought I was coming over to her section to step on her toes. Even after she realized he knew me and wanted me there, she had an attitude. Then the dancers were mad, and I really couldn't understand that, simply because I AM NOT A DANCER! Sorry, y'all, I had to capitalize that.

At the end of the night, when I walked into the dressing room, I walked into all the girls talking about Mat.

"Girl, that nigga's dick is so good" and "I heard he gave Moriah ten grand to pee on her" and "I heard he's bisexual" and "Girl, I don't give a damn what he's got going on or what he wants, as long as he's paying, I'll be and do whatever he wants."

It was like there were five different conversations about Mat at once. I couldn't believe what I was hearing. Then again, those girls were drunk. Anything came out their mouth when they were drunk. The Mat I knew did not grow up to be the person they are talking about.

I can't even explain how anxious I was for Mat to call me. So, when he didn't call me for a few days, I was kind of sad. Then, one day while I was showering, my phone rang. It was Mat!! His voice was soothing in my ear. I wrapped my shower up so he could have my full attention.

Our first conversation went well. We talked for a few hours. He told me he had to go to practice and that he would call me after. I felt a sense of relief to have someone I really knew, and who knew my story, to talk to. It was like I could let my guard down with Mat, even after all those years.

I spent the hours he was in practice waiting for his call. I was in high school all over again. He still had that same effect on me years later. Just like he said, after practice, he called me.

"Let's go to dinner," he somewhat asked.

I looked like a hot mess, so I hesitated before I answered.

"What, do you have a man or something?" he questioned.

"Hell no! What would make you say that?" I blurted out. I had to calm myself down. I did not want him to think it was anyone else. "I was second-guessing myself because I look a hot mess. My hair isn't done."

"Man, I know you from high school before makeup was invented, damn near. Throw some clothes on and send me your address."

I excitedly got myself together. Threw my hair in a cute bun and threw on some tight jeans with a simple pair of heels. When he pulled up, he was in a two-seater, and when I read the name, it said

MCLAREN. I had never heard of that type of car, but it looked expensive as hell.

We cruised and talked all the way to a high-end restaurant on the beach. He went into a little more detail about how he got into baseball, also letting me know he lost his mother not too long after he graduated. He said his mother's death had taken a toll on him and altered his life.

We had some vulnerable talks over dinner. Just catching each other up in detail while also sharing some laughs over memories.

"I really appreciate you letting me vent, and I'm happy I feel like I have a safe space with you," he said while looking into my eyes.

I let him know I felt the same. Looking back in his eyes, I realized Mat was not a boy anymore. This man was fine as hell! His skin was smooth, accentuating his perfectly straight teeth. Not to mention his body was in tip-top shape. Jesus!

While we rode home, I mustered up the confidence to ask if he had a girlfriend or a wife, to which he answered no. I was happy about that. Again, there I was daydreaming about him being the President and me his First Lady.

"Do you have to go home now? Let's go get some more drinks." He interrupted my daydreaming, but of course, I was down.

We went to this secret cigar bar inside this casino. Nothing but rich white people and, of course, everywhere we went, people noticed him. However, y'all know how white people are with black athletes. The attention was a bit overwhelming for me, but he seemed to handle it very well.

We stayed a couple of hours, enjoying each other's company.

"Let's sleep together tonight."

Once again, it was more of a demand than a question, to which I felt like I had to say yes. I was a little nervous because I didn't want this to end with sex, but I calmed myself down. Again. It was only Mat. We had history, and he was one of the few people I had opened up to in my entire life. I can trust him.

Of course, he pulled up to a luxury hotel. The view was an amazing one over the ocean. Mat turned on some soft jazz music before he stepped into the shower. I really couldn't believe the luxury he was able to afford. I never thought I would even see a lifestyle like this, let alone know someone in it. This was really next level. From the fans to his car to this very hotel room. Definitely out of my league, but I enjoyed it.

I don't know what got into me but I headed to the shower with Mat. I walked in butt-ass naked and stepped in. He immediately grabbed me and began aggressively kissing me all over. I matched his energy. It was like in those movies where the couple couldn't resist each other.

Matt lifted me as my legs straddled around him. Next thing I knew, we were fucking. We started in the shower, then he pulled me to the balcony. He made me hold onto the railings while he pulled my hair and smacked my ass overlooking the ocean. Mat was an aggressive person, so the sex matched his demeanor. I thought we were gonna make love, but I guess aggressive was his love language.

Once we were done, he fell asleep. It was like he went cold on me. I sat up thinking about how he had stretched my vagina out. I had only had sex (if that's what we want to call it) once. It was definitely not like what I just experienced. At least I got an ending this time!

The next morning, Mat woke up early, claiming he had practice. I was shocked that he could function after drinking so much the night before. As I got dressed, he pointed to a paper on the table and asked me to sign it. Confused, I read the paper, which turned out to be a non-disclosure agreement (NDA).

Mat explained that it was to ensure I wouldn't talk about anything concerning him, especially our sexual encounters. He mentioned that he trusted me and had gone as far as having sex with me before making me sign, which he did with everyone else. Feeling blown away, I signed the paper, and he dropped me off home. I couldn't help but still be stuck on the NDA.

The previous day, I had eagerly awaited Mat's call, but today, the butterflies were nowhere to be found. The way he had switched from being sweet and relatable to a cold monster was shocking. It reinforced my belief that men change after having sex.

I was going about my day when Mat unexpectedly called me. He demanded that I be ready at ten, without giving me a chance to contest. Despite my own reservations, I found myself preparing for Mat at eight. He arrived at ten sharp and explained that we would go to dinner and then stop by a teammate's gathering.

When he picked me up, he couldn't keep his eyes off me. He was back to being the sweet Mat. We went to a members-only restaurant, full of rich people, where everyone knew Mat. He introduced me as his girl, which both flattered and scared me.

We enjoyed our meal and wine. It felt like last night had never happened. I began to think that maybe his behavior was due to being drunk.

On the way to the party, Mat played music and rubbed my leg sensually. We stopped at a light, and he suddenly blurted out a demand for me to perform oral sex on him. I hesitated before reluctantly complying.

As I fixed myself up afterward, I felt violated. Mat led me to the party again without a word. The teammate's house was a luxurious mansion, filled with celebrities. The atmosphere was colorful and vibrant, with waitresses serving drugs openly. I couldn't believe what I was witnessing. Mat insisted that I take ecstasy, but I quickly denied, having never taken drugs before. He seemed mad at my disapproval and aggressively confronted me, asserting that I was his girl and that I should do whatever to make him happy.

Feeling pressured, I reluctantly agreed. Soon, I found myself naked in the pool, surrounded by people freely touching each other. Mat's possessiveness and jealousy flared when someone grabbed my ass. He confronted the person, and a heated exchange ensued, only to be diffused by security.

Afterward, Mat resumed his affectionate behavior. Soon performing oral sex on me in front of everyone, while some random girl was caressing my body. We eventually left the party, and on the car ride home, Mat asked if I was a lesbian. I clarified that I had only allowed another girl to participate because he wanted it. This seemed to anger him, and he drove recklessly to my house. He demanded that I get in the back seat and have sex with him, despite being in front of my building. Feeling trapped, I complied, and he aggressively fucked me leaving visible marks. Emotionally drained, I cried myself to sleep.

When I woke up the next day, I realized the whole day had passed, but I was greeted with a pleasant surprise. Mat had sent me three thousand five hundred dollars through a Cash App, labeled "MY GIRL." I was ecstatic. I had never received this much money from a man before, let alone had so much money at once for anything outside of bills. I also noticed that I had missed five calls from him.

He seemed happy when he finally reached me. Once again It was as if last night's events were forgotten, and I couldn't comprehend how he could function so normally after our wild nights together. He informed me that today was a good day for shopping and that he would pick me up at five after his meeting.

I quickly got ready, threw on some jeans and a top, and covered my bruises with makeup. Mat arrived, and we went to a high-end mall filled with top designer stores. Mat took charge and picked out most of the clothes for me, which I didn't mind since I had no clue about fashion. The price tags on the items scared me, but Mat insisted on paying for everything. By the end of the shopping spree, I estimated that he had spent twenty-five thousand dollars. Mat had other things to attend to, so he dropped me off afterward, leaving me disappointed that I couldn't spend the night with him.

That night, Mat consumed my thoughts, but I vowed not to bother him. Perhaps he needed some rest. With the money he had given me, I was able to call in sick for the entire weekend, something I had never done before. Over time, I found myself going to work less and dedicating most of my time to Mat and his needs. A few months later, Mat upgraded my living situation, moving me into a luxurious condo near his house. He wanted me close to him. In those moments, I felt loved, wanted, and needed. I couldn't resist him, and he had completely transformed my life. I was now living a life filled with fancy dinners, shopping sprees, and luxurious travel. I was accepted by big-name celebrities because I was "Mat's girl." However, amidst all the happiness, there was a dark side to our relationship. While we had many joyful moments, they were only possible if I did exactly what Mat wanted, when he wanted it. It took me a while to realize this, and by the time I did, I was already deeply entangled in the lifestyle.

The parties we attended turned out to be "Swingers Parties," but Mat only wanted me to engage with the females he chose. I was fine with that, especially considering my aversion to the drugs present at those gatherings. I was always taken aback by the sight of various celebrities, politicians included, indulging in drugs and engaging in sexual encounters with different partners. It felt like being part of a secret society. However, whenever I mentioned these parties during our personal time, Mat would get angry.

One night, as we were lying together, I mentioned seeing a politician taking cocaine and engaging in sexual activities with a young-looking girl. Before I could finish my sentence, Mat punched me so hard that I blacked out for a moment. He reminded me of the non-disclosure agreement (NDA) I had signed and made me read it aloud. From that moment on, I never mentioned anything or anyone I saw at those parties again.

Mood swings were typical of Mat. I had gotten used to them. I just felt like he had a lot of anger from losing his mom and I understood. I wanted to be there for him. After all, he was making sure I had everything I needed in life.

By this time I was doing Cocaine with Mat. It was a shorter, more controllable high than taking ecstasy. It helped me deal with all the publicity I was getting from being his girl. I mean, there were paparazzi everywhere and my social media was blowing up. Whenever we stepped out, I kept a pair of shades so fans wouldn't notice how high I was. I started even doing it by myself just to put up with Mat's mood swings. Cocaine made me more "Nice." It also helped me with the party lifestyle I had grown accustomed to. Before, I couldn't understand how Mat could party so hard but still function with only two hours of sleep. Now I was able to do that as well. The only downtime I had would be when he went to his meetings and practices or when I decided to pop into work. With Mat's jealous ways, I felt like work was almost forbidden, but it was okay because Mat made sure I was well taken care of.

Soon, my birthday had come around and Mat surprised me with a party full of my new celebrity friends and a few coworkers. Truth be told, Mat's friends were my only friends. The gathering was held at this prestigious hotel. I was super excited and overwhelmed with love. Mat also surprised me with a new Porsche Panamera. My night couldn't have been better! We enjoyed a night full of performances, drinks, good food, and music.

When the party began to clear out, my coworkers wanted to continue partying and go to my job to hang out. I told Mat I wanted to go, and he told me that he didn't. I told him he could go get some sleep if that's what it was, and I could go enjoy some time with my friends, then come back after. I also expressed that I wasn't ready to stop partying. After all, it was my birthday.

"I'm done partying. You don't want to end your birthday with me?" he sternly said.

I was confused at the mood swing. However, before things could take a turn, I dismissed my friends by telling them I was suddenly tired. Confused, they all left.

"What the fuck you want to hang with those whores for? You miss working? You want to go show your ass for other niggas?" Mat yelled as soon as the door closed behind my friends. He grabbed my neck and pushed me back into the wall. "You are living a life of luxury now. Don't ever ask me about hanging with those low lives," he yelled furiously. I nodded in agreement, then silently began to cry. Mat began trying to wipe my tears and console me. "Don't cry, baby, I got a surprise for you. You're gonna love it. A special way to end your birthday," he said offering me a large bump of Cocaine before taking one himself.

Next thing I heard was a tapping at the door. When Mat opened it, in the midst of my breakdown, in walked a man I'd never seen before. This man definitely was gay. I didn't even know Mat had gay friends. He wasn't wearing tight clothes or anything, but his eyebrows were done, and he had a girl purse on with makeup and a full beard. Despite me not knowing him, he greeted Mat as if they knew each other well. I went to freshen myself up while they talked in the living room. When I came out, they were both taking bumps.

"Here, take some, baby," Mat offered me.

I told him I wasn't in the mood and that I was going to bed.

"What the fuck did I say to do?" he yelled.

I stopped in my tracks, turned around, and did as I was told.

"Take a piece of this ecstasy too," he demanded.

I did as I was told to avoid a beating.

His friend, who he didn't even have the decency to introduce me to, came over and started rubbing on me. Mat, now smoking a cigar, watched. To my surprise, he let this man continue to rub all over me, eventually slowly undressing me. The feeling of euphoria had a hold of me. The touches were so sensual and felt so good, I began touching him back. Soon we were both fully naked and kissing all over each other.

"You like that big black dick, don't you?" Mat asked.

I moaned yes, then started sucking this man's dick as Mat watched. Moments later, Mat was now naked and told him to fuck me. He did as he was told. He fucked me like he loved me, and I enjoyed every bit of it.

"Get the fuck out," Mat yelled out of nowhere. Like literally stopped us. He threw his clothes at him. "Here's your money, nigga, get out."

Mat threw a wad of money at him as he quickly got dressed and headed out the door. Mat walked to me and aggressively spread my legs. "Your pussy wet for someone else?" he questioned.

I was scared to death of what Mat would do to me. Although he orchestrated this shit to happen, I couldn't remind him of that. He quickly slid his dick in me and fucked me while biting and smacking me all over.

"Happy Birthday," he said when he was finished.

He left me on the couch, went into the room, and closed the door.

The next afternoon, when I woke up, I spotted an envelope full of money on the table. There had to be about ten thousand dollars. I wanted to show my appreciation, but Mat was nowhere to be found, and when I called him a couple of times, it went to voicemail. I was still feeling a little groggy from the alcohol and drugs, so I went home to sleep it off. While lying in bed, I replayed all the events from my birthday party over in my head.

It was easy for him to pull off a surprise party. I really had no friends except Melissa, who over the course of time, I stopped communicating with because she didn't like how controlling Mat was in our friendship. Which was why out of the few friends I had, she wasn't there. Out of everyone who was there, even if they were celebrities, she was the one I would have wanted there the most.

However, knowing Mat, he didn't even try to reach her. I'm almost positive that's the only reason she wasn't there. Then the fact that all his friends were there was a bit weird. Like sure, I felt cool because of his celebrity friends, but let's be real, I only knew them because of him. It wasn't like a real genuine friendship. Now I'm thinking they only came out because it was a party thrown by Mat. That usually meant drugs, alcohol, and kinky sex, which was what all of them enjoyed. It wasn't really about me.

The car really blew me away, but he knew what I was putting up with behind closed doors. Despite the NDA, the car was a hush gift and a tax write-off. It was like the more I sat in silence and thought things through, the more I realized this wasn't a relationship based on love. It was about control and power. I had genuine love because I was swept off my feet and introduced to a life I never could imagine. Do I think I would have loved him the same without the celebrity status, money, and lavish life? I can honestly say yes. I was with Mat because of the boy I remembered him to be, failing to see him for the man he grew up to become. I was blinded by the gifts and the money and the person he was during our many sexcapades. To be honest, during those sexcapades is when he was the happiest. He would get up and jet to practice and be gone all day for the meetings. I was only allowed to his house when I was called. He moved me five minutes from him for convenience. He drugged me so I could enjoy what he enjoyed. Oh, and the money, that was just to keep me in line. How could I be so blind? This wasn't true love; this was just like he said from the beginning. BUSINESS. Now it was all coming to me. I called Mat a couple of times before I passed out from crying. No answer.

It had been months with no response from Mat, and honestly, I was happy to get my life back. I was happy I was able to return to my job. I left the apartment Mat got for me and moved into a smaller one that I could afford. I was free. I kept the car, but I feel like I deserved that much. I rekindled my relationship with Melissa, who was now pregnant, and I was to be the godmother. I was not in a rush to date. Hell, I never was into dating in the first place. So, it was easy to get back to the old me.

"Girl, why are you not dating? Despite how strong you are showing to be, I know without any distractions you think about Mat. Don't let that lifestyle or him block your heart from knowing that there is real love out there and you are deserving of it. No, you don't have to rush, but it's been nine months and all you do is work, then go home to eat ice cream," Melissa said to me over the phone one day.

I mean, Mat had fallen off the face of the earth. I hadn't seen him or heard of him at all. I did think of him and the few good moments we had. I had been introduced to a whole new lifestyle so, of course, I was going to think about it. I mean, there wasn't even any recent post about him on social media or anything. I was a little worried. However, I was not going to even attempt to get through the gate at his house. I had to let time heal.

Not too long after I decided to take Melissa's advice and not slump around the house, I started to do small things for myself. I would hang out with her for a few, you know it's only so much pregnant women can do. I would also go to brunch and enjoy my days instead of sitting in the house outside of work.

One day, while eating at this local brunch, the main topic on TV was Mat. He was battling drug addiction. He had enrolled himself in a drug program for six months, which helped me understand how he could fall off the grid like that. The final part of the news shocked me. He had gotten out of rehab but in no time was back on drugs and died from an overdose. They said his cocaine was mixed with fentanyl unbeknownst to him. The "unbeknownst to him" part was questionable to me. Mat had a strong appetite for drugs, and I kind of knew he would only go stronger. So, to me, it was possible he may have asked for the fentanyl.

Crazy thing was that had I been with him, I would have done any drug he wanted me to. It was our relationship dynamic. Many people would say that I knew what I was doing or that I was doing it for the lifestyle. I don't agree with that. I went into the relationship to be in love. Not to be forced to do drugs and have kinky sexcapades. I was lured in and possibly groomed.

Everyone can have their opinion, but that's what I know about me. I was young and innocent, coming from a messed-up childhood, and things I used to dream of were given to me at my fingertips. That was like a high, waking up every day not going to work and being taken care of as long as I did what I was told. I was used to that as a child doing every and anything to please my mom , in order to not get a beating. It became a way of life, and it was so easy. It was also with a person I was familiar with. I fell for someone I had loved since high school. I lost myself. I got lost amid the glitz and glamour. No, it wasn't about money. I was chasing love. So, for me, love was THE BOTTOM LINE.

ABOUT THE AUTHOR

Kenisha Myree, professionally known as MIAMI TIP, is a vibrant influence in South Florida. Originally from Long Island, New York, Miami Tip is one of Florida's greatest gems. Miami Tip, formally known as "TIPDRILL" rose to fame after becoming a Miami attraction as a professional exotic dancer. Known for her acrobatic skills and mesmerizing personality, Miami Tip became a worldwide sensation. Aside from releasing her books, she has also released music, which boosted her rise to fame. She is also a reality TV star on the VH1 platform. Known for her comedic and transparent personality, Miami Tip is also an advocate against domestic violence, HIV awareness, and has a nonprofit organization catered to foster children. Miami Tip is the perfect example of an empowered woman who is not confined by society's norms and lives in her truth. All social media handles are @Miamitip305

Made in the USA
Coppell, TX
08 August 2025

THE DESCENDED

MICHELLE PARK LAZETTE

The Descended

Cover design by Coverkitchen

ISBNs: 979-8-9988428-0-1 (paperback), 979-8-9988428-1-8 (ebook)

❀ Created with Vellum

To you, the reader, who's giving this debut author a chance. Through the years of work, litany of rejections, and umpteen edits, the idea that you would someday sit down with this story kept me forging ahead.

PROLOGUE

August

One year, nine months before

The rain came down sideways the day they showed up with his assignment.

It was the kind of summer thunderstorm he'd loved watching from his front porch while he dragged on a cigarette. Booming thunder, flashing lightning, and the earthy smell of land drinking the rain. They knocked several times, and he knew immediately through the storm door who they were by the emblem on their jackets. He thought the knock yesterday might've been theirs, but instead he'd found an Amazon box—thank God. He'd known to expect them but not precisely when, and the waiting game had been one of dread and anticipation.

He opened the door, stepped aside, and they stepped in. His heart thudded hard, his gut clenched. His life, as he'd lived it for decades, was over.

"We understand you've been briefed on the nature of our visit?" one of the three asked.

"Yes, sir," the man replied. He kept his gaze low out of respect.

"We are so fortunate for people like you," an older woman spoke softly, her blue eyes kind. She shook off her jacket. "May we sit?"

"Yes, by all means," he replied, offering the worn sofa in his front room.

They sat for hours, explaining his mission. He must keep the vow: no one, not even his family, could know. There'd be regular meetings, at least monthly, and more often if his mission required them.

"We must know immediately of problems," the woman urged, still softly. "Left unchecked, *these* types of problems can abruptly implode." She handed him the front page of a newspaper from the early 1900s. It pictured a mourner, her hair drawn back loosely and her face dropped into gloved hands. Behind her rose an enormous, mushroom-shaped plume of dark smoke.

In conclusion, they reminded him of the sacrifices the mission would require. He would never marry for love. He must never have children. Love, he didn't give up lightly, but he'd never wanted kids. His childhood at the hands of a cruel father was the only one he cared to know intimately.

"You wouldn't be the first person to change his or her mind," the woman assured him. "But we need your commitment now, or you'll need to forget this meeting ever occurred."

He knew they didn't mean they'd *leave* him to forget. They'd *make* him forget.

Was it wise to engage with them further? Wasn't there another way?

But he'd come this far, so he lifted his gaze and nodded. "Yes. I understand, and I accept."

1

May 26

Four hours before

If she'd been on assignment this night, Audrey Kelly would have asked each witness, be they first responders or nearby residents, two questions: where were you when they landed, and what do you think is going on?

Eh, fuck that. If Audrey had been on assignment this night, she would have ghosted the editors who refused her a living wage and saved herself. Or tried to.

But she wasn't on the clock when it happened. She was on her way home from the supposed-to-be-merry-but-actually-pretty-triggering Kelly–Mission wedding.

Although it had been more than a dozen years since her father had fled the cabin, he was all Audrey could think about as she watched her uncle lead her cousin, lace train trailing, to the dance floor. She swallowed, a raw ache drying up her throat, and blinked back tears. She forced a distraction, toying with the capers on her plate, squeezing the lemon on pasta she no longer had an appetite for, trying to focus on how she would attempt to recreate the dish.

Beneath the canopy of warm globe lights near the lake, her uncle and cousin had begun to sway to a ballad. The same uncle who grittily worked the farm, killing animals when necessary, held his baby girl tightly as Celine Dion sang. His lips moved near his daughter's ear.

You're supposed to watch the father–daughter dance, Audrey knew, but she needed air.

"It's an outdoor wedding," Kevin whispered back when she told him.

She nodded, standing with her back hunched so as not to call attention to herself. "I know."

"I'll come with you." They stopped at the bar. Drinks in hand, they sat on a bench, and Audrey stared out at the dock. The wedding's setting was so Ohio: a summer breeze that didn't make one swelter, a secluded lake found only after driving through acres of soybeans and past red barns. Audrey's drink was gone fast, but Kevin's, faster.

"You promised you'd drive us back," she reminded him.

"And I will." He paused and placed a hand on her knee. "I know weddings aren't easy for you."

Audrey scratched her head, carefully, to preserve the braided updo. She was sad at weddings, but this one had her angry, and her willingness to bury the feeling dissipated with every swallow. "Weddings would be easier if I thought I'd ever have one of my own." Her family was broken, and she wanted with every fiber of her being to build one that wasn't. She had to do it. Her happiness, her sanity, her belief that she could persevere despite her father's abandonment, hinged on it.

"I didn't say never to marriage, Dree. I said I'm not sure."

"You're nearly forty, Kevin. And you didn't say 'not sure.' You said, 'not ready.'" Audrey stood and sighed. "'Not sure' is worse." She left him on the bench.

The next time they spoke, he had the kind of glassy eyes that come from drinking one too many. She tried to ensure he was the only one to notice her irritated, cut-that-shit-out glances. Only gritted her teeth and swiped her fingers, right to left, beneath her chin when the coast seemed clear. *Stop. Drink water.* She knew well he saw. Knew well he thought he was *just fine.*

This was her cousin's wedding. *She* was supposed to be the one who got to let loose. Other family may not have realized Kevin was making good use of the open bar—probably its high-octane bourbon and craft ales—but they would know it soon enough if Kevin didn't cease. She didn't want to be the one with the puking boyfriend, least of all at their age. *Leave that to the twenty-year-olds.* What she did want, fervently, was for him to change his mind, and not for her but for him. He was pulling away, like her dad had.

"Kevin," she hissed, flanking him at the bar. "Cool it."

"I'm fine," he replied, slurring a little.

"Kevin—"

"Audrey, it's our song!" her cousin squealed from behind, grabbing her elbow. Tapping Kevin's arm, she added, "When will you lovebirds seal the deal? It's been long enough!"

Audrey couldn't flee that line of questioning fast enough, and the mid-90s rap song drew the millennials like the strung lights drew the bugs. Plus, a guest must oblige her bride. She straightened. Blinked pointedly at Kevin. Turned to her cousin in the wide ivory gown, face bright, smile forced though hopefully not obviously. "Coming, coming," she said.

Though she giggled, looped arms, and butchered numerous lyrics, the potential for Kevin to embarrass them both weighed on her mind. Gnawing away at her more was the realization that a night like this might never be hers. Theirs.

Audrey wasn't sure if Kevin drank this way before her. Tonight, he'd uncharacteristically laughed at an uncouth joke. He'd stumbled to the bathroom. This kind of drinking, even at a wedding, couldn't be healthy. It scared her.

To his credit, Kevin stopped drinking alcohol and switched to coffee. Nearly two hours later, by the time the first guests left the glittering lakeside nuptials, he insisted on driving. Though it bugged her that he drank that way, the way he slowed down made her feel heard, especially tonight, it being the first wedding she'd braved after he said what he'd said at that diner.

"Kevin—" she began from the passenger seat.

"I know." He loosened his tie, a forest green that really accentuated his eyes.

"I'm beginning to wonder if you need to stop."

"I'm fine, Dree. I don't want you to worry."

"I need to know that when we're around family, you can control yourself."

"It's not like I was the only one getting after it, right?" He cast her a sheepish look, the one he offered when he wanted to make things right, cracking the crooked grin they both knew could thaw her iciest moods.

She turned her face to the right, to the dark forest outside. "I don't want people thinking we're drunks."

His eyes were on the road, but his hand moved to her knee. "I'm sorry."

"Thank you."

She knew he hadn't meant to put her in this headspace, and if she was honest, it had been a relief to her, too, to drink away the questions and pressure about their future while watching two people seal theirs. She kept her eyes on the darkness outside. Pondered a moment. Swallowed the rest of the rebuke she'd been rehearsing.

A thunderous sound boomed in the distance. Followed by another. And another. Flashes of light were visible, but not in the clear summer sky. Closer to the ground.

"Yikes, I hope everyone's okay," Audrey said. "I remember reporting about the only female pyrotechnician in Phoenix. The fireworks exploded on the ground during the finale. Miraculously, no injuries."

"That's lucky," Kevin replied. "I forgot you were a reporter there. What was that, do you think?"

"Fireworks?" Audrey gripped her thighs, nervous. The sounds seemed more foreign than fireworks, not that she cared to admit it.

They drove without words on the two-lane highway for a handful of minutes before he suddenly slammed on the brakes. "Oh, shit!" He said it, screeching to a halt in the middle of the road.

Before them, fiery debris lay splintered across the road. She grabbed the panic handle above her right shoulder.

"What the hell?" he said, his voice rising.

Is he panicking? Audrey's pulse rose, too. It was unlike him. Kevin didn't sweat much. She followed his stare and raised a hand to her mouth. Shapes and shadows *(people?!)* dragged across the road. Savagely, they *(no, not people)* catapulted into the air, rabidly reaching and stabbing. Guttural screams pierced the night.

Audrey, now definitely dead sober, watched dark fluid rain down on the pavement.

"No, no, no," Kevin said, throwing the car into reverse. He slammed his palm on the steering wheel. "God." His eyes were on the rearview.

Audrey turned around and caught, despite the dark, movement in the air. Something of monstrous proportion descended fast, severing and blowing from their roots the trees and shrubbery beneath it. An intense humming sounded, and she squeezed her eyes shut against a sudden, blinding light.

"Can you see?" he asked.

"No," she said before she pulled one eye open. "Wait, sort of."

The aircraft met the pavement with a thunderous boom.

"Those booms weren't fireworks," Kevin said, echoing Audrey's own silent realization.

Audrey nodded, not that he saw. She peered all around, mouth ajar. One, two, three—she turned backward—four. How could there be four downed aircraft on one country road in Ohio? *Terrorists.* Her body went cold, but she sweated profusely. She wondered where her mom was. She'd been on her second tour of the cupcake table when Kevin and Audrey had left.

Audrey froze at the sound of an intense crunching and squinted.

"I cannot fucking see. What is that?" The entire span of highway rumbled, and the brush along the country road caught fire. "Oh my God ..." Audrey's voice was barely a whisper. Against the orange glow, something crawled from the aircraft, which had slammed craggy roots into the road. In the burgeoning brushfire's light, she could see better, and she gasped. Whatever crawled from the craft appeared to have scissorlike appendages and a mess of horns atop their heads. "Oh my God," she said again.

Kevin undid his seatbelt and hers. "We're surrounded. We have to go."

Audrey stared. *Out there? With those?*

Kevin jostled her. "Now."

She tumbled out of the passenger side, and he followed, falling atop her. When she yelped, he reached his hand clumsily over her face until he muzzled her mouth.

"Quiet," he hissed in her ear, and she heard him fumble for his footing. His hand snatched her arm and yanked her to her feet, then rubbed her arm. Ever her savior, even—no, especially—when life was scary.

She stumbled and grunted—regrettably—when her heel stuck in the muddy berm. "Wait," she whispered, and she ripped both shoes off.

They tumbled at times over rocks and thick tree root, stopping to pick each other up. Screams rose all around, subsiding some as they fled.

"Look, look." Kevin pointed up at a hill of trees to a home. Large and lit from within. "Come on, come on."

Audrey's legs burned with the effort. They chased the closest home. Upon approach, Kevin held his index finger to his lips. She nodded, sorry but also not sorry that he always proved the braver of the two. She held a nervous fist to her lips as he crawled up the back deck. Audrey heard nothing nearby. Kevin disappeared for half a minute, but it felt like twenty. Her eyes darted left and right, down the hill, up the deck. No matter: the darkness let on so little. She heard more booms, and she shrank, her heart thudding impossibly, her breaths wildly inefficient. It felt like at any moment, another monstrosity might plow into earth, rendering whole pieces of the planet gone.

At last, Kevin peered back over the deck to her. "C'mon," he hissed. He held an arm across her as they approached the back door. The sliding doors' glass gaped like a busted, jagged jack-o-lantern. They'd step over this—it didn't feel safer to remain outside—but they needed to be careful of shards. They needed to be careful, too, of the unknown inside.

As they confirmed with relief the rooms were empty, they turned off the lights inside. It made her anxiety climb, but it could mean they wouldn't be detected.

A part of Audrey doubted they should corner themselves. Another part of her couldn't make the call. She was far more comfortable following Kevin than navigating whatever this all was. He was pragmatic when scary things happened. Audrey remembered the night her ADT alarm had sounded. Kevin hadn't hesitated to pick up her bedside bat and carefully step down her century home's creaky stairs. It had turned out she hadn't actually locked the door, and the wind had blown it open, past the sensor. True to form, Kevin had forgiven her carelessness much more swiftly than she would have forgiven him.

In the nearly two years they'd dated, Kevin had made sure she had her coffee with the flavored creamer of the season—more accurately, her creamer with coffee—her multivitamin, her pills. He'd been her human clock because she'd found the blare of an alarm jarring. And now he led her into the unknown, with care and without second thought.

They'd left the wedding at around midnight. Their phones, bars unsettlingly nonexistent, told the time—4:47. Summer's early dawn couldn't come fast enough. Or maybe they didn't want to see what darkness now enshrouded.

Every so often, screams pierced the night, and twice, someone ran beneath the lone street light outside. The area appeared remote; they couldn't see another home. They didn't know exactly where they were, but they suspected they were in or near Kirtland. Over a fifth of the place was forest preserve, her cousin's wedding website had boasted.

The windows began to shake, and Audrey sank down deeper. *Not again.* The whole house began to reverberate, and she clutched Kevin's arm. Would this one be the one, the obliteration that erased this house? The last had sounded so close, she'd cried, sure their lives were over.

A thunderous sound built and built until her ears ached and a prickling sensation crawled the length of her spine. They didn't know where the things would fall. She pressed her palms into her ears and squeezed her eyes shut. A moment later, all was dark and quiet.

"Did you see them?" she dared ask. She could feel him eye her before turning back to the window.

"Who knows what we saw."

"I think I saw horns. It couldn't be, could it?"

This time Kevin didn't turn his eyes from the darkness outside. "We need a weapon." His voice sounded resigned. "Whatever we saw, they're dangerous, and we need a weapon. Stay here."

"No fucking way," she hissed. "We're not splitting up."

He gripped the windowsill and stood, pausing when some body part cracked. Audrey barely breathed but heard nothing more. Kevin offered her a hand, and they crept to the next room, mercifully the home's kitchen. They didn't open the fridge—a light could draw attention as could the sound—but a few bottled waters and a knife block were a most welcome sight. Children's artwork, painted and dotted with fluffy cotton balls, hung on the appliance's stainless steel face. A veterinarian office magnet held up a family photograph. *They look friendly enough*, Audrey thought, relieved, unsure whether any smiling humans were upstairs. If they were, Audrey and Kevin didn't know it.

A dish clanged against another, and Audrey jerked her face toward the noise.

Kevin's palms were in the air. He mouthed words to no avail, then pointed.

Audrey nodded and helped extricate a cast iron weapon from a teetering pile of pans. God, it was heavy. They tiptoed back to the window, and he gave her a knife she'd never effectively wield.

Their phones still showed no reception, and it had been silent for another hour before she suggested they turn on the TV. "See what people are saying? We can mute and turn on the captioning. Can't get anything else to load."

Kevin inhaled deeply and nodded. They sat still for another few minutes, listening, before he crawled from between the curtains to a set of couches and a coffee table, pawing from the floor for the familiar feel of a remote.

Glass shattered nearby. Alarmed, they eyed each other. In a home this large and unfamiliar, it was impossible to tell whether the shards clattered inside or outside. He crawled back to her, and they stilled the curtains.

Clumsy footsteps scuffled on the floor nearby.

They were definitely not alone.

ONE MINUTE, a crash sounded. The next, figures descended upon the living room, assailing the furniture in the room where they'd hunkered down. Kevin and Audrey watched from either side of the curtain that separated them from certain death, and she couldn't look away, though she desired nothing more than to shut her eyes and not have to know what was in front of her.

The creatures lurched and drooled and stank, and their eyes, teeth, and lips seemed black, but what wasn't black in this lightless room? Audrey shook so much and so hard, she could see the curtain pulsating. She tried to steel herself. Couldn't.

Kevin silently turned to Audrey, placing his finger on his lips. He raised his palm to cup her cheek and nodded at her, confirming some plan, and moved to stand, gathering a knife in one hand and the skillet in the other.

Dread washed over her. Was he planning to go somewhere?

Something tumbled to the ground nearby, and the creatures shrieked and descended upon whatever had shattered. Audrey shook her head vehemently at Kevin, clutching his arm.

Kevin turned, his green eyes wide, and shook his head back at her. He raised the skillet over his head, between the curtain and the window. He raised his chin, too, his eyes forward. She could hear him swallow.

Audrey blinked, tears burning down her face.

Kevin burst forward, screaming at the figures and running across the room toward a staircase. They swarmed in his direction. "Run!" he shrieked at her.

She didn't have time to think. Kevin banged the cast iron pan against the walls, and she slid along the edges of the room, then across it after the beasts gave chase as Kevin made it to the stairs. Not one chased Audrey when she fled and bumbled to the kitchen, where she frantically spotted a door.

She swung it open and stopped, peering behind her, watching with horror as Kevin tripped up the staircase, cracking his head on a wooden step. He scurried up, two creatures an arm's length behind, and screamed again at her to go. Audrey stumbled her way into a basement and scrambled now, clawing up earthen walls toward windows. They seemed her only escape route. Whatever those creatures were hadn't followed her, but she could hear their skittering and shrieking, the shattering of glass, a human screaming with more anguish than she'd ever heard, and a shockingly loud thud, followed by falling bricks outside the windows. Tears spilled down her cheeks, and her hands shook violently. *Come on, please, come on,* she willed the window, twisting it open and flinging out its screen. She squeezed herself through and instantly regretted it.

A crowd of *them* staggered nearby. Audrey dragged her body quietly toward a prickly bush. *Please let me fit,* she begged silently as she worked to force herself beneath it. She winced as its branches scratched her skin and snagged her hair. Daring a peek up through the branches, she sobbed at the sight: through a collapse in the home's exterior, she saw a creature flinging Kevin around like a rag doll.

"This way! Come on, come on!" A group of people sprinted by, and Audrey reached for them and yelped before thinking better of it. The creatures snarled impossibly close to Audrey, flashing rotted teeth, snagging at least one person, who screamed until she couldn't. It hollowed Audrey out to realize that asking for help was the last thing she should do; her odds of survival were better if she stayed unnoticed, without joining or attempting to save the others. She resigned herself to going it alone and tried to draw her feet in farther. People and creatures fell upon the flower bed near the bush. Audrey felt wetness on her legs. She turned her head, mouth against the chalky soil, and squeezed her eyes for the end. *Please help me. Please, God.*

"Get up. Fast."

Audrey turned, bewildered.

A man pulled on her foot insistently. "Get up."

Maybe he had a plan, this person who spotted her, didn't leave her, and dared to speak during this carnage. She inched backward, out from under the bush, its branches tearing her hair and raking her skin.

The man helped her up and pulled her forward. Scattered sequins covered the ground.

Audrey scanned, desperately combing their surroundings for Kevin, a futile last act. The way his body had hung from that monster's claws, she knew her Kevin was gone. *She*, then, was gone. What even was the point?

"Come on," the man said. His voice was gentle. His pull was not.

2

Audrey rode the bike daily, but she still struggled to run at the stranger's pace. She didn't complain, and she possessed a stamina she hadn't realized, especially the first few minutes when people's screams and a horrid crunching filled the air.

The man hadn't let go of her hand. He also hadn't spoken much. A "watch that ditch" and a "we're almost there"—the latter a lie spoken what felt like miles ago.

Where are we going? We should take cover. I can't. Kevin. Audrey snatched her hand from his, scurried behind a tree, and heaved for air. She grabbed and turned her foot inward. Both her feet burned with pain. She licked her palm and wiped the foot, inhaling sharply. She couldn't do this. When she righted herself, hands on her waist, she found him watching. Waiting.

"Who are you?" she panted.

"Not the time." Again, soft but demanding.

"Go on. I need—" She paused, gasping for air. "To go back."

"You shouldn't."

"Listen to me!" Audrey wiped sweat from her forehead and met his eyes. In the dark, she couldn't tell their color, but she could feel the intensity of his stare. "I left someone." She could *not* catch her damn breath. "I need to go back."

"What's your name?"

"Audrey."

"Audrey, we need to go."

Audrey pitched her chin to the sky. "Are you not listening? I need—"

"No." His voice was flat. "I know what they are."

His tone silenced her the way a parent's fear can immediately quell a child, the way her own mother's tense tone had quieted her the day they'd left her father in the divorce. She inhaled deeply.

They ran, Audrey wincing and stopping at times, past houses with reaching drives and one "fresh eggs" sign. She could read it now that the sun was up.

OHIO IS KNOWN for its flat heartland, but this forest—Chapin Forest, another sign she could read—mercilessly climbed. Her calves burned. The gravel on the trail crunched beneath the man's feet until he removed his shoes. She'd envied that he still had footwear more than once. Of course, she never could have run in those heels.

"Quieter," he explained in a whisper. "You can hear anything that moves here."

Away from the residential road and inside some nature preserve, he raised a palm, indicating they could pause and catch their breath. Audrey tried to do so quietly, but the quieter and calmer she tried to be, the harder it proved. She'd never proven steady in the face of chaos. After a few minutes, though, she could hear the truth he spoke. The forest was still, save for the tweeting of birds and the morning breeze through the foliage, a green covering so lush the rising sun illuminated none of the trail before them. She winced at the trail's pointy rocks.

The man motioned for her to follow and began to jog, leading her thankfully off trail.

Her eyes caught the carving of a heart and initials in a tree and a sign on the log fence they stepped over: "Restricted area. Keep out. Violators prosecuted." They now traversed leaf-laden forest floor, gentler on her bare feet, toward a strikingly large boulder. An insect buzzed near her left ear, and there came another sound: some vehicle, somewhere.

"Hey," she hissed.

The man turned, index finger to his lips.

She pointed to her ear. Someone, somewhere close, was on wheels. What she would give to climb in with them and go.

The man nodded at the sound.

"Maybe they can help."

The man stepped back toward her and placed his lips near her ear. "They cannot." He resumed his quiet maneuvering over moss-covered rocks and past thick, brown grape vines. Audrey followed, and clear of the vines, they ran.

Mere moments later, Audrey's body was flying forward when suddenly he yanked her back. She'd had no warning but made no sound. She met his eyes and found them intent, his index finger perpendicular to his lips. The man pointed to a tree collapsed across the forest floor, one of many she'd seen, and they crept behind it. He crouched, head low and toward her; she copied.

Not standing for the first time in hours, Audrey grimaced, exhaled shakily, and dared to look. They were as torn up as they felt: the shoeless running had bloodied the bottoms of her feet with deep gashes and puncture wounds. Dirt and leaves caked them, and they stung intensely.

The man stared wordlessly at her feet.

Then she heard what he heard: movement. A growl. No. Growls, plural.

The man pulsed a palm in the air—*stay*, the message—and she did. He moved his chin up slightly and turned his face stiffly to the left. As he turned it back to the right, back toward her, he stopped. His eyes looked black. Startingly black.

Audrey dropped her head lower, concentrating on her breathing.

The man suddenly exhaled and sat back on the forest floor, shaking. *I do not want to know,* she thought. She did nothing, waiting.

Only when he steadied his panting did he meet her eyes. "There's a cliff. We're going to walk to its edge and climb down."

Terrified of heights, she managed a nod, then stood, bending forward with pain as she placed her full weight on her mutilated feet. He offered her an arm, and she accepted it, righting herself. Immediately she gasped and nearly fell, tripping on branches behind them in an attempt to put distance between her and *them*.

On the other side of the fallen tree, a few yards away, lay two *things*. They didn't move. In the morning light, she could see what she hadn't in the dark. The creatures' hands were the size of human calves and had only two digits on them, scissorlike, each blade coming to a sharp, black point. Their bodies—*was that a tail?* she wondered, inhaling sharply and turning away.

The man kept his eyes on them. "They're strong," he said, scratching his head. "Really strong."

Together they looked, Audrey watching for any evidence of life. Then, together, they ran.

~

SILT AND ROCKS TUMBLED OVER, into depths Audrey didn't dare investigate, as the man stepped to the edge. What Audrey could see were treetops below. *Treetops. Below.*

The man lay down, his front to the dirt and one hand clutching a nearby tree root, and scooched his body back until his feet and legs dangled. Then he stood, seemingly suspended in air. He curled his hand toward himself several times, beckoning her.

Audrey winced as she knelt on the dirt, her feet insistently reminding her of how torn up they were. She crawled close.

"I'll climb down enough to guide your feet to the first one." He didn't leave room for questions or protest or fear. His face disappeared downward.

Audrey copied his movements, her heart's pounding more

pronounced with her chest against the earth and faster once she felt nothing but air beneath her ankles and legs. Her waist at the edge, she reached her feet down. Her toes clawed at the wall before her, and it felt smooth.

His hand caught one of her feet, and she whimpered. They hurt so much. The man pulled her down a touch and pushed her foot forward, and she felt it: a cool, metal rung. Someone had built a ladder into this earthen and stone wall. One rung after another, they descended into the forest below.

Nestled past thick, tangled tree roots and built into the side of the summit was a red door, taller than two men and in plain sight, but in a place no one would ever expect. The door looked smooth, but the mountain around it retained its craggy wilderness. Audrey felt anxious and relieved. She was tired of this unrelenting tide of conflict, her competing emotions the very least of it. She peered at the man and then behind them, her hands clutched in front of her. Here she stood, alone with a stranger. Yesterday, she would have *never* gone *anywhere* with a strange man. *Kevin.* How she wished for the safety of his presence.

The man knocked in a particular way, softly and four times, and the door opened immediately. Another man, hefty and silent, reached around the two of them, beginning to close the door. It looked military-strength.

"Wait," Audrey blurted.

Both men stared at her.

What if she'd made a mistake, blindly trusting him? She should run. Leave, trace back their steps, find Kevin and her mom. The hefty man proceeded, and the door closed with a heavy click followed by the sound of multiple locking mechanisms. Now she was definitely stuck inside whatever this place was with whomever these men were. Audrey swallowed hard.

"H16," the man who'd dragged her here said to the hefty man.

"I'll report you're here, Mitch," the man said, fingering a touch screen at the door. "And her?"

Mitch. Report to whom? There are more people down here? Who?

The stranger peered at Audrey, then at the man. "A guest."

"A guest?" Hefty Man raised his eyebrows.

"Audrey, what's your full name?" Mitch asked.

Should she lie? Why did they need her name? Audrey opened her mouth to ask the second question but thought better of it. She had to weigh the risk of not complying. If she revealed her distrust, they might do the same, and she was locked in *their* cave. Trapped inside their cave.

"Audrey Ana Marlena Kelly. Ana is A-N-A. Kelly is K-E-L-L-Y." A journalist spells names out.

Hefty Man typed in the words, and the device's screen turned fire-engine red. "Sir, this will require elder approval." His eyes darted toward Audrey.

"Mine will suffice for now."

Standing still for the first time in an hour, Audrey took in the man named Mitch who'd retrieved her from under the bush. He bled from a wound beneath one eye. His stately, brown uniform had been sliced open in multiple places. Like her, he stood barefoot. Like her, his palms looked black.

"Yes, sir. I'm reading." Hefty Man's eyes scanned the screen. "They require your attendance tonight."

The stranger nodded. "Status of the team?"

What team? Who requires his attendance, and what for? Audrey bit her lip, attempting to keep her rapid-fire line of questions off her face.

"All accounted for. Several minor injuries. One severe. In surgery now." Hefty Man eyed Audrey, then Mitch. "Do you require medical attention, sir?"

Mitch shook his head.

"Does she?"

Mitch's eyes met hers.

Audrey shrugged wordlessly.

"She does." Mitch tilted his head, motioning for Audrey to walk. He offered her an arm, and she accepted. "I know they hurt," he whispered. "Mine do, too."

Hurt was an understatement. The adrenaline had worn off, and she limped. She hoped they wouldn't need to walk far. The scene ahead frightened her. Mitch led her into a narrow hallway, dark save for the flickering light of a few candles on the earthen floor, foreign, and descending into the unknown. "This way," he said when she hesitated.

They took a sharp left turn into a somewhat brighter space. The corridor floor changed from dirt to smooth, light stone. Overhead was a crisscross design of diagonally laid wood planks and mirrors, and, ahead, another door in the distance, blood-red and with a circular door pull. He didn't use it. Again he knocked four times, and it swung open.

"H29," Mitch spoke, holding his arm across the door to let Audrey in.

This was the second person he'd called by a letter and number. *Do these people not have names? What kind of people don't have names?* Audrey wiped a bead of sweat off her forehead. She wanted to turn, leave, hide, but she couldn't know how they'd react. Exposure to hard circumstances as a journalist—fatal car crashes, murders, bitterly defensive politicians—had equipped her with one necessity for this moment: the ability to compartmentalize, to appear calm when absolutely not calm.

"Sir," said the man, uniformed like Hefty Man was. "I'm sorry to inconvenience you, but the elders convene now and they immediately require your attendance."

Mitch nodded and led Audrey past him and down several long passageways, which sank steeply into the earth. The farther they walked, the cleaner and more modern the place became, until they entered a mammoth room with plush couches, mounted televisions, and a hearty buffet of food.

What the fuck? Audrey didn't know him, and she got the distinct impression that she wasn't expected here, so she didn't feel comfortable asking. She was barefoot in a tattered gown, her skin wore a crust of mud and blood, she could smell herself, and she felt spent.

"Sir, would you like a plate?" A woman dressed in pristine white, her hair in a tight bun, approached. "We can imagine..." The woman noticed Audrey, paused, and trailed off. "Well, we were able to whip up chicken paprikash. I know it's breakfast, but we couldn't be sure when, well, we'd all end up here, so."

Chicken paprikash was the first homemade meal Audrey had made for Kevin. Loads of paprika. An entire container, of course, of sour cream. Store-bought spaetzle because she took cooking only so far. The chicken had turned out dry, but Kevin had been generous and kind, praising her effort. She winced. *Is he alive? Is he hungry?*

Mitch turned to Audrey. "Hungry?"

"Yes," she whispered, turning her head to hide her tears.

"Marney," he began, his eyes on the server's uniform, "I've got a matter. Please see to it that Audrey has her fill?"

"Of course, sir."

Mitch met Audrey's eyes. "I'll come back for you."

Audrey peered around the room, shockingly lavish for an underground place. What had she expected—mud floors and damp air? Who knew. She hadn't expected to walk through a red mouth into the belly of Ohio to begin with. She returned her gaze to Mitch. Did he really have to leave her? His was the only name she knew in the place.

Audrey sat. They served her paprikash and vegetables, and she drank water like she'd walked miles through a desert.

Mitch wouldn't return for hours.

3

Audrey ate until her underwear bit into her waistline. She'd been served like any other, but she wasn't like the others. They knew each other's names, chatted and milled around to each other's tables, hugging and asking about friends and families. Since Mitch had left the room, many others had entered the hall—men, women, and children, all disheveled like Audrey, but relieved. She didn't feel relieved. She didn't know how her mom or Kevin were, and she figured, if for no other reason than they weren't greeting her, that these people were aware she was an outsider.

Her appetite turned to unsettled nausea when the news anchor on TV cut to a TikTok. A reporter using her cell phone shakily whispered from wherever she was that she didn't know what had happened to her cameraman. She told the world she'd fled a bloody and frantic scene—"creatures," she called them. A guttural cry rang out, and the woman screamed. Her phone dropped, and nothing but the siding of a building could be seen. The TV picture flashed to a blaring emergency tone, and everyone stopped eating and talking, eyes and ears trained on the screen. Audrey immediately missed the chatter she'd initially resented.

Marney returned to her a half hour later, clearing her dishes, her eyes nervous. "Miss, can I get you anything?"

Audrey realized that there, surrounded by a few dozen strangers, she'd curled up on the couch. She shook her head.

Marney quietly disappeared.

When Mitch returned and woke her, he looked paler. Grave. "You all right?" he asked.

No. She was surprised she'd drifted to sleep surrounded by strangers and worried she'd hurl the paprikash. *I want to leave.* But again, she didn't. She didn't want to stay. She didn't want to go. Audrey inhaled, swallowed, and lied with a nod.

Mitch led her away from the brightly lit room down another corridor, also brightly lit. Now that it was the two of them, Audrey found the courage. "What *is* this place?"

"It's a shelter."

She peered at its walls. Signs directed their way. Suites one through twenty were to the left; suites twenty-one through forty toward the right. An arrow forward promised suites forty-one through eighty. Other signs announced the existence of a pool. A library. A planetarium?

"What kind of shelter?"

He stopped walking. His eyes were a green gray. His dark hair was a tousled mess. He looked tired. "It's a shelter that people arranged for times like these."

She returned his words with a confused look.

He walked.

She obliged him, shuffling forward, wincing at every step. She wasn't leaving behind her line of questioning, though. "Times like these?"

"People worried something would happen. They built this place. Families who also worried have, let's call them, timeshares in the shelter. They're reporting to survive here."

"What's happening? Do you know?" she persisted.

Mitch turned to face Audrey and exhaled. "I know we can't be above ground."

"I saw a newscast. This woman, she, um—" Audrey paused, her lip trembling with emotion. "She described the creatures. You and I saw them." She felt light-headed. She paused, placing a palm heavily on the wall while shaking her head. "I left him." Try as she did to avoid it, she cried, and once she started, she kept crying. She pressed her hands to her face, messy and snotty, and turned away, sliding down. Her sobs echoed in the corridor.

Mitch sat down with her. "I'm sorry."

She cried harder. After who knows how long, she raised her face to his. She needed to know. "Why me? There were so many people," she began haltingly. "Why bring *me* here?"

"I saw you," he replied, his eyes on the wall opposite them. "I couldn't leave you."

But he did leave so many others. Audrey decided to leave that unspoken.

Beggars can't be choosers. Audrey's eyes burned and her head pounded, the life she'd once lived a loss. When Mitch keyed open the door to where Audrey would sleep, she didn't give a damn what lay inside. A sleeping bag on an unforgiving floor would do.

The room was bare but comfortable. A full bed in one corner with a lamp on a simple nightstand. Near a mirror, a white wardrobe. Audrey absentmindedly pulled its silver, vertical handle. There hung no clothes inside, but shelves held folded towels, slippers that probably wouldn't fit her feet (*Who cares?*), and a unisex robe. Beyond the wardrobe was a simple, private bathroom, and she was grateful. She had never needed hot water more.

"I don't know what to say," Audrey began. "Thank you."

"You're welcome."

"I—uh, would you mind coming to me tomorrow morning? If you can spare the time?" She bit a fingernail and cringed when she tasted salt. *What did I just eat?* "I don't know my way around this place or, well, *my* place in all of this. I don't want to mess up."

"Sure," Mitch said. "I'll make it later in the morning. We all need sleep."

He eyed the room but didn't eye her, and she was thankful. She was dirty with mud, and she was sure her eyes were red and puffy from crying. She barely made eye contact.

Audrey wrapped herself in a hug.

He touched his palm to her elbow. "I'll get you help for your feet, too." And then he was gone.

Audrey pulled the shower knob and turned it to red. She tried to take her hair down and grunted when it proved such a knotted, dirty mess she had to rip the hair tie and a litany of bobby pins out, a mass of tangled frizz in tow. The steam began to streak up and down the mirror across from the shower.

She immediately stripped off her muddied dress and numbly realized in her reflection that half her face was so dirty it was unrecognizable. She bled from gashes down her arms and a nasty cut across her collarbone, and her skin had been battered a horrifyingly deep purple up and down her ribs and thighs. She turned the shower temp down, stepped inside, and sat in the tub for what could have been an hour. She rubbed and scrubbed to clear the dirt, and it stung, but nothing was going to wash this night from her life.

4

Mitch slept that morning until nine, hours later than usual. Ever the early bird, he had earnestly helped his mother as a boy around the sprawling Graylock Mansion: watering the potted herbs, setting the table for breakfast, kneading the bread dough every few days. *You can buy a loaf,* his mother said, *but serving homemade tastes and feels different.*

He imagined she wouldn't blame him for this late start. Last night's meeting had been a prosecution unlike any he'd endured. *You should have* never *stopped and brought her here. You've altered how we survive down here. You've endangered whether we survive. How could you?*

He picked up the phone near his bed, and it automatically dialed.

"Sir?" a male answered.

"Overnight report, please," Mitch replied. His stomach roiled.

The man put him on a brief hold. The report, three minutes later, proved grim. Mitch hung up and rubbed his forehead. He was confident they were doing what they needed to, but conditions were deteriorating. He swung his legs over the bed, showered, and dressed in uniform. The apocalypse raged, and he needed to stay ready. He also needed to look responsible; he was not well understood right now. He'd brought *her* underground, and even though he'd known he would bring her here, that he had to bring her here, he didn't have a plan for her. He'd been too busy planning everything else: training his body and his mind, ensuring the shelter would be ready when the shoe dropped. He wanted to be remembered for fulfilling the duty they imposed upon him. He needed to honor his parents.

Mitch's suite was in a private, locked section of the shelter. Departing the corridor, he nodded at a Descendant. He knew her name and he knew about her, but they'd never met.

She, like everyone down here, knew who he was. "Sir," she greeted him, walking by, her hand on her holster. Unexpectedly, she paused. "Sir? Do you mind?"

"No," he replied without hesitation.

"How might I go about joining you on runs? I want to help. I've heard about what's happening, and I feel compelled to do something. *Anything.*"

Mitch blinked rapidly. He pictured her with the team, hiding, running, killing. "It's dangerous," he began. "What's your background?"

"Joined the Army after 9/11, sir. Served in the War on Terror."

"Please, call me by my name," he said. "Approach the elders. Tell them we've spoken."

She saluted him. "Take care, sir—Mitch."

He dipped his head, affirming her. "You do the same."

He walked for ten minutes and knocked three different times, but Audrey didn't answer.

AUDREY LURCHED awake hours before dawn—not that its light reached down here—her heart racing and her robe drenched in sweat. She'd had a nightmare, and she refused to revisit it. It had been the kind that made you heave with relief when you awoke and remembered none of it was real and you were absolutely safe, only she wasn't safe. She didn't really know where she was, she didn't know whether her burning feet were dangerously infected, she might never know where her mom and Kevin had ended up. She shook, pulling the blanket atop her, and sobbed with inhibition.

By the time someone first knocked, hours later, she'd been crying much less loudly and scrawling memories for hours. On the notepad she found in the nightstand drawer, the way Mom tucked Audrey into bed when she visited, even as an adult. On another, the way Mom used to gleefully hide chocolate bunnies in unreasonably difficult places on Easter Sunday. One year, Audrey found a bunny behind books on a shelf.

She scribbled memories, too, about Kevin. Without these pages she filled, would the memories slip from her mind like angel hair slithering through a colander and down the drain? *Could* she forget?

Audrey sank her chin into her chest and paused her record-keeping when knocks sounded—presumably Mitch's. She held her breath.

"Some food," a man's voice said.

After a while, Audrey cracked open the door and pulled a paper bag of food inside. Her fingers shook as she pulled apart a crumb muffin. She silently thanked Mitch for affording her the space, but she also bit off her fingernails. She wouldn't know where to find him when she dared to face whatever this place was, and she realized only now she'd been without her medication for too long. Anxiety threatened, so she resorted to her five Ws.

Who: Underground people. Can't be villains, right? Feeding and clothing a stranger.

What: Like an anthill. Complex. Where do all the hallways end?

When: How long has this been here? Probably not long. Has amenities like smart TVs; think I saw someone on a VR, too.

Where: Where's Kevin? Mom? Not helpful. In Ohio. Why build this in Ohio?

Why: Why me? Because I'm a journalist. I can handle exposure to things others can't. Should investigate.

MITCH WOULDN'T LEAVE it to her to find him. He couldn't. He needed to advise her of the expectations before she had time to inadvertently violate them. He knocked that afternoon, her first in the Underground. The hallways were clear where they'd housed her, at least for now. He checked his watch. *Soon.* He'd have to be quick if she answered, and that didn't feel fair.

This time she did answer, propping the door open for him to hold before limping to the bed.

He entered but stayed near the door to respect her space, a pile of clothing in his arms. "I didn't know if you've had a chance to gauge how deeply your feet are cut. Our medical staff can come, but they're overloaded."

Audrey pulled her legs up and crossed them in front of her, handling the tops of her feet but not their bottoms. She peered at them, and, stepping closer, so did he. His, like hers, were deeply gashed and stained dirty. Bandaged with gauze, his hurt with every step.

"I don't think they warrant stitches."

He nodded. "Mine didn't. Are you okay with them taking a look?"

"I can deal."

"I brought supplies." He set the pile of clothing on a nearby table and pulled medical tape and gauze from between its lower layers. He retrieved several square wipes, too.

"Thank you."

Mitch scratched the back of his neck. *No easy way to say it.* "You remember how we got here?"

"The woods?"

"No. Where the cafeteria is?"

"No. But I'm a reporter. I can find most things I want to."

He winced at the revelation; the elders would not tolerate her pawing around. "There are signs."

"I noticed."

She hadn't come here by choice, but it still needed to be said. He cleared his throat and bit the inner corner of his mouth. "Certain wings are restricted. Please steer clear of them."

"Will I know which ones?"

"I can give you an idea. Not today," he added, checking his watch. "Tomorrow? I'll show you what's—" *What's the right word? Had he not brought her here, there would be no need for a right word because everyone permitted here knew which way was north and which way was south.* "Unrestricted." *That one would have to do.*

"The restricted wings,—are they restricted to all?" She tilted her head.

"Does it matter?"

She shook her head. "Suppose not. So I stay in this room until what? You come get me?"

He didn't know her, so he couldn't read her tone. "No, help yourself to things you need. Food. The pharmacy."

Audrey stared at him. "Okay."

Mitch exhaled. Best to be clear. "We're asking that you don't go exploring. We'd hate for you to get lost."

She blinked. "Who's we?"

She asks a lot of questions. If she persisted, it would make it harder for him to protect her. Defend her. "The families."

She merely stared.

He could tell his bland, nonspecific answer didn't meet her expectations. He couldn't do better in this moment. "I have to run. I brought you various sizes—wasn't sure which would fit," Mitch said, pointing to the pile of clothing.

"Thank you."

He nodded and left. Hours later, he stepped inside the meeting room, beyond the underground spring they'd chosen to build around and inside the wing Audrey was most forbidden to enter, and they'd already commenced roll call.

"Palm Springs, reporting," an unfamiliar voice said.

"St. Petersburg?" one of the elders called.

"Reporting," another unfamiliar voice said.

"St. Louis?"

The line crackled. No one replied.

"St. Louis?"

Mitch crossed his arms despite the stiffness of his uniform. He could feel their eyes on him before he raised his own to meet their worried faces. "Give them time," he said. "It's been a little over twenty-four hours."

Twenty-four hours since it actually happened. Twenty-four hours since May 26, most assuredly a date for the history books—if people continued to write them.

5

May 28

Two days after

The place smelled new. The few places Audrey dared to venture smelled fresh, and now in a back aisle of the library, she was inhaling crisp books. She found the chemical scent of a new book irresistible, and in the here and now, she found it comforting. *This place,* she thought. *Nicer than any place I've lived, yet used only what? Once? Now, when the world is ending?* She shook her head.

She welcomed the library's privacy on this, her second day here. The shelter was teeming with people, and most squinted at her or stared for longer than normal. She was unfamiliar. She'd waved and offered hellos, but they were returned half-heartedly, if they were returned at all. Tapping book spines as she walked, Audrey shook her head. She was alone and insecure enough without all of that.

"Hi," chirped someone behind her.

Audrey turned, startled.

"Looking for one of those? Don't blame you, girl. Who knows how long we're stuck here for." The Chirper, a curvy woman about Audrey's age, winked.

Confused, Audrey followed the woman's gaze and felt her face burn the color of the library's scarlet carpet. The book spines rattled off titles like *Dirty Talk*, *Fifty Shades of Grey*, and *The Feather*. She grimaced most at *Taking the Nanny*. "No, no, I'm just walking," Audrey said, a defensive palm in the air.

The woman pitched a thick eyebrow and feigned a nod. "Riii-iiiight."

"I mean it," Audrey said.

"Betty Jane," the Chirper said with a wave of her hand. "I wouldn't judge ya."

"Audrey. Erotica was never my thing."

"If my ass is stuck down here for too long, *everything* will be my thing." Betty Jane burst into loud, confident laughter.

Audrey smiled faintly. *Smiled.* She raised her gaze to Betty Jane with unspoken appreciation.

"Coffee shop?" Betty Jane suggested. "If you're not busy."

"I'm not busy." *Understatement.*

Half an hour ago, Audrey had left her suite alone. Now she was ordering a latte at a coffee counter shoulder to shoulder with only the second person in the shelter to know her name.

IT'D BEEN imperative for Audrey to get names right when reporting, to know when a Tom spelled it Thom and an Anna spelled it like her mom did. It ruined a story for her to get something so simple wrong. The rest of the time, though, Audrey failed miserably at remembering names. *Betty Jane, Betty Jane.* She wanted to commit this woman's name to memory.

"Funny," Betty Jane said, staring into the tea she stirred. "I'm living better *after* it happened."

Audrey furrowed her eyebrows.

Betty Jane shrugged. "It's true. I didn't have a gym membership before. I wasn't frequenting coffee shops. I was working two jobs to pay rent and keep my hoopty running."

"What'd you do for a living?"

"I taught preschool. And waited tables."

Betty Jane. Betty Jane.

The woman squeezed a lemon wedge into the mug. It squirted disobediently. "Whoops," she said, looking up. "Did I get you?"

Audrey shook her head. "All good."

"How 'bout you?"

Audrey cocked her head and stared.

"What'd you do for a living?" Betty Jane shook her head. "Weird that we're asking in the past tense."

"Yeah." Audrey sipped her drink. "I'm a newspaper reporter. Well, was."

Betty Jane raised an eyebrow. Hers were the attractively thick kind. "Cool gig."

"It had its ups and downs." Audrey never was one for small talk when questions needed asked. "You spoke in the library about how long we'll be down here. Does anyone have a sense for how long that'll be?" Audrey's heart raced. Nerves, yes, but—it dawned on her now—caffeine without her meds wasn't a good call. She set down the cup.

Betty Jane shook her head and stared off for a time.

"I mean, there's a limit to how long we can survive underground, right?"

Betty Jane met her gaze. "If we need it, this place is built for the long haul."

Frustrating, the similarities between this conversation and some interviews of Audrey's career. The friendliness with limitations. The answering of questions, but not really. Mitch had used the word, "timeshares." Timeshares were expensive, weren't they? She cocked her head. "How'd you afford to buy into all this if you were broke?"

Betty Jane either didn't hear or ignored the question. She seemed somewhere else, not on these couches near a faux fireplace underground. "Can't believe I didn't say goodbye."

Audrey looked at her.

"I was so angry with her, I didn't say bye. Left in a good old, self-righteous huff. They say don't leave things wrong with the people you love, and still we do it."

"Who?" Audrey knew about sudden and lacking and needed goodbyes. *Dad.*

"I assumed I'd see them again, you know? But if they're not here by now..." Her voice trailed off.

Audrey didn't repeat the question. It was now she who sank someplace different, inside a log cabin behind a brittle curtain of shriveled vines, the last place she'd seen the man who was half the reason she existed. She knew how it felt—to live a final moment with someone without knowing it—only she wasn't the one who hadn't said goodbye.

May 30

Four days after

Audrey had stewed over asking the question for the few days since Mitch let her into the suite. She'd bitten her fingernails so short, they hurt. She'd barfed after nearly every meal, save the paprikash that first day. Her chest felt tight. Her body couldn't take it anymore.

"You mentioned this place has a pharmacy?"

She'd lived with the anxiety for the past year or two, and Kevin had been supportive. He'd introduced her to his doctor after she'd admitted she didn't have a primary care physician. She'd been a healthy, active woman, and frankly, her health insurance left a lot to be desired. Kevin's doctor had quickly diagnosed her.

Mitch met her gaze. "Yes. Need something?"

"Lorazepam," she said, her cheeks flushing red. "It's for—"

"None of my business," he said. "Excuse me for asking." He nodded to the right. "This way."

They walked, and she took mental notes. *A full wing sprawled to the right. No signs. What's there? People nod at him like he's some boss. I count exactly one clock so far. No calendars, though.* Behind glass doors appeared a room with a grand counter, behind which were shelves lined with bottles and boxes. A white-haired, bespectacled man greeted them eagerly. He'd been stocking other shelves. "Mitch," he said. "Sir," he corrected.

Is he a boss?

"Long time no see."

Gosh, does he know everyone? It surprised her more that everyone, the brawny guards, this older man, the waitstaff, showed such consistent deference to a man about her age. *Who is he?*

"Hey, Walter."

Walter pushed his glasses up and acknowledged Audrey. "Hello, Miss."

"Hi!" she chirped and cringed inwardly. She overcompensated when embarrassed.

"What can I do for you two?"

"Audrey, meet Walter; Walter, this is Audrey," Mitch said. "She needs medication."

"Sure. What can I fill for you, dear?" Walter walked behind the counter and placed his palms on it, expectantly.

Audrey glanced at Mitch, and he walked to the left. She appreciated his attempt to afford her some semblance of privacy. "Lorazepam," she said. She tried to fight the shame, but it won. It often did. She believed there was nothing wrong with mental health meds, but her mom discouraged it. *Mom.*

Walter returned, a few bottles in his left hand and one pill in his right. "This should do it for a few months."

"Sir?" she began, confused. "Thank you. But that doesn't look like what I've been taking."

Walter tilted his head. "What was the color and shape of your medication?"

Mitch reappeared.

Audrey forged ahead anyway. She hadn't come this far not to feel the relief she needed. "I thought it resembled the earth," Audrey said. "Blue and green. Round."

Walter nodded. "My apologies, Miss. My mistake." He paused,

seemingly unsure. "One moment, please." He disappeared behind the counter.

Audrey's stomach sank. *What was he about to give me? Do they not have it?*

The instant he returned with the pills she'd swallowed night after night, Audrey calmed. He had several bottles in his left hand, one pill in his right. "Is this it?"

"Yes, thank you. Gosh," she said, reaching for a purse she hadn't carried in days. "I actually don't have my wallet. I—" Audrey trailed off, her gaze and thoughts somewhere else. She swallowed. "I lost it," she finished plainly.

"Miss, we don't charge down here. Be sure to let me know if your needs exceed what I've provided you."

Audrey glanced at Mitch, and he didn't bat an eye. The cost of her medication had often weighed on her mind. She exhaled.

Satisfied, Walter turned to Mitch. "Before you go, sir, would you please speak to the eld—"

"I'll stop by later," Mitch said.

Walter nodded. "Thank you."

Outside the apothecary, Audrey cracked open the bottle the pharmacist had given her. He'd given her one pill and that was her usual dose, but she wanted two.

6

Mitch and Audrey polished off tuna salad sandwiches made memorable and crunchy with diced, horseradish pickles. The food didn't suck, a small, welcome comfort, and Audrey hoped her barfing days were over now. Tuna stank enough going down.

It was an odd, off time for lunch—2:42—but that's how the day had unfolded. Did it matter what happened and when down here?

Audrey stopped to examine one of many composite pictures on the walls. She remembered dressing for sorority composite pictures, each young woman draping the same black, V-neck cloth across her chest, a shared string of pearls along her neck.

"Who are these people?" she asked. "Are they down here?"

"Yes and no." Mitch looked on with her. "They're the families who have space in the Underground."

The Underground. It was the first time he'd called the shelter by a formal name.

"So they paid for their spots?"

"Well, no."

Mitch was a man of few words. She'd encountered people like

this as a reporter. It wouldn't stop her. It never had. She'd been the newsroom's bulldog more times than she could count, and she'd worn it like a badge of honor. She unleashed her questions on him because she had to. *Mom is up there.* "What's happening? What are those creatures? How does this place exist, as though you people *knew* this would happen?" She winced. She hadn't expected to ask the last question so confrontationally.

Mitch regarded her silently before he spoke, as though he studied her. "What makes you think we know what they are?"

He had her there. Audrey wanted to push, but she was alone in a foreign place with strangers she wanted to help find her family. *You catch more flies with honey*, her parents used to say. She focused on a memory, desperate for a distraction.

The composites on the walls of the Chi Omega basement contained scores of pictures of young women, their hairstyles a quick tell of when they attended the university: the lion's mane bangs and side ponies of the '80s, the crowned headbands of the '70s.

Here, the oval-framed faces behind the glass were of men and children, too. At the tippy top were two stoic faces and two names: Puck and Raven Gray.

"What a pretty name," Audrey said, attempting an inroad. "Raven."

"Yes," Mitch said. "I have a half hour and thought of something I could show you."

"Okay," she replied, glad for another distraction.

Calmer than she'd been the first time she'd walked these halls, Audrey couldn't help but marvel at the place. It smelled like fresh paint but was built with intricate, old-world touches: decoratively timbered walls, leaded glass in arched doorways, older stone. Every so often, they passed large machines with grates that hummed. "What are those?" she asked, pointing.

"Dehumidifiers," he replied. "Can't have the steel rust."

Audrey cast him a wide-eyed stare.

"The steel isn't load-bearing. They used structural concrete because it maintains its strength under the weight of the earth."

Audrey looked now at the wood-beamed ceilings, above which she remembered lay a crushing amount of soil. The trusses vaulting the space reminded her of Cleveland's industrial bridges and made the space feel more open, another welcome comfort. Signs pointed the way to a swimming pool. A gym. A library. A theater. All underground. "This place is ... nuts."

"How do you mean?"

She traced her fingertips along the wall, lined with modern lights. "How on earth did this get built without more people knowing about it? I read the news. I would have thought it would have made a headline or two."

"The land is privately owned, and the owners did it under the radar."

"And the families who have space here, what? Were sworn to a blood oath?" She chuckled. "Also, I highly doubt blasting and building underground without permits is legal."

"You assume there were no permits."

"Permits are public record. Reporters would have reported them."

"We all miss things." They walked in silence for a bit before he spoke. "There actually is a nondisclosure agreement. For the families, I mean. And yeah ... I'm no expert on legalities." He pointed to the left. She followed.

Mitch piqued her curiosity. He didn't offer more information than she asked of him, and intriguingly, he possessed some stature down here. *Who are you?*

They turned down another corridor, and she gasped. The walls were glass, and on the other side of the double doors, green stretched as far as the eye could see. A *living* green she hadn't thought she'd behold until the world was safe. If ever it would be. "Oh my God." She exhaled.

"We didn't want to try to raise livestock in closed quarters," Mitch said, walking her into the dirt-floor greenhouse. "But we did build a farm."

Red and green tomatoes on the vine. Corn stalks taller than Mitch. Pots, dozens of pots, with herbs such as basil, cilantro, and puppy-ear-soft sage, all plants Audrey had inadvertently (and lazily) killed year after year in her attempts to emulate her mother, who'd not only successfully harvested vegetables and fruit but who'd often grown such a bumper crop, she canned them for winter use.

Some plants' vines crawled the land. *Land.* She crouched down and touched it to be sure it was real.

"Come look here," Mitch said. He walked her past cauliflower and watermelon and squash plants, identifiable to her only because she'd failed at gardening so many times. All the way down, a football field's length, there was a small, open room. Inside, around two vertical hives, bees buzzed all about.

"Of course," she whispered. She felt like a kid at the zoo.

"We can't do it without them," he said, and the respect in his voice for the insects struck her.

"Will you use their honey?"

"Sure. Most important, though, is the pollination. And bees make a resin that fights microbes."

"Propolis."

He turned to her, an eyebrow raised.

"Wrote a story about a local beekeeper once. Did you know they're considered livestock? This lady's neighbors argued she shouldn't keep the hives because her land wasn't zoned for agriculture."

"The things we used to fight about," he replied. "We'll use their propolis for wounds and their beeswax for lotions, depending on how long we're here as well as how well the colonies sustain themselves."

"How many are there?" The bees' frenzied flight paths mesmerized her.

"You'd have to ask the beekeeper."

There is something you don't know. "The beekeeper? What doesn't this place have?"

He fingered a plant to his right, lowered his glance to her, and smiled. It was the first time she'd seen him smile, and the way his full lips turned up more on one side than the other was so handsome. "The sun. The moon. The stars."

She nodded, and they stood for a while, her palms on the glass, his in his pockets, both shrouded in vegetation, watching the bees fly around. They looked so free.

7

Some date in June

One week after

Audrey awoke on who knew what day. Life underground had its way of stripping her appreciation for the passage of time. The sun didn't rise and set to signal what time of day it was. A regular work schedule didn't keep her keen on Friday. Were it not for her promise to hit the gym, she might have passed the day in her suite. Life was scary. Life hiding from scary was scary. Every time she laughed or smiled, she felt whiplashed by the cruel reminders. *Mom. Kevin. They're not here. They're not protected.*

The pills were on the simple nightstand. She used to worry she'd be the one to embarrass herself with an ambulance that flashed her business up and down the street if she didn't keep to her regimen. She didn't want to be a spectacle, least of all to the people who saw her on the regular. With gratitude to the pharmacist, she shook a pill from the bottle and tipped her head back.

A knock sounded at her door.

"Coming," she called. Audrey got briefly stuck, as always, in the sports bra she pulled on and yanked a hoodie over top. She opened the door.

"Hey," Betty Jane greeted. "Let's get 'er done."

The fitness center was unlike any gym Audrey had frequented. She learned today towels were heated. Green uplighting brightened the room and chandeliers hung. You couldn't stream workouts or music or podcasts because there was no signal, but they had their pick of Blu-rays on shelves spanning a wall from rubber gym mat to ceiling. They were the only ones there, and Betty Jane wiggled her eyebrows and chose *Cruel Intentions*. Audrey wordlessly approved and fingered the up arrow on the treadmill.

"So, are you not from around here?" Betty Jane asked, running at a clip Audrey wouldn't dare attempt.

"I actually am," Audrey replied.

"Your last name isn't familiar," Betty Jane said. "Most of us know each other."

Aren't you direct? Ever the direct one in any newsroom and friend group, Audrey appreciated the woman's candor. "Yeah, I feel weird," Audrey admitted. "I know the rest of you have your place down here." She turned up the treadmill a touch.

Betty Jane did the same. They ran for a while until Audrey slowed to a walk. She had so many questions, and she felt safer asking them of Betty Jane than of Mitch.

"So, who knows about this place? How long has it been here, do you know?"

Betty Jane left the treadmill's belt flying but hopped her feet to either side of it. She took a swig of water and panted. "It's new. Built in the last ten years or so."

"Do you know everybody down here? Am I the only, I don't know, guest? It's uncomfortable, if I'm honest." She thought better of what she said and waved a hand. "Not that I'm not grateful to be safe."

Her acquaintance took another swig of water and tightened her bun. "Most of us know each other, yeah," she repeated. "My sister and brother are unaccounted for. They were supposed to be here."

"I'm sorry."

"I feel like I'm the only one of us with family above ground." Betty

Jane turned her face toward Audrey's. "It's not what I want to have in common with anyone, but here we are."

Audrey nodded, further slowing the treadmill. "Everyone I know is up there."

"I know. I'm sorry, too. Just can't believe I didn't say goodbye."

"None of us knew this was coming. And beating yourself up achieves nothing. Been there."

Betty Jane jumped back on the running belt.

"Aren't you afraid?" Audrey asked. It felt the most forward of her questions, but she couldn't help it. Everyone in this place seemed to do precisely what Betty Jane did: jump back on the conveyer belt of life—eating, working out, relaxing, even—while she trailed them, the place's lone embattled and winded witness.

Betty Jane answered her question with a question. "So how *did* it happen?" she asked, running. "How did you wind up here?"

Audrey wiped the sweat from her neck, draped the towel on the bar in front of her, and started to jog. "It's a blur." She shook her head. "I was on the ground, and Mitch found me and told me to get up. Do you know Mitch?"

Betty Jane laughed. "Yes, I know Mitch." She didn't elaborate.

Audrey wondered if her new acquaintance knew Mitch in *that* way. She didn't feel she should ask about him. Maybe later. Much later. She accelerated the conveyer belt beneath her. "How do you think it is? Up there?" She pointed an index finger.

"I don't let my mind go there, especially not with them missing," Betty Jane said. "I'm not one of—" She looked at Audrey. "I haven't been above ground."

"Wait," Audrey said, breathless from her interval. "Do people down here go up there? Is it those people who wear the uniforms? The ones who don't wear names, just the letter H and a number? What's the H stand for?" *Too many questions. Slow down.*

"Handler. A title, that's all." Betty Jane paused. "I don't go up. I like to think I would if I could. To help."

Same, Audrey thought, left with another unanswered question she wouldn't ask again, at least not immediately. *Do people go above ground? If yes, what do they do? What do they know? Can they save survivors? Would they bring them here?*

She pressed the down arrow until the treadmill slowed to a crawl as a familiar, unwelcome ache consumed her and the merciless questions intruded.

Are there survivors? Could Mom and Kevin be alive? If they are, how much time do I have to save them?

AUDREY HAD every intention of retreating to her room. Her collar and pits and back and crotch were steeped in sweat, and she could smell herself.

But she saw a sign for "the spring" and paused. Audrey looked forward and backward and saw no one. She risked getting turned around, but she wouldn't fight her curiosity. What she would fight was her deep, well-earned fear of water. She took the slight left and walked. Her legs burned slightly, but she couldn't tell if it was fatigue from the run with Betty Jane or if this hallway actually climbed. The narrow corridor reached a fork. She split left, following an arrow for "the spring," and again the walk felt uphill.

She arrived at the next clearing, instantly sorry she'd given in to her curiosity. Somehow she'd found herself in a hallway that felt familiar, and if it *was* familiar, she suspected it was because she was close to the entrance where she'd first stepped into this place. The giveaway was the ceiling, with its design of diagonally laid wood planks and mirrors she remembered from the morning she'd limped in after the world changed.

"Move, move, move!"

Audrey jumped and pinned herself against the wall as bodies poured into the clearing. She shut her eyes, afraid, expecting to be grabbed and detained, but the mass of people didn't touch her. She darted behind a corner, sure she'd be chastised, but when no one said a thing, she crept forward and peeked. Their focus was on their center, and quickly Audrey's was, too. She gasped. A man laid a leg

—a leg—down on the floor. And in the center was a man whose uniform was splattered red and whose pantleg lay deflated on the ground.

"Get Walter!" one person yelled.

"He's on his way! Move, move!" another responded.

"Stay with us, Bram," urged a man as a woman, also in a uniform stained red, ripped the deflated pantleg up the middle and began crafting a tourniquet.

What remained of the man's limb was pulp. *His leg is off. It's off his body. He's going to die.* A prickling sensation washed over her, and she gripped the wall, worried the tingling meant she might pass out. She couldn't believe no one acknowledged her. It was possible they knew they didn't have the time.

The man's skin was gray and he shivered mercilessly, but his eyes remained open. Another patted his cheek gently and spoke constantly to him.

She'd seen a lot in her years of reporting but never a wounded person this close. Back against the wall, standing there doing nothing helpful, she felt bad for invading the man's privacy, for gawking at his deathly state. But bodies crowded her to the wall, and she was near enough that her options were to look down at him or look up and see it all in the mirrors above. She presumed this would be his end. Who survives a torn-off limb and blood loss so immense a current of it flowed down the hallway floor? Especially when they all were down here, presumably without a trauma center and surgeons?

"We can't lose him. He's the strongest."

"Walter will save him. What the hell happened?"

"We can't lose him." The woman's voice was increasingly shrill.

"Calm down. We don't resurrect."

"We'll lose him."

A white-haired man bounded in, and the commotion grew at first before the crowd parted around the bloodied man.

"What happened?" asked the man.

The pharmacist, Audrey recognized.

"We didn't see it coming. We were following protocol—"

"No one's blaming you. What happened?" the man persisted.

"Out of nowhere, I don't know, came these scissor hands and the thing cut his leg clean off," said the woman, so covered in blood that the only recognizable part of her face was the whites of her eyes. "It came out of nowhere," she repeated, staring in the direction from which they'd all run. "What if they get inside?"

"The fire team's up there," another man said.

Audrey couldn't believe no one insisted she leave. Her eyes followed the woman's gaze only to snap back to the carnage before her at the sound of a thunderous clap. Others had emerged from the hallway, carrying a stretcher. The wounded man seemed more alert now, and they placed his one-legged body on it.

"You'll be all right, Bram," the white-haired man said, removing his spectacles and wiping blood from his lenses. "The others are ready."

The pharmacist was in control. Almost all of the crowd followed him, several carrying the stretcher and two with the unfortunate task of carrying the slippery, detached leg. Two remained in the hallway upon which Audrey spied.

"Well," one said to another.

"Holy hell. If Bram can get demolished—" The person paused and exhaled. "Holy hell."

"I wonder if Mitch knows."

"If he didn't, he does now."

The pair left the hallway. When there sounded no more footsteps, Audrey started to follow their path, back the way she came. She slipped but stayed upright, and she gagged twice at the blood on the smooth, stone floor.

For a few nights, the carnage in the hallway replayed in Audrey's mind whenever she lay down to sleep. It made her physically ill. She attempted to will it away, to lead her mind to happier and comfortable memories, but gore had a way of sticking. For a few days, she theorized what had become of the man, though most of her theories hinged on conditions of a world and of a healthcare system she presumed ceased to exist. The pharmacist had told the wounded man he'd survive, but people lied in dire situations. The pharmacist had also told the man the "others" were ready. *Others who? Ready how?* How could anyone address a severed limb without the unrivaled medical care Northeast Ohio used to count on? She'd interviewed many who'd traveled continents to be treated at the Cleveland Clinic.

Eventually a monotony set in. She woke up. Ate. Read more books than she ever had time for before. Worked out. Sometimes saw Betty Jane. Invariably contemplated asking Betty Jane questions she suspected she shouldn't. Woke up. Ate. Tried new genres. Started lifting weights. Small variations aside, each day echoed the one before it.

The sameness would have depressed Audrey if she'd let it, but she was more self-aware than that. People above ground would kill for the liberty of being bored. She refused to stew in useless self-pity.

She couldn't as easily ignore the alienation. She didn't feel welcome to ask questions in this place, and it contradicted her very nature. She'd lived a life where asking questions was the meat of her meal ticket. Hell, she'd brought a pen, reporter's notebook, and twenty-seven questions to the venue she'd ultimately hired for the only baby shower she'd ever planned. If people here were so bent on ignoring her, she couldn't help but wonder again: why had Mitch brought her here?

This afternoon, she'd taken to pretending to read a book and people-watched. It was another thing about her reporting past she couldn't do anymore: overtly observe others. If she wasn't asking questions, she would unearth answers in other ways.

Today, amid the books, she wondered about the expectant mother who cradled her swollen belly, draped in a flattering mustard-colored dress. Audrey felt two conflicting emotions: envious of the fresh chapter unfolding for her, but also glad she was not growing a baby. *Who wants to have a baby with the world ending?* She pitied the woman.

A short man brought the pregnant woman a lemonade, and

Audrey guessed at how they'd met. The woman used to teach, she decided. He had been her boss. No, maybe he'd been the parent of one of her students. Audrey cocked her head behind the worn book she held. Couldn't be. The only kid with them was the one in utero.

There was a child in the library, though, and what a curious little thing. She was grade-school age, judging by her puffy, black pigtails and height. The girl's fingers were covered in blue and white finger paint, and she put them to a surface on the table, moving them up and down and left and right. Audrey wanted to see what she was painting, but she also didn't want to appear to spy, so she stood and perused a bookshelf nearby. Fingering a book spine, she scanned the room and when no adults appeared to be with the girl, she peeked.

The girl painted a dark blue sky, peppered with a blizzard of fingertip-shaped snow. She swirled her pinky around, too, creating a windy scene.

Audrey turned away from the painting, flooded by the memory of when it snowed so much one middle-school year that a two-week winter break became a four-week winter break. She remembered, smiling at the library floor, mornings awaiting (and cheering) the school closures and days with few rules. Her dad and mom had taken turns with her, given the divorce and their work schedules, and she had loved every minute. She and Dad would sled down the steep hill at the nearby park until their fingers, though mittened, burned from the cold. He'd dubbed them the "Cascading Kellys." She and Mom watched Home Alone and sipped hot cocoa upon which mini marshmallows buoyed.

Her mom and she kept up that tradition after her dad disappeared, and it had offered measured comfort. Years after he left, and as Audrey was moving out, her mom had asked Audrey to sift through her childhood toys to decide what she wanted to keep. Audrey had found the wooden sled her dad and she used. Initially, she'd left it behind, destined for the trash. Two minutes into her drive back home, she'd turned around, wordlessly climbed the attic stairs, retrieved the ornamental slab, and stuck it in her car. She wasn't ready to part with all of him.

Staring at the girl, who now turned to creating some new green and yellow canvas piece, Audrey wondered whether Audrey would ever return to her home and collect remnants of the life she'd once lived, reminders of the people she'd loved. She'd intended to create a family where hers had ceased to exist. It felt unwise to continue believing that was possible.

8

Another date in June

Two-ish weeks after

The room felt suffocating and also, incongruously, like a warm hug. For the first time in weeks, Audrey's muscles relaxed. She lay naked beneath a soft towel in the pool's steam room. She felt guilt. Heavy, unforgiving guilt. *People above ground are dead and suffering, and you're steaming your pores.*

The door opened, interrupting the thought.

"Oh, hey," someone greeted. "Mind if I come in?"

"Not at all," Audrey said. The steam had turned back on.

"I'm Bram," the man said. "Have we met?"

An introduction? A question about herself? This was new. "I'm Audrey, and no, we haven't," she replied. "Nice to—"

The question scrunched up Audrey's eyebrows before she thought to hide it, although she quickly realized he couldn't see her through the steam. It couldn't be the same Bram. There was no way a man whose leg had to be carried separately from his torso could stand and stroll into here a week later.

"Hey, how's your—" She stopped, cringing. She shouldn't ask. Her knowledge of his injury—amputation—placed her in a hallway and a frantic scene painted in his blood that she'd had no business witnessing.

"How's my what?"

She chuckled nervously. "Sorry, mixing you up with someone I've met."

"Nice to meet you."

"Same." Now it was her thoughts that became suffocating.

She realized the man was leaving because the door opened, and with the steam escaping, she could see him. His eyes were astonishingly blue, and his teeth spectacularly white and impossibly straight. He was huge, too: noticeably tall and very noticeably muscular. "Coffee sometime?"

She pushed her matted curls off her shoulder. "Sure." The only people she knew down here who'd speak to her were Mitch and Betty Jane. It couldn't hurt to branch out.

Bram caught her gaze. "You said you've met people here. You're not one of the families?"

Audrey shook her head.

"I'll explain—I bet this place can be pretty confusing to the uninitiated," he said with a warmth she appreciated.

She nodded. *It's downright confounding. Why was I brought here only to be stared at and ignored?*

They made plans, and she looked forward to them. Mitch never offered more than what she asked. She hoped Bram would prove to be much less tight-lipped.

Bram leaned in to touch her shoulder, and she blushed at his simultaneous eye contact. Kevin used to have that effect on her. Audrey gave a slight wave and stood as soon as the door closed. She peered out, watching. It was only a few weeks ago that Kevin and she had been separated, yet Audrey was blushing at another man, staring at another man. She disappointed herself. But another, more important emotion barged in. If she was honest with herself, and lately she really didn't want to be, she was frightened.

What she witnessed didn't reduce her anxiety. The man named Bram wasn't limping.

Some date in June

Three-ish weeks after

Audrey moved the straw in circles, sipped, and closed her eyes as the warm memory washed over her. Her mother used to man the juicer for Audrey's lemonade stands, "carpal tunnel be damned." It would be decades later when Audrey understood what carpal tunnel had to do with lemons. She remembered thrilling at how much money she could make, peddling cups of sunshine to passersby on a blazing summer day. Her highest daily net, thirty-seven dollars, more than covered a couple of Blockbuster rentals, popcorn, and candy. Her friends had talked about her bounty for weeks.

Today, she didn't know if her mother was alive, and Audrey lived with the "families" underground where the seasons were depressingly out of reach. There was no balmy breeze or cracking and rumbling storm this summer.

But the Underground tried. One morning, Audrey opened her suite door and found the halls lined with county-fair posters. While it was abundantly obvious that the salty beach smell emanated from candles, the little touches lifted her spirits. She missed the world. She bent to touch a potted cactus, and it poked her. *Wow, you're real.*

The menu shrugged on summer, too, the way young women shrug on light sweaters when summer days slip into cooler nights. Among the items that night was the lemonade she now stirred, honey barbecue ribs, and feta pasta salad. Mitch ordered a dinner portion of ribs, and she couldn't resist the bacon cheeseburger.

"So, do you know everyone down here?" Audrey asked, sipping the lemonade.

"I do." He tore the ribs with his teeth. They were nice teeth. "My family is one of them."

"What about right now? How many people in the cafeteria do you know?"

Mitch scratched his head. "In one way or another, most."

"These are *all* your family?"

"No, that'd be weird." He chuckled. It was a nice chuckle. So much about him was nice. She could press him without too much worry, right?

"Why?" she asked.

"I dated one."

Audrey's eyes widened. "Who?"

"She's seated alone by the 'window' on the far left," Mitch replied. "Black curls."

When the seasons changed, the Underground swapped out the "views" on the cafeteria's canvases, painted like windows in the room and flanked with floor-length curtains. Recently, ocean horizons had replaced fields of tulips and daffodils.

Audrey dared a peek. The woman wore a white jumpsuit that flattered her olive skin and black locks. She was a looker. *I wonder why they didn't work out.*

Audrey felt Mitch watching her while she peered at the woman. "If it were up to my family, we'd be married," he said.

There you are, Audrey thought, satisfied he was opening up, if a bit. Audrey ducked her eyes. Before an apocalypse separated her from Kevin, she'd had the sinking feeling he wasn't on the same page as her. "That's hard," she began. "I wonder if love would be easier if our choices were more limited. If, you know, people who know and love us guide us toward good fits and away from, well, the wrong ones. A courtship, if you will, but with way more ... together time." She laughed.

Mitch sipped his own lemonade. "I don't know what a courtship is," he admitted.

She waved him on. *Not important.*

"But I do know people who live that way, and it doesn't work as well as you might presume."

"I guess we're all fuck—," Audrey began. "Doomed." Mitch didn't cuss, so maybe she shouldn't either.

"Could be."

Audrey decided in this moment she would press him, but she'd do it strategically. J school hadn't taught her this, but terse conversations with embattled sources, particularly a series of them with one bitterly mean superintendent, had: if a journalist suspected certain questions would spook a source, prompting them to end an interview prematurely, she had two choices:

1. Get down to business and ask the hard shit first because some sources would tolerate only a single question before hanging up or declining to comment. Best to be able to report that you asked the question that mattered most.
2. Delay until the very end asking the question the source likely hopes you won't, so you draw as much from them as possible before they call it quits.

Audrey had been underground for weeks, and asking questions here felt more uncomfortable than asking them of families in the throes of tragedy, even the several fatal car accidents she'd covered, because asking questions here potentially endangered her living situation. That was new. But she wasn't waiting another minute, especially when Mitch's availability was such an unknown to her. Some days, they could grab a bite. Others, he seemed able to spare only a handful of minutes. So in this moment, yeah, she would press him.

"Do people down here go above ground?"

He put his rib down. "Why do you ask?"

It wasn't Audrey's style to beat around the bush, and she felt less willing to "behave" as the days here stretched into weeks. *He* had brought *her* here. She swallowed a bit of burger and the lump in her throat. "People I love are up there."

"Yes, people down here go up."

"You?"

Mitch averted his gaze. "I do."

"Can you check an area for people I know?" Had it happened any other day, Audrey's faulty memory would have invariably forgotten what Mom and Kevin were wearing. Luckily, they'd been at a wedding. She remembered his suit, the way her heart had skipped a beat at how fine he'd looked, and she'd been with her mom when she'd bought that flowered gown. It was entirely possible they hadn't had the chance to change. That fact all but took her breath away.

Mitch met Audrey's eyes. "At present, we're staying close. Patrolling for threats that might stumble upon our doors. Sorry."

"Doors, plural?" Her career had required this of her: watching for the truths that single word choices could reveal.

Mitch didn't break eye contact. "Doors plural," he confirmed, wiping his fingers clean. "Do me a favor, Audrey."

Audrey nodded her cooperation.

"I'm fair game, but careful who you interrogate. Some will view any question as an intrusion."

The very next person Audrey encountered made that uncomfortably clear.

Fresh-squeezed lemonade made her happy and nostalgic, as did asking questions without repercussions, so Audrey walked the halls with a brighter air than usual. Smiled at the children. They were fun, and she could be, too, again. Maybe. She told a woman she liked her dress. "Thank you," the woman said, though she darted quickly away.

Audrey's mistake was daring to speak a casual "How are you?" to someone older in a curious cloak.

The wrinkled woman stopped and frowned. "Know your place," she replied.

Audrey's cheer dissipated, her jaw dropped, and she shrank away. Embarrassed, she resumed walking, but the woman wasn't done with her.

"You," Audrey heard her say. Audrey swallowed and turned to face the one she'd offended.

The woman pursed her lips. "Make no mistake. Just because you ended up here doesn't mean you are welcome. We allow it because he allows it. No more, no less."

He? She must have meant Mitch.

"You're a drain on everything *we* prepared to survive. You eat our stores, you inhabit our room, you use our water and supplies. Your gratitude is expected, and you can show it by proving invisible." The woman blinked pointedly and turned with a swish of her cloak. "We can and will require your compliance."

Audrey watched her depart, and her hands shook. She felt low and little. The woman turned left, out of the hallway, and another trio of people passed. Two women and a child. The women didn't wave, but they smiled.

Audrey didn't return the smile. She felt thrust into a fog, into the memory of the only other time she'd felt this unwelcome: sitting there, mortified, as Principal Haggan viciously slut-shamed her in front of her dad. She stepped through her suite door and into the room she didn't deserve, and her breaths became short and insufficient. She inhaled, her face to the ceiling. *Steady yourself.*

Who: Me. I'm my mother's daughter. I'm kind because people deserve kindness. They just don't know me yet.

What: Underground. May be time to find a way out. If I go, how do I stay alive? What do I take with me?

When: Will she kick me out? Can *she kick me out?*

Where: Earth is under siege. Will there be a place that's safe? How do I find Mom? Audrey's heart sank, and a sob escaped her mouth. Kevin wouldn't need finding. She had to face he hadn't survived; there was no way. She knew what she'd seen. How does a person survive an apocalypse knowing the person she lived for is ... gone? *Stop. Those thoughts won't help.*

Why: Why should I allow them to push me out? I didn't ask to be here. Gather info. If push comes to shove, and I have shit I can use to expose them for illegal building or for watching movies and reading books and eating seasonally themed ravioli while others met violent, preventable deaths above them, I'll have a hand to play. Leverage.

Audrey stood, unsteady, despite the mental exercise that usually braced her. She pulled on a fluffy robe and stepped to the bathroom mirror. Her face looked swollen and ugly; never failed when she cried. She bent down and rubbed her cheeks and forehead and nose with soap, and as she washed her face, the memory washed over her. She wished it wouldn't: it still made her feel dirty if she let it.

The blinds were drawn as if Principal Haggan wanted the room to be as devoid of light as Audrey was of hope. Her heart thumped when her dad stepped inside. He didn't know why he'd been summoned, but she had every reason to fear he would shortly.

"Principal Haggan," Charles Kelly began, sitting and peering at Audrey, and Audrey whipped her head away with dread and shame. *Just let me die*, she thought. Were it Ms. Reynolds, her sex-positive physical education teacher, she'd have entertained a sliver of hope that the whole of her crime wouldn't be revealed to her *parent*. But seated before her was Principal Haggan (Haggard, the kids called him). She might as well be a hunk of meat, thrown to the most blistering of fires. Nothing of her would be left unsinged, and Audrey sweated down her back and in her pits. She dared to peer at the man who held her secret in his hands, and her fears were confirmed: he looked bitterly mad and simultaneously smug. She was toast.

"I've got to tell you, Mr. Kelly," the principal began, his tone condescending to her *father*. "This is a new one, and I've been at this for thirty-four years." Principal Haggan tilted his head, and Audrey could feel his eyes on her. "Would you like to tell him, Audrey, or shall I?"

Audrey weighed her options. Would it go better if she told her dad she got caught going down on Phillip Freyer, or would it go better if the principal did?

But Principal Haggan hadn't meant it when he floated the option. "Mr. Kelly, your daughter was caught today, during fourth period, with her mouth on a boy's private parts in the locker room."

Audrey now thanked the room for being so dark. She didn't want to look at her dad, but she wanted to look at the principal less. Audrey peeked. Her dad's eyes blinked rapidly, and his mouth formed a stern line across his face.

"I'm sorry to be the bearer of such lurid news about your daughter's character and behavior, but this is grounds for expulsion, so it's best you embrace the full picture."

Expulsion? Audrey hated herself even more now, however that could be possible.

The principal's eyes moved from her dad to Audrey and back to her dad, and Audrey saw it as a challenge. Slut-daughter and slut-daughter's dad, meet your maker. Principal Haggan was leaving out the words he hadn't minced when he'd caught her. *Who raised you? What kind of household do you live in that you think you can engage in sexual acts at a place of formal education? I've got to say, I'm the father of three daughters, and they would* never *do this.*

Audrey had died inside when she wiped her mouth and stood, eyes down, and she'd nodded vigorously at his every point, hopeful that if she proved as contrite as the man demanded, he would sentence her to detentions she could explain away as, "Oh, I was too talkative, you know." Her contrition had apparently bought her nothing.

Principal Haggan had merely brandished a hand at Phillip, who zipped up his jeans and stepped out of the room.

"Who is the boy?" her dad asked.

"I'm not sure that's relevant to your daughter's punish—" the principal began.

"I'm not asking you," her father interrupted. "Audrey, who were you with?"

"Phillip," Audrey replied immediately, because what was the sense in fighting the train that barreled down the tracks?

"Hm," her dad murmured, rubbing his forehead.

He worked so hard. Audrey regretted so much that he was here, at 2:37 p.m. on a workday, dealing with her slutty mistake. He must be embarrassed and disappointed, and, God, the thought of his daughter doing that. A principal with three daughters had never—

"Audrey, we'll have a conversation later," her dad began.

She shrank, her shaking hands bound in a knot on her lap.

"Principal Haggan, I'm sorry. I raised her better than this."

She shrank some more.

"But I will say, and Audrey, you look at me when I say this," her dad said. "Was your act consensual?"

Audrey complied and nodded.

"Let's be sure we get this on the record. Was your act consensual?"

"Yes, it was."

Her dad turned to the adult man seated before him, but she realized he was still speaking to her. "Sexual behavior, done privately and consensually, is not anyone's business. Unfortunately, you chose to engage in it in a place where there could be witnesses, and there were witnesses. As I said, we have a conversation to have. But you, sir, are an adult, and you will not slut-shame my daughter. You also will not expel her without expelling her willing, consensual partner, even if he is the one presently leading this school to its first championship in, what did the headline say? Four decades? I presume you've talked to his parents, too? Lamented his lacking character and threatened expulsion? Yeah?"

Audrey's eyes widened. She tightened her ball of fists.

Two adult men in her life, both with abundant authority to punish her, looked like they wanted to tear *each other* apart. Principal Haggan obviously seethed, his wrinkled jaw hemming and hawing. Her dad crossed his leg over the other and tapped his finger on his knee. He didn't seethe outwardly, but it was clear he was in his take-no-bullshit mood.

Principal Haggan stood. "I see now why we're in this predicament. Parents who don't enforce consequences—"

"My consequences are a family matter," her dad interrupted matter-of-factly. "But your punishments and the equity of them are a matter of public interest. So, you tell me which it is: we're looking at a dual expulsion, or we're looking at misogyny, and if it's the latter, you can find me next Wednesday telling the school board of *your* behavior."

Audrey's head spinned. Her heart boomed.

The principal ate his words that afternoon because as often happens, Ohio protects its football players, and men protect men.

The words exchanged between 2:37 and 2:52 on a Tuesday afternoon fueled so much self-love in Audrey that she knew she could never repay her father. It wouldn't have been the same had her mother done it, she realized only decades later. Charles had been, in that moment, an ally before allyship was a term. He gave her in those fifteen minutes the permission to be a full, smart, and sexual woman, to demand fairness, and to reject slut-shaming in a world that sure liked its women erotic but also wanted them demure. At eighteen, she'd gladly shrugged on the confident go-fuck-yourself demeanor of a woman decades older.

For the five months after it happened, Audrey felt wrapped in a warm, impenetrable hug, one that she extended to herself and to other teenage girls clawing their way to adulthood.

Then, five months and two days later, her father left, and everything that forged the strength in her felt fragile, listless, and nearly gone.

9

July

Five weeks after

Audrey knew her grandmother would blink pointedly, raise her gray eyebrows, and tut in her way before launching into a monologue. Snooping is low. A person must respect the right of another to have privacy. A woman, especially, should have the class to resist the urge to stick her nose where it does not belong.

But her grandmother had never stepped foot in this place, a curious and luxurious Underground beneath an unassuming slice of Ohio. A place that teemed with everyday activity while so many probably suffered. That man, Bram, walked though his leg had been severed. *What else didn't make sense? What else proved this place was unnatural?* What secrets could she sock away, just in case?

She chose 3 a.m., thinking the coast would be clear. Audrey's jitters climbed but not because she doubted herself. She knew she was capable of finding answers, especially when they weren't easy to come by. It had been a point of pride that her newsroom colleagues consulted her when they hunted something but hit dead-ends.

The lighting in the Underground's corridors was dimmest in the mornings and brightened as it would be expected to at dawn. It was a handsome place, and more alone than she'd been in its public spaces, she noticed again its intricate details, its crown molding and ornamental light switches and doorknobs. Within minutes of turning down a hallway she'd never been down, footsteps came from a connecting corridor. *Fuck!*

Even before that witch of a woman told her to "know her place," Audrey knew she was an outsider. People didn't complete sentences around her. She wasn't greeted. She was *watched*. People weren't rude; she figured they simply didn't know what to make of a woman they hadn't expected to be safe alongside them sleeping in one of their beds and eating their food. They would probably not appreciate discovering the outsider sneaking around.

She tried a door handle, held her breath as the door gave way, and stepped swiftly inside. She backed against the door and listened. The footsteps stopped outside the room, and someone fiddled with the door. Audrey quickly tiptoed to a corner between two filing cabinets and slowly, her back to the wall, slid down. Her mouth dried, and her heart felt like it had catapulted someplace new within her ribcage, an angry tiger thumping, thrashing on its prison.

The door clicked open. The lights flicked on. Audrey's alarms were now full on tornado sirens. A woman with midnight hair to her waist stepped inside, cradling a cordless phone to her face, and it was merely a matter of time before Audrey was caught.

"I'm sorry, I just can't fathom it," the woman hissed. Silence reigned while the woman listened. She stepped to a filing cabinet and rustled through some papers. "How realistic is it that we stay hidden now that—"

Audrey slowly pulled her feet inward in an attempt to further conceal herself. She didn't see the cord beneath her. Something nearby crashed to the floor. *Shit.*

The woman's face snapped toward Audrey. "Hold up."

Audrey froze but poorly. Her body shook so disobediently she worried she'd clang against the cabinets to the left and right. Her eyes locked with the woman's. Terrified, she stared. Her body tingled and not in the way it does when a foot falls asleep. She'd felt this tingle a couple times before.

The woman's eyes immediately left Audrey's person. Darted up. Down. Focused on the item tangled on the ground. Her brow furrowed. "All I'm saying," she picked back up, selecting a forest green file folder and closing the drawer, "is I worry. It's enough to juggle with the Handlers down here. I worry we're not equipped to manage this additional risk." Silence again. "Mmmk, well you can tell them what I say, if it would help."

Away the woman went, lights off, leaving Audrey alone. Audrey exhaled with relief and suspicion. Why hadn't the woman demanded to know what she was doing there? Why had she looked straight at her but acted like Audrey was a ghost? Maybe the woman was afraid of the outsider who had strayed from where she was told to stay, and she was enlisting reinforcements to dispatch her. Audrey kept her legs tight to her chest until the click of heels had long disappeared and she felt reasonably confident the sound wouldn't return.

Audrey pulled on a handle. No dice. She tried another, the one she believed the woman had opened. It wasn't completely shut and slid forward. Inside were dozens, possibly hundreds, of file folders. She pulled one out. Rosalia Green was written on its tab.

Inside was a stack of paper, all dated and some time-stamped.

Rosalia got a new job today.

Audrey flipped forward. More notes. Tons of notes.

She's taking 200 milligrams a day, and that is working for suppression.

Audrey paged nearly to the end.

Rosalia has been having an affair. Her pairing is at risk, as is her continued medication.

Audrey flipped to the last page and frowned. She reread the sentence, but she wasn't mistaken. She cocked her head. *What does* "Rosalia's wipe complete. New pairing commenced" *mean?* Audrey flipped all the way to the front again. Rosalia Green was Audrey's age. Who was she? Where was she? What Audrey wouldn't give for Google right now.

Audrey dropped the file folder back where she found it and picked up another belonging to a Sebastian George. The first page was a copy of a birth certificate; Sebastian had been born at eight pounds, thirteen ounces, in Phoenixville, Pennsylvania. Audrey paged ahead.

Sebastian is proving to be an extremely difficult and volatile case. Attempts to medicate him have failed. We may need to consider other approaches.

She flipped all the way to the end and lifted her palms. She swallowed, scanning Sebastian George's death certificate. Manner, accidental. Decedent's usual occupation, bartender. Cause of death, fall.

Audrey shook her head. Who were these people, what medications were they taking, and why were they under scrutiny? She didn't keep files this thick about herself. Why did a luxury shelter have them for—she let her thumb ripple across the folders' tabs—dozens of people? Why was none of it digitized?

These were the kinds of crumbs she would have chased on assignment, jotting down questions to ask sources in an attempt to piece together an unbiased and complete picture. Above ground, she'd unearthed the stories behind company bankruptcies and unprecedented public utility investigations and insider trading. SEC filings were a truth trove if one knew what to search for. Below ground, she wasn't on assignment, but she would take an insurance policy.

Her heart raced, and she could feel her profuse back sweat as she extracted a few pages from the Sebastian George file, folded them, and stuck them in her pocket. She worried about getting caught with the pages. She worried more that no one knew where she was. Would anyone ever? *Mom will never think to search some cave.* She needed to lie down. She shoved the folder back into the drawer, did a once-over of the room, and left, not at all confident she'd find her way back. She felt both increasingly unsettled and afraid to be caught for snooping, having strayed farther than she remembered from the suite she'd been given. *Given.* These people had taken her in as the world above devolved, and she'd repaid them with sneaking and stealing.

Navigating the Underground's many tunnels proved way harder when she was fighting to navigate her thoughts, too. Had the woman with midnight hair pretended not to catch her? Why would she do that? To send her a message? And what had the woman meant? "It's enough to juggle with the Handlers down here." What was a handler? Betty Jane had mentioned the term. Audrey figured she'd know if she was one. But would she?

She turned a corner and collided with Mitch.

"Up early," he said.

Mitch must know. He brought her here. Audrey forced a smile. "Hey Mitch. Yeah, I'm feeling *so* sick. I need to lay down. I didn't mean to, I was looking for medication, and I got turned around." She actually did feel ill—dizzy, physically and emotionally. Her new underground world was spinning. She didn't know if her mother was alive, the ache that Kevin was gone threatened to drown her at every turn, and she felt more confused than she thought possible about what this country club-like Underground was. *Why all the records?*

"Hey, hey, hold up." Mitch put his hands on her shoulders and peered at her. She could barely meet his gaze. She felt the horrifying creep of warm saliva in her mouth, a sign vomiting was near. His eyes flashed with, strangely, realization. "I'm sorry you're dizzy."

Audrey lifted her face. She hadn't told him that, had she? "Yeah, I need to lie down." *And figure out what this place actually is and who you all actually are.*

Mitch exhaled and paused, his eyes boring into her. She couldn't remember his ever peering at her so intently. "This is the Underground. I'm Mitch."

Alarm spread hot throughout Audrey's body. He was answering her *unspoken thoughts*. Her face flushed. "What? I just need to—"

"We need to talk. Privately. Let's get to your room."

Audrey didn't dare say no. The warm saliva refused to retreat. Before this, she would have focused on anything until the urge retreated. But her heart pounded. Her head pounded. She now questioned whether the man leading her to her room was a liar—and a dangerous one. Their walk through the tunnels wasn't unlike their frantic run to the Underground away from the end of the world. They didn't speak. Mitch led the way, and Audrey was in the dark.

It took them ten minutes to walk back; Audrey counted it instead in the times she successfully didn't puke. (Three.)

Before the door to her suite clicked closed, she pressed him: "Mitch, how do you know what I'm—" She stopped. "It's like you know what I'm thinking?"

"I've been able to read minds since birth."

It was a miracle she didn't spew all over the floor. She peered at him intently, but he cracked no gotcha grin. There was no punch line. He couldn't be serious, right? *I'm so confused.* "I'm—"

"Confused," he finished for her. "I'm sorry. There were things I couldn't tell you. Where were you just now?"

Her thoughts flashed back to the room of filing cabinets.

He inhaled. "I could understand why the vault could prove ... unsettling. Frankly, you shouldn't have been there."

"Mitch, I'm freaking out," Audrey said, beginning to pace the room. "Please, be for real. Are you reading my mind?"

"It's an ability I was born with," he repeated calmly.

"So, wait—you've been reading my mind since we met?" Audrey's cheeks grew hot. It wasn't the time, and she had so many other more important questions, but please no. *Has he heard every way I've thought about him?*

Mitch blinked slowly and exhaled.

Audrey's eyes met his.

"Yes," he said. "I don't listen intentionally, to be clear. But I can't turn it off."

Audrey closed her eyes. "Mitch...I don't know what to say." Usually a woman of words, and in her life before this, paid to communicate, Audrey stared at the ground.

He put his hands on her hands.

She raised her face to his.

"I'm going to tell you something I shouldn't. No one can know."

Audrey nodded slowly, blinking rapidly.

"You need to start covering your thoughts, Audrey. Otherwise, you'll repeat what I'm about to tell you without saying a word. I'm not the only one around here who can read minds. I'll teach you how to block them."

Audrey's eyes widened. She pulled her curls into a sloppy bun high on her head—her hair was increasingly sweaty—and lay down on the bed. She felt *exhausted*. All she could think to do was pull the blanket to her chin and nod.

The nausea was here to stay, but it wouldn't stop her. She would vomit questions as they came, and, to her surprise, Mitch kept talking.

10

Mitch's family had *lore*, stories and secrets passed with rigor from generation to generation. His ancestors had left to their bloodline enormous wealth and strict creed. Mitch, like his cousins, and they, like their parents, wouldn't intentionally stray from it: know the rituals. Defend. Grow the family branches judiciously. Assimilate into society and leave it better. Outsiders must never know.

The family's silence wasn't rooted in elitism. It was rooted in a fear of discovery. A fear of persecution. A need to maintain what generations and generations had preserved.

The elders had convened a meeting weeks ago, immediately after Mitch introduced a threat named Audrey into the Underground, and they'd made it abundantly clear. Keep the oath. Mitch had nodded. She was his first "mistake." Plenty of family members hadn't made it to thirty-five years old without committing some act that had them summoned. He feared, though, his was the most egregious. Given the circumstances, his action had created quite the security threat. No doubt about it, the family couldn't fathom his behavior. *You should have* never *stopped and brought her here. You've altered how we survive down here. You've endangered whether we survive. How could you?*

They didn't know what he knew. They couldn't know that he was supposed to bring her here.

"We cannot be responsible for others' treason. She only exists because *one* of us betrayed *all* of us, and we handle those mistakes. Mitch. You are of Puck and Raven. You were raised better. She's a danger to us all, and now she's down here when we have *nowhere* to go. Let me be clear," the elder had seethed weeks earlier. "She is your responsibility. We'll assign controls, but you will mitigate this risk. Or we will."

Mitch searched the faces around the table for empathy. He expected and found none. He pitched his chin down. They excused him.

For all his years, stories of men and women before him who tangled with outsiders had kept him faithful. He knew the gory details, but when he heard and found her, terrified and curled in a ball in a tattered gown beneath the bushes, he'd stopped. Worse yet, he'd brought her here.

In many moments since, he'd wrestled with his core teachings. She wasn't so different than him. She just didn't know it.

Audrey cleared her throat, pitching Mitch back to the present, inside the tense room. She wore the woven blanket, an attempt at protection. He could hear her fear, and it made him miserable. It occurred to him now that he hadn't planned for the after: for after he brought her here. He'd been so determined to find her, and that had been the extent of it.

"Okay..." He trailed off. *This, if done, is a mistake you cannot right. If she knows, she's a danger. If they know, she's* in *danger. But you have reason to tell her, elders be damned.*

"How, Mitch?"

Her tone dripped with impatience, and he understood. He had forced this upon her. She would have gone back, had he not interfered. She'd left someone. Neither one of them knew if that person, her lover, was dead. She didn't know Mitch knew his name. *Kevin.*

"How can you—how can you read my mind?"

Mitch met her eyes. He rubbed his forehead and breathed deeply. "I can't say."

"I'm so sick—" She sat up. Covered her mouth. "Mitch, I need to leave."

"You can't."

She sat silently, mouth covered. Breathed and exhaled a few times. "I think I might get sick."

His eyes darted left. Focused on the rug. He didn't know if more information would help. "This place isn't what I told you it is."

She inhaled, mouth still in her hands.

He stood and sat beside her, eyes closed. "I'm—we're—different than you."

"How do you mean?"

"My family has ... abilities."

"What do you mean? Please, please stop making me ask."

"We are Descendants. We can read minds."

He'd done it. His family would never forgive it if they knew.

"You read people's minds? Like actually? You just said this place isn't what you told me it was. What is it?"

"It's built for times like these, for people like me."

"Not for people like me?"

Mitch heard her worry again she would puke. Heard her wish to escape, fearful of him, fearful of all of them. He regretted her fear. They were a month into this disaster, one the prophet had estimated could span years, and he tired of so much already. He wanted to tell everyone everything and focus not on keeping his secrets straight, but on the mitigation and dominance required above ground.

Mitch looked aside and just said it. "Audrey, you are not who you think you are."

11

Inexplicably, despite or perhaps because of how her thoughts raced and her nausea roiled, Audrey had fallen asleep for an hour. She awoke with a start and immediately felt conflicted about Mitch's remaining in her suite. On the one hand, she had *so. many. questions.* On the other, she'd drifted, thinking about which ways she might escape if only she could lose him.

"Not trying to scare you, but you'd be hard-pressed to lose me down here," Mitch replied to her thoughts.

Her jaw dropped.

He walked toward her and knelt by the bed. "Try this, Audrey. I want you to visualize a door—doesn't matter what door, but it's got to be what occurs to *you*. It has to be your original thought. Now slam the door on my read." He nodded at her, prompting her to do it.

She sat up. The first door she saw was that of the apartment building where she'd stayed with her father every other weekend after her parents' divorce. Theirs had been a fairly cookie-cutter separation to Audrey. Her parents spoke little ill of one another, and in some ways, that was more confusing than the angrier schisms she'd heard her classmates live through. The door was a soft blue, wooden entry with a gold deadbolt and an additional lock on its gold knob.

"It's light blue with gold hardware," Mitch said. "Slam the door on my read, Audrey."

She shut her eyes.

"No. You need to learn to do it without closing your eyes. That's a tell around here."

She stared directly at him. She felt angry at, afraid of, and thankful to him—and now she needed to summon the strength to do this fantastical thing he demanded of her. She inhaled and envisioned the light blue door slamming in his face. She'd thrown that door shut when running from friends in the neighborhood during many summer breaks, and she could hear its sound now.

"Good, I can hear less," Mitch encouraged. "Now lock every lock."

She stared at him and nodded. The deadbolt turned right, and the lock on the doorknob twisted. She blinked.

"Well done," he said. "Your thoughts will remain secured unless you open them for someone."

Not going to happen, Audrey thought before catching herself mid-thought, instantly nervous.

Mitch seemed to register nothing—or at least gave away nothing.

"Thank—" Her voice cracked. She cleared her throat. "Thank you. Do I, what? Imagine that with everyone over and over down here?"

"It shouldn't be necessary person to person, but it wouldn't hurt to close it nightly or weekly at a minimum," Mitch replied.

"And why and how would I open my thoughts to another?"

"It's the opposite of what you did: you visualize opening the door to only the person you want to hear your thoughts. I advise you keep them closed down here," Mitch said. "You're new down here; those who can read minds may not know you've turned yours off, and that's ideal. We don't want them realizing someone's taught you to block readers."

Audrey wrung her hands. "As if my anxiety wasn't peaking like a motherfucker," she murmured.

"Do you need more medication?"

"Nah, I've been weaning myself off it. If we're down here for the foreseeable future, I need to cope better."

Mitch raised his eyes to hers. "Ah," he said. "You needn't worry. Our pharmacy is stocked."

"Mitch?" She leaned in toward him.

His eyes remained trained on hers.

"You said I'm not who I think I am. Who am I?"

SIXTEEN YEARS *before*

When Mitch used his abilities to read the adults' minds before he snuck out, he didn't lie. Not about reading their minds (which was expressly forbidden and usually something adults prevented) and more impressively not about why he committed the crime (to skinny-dip in the unnamed, bubbling creek, and yes, with girls, too). Mitch Gray could be counted on to be honest, even in situations when adults knew, were the tables turned, they would have lied. The elders recognized his was an old soul, but all he knew was that he didn't feel drawn to lie, even to Theodora when their future was all but ordained.

It all began with that year's Feast of Maturation. The Feast marked the first time the oldest youth were asked to serve the meal. The first time one's name could be called.

In some ways, the feast was no different than the quintessential American Thanksgiving. An abundant spread of food. Family, some not seen in a year. Warmth from the hearth—and heart. A return home.

For more than 200 years, seven generations had called Graylock Mansion home. At the end of a long, straightaway road lined with a tunnel of girthy, reaching oak trees stood the sprawling stone home with its slate gray brick and five chimney stacks. It evoked presumptions of secret passageways and clawfoot tubs, and the mansion actually had both if one knew where to walk.

That year, Mitch returned to the Graylock Mansion a man. He

was attending college, and at nineteen, he was prime age to be betrothed, should the elders deem it fit.

Mitch reveled in his freedom the way many college freshmen do. He was a young man living on his own. He drank, ordered too many late-night pizzas, and skipped class to duel buddies in video games and play ball. But his freedom stopped short of the others'. They slept with whom they wanted; their bloodline didn't demand extreme compliance. They teased and called him a prude because they didn't know better.

When it came time to return home, it felt comfortable. Warm. And family did know better.

The Descendants cooked up a spread, and it smelled and tasted like *before*. They roasted meat they'd hunted themselves: turkey, pheasant, and deer. Above bright, licking flames stewed carrots, potatoes, and onions, vegetables they'd grown themselves, made thick by starch and flavorful by herbs such as thyme and sage. Salty because the family liked it.

Across the table, surrounded by familiar faces, they'd chosen Mitch.

"Descendants, the occasion has come to speak of love," the elder at the head of the table began. The woman seated directly across from the elder nodded.

"Mitch Gray, we believe it to be true. There may be a union that speaks to you today."

Mitch had sensed it coming. They'd known he would. But with all eyes on him and voices reverently quiet, the moment felt heavier than he expected. "Theodora Bishop, have you the heart and interest to explore a union with Mitch Gray?"

"Yes," the tall girl down the table said without hesitation.

And they did explore.

Theodora Bishop had not a mean bone in her body. She'd grown up, soothing six little sisters, dabbing hydrogen peroxide on boo-boos, gently applying Mickey Mouse Band-Aids as little sobs subsided. She was the type of person who cradled an injured bird and stopped during a jog to help a flailing beetle off its back. Mitch admired her. Still did.

They'd grown up thick as thieves. As middle-schoolers, they'd eaten together, attended school together, played in her family's treehouse together. She'd changed the summer when they were freshmen in high school. *They'd* changed.

"Password?" she said, peering down, her dark eyebrows raised.

Her family's treehouse was so shrouded in lush green canopy, one couldn't tell it was there unless directly beneath it. Generations had climbed to the treehouse as they themselves had grown tall. Much more slowly, the trees around them did the same.

He scoffed and flew up the ladder.

She smelled of watermelon bubble gum and sweet body spray, and she insisted, "Password?"

"Please," Mitch said, smirking.

She relented.

"Can you believe he's getting married?"

"About time," he carelessly replied about her uncle. He handed her the popsicle he had fetched.

"He waited for her. It's so *romantic*."

Theodora's eyes met his.

He sat cross-legged, crunching red sugar ice from the plastic wrapper. His mouth slowed.

She moved closer. Closer than their faces had ever been, save when they whispered secrets. "Mitch," she said. "I—" She averted her eyes to her own lap, smiled sheepishly, and leaned in.

Her kiss was soft but not timid, and he returned it insistently. She pulled away and bit her lip. She knew well it was his first. *She* now was Mitch Gray's first.

Years and many incredibly tempting situations later, the elders named them. Two Descendants who were asked to explore a union and agree were expected to explore each other physically. That instruction came privately, as the youth cleaned up the year's Feast of Maturation. Theodora and Mitch followed an elder couple to a sitting room inside Graylock Mansion. The male elder gestured to a plush, antique couch, and they sat. The man placed Theodora's hand on Mitch's thigh and Mitch's hand on her thigh.

"Sex between man and woman is expressly forbidden outside of two arrangements," the elder began. "Wedlock and exploration. We cannot have our family grow in accidental ways."

This was not news to Mitch; it was a refrain from his childhood.

The man and woman elders sat before Theodora and Mitch on a couch facing theirs and joined hands. "We first slept together when we explored our union. It was the 1950s, and we were interrupted during a drive-in movie," the man divulged ruefully.

His wife chuckled at the memory.

"You'd be wise to explore each other in this way," the man said. "Mitch, seek her satisfaction before yours."

"And Theodora," the woman said, "teach him to satisfy."

Theodora averted her eyes. Her cheeks flushed. But the next night and for months after, they did what was encouraged, fueled by needs neither had fully explored before. Mitch consumed her. He'd casually wondered for years what the girl who knew him best would be like in these ways: how her face would look and how she'd sound when a man satisfied her. Now he eagerly discovered both. And Theodora was in no way shy: she often put his hands on her, his mouth on her.

One night, four months later, she turned her face from his advance and sat stiffly. "Were you just not going to tell me?"

Instantly, Mitch's neck felt ablaze. "What?"

"Mitch." Her tone was different. Distant.

Mitch hung his head. "I tried, Tee."

"What's wrong?" she insisted. She sounded uncharacteristically insecure, and she refused eye contact.

"Nothing. We're just *us*, and I—" He shook his head and exhaled. "I'm sorry."

"You slept with me for months. You *used* me."

He hadn't, or at least he hadn't intended to. But if she felt used, he wouldn't presume to argue the point. He had reached for her to fulfill a duty, an expectation, but no matter how he tried to beat it back or explain it away, a gnawing truth tunneled its way through his defenses. His love for Theodora wasn't the kind he wanted to feel for a wife, and sex hadn't changed that. He wanted a companionship, too, and theirs had stopped evolving at high school.

Mitch had begun mourning their friendship in the tree, the people they used to be when they were without complication. He wished they could rewind and relive the Feast, but to do what? The elders had asked them to explore. Descendants don't tell the elders no.

"Mitch."

He raised his head.

She was her courageous and generous self to the end, telling him calmly how she loved and wanted "every perfectly broken bit" of him, how she knew he hadn't intended to hurt her.

Mitch broke eye contact only when she said the words he couldn't: "You don't love me like that."

Theodora swallowed and lifted his chin to look him dead in the eye. "You will tell them. Good luck."

Mitch was unsure if she wished him good luck because he would be only the second to reject an elder coupling, or if she actually meant goodbye.

In the moments he watched her leave and for months thereafter, he deeply second-guessed himself. His family members disagreed with—and very vocally disapproved of—his decision.

Theodora was hurt and embarrassed, and *he* had done that to her. When the girl from the treehouse stayed away thereafter, Mitch understood.

12

August

Two and a half months after

Mitch and Audrey stood in the grill line, both in their thoughts, when a siren began chirping and red lights at the top of the cafeteria walls started flashing. Audrey looked up and around, her eyes wide, before uniformed men approached. "Sir, we need you to —" the speaker glanced at Audrey. "You're needed immediately, sir."

Mitch turned to Audrey. "Grab a bite. I'll find you when I can."

She'd clearly closed her door, preventing his read, but Audrey frowned, revealing her disappointment. He felt badly, but they weren't asking him. He jogged away as she ordered a cheesesteak.

"Brief me," Mitch said, jogging but not breathless because he trained for these situations.

A lurcher has found and recognized the mountain door as a door, one man began, his thoughts loud and clear for Mitch.

Mitch's eyes widened. "When?"

Roughly ten minutes ago. We waited, hoping it would simply walk away, but it did not. It's banging its head, drawing others' attention.

Mitch's jog turned to a sprint, and the fighters flanking him followed suit. The Descendants had evidence that the killers above ground communicated in hive mind, and they couldn't afford for one of the savages to tell the scourge about some door—*their* door—in the side of an Ohio mountain.

The thuds against the front door were audible now, and Mitch didn't stop running. An officer keyed in a code to open the door separating the team and Mitch from the ravaged world. First out, as he always was, Mitch came face to face with the gruesome savage. He ducked, ran to the tree line, motioning for the others to disperse to the north and the south, and turned quickly, but the lurcher lunged and caught Mitch in the neck before he could shove the creature away. Mitch groaned but stood his ground in the way only he could.

It happened when he wielded a power: Mitch's eyes darkened to black, and goosebumps spread across his skin. Clutching his neck wound, Mitch silently gave a quick flick of his wrist, and the lurcher flew twenty feet backward into a nearby tree. It began to scream—an unpleasantly shrill sound that caused the fighters to cover their ears and hinge forward, paralyzed with evident pain—and Mitch curled his fingers into a fist, his entire body shaking, and the creature quieted. Mitch nearly collapsed. Killing anything required an inordinate effort, but killing these things robbed him of breath and strength. This was the fourteenth he'd slain; he would keep count until he couldn't.

Mitch approached the murderous monster, his chin and palms up, his gait an exhausted stagger. He circled it quietly, carefully navigating its massive frame. Its body looked nine or ten feet long. Its skin appeared to be similar to a crocodile's armor, thick and scaly. Its face looked blood-stained—maybe it was—and its black eyes weren't closed. Mitch shivered at its mouth, agape with wickedly pencil-length fangs.

"Sir, are you okay?" one fighter breathed, carefully quiet. Mitch examined the hand he pulled from his neck. *It's a surface cut, I'll be fine.* It burned, though, and strangely.

Let's stick together, he thought to the team behind him.

They gripped their weapons. He could sense their fear.

Buckle up, he added, without speaking. *We can't risk detection, so we're out here until we're convinced they're not coming for us.*

THE NEXT DAY, after eleven tense hours above ground, a serious injury to one fighter's face, and six more kills far too close to what needed to be their safe and undetected shelter, Mitch, back underground, stepped inside the room lit by red sconces and lined with towering built-in bookshelves. He waited, wrists crossed before his waist, until another finished accounting for how the Underground's stockpile of food, supplies, and medicine fared now that so many were living there. Apparently well, was the gist.

"Our greenhouse has outperformed projections, and we're heartened by that," the woman concluded.

The elders voiced pleasant surprise.

"Mitch," one called.

He stood in the place any speaker does. "Elders," he began with deference, ducking his forehead. "What we observe of our earth is increasingly overgrown. Grass is knee-high in some places, it must have rained heavily, and it's introducing a hazard to our teams when they need to run. Lurchers are plentiful, unfortunately. We've not commenced comprehensive missions to gauge how many people are hiding out, waiting for relief, but we have seen lights flickering inside on occasion, so there are survivors. We've marked those buildings for first dispatch when reconstruction begins. That they've survived for months is incredible."

"Did you go inside any structures this time?" a male elder asked.

"Yes, we did."

Mitch would never forget it. The flags along the walkway of one house in particular—lit brightly by nothing but the summer moonlight—were a haunting reminder of the race to survive that began Memorial Day weekend. Mitch and his team had stepped to the yellow front door and found it ajar. Protected by Mitch, the team stepped inside. Though only the strongest men and women accompanied him on runs, several gagged at the smell.

"As you can imagine," Mitch began, "we found plates of half-eaten food turned black and people..." He swallowed. "I'll leave it at that." He wouldn't describe them. The child in red, white, and blue footed pajamas. The parents nearby, limbs missing. Mitch winced at the memory of splatters across the walls, then ducked his head toward the floor, clenching his jaw.

The elder woman, usually merciless and quick and terse in her questioning, allowed a full minute to lapse before asking him to speak again. "Any sign their approach abates?"

"No, ma'am," Mitch replied, straightening and smoothing his shirt. "We did try every frequency on a radio we found inside a diner to try to pick up on any messages. Nothing to report." The restaurant had smelled the worst. Flies had swarmed all over the plates and the bodies left to rot in booths, at the avocado-green counter, in the kitchen.

"Thank you, Mitch. We know it's not easy," one man said. "Our researchers continue to study the risk we face. Presently, they maintain the same as they first theorized: these creatures seek a new home, and they assumed all on Earth are merely human."

"They'll die for the underestimation," Mitch replied. He clenched his teeth at the memory of all the bodies, strewn in the street and down front steps, left to decay like they weren't someone's mom, brother, friend, child. *We will kill you all and take it back.*

The elders respected his ruthlessness in this moment; it wasn't often that this side of Mitch Gray reared itself.

"And Audrey Kelly?" the merciless woman asked, drumming her fingers impatiently on the table.

"Nothing to report except—" Mitch paused. "She's disclosed that she's stopped taking her meds."

"Pardon me, but nothing to report? That's not permissible," the woman retorted.

"If I may," Mitch began, his palm up in a deferential assurance.

The woman glared. A few around the table motioned for him to proceed.

"Cloaking as a power is less dangerous if a person realizes they're doing it," he said. "She's not going to implode the Underground if it intensifies absent medication. I'm keeping close to Ms. Kelly, and I'm monitoring what she knows and her activities below ground. You can trust me to identify if risks arise."

"We should move to more covert drugging," pressed the elder, ever critical and ever pessimistic. "If she drinks or eats something regularly—"

"I don't think it's necessary," Mitch interrupted her. "She's my responsibility."

"Well of course she is," the elder spat. "She wouldn't be here, in *our* safehouse, if it weren't for your losing your goddamned mind."

What he wouldn't do to tell them the truth, to extinguish the fire they held to his feet. All it would take was a couple of sentences, disclosing what he'd been told ten years ago. "Excuse me," Mitch said instead.

The woman quieted, but her face did not. Her eyebrows formed that signature, deep crevasse in the middle of her craggy face that warned all in her vicinity: she is next-level pissed.

"If covert control becomes a necessity, I'll recommend it. I will protect our interests. I will protect you."

The woman pushed back in her chair and crossed her arms. For good measure, Mitch slammed his own door—the tall heavy one to his childhood bedroom. Most elders were readers. *She is pissed,* he reflected. *If only she knew.*

Mitch was his father's son, so even after a particularly contentious meeting, even after an elder chewed him out that bitterly before the others, he didn't let anger show and actually didn't feel it much. For one thing, he could see where she would think he deserved her ire. And responding in kind would achieve nothing.

He did have someone to answer to now, and he had decided what he would say. He had reason to believe, based on what he knew about Audrey and what he learned ten years ago, that she could take what he was about to tell her.

13

None of it seemed possible. How could a person live for decades and not realize a truth so innate about herself as this? How could no one in her life have ever noticed when she did what Mitch was telling her she could do: be there one minute and gone the next?

The conversation began with his saying, "Do you remember when I told you I read minds?"

Audrey nodded. A new, heavy dread reached its fingers around her ricocheting heart, and her stomach clenched. They sat in her suite, ignoring the coffees he'd brought.

"The night when *it* happened, I heard you. I heard you screaming —*inside*."

Audrey tipped her head, confused, and it sank in.

"And though I couldn't see you, I thought I had the time." That night, Mitch explained, he'd heard a desperate, telepathic plea. *Please help me. Please, God.*

It had stopped him mid-sprint, and because she kept "screaming," he found her. He'd leaned down, between the houses, despite the commotion and the violence, and spoke to the woman he couldn't discern. "Get up. Fast."

When she'd responded, with a groan to stand, she'd become visible to him as happens when a cloaked one speaks. Mitch didn't know her, but he knew she was not family. Family knew to run for the mountain. In the middle of tearing flesh and screaming humans, she'd lain down and waited to die. She didn't know the threat; he did. She didn't know how to fight; he did. She didn't know where to go; he did. He had reasons he couldn't leave her. So he grabbed her and ran, and he'd spent the last few months—"Well, here," he said.

"You have the ability to cloak," Mitch revealed. "It appears you do it unknowingly. Is that true?"

"I can do *what*?" Audrey replied with disbelief.

"We call it cloaking. It's the power of invisibility."

Audrey snickered. "Right, and I can fly, too. You got a broom?" When he merely stared, she swallowed and shook her head. "How could you know that? How can you be sure?"

"I've grown up around cloakers," Mitch replied.

Audrey shook her head. She stood and staggered when a thought, a memory, occurred to her.

Mitch cleared his throat. "Want me to give you some time? Come back tomorrow?"

"How about tonight?"

Mitch scratched his forehead awkwardly. "See you tonight."

THE DAY after Audrey turned eighteen was the worst day of her life. The popular boy, the *most* popular boy, had asked her to senior prom. After the reason for her near expulsion spread like wildfire among chatty, cruel teenagers, Audrey didn't date. But this year, Jamie Patterson asked *her* to the dance. She ironed her hair straight and painted her lips cherry red. Her dress glinted in the setting sun as she stepped onto the apartment's front porch when he showed to pick her up.

"Have her home by one," her dad told him.

"Yes, sir," Jamie replied, and away they went.

Making out again was exciting. Jamie was no gentleman: he pawed her body and put her hands on him, too, and she didn't mind. She had spent her teenage years mostly playing it safe, particularly after her tryst in the locker room. It was beyond time to have some fun. She'd been responsible enough, and this was her reward.

The school gymnasium glittered black and silver, save a few mint green touches including confetti on the tables and uplighting along the walls. A sanitized version of a hip-hop song played as Jamie and Audrey walked in, and it felt like she was walking the red carpet. Girls who never so much as said hello to her were asking her where she bought her dress and gushing about her makeup. She carried a new form of credit, apparently, and she relished cashing it in.

They danced in unfamiliar and intimate ways, and she could feel his attraction when their hips came together. That he wanted her to know his physical attraction to her was itself attractive.

As the dance drew to a close, Jamie and a couple of friends started planning the after party. He lifted keys from his pocket, and Audrey felt a chill crawl across her.

"Hey, we shouldn't," she said. "We've been drinking."

"It'll be fine," Jamie insisted.

He'd done this before, he said, so maybe she was overreacting. She wasn't ready to surrender this new clout by unnecessarily being a worrywart, so she sat in his Civic and flashed a smile. "Let's go," she agreed.

She'd spent the rest of her life wishing she'd thought to buckle in and tell them all to do the same.

The next thing Audrey knew, she could taste metal and winced when she moved. She couldn't grasp her surroundings well because of the glare of red and blue flashing lights. She tried to pull up and winced again. She didn't know where she was, but she felt wet. Audrey groaned and tried to move, blinking rapidly. She felt smooth stones beneath her hands and face, and her legs floated. *Floated.* She was in water. She fought to lift her face from cold water, and the lights glinting off the black sequins on her gown reminded her. *Prom.*

She couldn't make the scene out well. As her focus sharpened, she realized paramedics and firefighters were crowded around and above and close to her. A car was on its roof, smoking. A paramedic pushed someone on a stretcher. She tried to speak. *Help,* she thought. *Help.* Though she was no more than twenty yards away, no one rushed toward her. Groaning, she dug her fingers into the wall of mud and grass before her. Pulling on it, she grunted toward the emergency responders before she slipped, bumping her lip on a rock and swallowing water. *Help,* she tried. She couldn't speak. *I'm going to drown.*

She dug her fingers into the rocks to her right, attempting to drag herself forward. They were small, pebbles even, so they didn't offer her a steady surface against which to pull. Audrey kept at it, kicking her feet in the water until she pulled her body several feet. A white van came into view. Coroner, it read. Fear rose from her stomach and screamed out through her throat. "Help me!" she finally said. "Help!" she screamed. Not one turned toward her. Could it be they couldn't hear her over the river's rush? Was it possible she wasn't actually speaking?

Muddy and bloodied, Audrey kept crawling until she couldn't. The paramedics and firefighters carted away three other people and cleared the scene. Her pleas for help went unanswered. She was crying hard as they packed up and left her there, wet, cold, and shaking in the dark. But she was grateful to no longer be in the water.

She would later learn that Jamie careened his Civic through a guardrail and onto the banks of the Rocky River. She would also later learn the police didn't have answers for Charles Kelly. Though he was positive his daughter must have been in Jamie's car, they'd found only three bodies. *Bodies.* Teenagers who should have had the rest of their lives ahead of them. He'd told her this the night she returned home, hysterical about how they'd left her there to die. Her father had insisted to Audrey he'd begged the first responders, "Did you find anything of hers in the car? Did you search the river?"

They had assured him, "No, nothing in the car, and yes, Mr. Kelly. Based on where we found the others, we don't have reason to believe anyone ended up in the river. We searched. We didn't find her."

She couldn't understand how they'd never hear her. The police combed the river bank the day after the accident and the next day. She was frozen, covered in blood, and in shock. No one responded to her. It was as if they were ignoring her, but they wouldn't. Maybe she wasn't actually speaking? Maybe she was too weak to utter a word? Maybe she imagined her protests?

By the time a man with a set of fishing poles stumbled upon her, Audrey had accepted defeat. She'd tried to keep count of the hours she laid out there on the ground, but her thoughts had become crossed. Instead, she started thinking her apologies and prayers.

"Hey, are you okay?" the man exclaimed, dropping his bait and poles and rushing to her side.

Audrey was slow to react; her body hurt, and she felt bewildered. *He can see me?* She winced and tried to sit up.

"Hold on, hold on," the man told her, his palm up and his phone to his ear. "Stay where you are."

The police couldn't explain it. How had they missed a bloodied teenage girl in not one, not two, but three searches? Charles was furious, but his daughter was alive, and he was grateful.

He cooked her favorite—honey biscuits and spicy gravy—and kept a written log of when she swallowed which medications. Left for as long as she was, she'd developed a nasty, persistent infection.

After about a week, the police asked to interview Audrey about what had happened during those hours she was missing, and because she swore she felt up to it, Charles obliged them.

When another set of officials showed up at his light blue door, asking to do the same, he raised an eyebrow and hesitated.

"My daughter's already spoken for hours with the police, and she needs her rest," he said.

"Sir, we want to prevent this from happening again," the officials told him.

He nodded and stepped aside, and Audrey spent two more hours describing how she'd cried for help every morning the police had reported to the scene and, yes, within earshot.

"It's as if I were invisible," she told them. "I know that's impossible, but that's how it felt."

The interviewer kept scribbling notes. "Has that ever happened before?" she asked.

"No—well, come to think of it, yes," Audrey said, thinking of the stormy night her parents split up, when neither comforted her despite her hysteria.

"Can you tell us more about that?"

Audrey touched her forehead and exhaled. "Can we do this another time? I'm exhausted."

"Of course, Audrey. We'll schedule with your father."

14

Mitch wouldn't return for hours, but Audrey's appetite had roared back. The clock in the room told her she had time. She pulled on some clothes and stared at her reflection. She flipped her curls to the left side of her face and drew the mess up in a bun, tucking wild tentacles in and over and under until the mess appeared contained. Strange, to have nowhere to go but be surrounded by so many unfamiliar people, she felt the need to keep up appearances. Unsettling, to have a man she'd known for only two months inform her of things her own parents hadn't. Who else down here knew more about her than she knew about herself?

She glanced at her feet. At her hands. At her face. Supposedly, she could turn them all invisible. *What in the world.*

She kept her head down while leaving the suite, intent to follow her hunger to the day's menu, but there it was again: the sign for the spring. She shook her head. Why did she feel so drawn to it? She hated bodies of water. But she had just learned impossible things in this impossible place, and her desire to explore felt righteous.

She peered around while acting like she wasn't peering around. It did feel wrong. Her grandmother had taught her better, plus a trained journalist knew not to enter spaces without authorization; it was unethical and what one discovered while trespassing was unusable. She didn't carry a reporter's notebook today, though. And information was power. She had to seize whatever power she could while stuck here.

She traced her finger along the right wall. Strange to know that areas of the very place she lived were forbidden. It hadn't happened much that places were off limits to her when she was a reporter. Car accidents and court proceedings and zoning-variance-hearings-turned-spats were accessible because public property is public property.

She tried a doorknob. It refused her, unlike most people who had eagerly opened the door to a journalist, raring to snatch an irresistible fifteen minutes of fame, even if that fame came printed inside the woefully thin Metro section of the local paper. In places where she was obviously unwelcome, a press pass often gained her entry. Upon viewing her badge, the most curmudgeonly firefighter Audrey remembered had flicked his hand, his resentful exhale visible in the frigid night, allowing her past the tape cordoning off a memorable four-alarm fire in, ironically, Bernville. That was the only time she'd reported an arson.

The farther she climbed, the clearer it became that this was one of the wings Mitch had called restricted. Fewer signs, which meant those who walked this way knew what was here but didn't advertise it. The hall felt darker, too. The two doorknobs she'd tried so far didn't give. She wanted only a peek, not to touch or take something. And the underground spring wasn't a secret; signs in public parts announced its location. Well, more public parts. Nothing here was public.

She kept walking, and the third doorknob did give. Audrey raised her eyebrows in surprise and tripped inward. She really had not expected any forward motion. "Oof," she murmured.

"Excuse me?"

Audrey blinked, and her stomach sank. *Oh, fuck.*

Three adults advanced toward her, and one took her arm and began to turn her around. Audrey pinched her eyebrows together.

The adults wore long, crimson garments. The room was darker than the wing and something herbaceous burned. A person lay on a platform atop some white material. She turned her face to get a better look, but one of the cloaked adults, this one a man, blocked her view, his lips tense. The trio led her out to the wing.

"I'm sorry, I got turned around, and I couldn't find any signs," Audrey sputtered, attempting to defend her curiosity.

"You can't be here," the woman said through gritted teeth. "Leave this instant."

Audrey's breath was hard to catch and she held up her palm, a white flag. She felt sorrier than she thought she would. She bit a fingernail. "Yes, no problem of course. My name is Audrey Kelly, and my suite is—"

"We know. I'll show you back to the main corridor." The man spoke less crisply than the woman, and she gave silent thanks that he would take her back. The third adult never spoke, eyes on Audrey and on the other two for longer than seemed natural before turning, opening the door a mite, and disappearing.

The man didn't speak to Audrey, and she didn't break the silence. She did steal a glance at the emblem on his robe, though she definitely wasn't asking about it. It looked like an infant whose head contained blue and green shapes, possibly Earth's continents. She didn't attempt a closer look, given the deep trouble she was in already.

The man stopped, his eyes forward. "That wing is off limits," he said. "Be well." He turned and walked back the way they'd come, his cloak dragging behind him. "Oh," he uttered, turning around, his hands clasped before him. "Just because there are signs doesn't mean they beckon you. If you're unsure whether you're welcome somewhere, assume you're not."

Audrey licked her lip, not that her dry tongue helped much. She really screwed up, and she rubbed her forehead, miserable at the thought of admitting it to Mitch, who definitely told her not to explore. She walked briskly and knocked constantly until her only other friend beneath the surface answered.

Acquaintance. Could she really count anyone here as friends?

"Jesus, bitch. Is the place on fire?" Betty Jane spilled out of a sports bra and yoga pants.

If it were different circumstances, Audrey would have laughed. "I need to talk to you."

Betty Jane bowed with a flourish. "Be my guest."

"I fucked up. I really did it this time, and I'm worried." Audrey's anxiety dominoes cascaded relentlessly. Where would she go if they threw her out of this place? How long could she live? How would she die? Her feelings about the Underground were valid, but staring down the barrel of surefire eviction, she shuddered.

Betty Jane sat down. Audrey didn't know the woman could look so serious. "Can't be that bad, right? All of us being stuck down here and all."

Audrey inhaled. "I went walking. Toward the spring. And I opened a door and there were these people in robes and something was burning, and, I don't know, there was a person lying on white stuff, and I'm wondering now if they were dead, or if they needed help. This woman was super pissed, and I know they're going to tell Mitch, and Mitch told me not to explore." She took a breath. "Do you know what they were doing? What's Mitch going to say? What's he going to do? Should I be running out of here right now? What if I saw something they want me to unsee? I can't take it back, and ... I'm scared."

Betty Jane blinked several times. "That was a lot." She stood and poured Audrey a drink. "I can't say what Mitch and the elders will do. And I shouldn't tell ya, but I don't know." Betty Jane shrugged. "I suspect what you do and don't know won't matter much anymore."

Audrey finished the lemonade in less than a minute. Her mouth was so dry.

"You walked in on a natal day recuperation."

"A what?" Audrey shook her head. The code speak of this place and its residents tired her.

"They were burning sage, and it was salt under the person. That's what you saw. The person is healing. They survived a birthday."

Audrey stood back up and began to pace. "They survived a *birthday*?"

Betty Jane started to speak and stopped. "We do." She stared off for a time, before meeting Audrey's eyes. "They can't think they're going to preserve every secret with you down here, can they?" She didn't wait for an answer Audrey was sure not to have. "Most of us, the sane ones, straight up fear our birthdays. You never know when the test is coming and what it will be."

"What test?"

"I've been wondering how they'll administer them down here."

"What tests, Betty Jane?"

"They test how we've grown, how our p—" Betty Jane stopped. "Our capabilities. They test whether we can do certain things every year."

"How do they do that?"

Betty Jane cocked her head and raised an eyebrow. She cracked her neck and moved her head from side to side.

"You can trust me," Audrey said. "I won't let on we talked."

"You can let on in ways you don't realize."

Audrey knew precisely what she meant and hurriedly visualized the light blue door closed shut, the gold deadbolt twisted locked. *Oh no. What if Betty Jane can read minds?* She blinked. *What if she's been reading my mind this whole time? Have I thought ugly things about her?* She shook her head, relieved. She didn't have anything ugly to think about Betty Jane. She was the friendliest she'd met here.

"Talking to yourself?" Betty Jane teased.

Audrey laughed. "I was. I'm done now. Tell me."

"You tell me this first."

"Tell you what?"

"You didn't ask what they're testing for." Betty Jane's eyes bored into Audrey's. "How'd you know? About us?"

Oh, shit. Audrey wiped her clammy hands on her pants. She couldn't give him up. It could mean he would tell her nothing more and retract her welcome to this place—if that welcome remained after what she'd done.

"Fucking Bram." Betty Jane smirked as if she were satisfied. "You told me about your coffee, and I knew it. He struck me as a guy who'd say too much for attention. He's tough, I'll give him that. Hot, too."

Audrey stared. "A journalist doesn't give up her sources."

"Uh huh. Be careful, though, Audrey. Some families protect their secrets at any cost."

Is that a threat? Betty Jane had befriended *her*. Had Audrey missed how obviously this could be a setup? *How to proceed without being paranoid but while also being careful?* "Listen, I'm not here to get anybody," Audrey began. "I'm afraid. I'm literally the only one in the dark down here. And what I walked in on—it looked ritualistic."

"It is," Betty Jane replied. She sat next to Audrey. "Our ... capabilities, if they grow, it's only ever within weeks of a birthday or when pregnant, not that I'm ever doing that." This time Betty Jane poured herself a drink, and not a lemonade. "The thing is, you're never told it's a test. It's unfamiliar people who test us. You don't know it's *the* test or *them*, so you don't know if you fail to run or to escape or to crack open some new power if they'd actually let you burn."

"Let you burn?" Audrey dried her palms on her pants.

"For me, yes, once they did let me burn. A man came for me, slipped into my bedroom window and slithered a grimy hand over my mouth. His stench woke me before his hand did. He reeked of cigarettes and hangover. He tied me up, stuffed me into the trunk of a car, and dragged me into some house in the hood. He lit the place on fire. I smelled the wood burn before I saw the flames." Betty Jane shook her head. "Bonfires and fireplaces nauseate me to this day. Can't really stomach a cookout."

"I'm so sorry. I'm sorry that happened to you."

"It had its purpose. I learned that night I could make it rain." Betty Jane tossed back the drink. "That, Audrey, is why we have natal day recuperation."

Betty Jane pulled up her pantleg and turned her leg to Audrey. A shiny, raised scar reached its tendrils up the back of it.

Audrey blinked rapidly as the pit deepened in her stomach. If these people could do this to family, what could—would—they do to her?

"You made it rain? How do you know it wasn't coincidence?"

"Girl, I never get that lucky."

Audrey's lip curled up.

"It was December in Ohio. It was a 100-year storm in December. Meteorologists talked about it for a week."

"You're telling me your family set you up? Your family let you burn? To test your capabilities?" She was careful to use Betty Jane's word.

"It was my natal day test. That year, anyway. I was ten."

Audrey covered her mouth. *She was ten.*

When Audrey was nine and blew out the candles on the chocolate chocolate chip cake her dad baked annually, she wished for one of those fluffy cat robots. She shrieked when her dad handed her the unwrapped creature. She walked it inside and out, pressing the switch on its pink leash constantly for weeks. Slept with it, too, though its mechanical parts made it a bony bed partner.

When Audrey was nineteen and blew out the candles on the cake her mom brought despite Audrey's insistence otherwise, she wished for her dad. To know where he'd gone, why he'd left. When she'd cut the first slice, she'd doubled down on the wish, pleading with the universe to reunite them so they could accept his disappearance as a blip, a mistake. Anything but his intentional abandonment of his family, of her.

She didn't wish for him again until the first birthday she spent with Kevin. She blew out candles that drooped precariously atop a sloppy lattice pie Kevin had baked, and she wished for her dad. For them to accept together the milestones missed and relearn who they were. To find forgiveness.

Kevin brought it out of her, the vulnerability. Before she fell in love with Kevin, she'd spent years refusing to wish for Charles Kelly. Her ache for him had hardened, and she wasn't tempted much to pick the crust of that scab. But when someone close to you picks at scabs similar to your own, you become tempted to do the same.

By now, Audrey believed less and less that she'd see her dad or her mom again. Things felt grimmer every day she remained here instead of reemerging where the sun shined. But if Kevin were down here, he'd urge her—no, he'd convince her—to keep wishing. It'd be too damn sad not to, he'd say. And she'd be glad he'd convinced her to keep the faith.

15

Audrey had never before felt nervous to go to a planetarium. Mitch had invited her, and she worried he did so to address her transgression.

"This place reminds me of this lecture hall at college," Audrey rattled on, lying on the floor arm to arm with Mitch beneath the constellations. "I got an A, even though I skipped so much. Did you go to college?" She paused but only briefly. If she kept talking, he couldn't. If she kept blabbing, he couldn't tell her the news that she would be cast outside, almost certainly to her untimely death. "Can't believe how cavernous this place feels—*down here.*" She picked at a nail cuticle. "I miss the moon."

"Me too."

She propped herself up to look at him. "Crazy the things we took for granted. The sound of the wind. The birds and squirrels. The seasons. I miss most the freedom to ... *go.*"

Mitch propped himself up to look at her. "Me, too."

"I've been wanting to say thank you," Audrey said. "For bringing me here. Who knows where I'd be if you hadn't." She bit her lip. Hopefully he wasn't about to rescind her invite.

Mitch didn't say, "You're welcome," and Audrey picked another cuticle. "What do you think it's like?" she said.

"What?"

"There," she said, lying back down and pointing to the stars, which didn't actually burn. Audrey dropped her hand, and in the dark, it landed on his thigh. His big, muscular thigh. She moved it quickly to the floor and blushed, thankful he couldn't see her face.

"Violent and vacant."

Audrey bit her lip and blinked rapidly. She crossed her arms, hugging herself. She pushed her chin up, but it trembled. She fixated on the Big Dipper, the only constellation she could identify, trying to beat back the tears. So much of life in the Underground felt like these phony stars, a shadow of the life she knew, and the worst part for Audrey was how life went on for everyone else here. They knew each other. Many were in love, making love, had families to love, and all the while, her life felt paused without a play button in sight. These people didn't worry over how their loved ones were going to survive the violent and vacant.

"Sorry." Mitch reached for her hand, and Audrey's heart skipped. *He's touching me. He's not going to kick me to the curb.* "Sorry. We do suspect there are survivors. A good number of them."

She squeezed his hand back. "I hope so."

He took his hand back. "We need to talk about it, Audrey."

She stiffened. Nope. She would not talk her way out of this. Would this be when she had to become the adversary and threaten to expose them and their file folders and their sick birthday rituals?

"You cannot trespass around here. I'm already navigating ..." He trailed off. "Have you ever betrayed someone you love?"

That's out of left field. Maybe if I answer, maybe if I show vulnerability, he'll reconsider what he's about to do. "I don't know that I love my dad. Not how a person should love a dad."

The room was necessarily dark—can't see the stars in daylight—but Audrey could hear him turn toward her. "That's hard."

She knew he couldn't really see it, but she nodded.

"When I brought you here, I betrayed someone I love."

Her heart rate picked up. Who did he cross? Were they down here, watching her? Were they angry that she even breathed? Was this where he returned her to the red door and let her loose into the violent and vacant? She winced. Flat tires and late-night deadlines used to leave her panicked. She knew she wasn't cut out to survive the chaos above ground. *Should have thought harder about that before you did this, idiot.* She opened her mouth twice but didn't speak.

"When you trespass, it makes things worse for me. We're needing to do more runs than expected, and I'm fielding the calls, and the panic of both keep me so busy I can barely sleep. When I don't sleep, I can't ... perform. So please stop."

"I didn't mean to get you in trouble."

Mitch sat up and appeared to check the space. When he spoke, he kept his voice low. "I didn't want to bring you here, tell you that you have a supernatural power, and then expect you to sit still."

"Yeah." Audrey's spirits lifted. He afforded her compassion even in this moment. Maybe he wasn't kicking her out. Maybe she could change the subject. Maybe she could ask, though not quite yet but soon, what other powers she might possess and if they were able to bring people above ground down here. To safety.

"Who would you be if you weren't Mitch Gray?"

"Who would you be if you weren't Audrey Kelly?"

"How could I know?" She turned to her side to face him, her face in her hands. "Right. But seriously," Audrey persisted. "What if you were free to do what*ever* you wanted?"

Mitch exhaled. "Audrey, I've never considered it."

"Fine. Name three things you miss about life before this."

Mitch inhaled. "I already said the moon." He was silent for a few. "Quiet nights. My dad."

"Your dad." So he knew how it felt? She'd lived a lifetime without her dad and still missed him. In this moment, she admitted it to herself.

"Yeah. He died. Long time ago."

No, he didn't know how she felt. His dad hadn't chosen to be without him.

"You? What three things do you miss?"

"My partner. His name was—" Audrey stopped, disturbed. She'd been so angry, but what she would give to know Kevin had survived those hellish monsters. "His name *is* Kevin. I think I told you that. He knew me better than anyone. I miss him, and I miss the feeling of being home. It's hard being the stranger."

Mitch listened, quiet. He reached a hand, pulled it back, but proceeded, tucking a curl behind her ear.

Audrey shivered at his touch. "I worry I'll never find someone who loves me for me. But he could be alive. Right?"

Mitch paused for long enough that her heart dropped, knowing well his next word was a lie. "Right."

"I don't know what I'd do without him, up there." Audrey returned to lying on her back and wondered. Could Kevin see the stars, the real ones they'd lain on the grass to see during that one summer movie in the park? What did he miss about her?

THE SECOND TIME Audrey and Bram agreed to meet, she drew her eyes larger, painted her lips, and evened out her skin tone. Even if she'd had to pay the Underground for the makeup, she would have spent the money—not that she had any. The eyeliner, lip gloss, and foundation were her armor. *You're not trying to look good for him,* she assured herself. But she wanted to feel confident. She had plans to extract information from him. What exactly were the creatures above ground, and where did they come from? (Maybe enough time had passed that they knew.) When was this shelter built? (She had to imagine someone knew, but she'd been reticent for good recent reason to ask Mitch.) How long did Bram think they'd have to be underground? (She might be the only one, but she wanted desperately to return above ground. Maybe it was still possible to save Mom.)

The first time they'd met for coffee, the meeting had been cut short by a call he'd received. The name Bram appeared nowhere on this man's uniform, but the label "H7" did.

Now someone knocked, and her heart rate quickened. "Just a second," she called. Her nerves felt the same way they had when she was a reporter who knew she had to ask questions wisely to secure critical answers. She might never have this opportunity again, and she needed to not spook her source. She needed Bram to *talk*, and she needed him to talk *a lot*.

She opened the door to blue eyes and a wide, bright smile.

"Hey, you," Bram said.

"Hi," she replied, swinging her door open.

"Has anyone shown you the hall's private quarter?" he asked.

"No."

"Want to change that?"

"Sure," she replied.

Grabbing her keycard, she took him in. Bram was dressed neatly, in navy slacks and a white button-down with blue anchors stretched across his physique. No uniform today, apparently. He was *fine*.

So was Mitch. Audrey shook her head. Her attraction to both men made her feel guilty. Kevin. Wherever he was, dead or alive in the *violent and vacant*, he was not fawning over women, she was sure of it.

He walked her to the main hall, and when a server approached, he leaned in and said something out of earshot.

The server nodded at him, then at Audrey. "Right this way."

They followed the woman down a narrow corridor flanked with dim lighting. They entered a room with a single, candle-lit table.

"Oh, uh, wow," Audrey said. It was beautiful, but it reminded her of Kevin. He had served the only candlelit dinner of her life. Not a celebration meal—quite the contrary. She'd made a mistake that required the newspaper to run a correction, and her editor had fielded the nasty call from City Hall, then chastised her in front of the entire staff. As Audrey had shrugged off her jacket, she'd smelled steak. Turning the corner, she'd found Kevin pulling out her chair with the nerdiest of flourishes, a single candlestick's flame bouncing shadows against the walls. He'd served her that night what he dubbed a "today-sucked-balls" meal.

Bram pulled out a chair, and she obliged him. "How are you holding up, Audrey?" he asked, downing one of two glasses at their place settings.

Good. Get nice and buzzed and loose-lipped. She averted her eyes and bit her lip. "I'm okay."

"Rough week?"

"Aren't they all?"

"Want to talk about it?"

"Nah," she replied, flashing a smile. "It's not important." She leaned forward and blew out the candle. She wasn't ready for a second candlelit dinner without Kevin.

Bram raised an eyebrow but left it alone.

Through early, casual small talk, she learned Bram was not unlike her. He'd endured his parents' divorce. He'd worked in communications. He had family he worried about, up there. For a moment, Audrey felt guilty, knowing she'd agreed to dinner not for his company but for his confessions. But she would get what she came for.

"What exactly do you do down here?" she dared to ask as she sipped her drink, feigning nonchalance. "What's H7? I saw it on your uniform."

"You'd have to ask someone above my paygrade," Bram replied. "So much of this place isn't explained to those of us who aren't, well, the family. They're big on need-to-know policies."

"Wait, you're not family?"

He held up an index finger, chewing a bite. "The families," he amended. "The people who built the shelter. And no, I'm not family. I'm an outsider like you, only I work for them. I manage assets and help protect this place."

It occurred to Audrey now that she should ask Mitch to put her to work. Perhaps if she busied herself, it'd make people less mean toward her. More importantly, perhaps she'd gain access to more information she could use.

Audrey leaned in. Eyes scanning the space, she whispered, "Do you know when and why they built it?"

Bram didn't match her clandestine efforts when he replied, "It's a shelter, so I presume they worried there would be a need for it."

Audrey sighed as she sat back in her chair. God, the inability of people around here to actually answer a question frustrated her. She'd had more interviews than she could count that ended with her asking, "Do you not want to comment?" People, her career had revealed, would rather beat around the bush, would rather pretend to answer an inquiry, before they would state simply, "No comment." But the former wasted her time—above ground when she held a reporter's notebook, and below ground where she now held a spoon.

"Don't you ever want to know more? It drives me nuts, it's so, I don't know, secretive," she replied, motioning with her glass for him to drink more. "I'm tempted to go all investigative reporter. Already got busted for exploring, though."

"Oh?" Bram replied, finishing his neat drink. "What happened?"

Audrey waved off the question. "Let's leave it at: I was escorted out of a wing and told to steer clear."

Bram nodded. "That's best. They've got their reasons. We're safe. I just want to be safe, Audrey. The people I work with, they know what it's like up there."

"What's it like? Have they seen people? Are people alive? Are they taking names? Is the Underground going to help survivors?"

"Bram, sorry to intrude," a server interrupted. "It's closing time."

Bram and Audrey swiftly apologized and left, and when he asked to walk her back to her suite, she agreed.

As they walked, she peered at him. No limp, though he did stumble a little. Crooked smile. *Does he think we're hooking up?* All night, he had laughed and touched her, and she'd kept her eye on the prize and her responses friendly. She'd learned as a journalist that sources were more willing to divulge any little thing if they liked you.

She keyed into her suite. "Bram, I—" Audrey began.

"Cool if I come in?"

She hesitated. But she had so many other questions. And maybe his lips would be looser still, drinking a nightcap inside her room sans witnesses.

They sat, watching *The Goonies* DVD she'd swiped from the gym. She paid little attention to the show, mulling over which additional questions she could ask without showing her cards.

"Hey, have you ever met another Bram? Down here or up there?" was the first she asked.

He sounded sleepy, drunk. "No, why?"

"Unique name. I like it." *If there's not another Bram, that means* you *lost* your *leg. You couldn't have.*

"Thanks." His voice slurred enough that she dared to ask it.

"Hey, is there a way out of here that isn't monitored?" He didn't answer. "Bram?" Audrey's face fell when she realized Bram, H7, whoever he was, had fallen asleep. Another interview, thwarted.

A KNOCK on Audrey's door awoke her, and she sat up, remembering only when she couldn't exit her bed on the usual side that Bram had slept in her room. *Oh no.* Was someone looking for him? She didn't need to add slut to the reasons they disliked her. She looked at the clock. 8:17. Had to be a.m.

Another knock. "Just a sec," she called, carefully climbing out of bed to stand. She wrapped herself in a robe, eyes on Bram, who didn't stir. Then she opened the door a bit and instinctively retreated. Mitch. *Oh, shit.* Her cheeks burned hot, and her heart rate picked up. She would dissect why she felt this way later.

"Hey," she said, attempting to rein in her flush and stepping into the hallway.

"Breakfast?"

"I can't today," she said, worried she smelled of alcohol from the night before.

Mitch adjusted his weapon belt. "Lunch? I need to talk to you." He cleared his throat.

"Audrey?" Bram said, cracking the door open.

Audrey scratched her neck awkwardly. She really didn't want Mitch to think she'd fucked another man.

"Oh, excuse me," Bram said. "Morning, sir."

"Morning," Mitch replied. His tone was icier toward Bram than Audrey had heard it sound in three months.

The three stood for a moment before Audrey muttered, "Excuse me, I need to use the restroom." *And die.* She locked her suite's bathroom door, sat on the toilet lid, and dropped her head into her hands. *You had to show up now?*

AUDREY RAISED the fork to her mouth then exhaled and put it down. She wasn't even hungry, and she might as well get it out of the way. She kept her voice low. "So you know, I didn't sleep with him. We didn't even kiss."

Mitch didn't miss a beat. "I wouldn't."

Audrey's eyebrows rose. Best to be clear. "You wouldn't ..."

"I wouldn't entangle yourself with him."

"Why's that?"

Mitch shook his head. "This isn't the place to get into it," he replied.

"What *is* the place to get into it?"

"Try to stay patient, Audrey. I'll fill you in when conditions allow it. Can you trust me to do that?"

She didn't really trust him to, though; he rarely offered an answer she didn't extract. But she nodded and took a bite. "Can you make it sooner than later?" she began. "Also, I've got a favor to ask."

Mitch nodded her onward.

"I'd like you to give me a job around here."

"Why? Not everyone works. Not everyone *needs* to work."

"Right, but maybe if I helped clean or stock shelves or garden, though I must admit that gardening was never my forte, I'd feel less like a giant mooch." Audrey shrugged. "I can do *something*. You know, to earn my keep."

"I don't think that's a good idea," Mitch began before stopping.

"How could it be a bad one?"

Mitch pursed his lips. "Let me think on it."

Audrey could hardly believe it and also entirely could: this place, full of secretive people, totally *would* find some downside to the stranger picking up some work around here. *I cannot win here.*

She noticed the moment Mitch's eyes were on something else. He stood, and Audrey turned to see a middle-aged man approach.

"Sir," he began.

Sir. There it was again, the ubiquitous show of deference to Mitch. Audrey had never called him what the rest of the people here did. Did they resent her for it?

"My wife has gone into labor. As you know, they'd like you bedside. Said you needn't come now, but that you should know it has begun."

Mitch touched the man's shoulder, and Audrey could tell Mitch's elation was genuine. "Congrats will soon be in order. Duly noted, Christopher."

The father-to-be smiled the widest grin. Audrey smiled with him, and he departed. Her attention immediately reverted to Mitch as he sat back down. She sat, too. *Why would they need Mitch bedside? Don't they have doctors?* She cocked her head at him. *Who really are you?* "I used to say I wanted three," she began. "Kids," she added when he raised an eyebrow. "I would cut out the faces of models in those JCPenney catalogues—remember them?—imagining they were how my kids would look. What about you?" she asked. "Do you want children?"

Mitch chuckled.

She liked it when he laughed, even if his laughing at a question like "Do you want children?" struck her as odd.

"Who could want children with me?"

What a strange thing to say. "You rule this place. Powerful men always have a line out the door of willing lovers."

Mitch regarded her wryly. "I don't rule this place, Audrey," he began. "I'm responsible. And that responsibility doesn't care if I've got a wife and children."

For the first time, she saw the extent of his worry. Its weight. His shoulders looked sunken, his expression resigned.

"Were it not for that, would you want a wife and children?" she pressed.

"What I want is of no matter, and everyone here knows it but you," he began, lowering his voice to a whisper. He leaned over the table, and Audrey met him in the middle. "None of them would even acknowledge that I actually have wants." He shook his head and shrugged.

Audrey exhaled. Curiosity rose in her. "Why me? Why count me as a confidant if none of them are?" The cafeteria teemed, but they sat in its periphery, safe (she imagined) from prying ears. This man would never have talked with her this way if others could hear him.

"I'm just a guy named Mitch with you."

She nodded immediately because she understood. Sometimes being seen meant everything.

That said, Mitch was wrong. Increasingly, he wasn't just a guy named Mitch to her.

The similarity between Mitch and Kevin was specific and unexpected. Both thought they weren't cut out for families. Audrey disagreed with them, but did she disagree because she found both to be arrestingly attractive? Was she willfully blind, and they were right?

The way Mitch showed up at her door the next morning, offering coffee, and sheepishly smiling didn't dissuade her a bit.

"What's so funny?" Audrey asked, noticing he was way more cleanly shaved than usual.

"My face," he retorted. "Shaving mishap."

Snickering and closing the door to her suite, Audrey followed his lead to a brightly colored playground she'd seen before on walks in the Underground, but it was different this time. A winding train tooted and puffed white steam as it snaked through fall foliage-lined streets into a Main Street circa the 1950s, complete with vertical storefront signs and chrome-lined cars. Past Main Street, the miniature train met a line of people at a miniature depot. Audrey stuck her face close to the minute details, entranced, before they kept moving.

So long as no one asked for him, Mitch said he had time to talk, so Audrey decided she would reach for answers this morning. First, as she'd often done in interviews, she'd share something about herself to get information flowing. Seated in the library's private alcove, she leaned back against the wall, glad he watched her. "Trains were the soundtrack of my childhood. We didn't have AC, and we learned to sleep despite their horns blaring through our windows." She paused midthought. "They eventually built an overpass so you didn't have to sit forever while 100-car trains blocked traffic."

"Berea?" Mitch said.

Audrey grinned at the name of her hometown. "You've been?"

"Yep. The construction was a pain, I remember reading."

"We lived in a second-floor apartment near the Browns training camp. It was so hot some summers I would cool myself with spray bottles of water beside a fan. Open windows. Summer air."

"Yeah." Mitch seemed far away, too, maybe in some memory of his own.

Audrey loved the smell of this library, particularly here where they'd stocked the mustiest and oldest of the collection. She eyed the glass door of a room in the back she'd tried once and learned was locked. Why would the library have a locked room? Why did the word TOME span the width of the door? She returned her gaze to Mitch. *Less facial hair makes you less attractive*, she decided.

"I can hear you," Mitch said.

Gah, Audrey thought, quickly locking her blue door. *Kill me now.* She smiled awkwardly and laughed when he laughed. "Oops."

"Well, hey, you didn't say 'ghastly or repulsive,' so I'll take the W."

Audrey laughed. He'd just admitted he wanted her to find him attractive, and it puffed her up. "*Tome*? You all have a tome?" She pointed to the locked room.

Mitch shook his head. "That's a bore, trust me, and I've got to check in with staff." He started to stand, but Audrey hadn't asked a single question of substance.

"Wait," she insisted. "Answer a question for me. You brought me here, and I have questions. What's the latest? Are humans surviving?" *Mom. You cannot imagine how much I need to know I'll see her again.*

"They are, Audrey."

"And will you save them? Bring them here?"

"We will commence a reconstruction. We couldn't build enough space here for everyone, but we will help rebuild."

"When, though? How long will you people—" That felt too aggressive. "How long will you let them fight before you help? My mom is up there." She left out Kevin because Kevin was gone. Her stomach churned. The morning's mirth had dried up.

Mitch reached for her hand, and she let him. A star of emotion burst within her when their fingers intertwined. It felt so intimate. It had been months since she'd held hands with a man.

It proved short-lived, though, because he disentangled himself from her, looking around. "It might seem like we're not helping, but we go above ground to kill those monsters, and we're expanding our fight. I didn't tell you this, but we're marking the properties where we see evidence of life, and we will return to them. In the meantime, our work is killing. It has to be."

God, he punctuated that last sentence with force.

Be damned any watchful eyes, Audrey took back and squeezed his hand. He squeezed hers back, stood, and disappeared around the "boring" TOME room. She wondered if that same hand of his had killed any monsters.

16

"I'm glad we prepared," spoke the woman in a thick Spanish accent, "but we didn't anticipate it all."

Mitch steeled his jaw, knowing the elders listening to the status reports from Phoenix from seats inside their Northeast Ohio shelter would most certainly call the most unanticipated complication here the woman he'd brought inside with him. To avoid their stares—or more accurately, their glares—he focused intently on taking notes about Phoenix's condition.

"Philadelphia," a man's voice stated.

"Go ahead, Philly," Mitch replied.

"The natural gas wells are on line and stably producing. No electricity issues expected here for at least six months. Maybe longer."

"That was our smartest move," said an elder in the room. "We never could have stored enough diesel for the generators."

Mitch nodded. Fueling generators with gasoline would have been a short-lived endeavor in the world before and certainly now in the world they encountered.

"But, uh," the man continued.

"Proceed," Mitch replied.

"We are experiencing a colony collapse. If all the bees die, our rations will become limited."

Mitch looked at the elders surrounding him. Many had salt-and-pepper beards or locks, and all dressed in red cloaks. He remembered sitting with elders as a child and not understanding why he sat among them when other Descendant children did not. He would come to understand it was because he was Mitch Gray, of Raven and Puck.

He didn't have a quick answer for bee colony collapse, and the shaking heads around him echoed the same. No one would utter their grave worry to Philly, but their faces let on their anxiety.

"Philly, we'll connect about next steps," he said, not confident at all they could help. He muted his line. "H32," he said, "connect with BJ about possibilities."

The uniformed man to his left nodded.

"Palm Springs."

"We hear you, Palm Springs." He expected bad news, and he got it.

"It hasn't rained here in nearly a year. We can't flush toilets because we don't dare use water for that, so we're defecating in buckets. It reeks. Even though we tell people not to go on the land, we're nervous some will, potentially contaminating the water stores. What I wouldn't give for a wastewater treatment plant right now."

Mitch bit his lip and exhaled steadily. They always knew desert shelters would run into this problem before those in more temperate climates would. "You—we—are doing the best we can. Is your spring producing?"

"Yes," a woman from Palm Springs said. "We were wise to build our shelters near natural waters."

They'd had to. It was how civilizations had been located for millennia.

As Mitch called out the representative for each locale, the reports took on a clear pattern. So much was going wrong.

September

Four months after

He'd fully expected to be dead by now. The first couple weeks of life after the explosions, a part of Kevin honestly welcomed an end. There would have been a peace to not trying.

There was no peace on this earth. But four months in, there was community, and he didn't want to give up on any one of them. He wanted a future for them.

Little Amelia called them monsters, and no one in the house disagreed.

Not Marcel and Winston, who'd literally dragged others inside to share their home, splitting their food seven ways, this afternoon's meal canned chickpeas and teriyaki turkey jerky.

Not Maggie and Stephanie, the sisters who'd returned from military tours months before the invasion. The house's inhabitants slept best when those two took night watch.

Not Kevin. He hadn't divulged it to the others, but he suspected he'd come closest to the creatures. They *were* monsters.

Tearing at turkey and muscling it with his jaw, he wondered if this would be the last meat he'd ever taste. Six of them sat upstairs, fishing around in the bags until all that remained were those little packets of silica gel. Their seventh, the gentleman with the white ear hair who never spoke and still hadn't shared his name, currently kept watch. Kevin hoped, as he did each time he was their guard, they wouldn't encounter a reason for him to speak. Or scream.

Kevin swallowed and paused. Would this be the last week they could stay put and not go hungry? The motley crew household had rationed but nearly depleted the couple's stockpile, but Winston's prior dedication to collecting Bath & Body Works candles kept them well-lit. Several burned in the middle of their jerky feast.

Picking up a glass jar, Kevin skimmed the label. Bright berries. Juicy tangerine. Bubbly champagne. Champagne toast, its name. *Ironic.*

"Daddy?" Amelia began through a mouthful of garbanzo beans.

Marcel and Winston looked at their daughter.

"I'm bored."

The group obliged her as it did when it could, the deck of Go Fish cards shuffling in Maggie's hands, but Kevin waved off the game and stood, dropping the blanket off his lap, head ducking beneath the attic rafters. He sank near the west window, lifted a cracker-sized piece of tape and wrapping paper away from the glass, and peered out, squinting and blinking into the night.

The landscape wasn't as familiar to him as it was to the others, because he'd randomly landed here. But the snow proved bright. Even with the end of the world, Ohio proved annoying and difficult. Late September, and already snowing. As with every time he dared to look, he wished he'd see her and he wished he wouldn't.

His eyes stopped focusing, mind elsewhere, and he shook his head. *You were there, so close, and I spent our time so far away.* He bit his thumbnail, the one he was lucky to have, his entire left hand a mangled reminder of the wounds and infection he'd somehow survived after the monsters cornered him in that house.

Every crew member had seared into their psyches what the apocalypse had interrupted.

Amelia remembered very little, a comfort to them all—just that she'd awoken to her daddies filling the bathtub and racing food up to their room before stacking furniture "like Tetris" in the stairwell. Marcel and Winston had called the police three times, reporting the chaos outside, hearing assurances police were on their way. They stopped believing the police were coming when 9-1-1 rang busy. That's when they'd started racing many cans and boxes of food from their cellar stockpile upstairs. Amelia had been so happy they'd "saved" her favorite cookies, long since eaten.

For Stephanie, most unforgettable was the food left uneaten. She and Maggie had recounted the sounds: the shattering of glass, the screech of chair legs, the screaming as diners abandoned martinis and meals. Stephanie had taken only a single bite of her shrimp pesto pasta when shit hit the fan.

Ears only ever shook his head.

Kevin had never told the others about his bickering with Audrey.

Speaking it aloud would only deepen his regret. He'd chosen instead to share his moments with her at the wedding at a lake, and over the months, he'd come to find some solace in the fact that they'd shared that time, some togetherness, before it happened. He still hoped the distraction he'd attempted to create by running upstairs in that house had given her time to escape, but the more the days proved empty and the nights quiet, the less he found he *could* hope for anything.

She didn't know it, but he knew her better than she knew herself. *If one of us could survive out there,* he thought, his eyes on the house across the road with the black shutters on its face and the red barn behind it, their roofs blanketed in snow, *it's you. I pray you realize it.*

HE'D FULLY EXPECTED to be dead by now, and he would be, were it not for Winston.

"Run!" he'd shrieked one more time to Audrey, bounding up the steps in that house, three at a time after he tripped. He hadn't had the time or courage to see whether she escaped. Whatever these creatures were, they pursued so relentlessly and so closely, he could smell their rot.

He didn't have time to shut the door. He didn't have a prayer of shoving furniture and barricading it. In retrospect, neither would have made a difference. The creatures had slammed holes into the farmhouse's stone exterior, big ones, though not big enough for Kevin to fit through. He had tried.

His final seconds in that upstairs bedroom, followed by his fall from the window, made up one of those scenes in life that felt intensely lucky or unlucky, one for which a person, in hindsight, ran the many ways it could have transpired through his mind and shook his head, surprised at the unlikely way one domino fell just right into the next, which fell just right into the next, securing a reality unreal and almost unfair. *Why him and not so many others who'd begged to live?*

He turned around only when there was nowhere else in the house he could run, and a creature's teeth crunched into his hand before he could get a look at it or around the room. The pain seared, causing Kevin to nearly pass out. His other hand free, he began thrashing on the thing, first punching, next scratching, drawing quickly some bodily fluid from it. The creature's wounds oozed and stank like garbage exposed to summer sun. It shrieked and threw him over the bed. Kevin's peripheral vision faltered, threatening a blackout like those he had suffered when his father beat him. He attempted to crawl but fell forward, realizing only in this moment that his left hand was unusable. It didn't resemble a hand.

The second domino fell when another creature ripped him off the floor—carpeted forest green, he remembered for some inexplicable reason—paused to roar in his face, and threw him. In a stroke of luck, the thing hurled Kevin straight through the bedroom window. In another lucky turn, an enormous bush broke his two-story fall. That didn't mean it hadn't hurt.

The third domino came in the form of a tall man who burst onto the scene, gun barrel up, quickly yet methodically scanning for targets. The stranger found Kevin, who'd dragged himself to the mulch beneath an evergreen tree. Tucking the hefty gun behind his elbow, he pulled Kevin up and started walking him away. The man would later introduce himself as Winston Wallace the Third.

Though dazed, Kevin hadn't forgotten. He never would. "She's inside," he'd mustered, wheezing.

"No one but those monsters are alive inside," Winston replied. "Shh. I don't know if they can see or hear us, but the sun'll be up any minute and best to be quiet."

Kevin woke up later in a candlelit room, concerned. Had the sun stopped rising when the creatures started rising? He scrambled to sit up, unsure who the several figures nearest the candles were.

"Hungry?" one woman asked.

Kevin winced, first at the pain from his left hand and then at the sight: bandaged heavily, yet soaking and dark.

"Here," said a tall man he recognized, standing and carrying a candle to Kevin in a corner of the room. "It's got lavender. Supposed to be calming."

In the weeks that followed, Kevin had thought it but never spoken it: surprise, and a little disappointment in himself for feeling surprised, that a man with a passion for scented candles could be the same man who had burst into and out of his neighbor's stone farmhouse, determined to defend the life of a man he was sure he'd heard scream.

HE'D FULLY EXPECTED to be dead by now, so yes, Maggie, he would take a cigarette and a light. Of course, they wouldn't talk. They wouldn't dare, especially when they chose to smoke the cigarettes they carefully rationed. He stared at where they had discovered new bodies on the road outside their house. As grim as it was, he wanted to witness them. Acknowledge them. The night's inkiness would have made them impossible to see, were it not for the snow illuminating the dark. He was usually comforted by the way the snow made the night less bleak. Tonight, he didn't find it comforting.

A childhood filled with abuse and neglect had long ago dispelled Kevin of the confidence to assert himself, so he wouldn't ask Maggie to leave. He couldn't, really: the household members only spent time outside the house when with another.

In the time *before*, he might have boiled noodles, layered them with sauteed peppers and garlic and a ground beef and sausage blend, then dropped a foil pan to the grieving families of the dead. He would never forget the way Audrey had stared at him the first time she'd found him cooking a lasagna for someone other than her. She'd cocked her head and bitten her lip in that way she did, shook her head, and smiled. "You're good people, Kevin. I don't know how, but you are."

To Audrey, the "loss lasagnas" were a testament to his generosity. To Kevin, they neared on duty. He wouldn't have eaten in the month after his mother died were it not for the pans and pies and breads and gallon Ziplocs of food so many left near the goose garden statue on his father's front stoop. His father had willfully ignored his only son's needs before the woman died, and her death changed nothing. For Kevin, to not give to others in a way others had given to and sustained him felt criminal.

A throat clearing jolted Kevin upright. "You know what those mean," Winston said, now apparently outside, lifting his chin toward the bodies on the road.

The driveways in these rolling acres of Ohio spanned so long that one couldn't see much from the front porch, save the lack of movement from the bodies. The family didn't dare walk that far from the house, day or night, to check them for pulses. From this distance, there appeared to be three or four.

"What's that?" Kevin replied, exhaling cigarette smoke. He noticed now Maggie had slipped back inside.

"There are others," Winston said. "Survivors."

Kevin turned his face back to the road, licking his bottom lip. Could she be one? Was she out there?

Winston cleared his throat. "Marcel says it's time. He ballparks we've got only about a week's worth."

Kevin clenched his jaw. "I can't convince you to let me go alone?"

"Nah. You don't know these parts. I do. It's cold, and beyond that, we've got zero margin for error."

"When?"

"It's a full moon. We go tonight."

Kevin met Winston's eyes. "Go tell your daughter you'll see her in the morning."

"Can't leave you out here alone."

Kevin stood and dug his cigarette butt into one of the hanging dead plants and followed Winston inside, locking the deadbolt and dragging and tipping the heavy chair up under the doorknob.

17

October

Five months after

Though she assured Mitch, proactively, that they were not lovers, Audrey kept seeing Bram. They played poker. Watched DVDs. Ate. She could tell Bram was interested, flirting shamelessly. She encouraged it, wanting to learn more about him and this place. A part of her felt guilty, but not enough to stop. This man had no comprehension of her ability to compartmentalize. Yes, show me interest. Yes, give me answers. Yes, I'll let you stay with me. No, you can't have my body. No, you can't have my heart.

She'd learned a decent amount for her methodically spent time: Bram was mouthy when drunk. He'd confirmed to her the H on his uniform stood for Handler, but then he wouldn't explain what Handler meant. She could tell he regretted the topic—his forehead had sprouted sweat beads, and his chest had flushed hives—and she decided to keep trying to etch away at that rock. Eventually. A journalist had to read her source, know when she pushed too hard and when ingratiating herself was the better salve. She learned from Bram there were at least two ways in and out of the Underground, and no, they were never not guarded. "That's the point, Audrey," he'd said. Had Bram ever been injured severely? she asked one time over Uno. Yes, he'd conceded. I hurt my leg once. *Bingo.* Now, the investigation was getting somewhere.

Thankfully, the gruesome, cruel nightmares had slowed. A person cannot let grief swallow them whole, she'd learned from years of therapy after her parents' divorce, and she was committed to coping without pills. It made her feel more in control, even if that didn't make sense.

One morning, she awoke to him staring at her. "Hey," she murmured, smiling.

"Hey," Bram said, tucking her hair from her face. He was the first man she'd spent this many nights with without ... entangling. She was surprised he hadn't pushed the issue. It was almost as if he followed a rulebook titled *How Not to Alienate a Woman Who Won't Fuck You*.

"How long have you been awake?"

"An hour, give or take."

She turned away and cuddled a pillow. "I saw the new baby yesterday," Audrey said. "What a sweet little thing."

Bram stared at the ceiling. "Do *you* want babies?"

"I did." Audrey sat up, fingering the felt woven blanket on her body. "I'm not sure anymore. The world is different now, so dangerous, you know? And I'm not getting any younger."

Bram nodded.

"Do you want babies?" she asked, biting a fingernail and avoiding eye contact. This was the first conversation about children she'd had since Kevin.

"I do. But I've accepted it's not for me."

"Why?"

"Well, I'm older and can't imagine caring for a baby on top of it all," Bram replied. He laid his head back on the pillows. "What did Kevin want?"

Audrey stiffened. "What did you say?"

"What did Kevin want? Were you two going to try?"

She paused, unsure what to say.

"Audrey?" Bram pushed.

"Uh, we didn't have plans one way or another," she lied.

She remembered the conversation well, seated in the booth inside the diner whose neon green sign blinked the name Jenny's. They'd been dating longer than a year, and she thought it made sense to ask. "Are they everything you dreamed of?" she'd asked Kevin over greasy-diner omelets.

He'd tilted his head and grinned in the way she loved, a playfulness to those handsome green eyes. "Sure are."

"Mine, too," she'd said. She had thrown caution to the wind and ordered hers slathered in sausage gravy.

Kevin had smiled, his mouth full.

She'd reached her shoeless foot up to his knee beneath the table of their booth and winked. "Let's get married and make a baby."

His eyes had dropped. He'd fiddled with his omelet and eventually set his fork down. "That's random." His smile looked forced.

Audrey remembered biting a fingernail. "I'm thirty-five. You're thirty-eight."

"I know, Dree," Kevin had said. "But I've got a lot of growing up to do before a baby."

"Kevin, you don't give yourself enough credit," she'd replied. She'd thought what followed would be the kind of conversation most people have where one lover self-deprecates and the other affirms him as thoughtful and reliable and loving and convinces him he possesses the qualities of good fathers. What followed wasn't that. That morning, Audrey had realized if having a family was to be in her future, the love of her life might not be.

A type of dread built in Audrey then, and a dread built now. She felt clammy and borderline nauseated, but it wasn't just the memory. "I'm feeling queasy," she told Bram, laying back down. "I think I need rest."

"I got you," Bram replied, enveloping her in his arms. "Whatever you need, I'm here."

"Actually," Audrey said, hopeful her uneasiness wasn't obvious, "it's my period."

"Do you want me to leave?"

She mustered a familiar tone. "For a few."

He obliged her. "I'll come back later to check on you. The pharmacy will have something to help."

She tucked her face against the pillow.

Bram stood, pulled on clothing, and quietly left.

Once the door clicked behind him, Audrey exhaled and tried to steady her breathing. She stood and locked the door. A hankering for those meds grew potent within her.

Audrey was positive: she'd never spoken Kevin's name to Bram.

What are you doing here? Mitch thought as Bram closed the heavy door to the meeting room and fell in line. Mitch didn't sit with the elders—no one did—but on reporting days he stood against the left wall, listening for security concerns.

Bram didn't look to Mitch's dark corner of the room, but.

I know you know I'm here.

A teacher asked for direction, concerned about the children's growing restlessness. The novelty of their subterranean home and school had worn off.

A doctor updated the council on contagious and infectious diseases inside the shelter: "Our isolation has imparted one gift," he began. "Five months in, I'm unaware of a single concern."

The obstetrician disclosed the Underground's first birth, one new pregnancy, and said the other two women were experiencing no complications. One was due the following week, so it would be all hands on deck again, the M.D. explained.

Dressed in uniform, Bram stepped forward.

"H7?" an elder prompted.

"Audrey Kelly and I haven't spoken for seven days," H7 said. "I have knocked. I have left notes. I have looked for her in places she frequents. I believe she's avoiding me."

"Why would she do that?" the elder asked. "Last you reported, she'd taken well to you."

"I'm unclear on that." Bram paused and looked toward Mitch's dark corner. "Perhaps Mr. Gray knows."

Asshole, Mitch thought.

The elders craned their necks. "Mitch?"

Hands tucked beneath his armpits and in uniform himself, Mitch walked forward from the corner. "I have seen less of Ms. Kelly, but we have been busy above ground as you know."

"And you didn't bring this diminished communication to our attention?" The ever pessimistic elder's voice sounded sharp as usual.

"It is reasonable for a person to seek privacy, even—perhaps especially—here." Mitch regretted the words the moment he spoke them. The Descendants wouldn't agree.

"We don't afford *Audrey Kelly* privacy," the woman snapped. "H7 has tried to do his job. Fall back."

Mitch retreated to the corner while the elders whispered at the table. They didn't deliberate.

"Mitch, you have twenty-four hours to ascertain that Audrey Kelly's state of mind is stable and amenable," another elder began. "Fail, and we'll put her where she should have been to begin with."

MITCH KNOCKED and whispered Audrey's name again through the door before it occurred to him: *Marney would know. Everyone eats.* He went to the dining hall.

"You know that young woman who's not family?"

The server did, of course.

"Have you seen her here?"

The waitress hesitated. "Late nights, early mornings. Sir," Marney began, "she's looking *different.*"

Mitch staked out the dining hall, watching. It was dim, and no more than five people shared the cavernous space with him, all seemingly oblivious to his presence. He liked oblivion. What he wouldn't do to solve this terror and retire somewhere quiet, where no one needed or summoned or thought of him again.

A loud thud rang out, and Mitch shrank, his hands up. Gooseflesh spread across his arms and down his belly. He searched for the sound's origin and saw a few servers wrestling to rehang a large painting that had fallen. He peered at the other Descendants. Had they noticed? Would they realize Mitch Gray could be startled and worry: Who will save us now?

No.

His people expected stalwart, unshakeable strength. He needed to be their lighthouse in this scary, dangerous sea, and he would never not try—but lately, loud sounds below ground caused his hands to shake and his heart to palpitate wildly in ways he didn't like. He'd been waking from nightmares. He hadn't done that since his fifth natal day.

Mitch didn't need a therapist to diagnose these new manifestations. A pop or a snarl or a scream above ground left him mere milliseconds to spare his flesh or the flesh of those who patrolled alongside him. The shrieks, the claw pierces, the pencil-length teeth of those reptilian-skinned monsters kept him crazy ready, even in the Underground. The release of pop can tabs had begun to scare him last week, and it was just something he would have to cope with. His people needed to feel safe at home, even if their normal living made him bare his knuckles and shudder, ready as ever to kill. He was murderous and merciless, two things they'd trained him to become, but he wasn't allowed to be either most of the time. Turn it on when it's needed, they expected. But lately, he couldn't turn it off. He'd almost accidentally hurt people yesterday (a woman had screamed bloody murder at a spider), and this morning's thrust of his hands carried risks he didn't think the Descendants understood. Lucky for them, he maintained control. He couldn't predict how long that would remain true.

He slowed his breathing and waited in the dim room until he saw her. She did look different. Thinner. Paler. When Audrey left, a to-go in her hands, he followed. Five or ten steps behind and in a vacant hallway, he said her name.

She startled and dropped her dinner to the ground. Gravy splattered, and her eyes welled.

"Hey, come here," he said.

She obliged, sinking into his chest. "Would you please go get towels?" she asked, her voice small and muffled by his hoodie.

"I can take you away and call someone to clean it."

"No. I don't leave messes down here. Least I can do."

Mitch nodded. "Okay."

The scene he made out upon his return down the long corridor made his heartrate and footsteps quicken. Audrey had removed her own hooded sweatshirt and was mopping up the mess with it, and Vera's arms were crossed. Her voice sounded cross, too. The sight of her near Audrey made him nervous. She was very clearly the angriest about Audrey's being down here.

"We've got enough to do without you making messes," he heard her say as he neared them.

"It was an accident, and Mitch is—"

"Mitch is spending time cleaning up your mess instead of much more important—"

"Hi, Vera," Mitch interrupted, an attempt to deflect.

The woman straightened and smiled tightly at him.

"It was an accident, and we're handling it," Mitch continued, dropping to his knees with the towels.

"Girl should behave like she knows her place," Vera retorted. "Sneaking around and whatnot." She tsked. "Bet she wouldn't have told you that, but of course we did. Don't let her—"

Mitch stood. Audrey stayed on all fours, eyes up, looking humiliated. Any wound she suffered because of this place and its inhabitants was his fault. His pacification of Vera would end now.

"Vera. I have words for you, but they'll be spoken with the full council in attendance. Do we understand one another?"

Vera's eyes were the size of the clocks in the cafeteria.

"Leave us to it, please."

Vera did. Elders had voting rights, but Mitch had veto rights, and every one of them knew it.

Audrey shook like a terrified dog. Mitch scooped up the rest of the sausage gravy, placed the towels in a pile on the floor, and steered her away.

Audrey didn't say a word as he led her down hallways to a suite in a locked section of the shelter. His suite. Should there be an infiltration, they needed him to have more time.

Inside, she remained standing, hugging herself. "It's been years since I watched someone defend me like that," she said softly. She moved her body into his and stroked his cheek, eyeing his face with those uniquely silver eyes, and her touch sent waves of warmth and desire to every last cell of him. The sensation reminded him of how it felt to cast power, only she made him feel powerless.

When Audrey's eyes moved to his mouth, he inhaled sharply. Her gaze penetrated his defenses. He found it intoxicating to see how intoxicated she was by him.

"Do it."

"Do what?" he whispered.

"Put your mouth on me, Mitch." She had a curious way with words, and he couldn't resist. The storm in his body raged, and he let it. Mitch leaned into her, his lips sloppy and needy upon hers, and the tsunami only crashed harder to shore when she moaned into his mouth and wilted in his arms. He kissed her as though he had to eat her, to steal her, and they backed up to his bed. Audrey pulled off the scant tank top she wore after she'd used her hoodie as a rag, and he eagerly helped her rip off his own hoodie. He put his mouth on her neck and her ears, and she pushed her pelvis into his, growling. *Good God.* He laid into her, breathing hard, enthralled and at peace at last. He was giving in to it, the feelings he wasn't supposed to have, and it felt delicious.

"Make love to me, Mitch," Audrey said breathlessly, working beneath him to slip off her pants.

Her request woke him up in the worst of ways. A lifetime of

threatened consequences played back, first among them the nursery rhyme he learned as a child:

Our blood,
So preciously built,
Must ye preserve
Lest others' be spilt.

Audrey had wiggled out of her pants, and the warmth radiating from her, from *there*, drove him mad. But this was a crime he wouldn't entangle her in. Mitch stopped tasting her, stopped giving into it all, and pulled away.

Audrey heaved and tried to pull him back to her, but he resisted.

"Audrey, I'm sorry, I can't," Mitch said, breathlessly. He stood, adjusting himself. Sweatpants hid nothing, goddamnit. "It's not you." She pulled his blanket over her body, and he hated how she seemed to drown in humiliation anew. "It isn't you. It's us."

The Tome of The Descended

1907. The death of our Great Raven Gray. What was will be again.

They whipped Elijah's arms and legs and back and buttocks for a nauseating eleven minutes before he stopped chanting, groaned, and fell forward. An hour later, we stopped using power. Our brother was dead, his blood dried black in the street, and we rejected his name. *It is frightening,* we agreed with the townsfolk, feigning the commoners' fear. *We didn't know he was this way. How could we not have known?*

Of course, we knew.

He would have wanted us to save ourselves, and so we did.

The rites we Descendants used to teach and applaud would risk the deaths of our babies and the end of our way of life. One child in our community, so young he couldn't yet roll over, was secluded for levitating a bottle to his mouth. Cry and we'll feed you, we conditioned him. It took a solid month for him to stop floating the bottle to his cradle, and we felt both pleased and devastated when he stopped. What will his life be if he can't be who he truly is? Will he forget how to use his powers? If he does, if they all do, what is our future? Matchers were urged to extinguish the flames from their fingers and harnessers were forbidden from rousing wind and water. Casual uses such as making it pour when the crops needed sustenance weren't merely stopped. They were punished. Reading the minds of town council members to gauge how they regarded us continued but only by the most senior Descendants. It was believed the elders among us could best hide their abilities and their knee-jerk reactions to any upsetting revelations.

Years passed, and we loosened our grip, confident our work to conceal who we are had worked. Then it happened.

The news came crashing into our corner of town. Know that peasant woman, Emme? the townsfolk asked.

"Yes, yes," our Great Raven Gray stammered. Strange material fell from the sky.

Is she your kin?

"No, sir. No, ma'am."

How do you know her?

"The town is little," Raven said. "We know of everyone. I'm not sure a single member of my family has spoken a touch to Lady Emme."

That woman had been found guilty by the town council of thievery, and on this day, she was to meet her punishment: loss of a hand, maybe both, were she to fight back. At the time the town council members approached Raven Gray's doorstep, Emme hadn't lost a finger. Instead, she'd burst into flames and caught each of her punishers aflame, too, before all who gathered. People tripped over themselves and each other, fleeing the scene. An explosion thundered, and a mushroom cloud the size of the tallest building rose above the town, after which ash began to fall like snow. Ash continued to fall for hours. The townsfolk were sure it was witchcraft. Fueled by deep-seated suspicion of us, they interrogated our matriarch.

Raven Gray actually had no clue who Emme was or how she was capable of what the town council members reported. But that truth and the years between the Grays and their brother Elijah's unceremonious death didn't convince the townspeople.

This is your doing, town men and women and children cried.

No! the elders insisted. We know nothing of people's having powers. We lied. We had to.

In truth, Emme wasn't one of us—we thought—until Samuel, our plodding and dedicated brother, delivered a tearful admission.

"Brothers and sisters," he began, lit only by candlelight during the emergency meeting that night. He looked to his wife, Clara, in the corner. "Emme is mine."

Gasps sounded throughout the room, and Clara shrank, holding their babies, both under two years old.

"I have many apologies to give," Samuel began, his eyes trained on Clara. "But I cannot withhold the truth. Emme is my blood. Our blood."

Samuel had been a good husband. It's why it so overwhelmed his wife—and the crowd. He'd never intended to stray, but early in their marriage, he had, and he'd fought afterward to prove worthy to her and the family. He'd fought, too, to forget his first child.

Emme's mother had been stricken by his betrayal, begging him to love them, too.

Ultimately, his hatred for himself had nearly done him in many times. But he'd religiously told himself: your wife and children need you to be who you're supposed to be. In this moment, the man he was supposed to be collided with the choices he'd made. He had done the unthinkable.

"We can do nothing for her," one of our elders spoke immediately, resolute. Samuel was stricken.

"She couldn't have known. This, this, this is not her fault—" Samuel stammered.

"You're right, Samuel," the elder man said abruptly. "This is your fault."

Samuel looked around the room, filled with fathers, mothers, and the wide, unknowing eyes of our children, and he hung his head. Flames of candles flickered, and many whispered in the night air.

"You will never speak her name," the elder man said to the echoing chamber. "Not a one of you. We do not know this woman. She is an abomination. We will weep with the town, joyful, when she is no more."

Samuel didn't react. The town, our elders included, fought that night to rein in Emme, and she lit the town with rage and fear. Fifteen townspeople lost their lives before Raven Gray intervened.

Her dark eyes alight, her dark hair flying in the wind, she stepped before Emme as Emme raged. "Stop this at once," Raven told the young woman.

Emme cackled back. She was drunk with a power she'd only just realized she possessed, and she was angry. Emme lifted her palm and with a wave, threw Raven into the air, and lit her on fire.

We Descendants on the scene were distraught, unsure of how to react. For years, we'd been told not to use our abilities, but it was clear no one would survive Emme if we didn't fight fire with fire.

Raven, aflame, visibly shaken, and bleeding from her mouth, descended to the ground and stood. Townsfolk crowded the scene, and she knew that if she fought this fire with the necessary antidote before this particular audience, she'd die. If Emme didn't kill her, the townsfolk, upon realizing who she was, would.

She trained her eyes on Emme, and an extreme wind picked up. "I've lived a lie," she told our family before the townsfolk. "I am not who you thought me to be." Raven raised her palms, and Emme was in the air. The crowd shrank away, some screaming. Lightning crackled in the night, and Raven closed her fists. Emme's body distorted, and her insides began to leak out. Most below on the ground gasped in horror. Emme cackled once more and blew a fiery kiss to Raven. Raven bore the fire better than any of us could, skin bubbling and melting away from bone. The nauseating stench of burning flesh swirled. Raven managed the strength to strike down her fists. Emme exploded.

Nothing of Emme, not a limb, not a hair, was ever found.

Our people had instinctively run to where Raven stood, desperate to save our matriarch. But there was no one to save. For more than eighty years, she'd lived, and she'd loved. This lost match would be the end of an era for her and us all. And just as we had done with brother Elijah, we realized we needed to reject Raven, too.

We were not aware, we'd insisted.

~

MITCH HAD HEARD the lesson of Emme and Samuel all of his life. Be irresponsible with your body, and all ultimately pay.

The Descendants didn't set out to govern this way. But Descendants' behavior then ushered in an era of contingencies, and their mistakes now, in modern times, continued to require contingencies. No one, not even a fastidiously reared Descendant boy or girl, was perfect, it turned out.

Mitch flipped the page of the tome, the item preserved in the library's locked room, the place he'd called boring in an attempt to divert Audrey's curiosity. He stared not at the next page, though, but at his reflection in the glass door. Not even he had resisted a human woman, even when the world had come to this.

He continued to read. Maybe he needed the reminder. And then came another thought that shocked him.

Maybe he needed her.

~

THE TOME of The Descended

1907. Origins of the Handler protocol, derived from the personal diaries of twelve Descendants, two of them elders, and the transcript of the first Confessions.

Months after the tragic demise of our Great Raven Gray and our secretive and ritualistic scattering of Raven's ashes in the unnamed creek near which she meditated, we Descendants continued to light candles and chant, "What was will be again," willing Raven's soul to make the journey in which we believe.

Many blamed Samuel. But one elder knew better than to allow us to focus only on Samuel's transgression, and he raised the issue on a brisk winter day. "Samuel is unlikely the only one who's fornicated outside our bloodline," the elder said. "And the only way we prevent another Emme is honesty."

The men and women in the room peered at one another; those gathered were only a fraction of the Descendants. To protect privacy and to encourage honesty, our elders were conducting these meetings in smaller groups. Still, no one moved, and no one spoke a word. He urged the men and women to confess if we'd strayed from our Descended order, especially if we knew we'd engaged in an affair resulting in a child. Still, no volunteers. It remained so quiet, one could hear the candles flickering.

In the coming months, our elders hatched a more private arrangement. Confessions of affairs and illegitimate children would be heard by only one elder, who would privately consult with other elders on what we would do to confront the risk illegitimate children presented. In this way, husbands and wives wouldn't be forced to confess years-old adulteries, and unmatched Descendants wouldn't be forced to air transgressions they'd committed out of wedlock.

The elder, a stout man with a chest-deep, bone-colored beard and reliable composure, kept visiting hours in a dark room of the chamber so those appearing to speak to him could do so in a shroud of secrecy. In a week's time, he'd heard from so many of us that he saw fit to call an emergency meeting. As the elders took their seats around the ornate table, the elder's eyes gave nothing away. It was his way. It was why this was his job and no one else's.

"Brothers and sisters," he began. "We must remember our people descend, too, from human beings. We are imperfect, no matter how regimented and thorough and early our teachings are." He paused. "I've spoken to forty-two—"

One elder covered her mouth.

A man exhaled, exasperated.

"I've spoken to forty-two Descendants who are certain they've fathered or mothered a child who is not reared by us. It's been a *week*. That means we're grappling with a *minimum* of forty-two people out there, reacting to life's joys and stresses, unaware they've inherited powers they aren't taught to control. Forty-two people whom we don't know, and we cannot say if they will use those powers for good."

"Forty-two Emmes," one elder sneered.

"What are we going to do?" an elder wailed. She slammed her fist on the table, and a burst of wind extinguished every candle on it.

"First," the elder with the beard said calmly, flicking his wrist and relighting every wick, "we're going to control ourselves." The elder who'd blown them all out averted her eyes and nodded respectfully. "Next, we need to handle what we now know, and we need to do it immediately."

18

Mitch needed to address Audrey's radio silence with Bram, or the elders would throw her to the wolves—well, worse. He could barely bring himself to approach her suite, though, after what he'd done. The moment was seared into his brain: her primal growl, the way she'd panted when she'd removed her pants, the hurt and confusion in those gray eyes when he'd abruptly put a room's worth of distance between them. But his life had been full of these kinds of requirements, doing and saying things because the Descendants said so, and now was no different.

She answered her door in a robe, and he immediately wondered what she did or didn't wear beneath it. Her hello wasn't terse, and he felt relief.

The distance he held between them wasn't intended to further hurt or confuse her. It was his duty. "Did something happen between Bram and you?" The draw he felt toward her was a strong magnet, and getting right to it seemed best. The less time he spent in private with her, the better for them both.

"I told you, we didn't do anything. Is that why you stopped yesterday?"

Mitch fought the urge to think on the way her curls cascaded to her breasts. *Good God, you're beautiful.* "No. I mean, you two were spending time together, and now you're not." Should he explain further why he needed to know? Maybe she wouldn't push.

Her reporter self showed itself again. He should have known better. "Is this a matter of Underground national security?" She bit her lip in that way she did, and it reminded him of how she'd bitten his. He did and didn't want these memories.

"He's supposed to befriend you." Once more Mitch was divulging things he shouldn't.

"Supposed to?"

"Yes."

"Are you going to elaborate?" Audrey walked closer to him, and he could smell coconut on her.

"Can we start with you elaborating, please? Did he do something to you?" Now Mitch felt the flames of anger ignite within him. It hadn't occurred to him until now that maybe that pompous prick had forced himself on her—

"I'm sorry," she began, her voice shaky.

The flames grew hotter inside Mitch. *He better not have.*

"Bram said something he shouldn't have known, and I've been losing my shit. Thought about resuming my pills. He knew Kevin's name when I *know* I never told him."

She stopped and emphasized the point. "I adore Kevin, and I *never* spoke his name to Bram. Not because we did anything, as you know, but ..." She trailed off and blushed. "*No one* knows me down here like you, so I started thinking you set him up to something? Or this place did? I'm so unsure of everything, it makes me sick. I've been puking." She shivered.

Mitch grabbed a blanket and draped it across her shoulders, his thoughts racing. She sat on her bed, and he sat with her. So close to where he'd almost made love to this woman. This *human* woman.

"Your turn. Why did you stop? Us?"

"It won't happen again, Audrey. I'm so sorry."

"You presume I don't want it to happen again. I want you, Mitch."

Mitch raised his chin and put his hands on his thighs. "There was a time I served on a jury, and the case was full-on Orange Is the New Black. Prison guard was having sex with prison inmates, and we convicted him of felonies because those women could not have given consent, with their being incarcerated and all."

Audrey looked confused, but he knew he had a point.

"I brought you to this place, where you don't have the same rights or knowledge as the rest of us. I don't feel like I should be sleeping with you, given all that. I'm not a predator."

"Not exactly the same," she replied. "I mean, am I imprisoned?"

"Well, no." But there were restraints she couldn't see, and Mitch didn't know if he should tell her those controls, but he needed her to reengage with Bram. If she didn't, he wasn't sure he could protect her from the consequences. "I didn't tell you everything."

Audrey furrowed her brows. "What now? What more could there possibly be?"

He swallowed. His family would be horrified by what he now contemplated. No. If they knew, they would restrain him. But he couldn't stand the idea of them continuing to meddle in her life, causing her such confusion and self-doubt. She was *puking* because of them. She had a purpose here. She was paramount for them. And, he admitted to himself, she was extraordinary to him.

Mitch dropped the side of his face into his palm. Selfishly, he didn't want to be the one to tell her this. But Bram wouldn't let her go; he would follow orders 'til the end. And if she didn't fall in line, the elders would fight to cast her to the bloodbath outside. Her short-term behavior meant life or death, only she didn't know it. He had to make her understand. Mitch looked up to the ceiling again and inhaled. "What's going on above ground is not an unknown catastrophe to us."

Audrey's bottom lip fell.

"We believe the lurchers descended here—unaware that beings with abilities live on earth—thinking earth would be an easy rout. They believe we cannot retaliate."

"Lurchers?"

"Our name for them. Though fast, they have an abrupt, unsteady stagger to them. They're treacherous, but we're battling. The reason they didn't know people have abilities here is because our kind keep our powers hidden and because—" He fumbled for words. This was another line in the sand he couldn't uncross. "To keep the powers of people like you hidden, we interfere. We make it so people like you don't know the things you can do."

Audrey's lips parted, but she didn't speak.

"You know how the uniformed officers here wear labels?"

Audrey merely stared.

"We call them Handlers, and I need to tell you what they do."

A MAJOR FOCUS of Descendant history lessons was the fraught years after the Emme incident. Wives wondered if their husbands had fathered children unknown to them, and husbands wondered if their wives had birthed the same, before they'd become spouses. *It was a period of distrust and conflict,* Descendant children were told. *And all of it was preventable. Don't forget that we are not the victims. Humans and their children are.*

After a series of terse meetings, the elders reached a consensus (not unanimous) and began recruiting. While many bitterly lamented it as unnecessary, an elaborate program staffed by humans was established to manage the "half-breeds." The most progressive among them discouraged the use of that term, and a minority of Descendants questioned their right to meddle in others' lives in this way. But the elders declared it necessary. *The less Descendants engage in prohibited acts with humans, the fewer Handlers we need and the fewer lives we manage,* they reminded those opposed to the plan.

The Descendants paid the Handlers, but they marketed the surreptitious work, first, as service to country.

"They are assigned to people who aren't Descendants but have powers, to keep them unaware of their abilities," Mitch explained.

"For a long time, our family has believed those who have powers but not our upbringing and education are safer, and the world is safer, when they don't realize their powers and don't use them."

"Assigned to people like me?" Audrey croaked.

Her hands had begun to shake. He reached to grab them, but she withdrew from him.

"Is Bram *assigned* to me?" she asked, bending her fingers into quotation marks.

Mitch nodded. He felt compelled to tell her but also steeped in regret, while also believing in the reasons why they did it. "You don't need pills, Audrey. We convinced you to take them to suppress your abilities. Abilities grow with time. Can you imagine a world where people, angry about—I don't know—someone cutting them off in the highway merge lane—throw cars and buses with their minds? Where people shapeshift and read minds amid people who can't? At a minimum, our kind would be persecuted. At worst, mankind would suffer."

"And your family—*your family*," she said through tightly gritted teeth. "Your family orchestrates this unfair charade to keep power all to yourselves?"

He no longer worried she'd keep trying to sleep with him.

"No, it's safer—" Mitch began.

She slammed her hand on the nearby wall and glowered. "Don't you fucking dare make this some play to 'protect' me," she said. She must have unlocked the gold deadbolt and the doorknob to the blue door from her childhood because he reacted physically to her thoughts now. *The light blue door from my "childhood." Who knows how much of my childhood was mine to live,* she sneered, shaking her head indignantly at him.

Mitch blinked rapidly but didn't break eye contact.

Don't you ever talk to me again.

Mitch bit the inside of his lip.

Audrey spoke it, too, making herself abundantly clear: "Don't you *ever* talk to me again."

She stood. "Leave," she demanded.

Mitch stood. "Audrey, just make conversation with him, with Bram. You needn't do a thing more. If he can't engage with you, they will force you to leave."

Audrey scoffed. "Let them. I can't stand the idea of being here a day longer."

19

They would take nothing but weapons and bags. Winston wore a hiking backpack complete with a water bladder and dragged a rolling suitcase; Kevin wore the Lightning McQueen backpack purchased confidently for a kindergarten year that never materialized and carried a duffel bag. Marcel would stay back with Amelia, but he was a bag of nerves.

"I wish we knew more—*anything*—about them," Marcel said, following Winston and Kevin around the first floor. "We don't know if they can see us, smell us, hear us."

"We're just going next door," Winston said. He set the suitcase upright and hugged Marcel, whispering in his ear. "Now get back to Amelia. If she comes down here, she'll figure it out."

"Daddy," a small voice interrupted.

Too late.

Marcel dropped the angst from his face and his voice and smiled sweetly as he turned to greet her. "Hey, sugar snap."

"I have to poop."

Kevin cringed, and Marcel lifted his chin to the sky, drawing patience from nowhere. Taking a dump outdoors in the premature snow wasn't fun for the adults, let alone a child. But they had to go outside now. It wasn't that the toilets wouldn't flush; the property had a septic tank operating without issues (for now). In fact, after Kevin had mused, "Well at least I ended up with you in the sticks," Winston had explained that toilets could flush in the city, too. "Gravity sucks away waste when wastewater treatment plants don't operate," he'd explained, his impressive doomsday-prepper wisdom on full display. But they and public sewer customers faced the same problem: the toilets flushed only if you had water you cared to sacrifice to a toilet tank. Kevin remembered last summer when it had thundered, and they'd all excitedly awaited the storm, hoping it would deliver more than enough water in their rain barrels to use for drinking *and* the toilet. It had.

Though they had gathered and melted snow to enable flushing more times than they could count, they hadn't lately. They were more worried about addressing their food supply. When flushing wasn't possible, they pooped outside in a couple of holes they'd dug deep and away from the stream. They had to be careful not to contaminate the water source.

"Daddy!" Amelia exclaimed urgently, pulling Marcel's arm.

"We have to go outside, sugar snap," he said, and the whining began. Marcel turned to Kevin. "Make it so you both get back, all right?" he whispered, not that his six-year-old could hear him above her protests.

Kevin squeezed his shoulder. "You got it."

Kevin could feel his heart pounding, and his fingers shook as he and Winston crept down the porch steps. He winced at every creak and crunch of snow. His heart's pounding subsided a bit with the stillness their shoes met on the concrete drive, until the wheels began to roll. He immediately tapped Winston. The suitcase would not do.

Winston set the bag aside, and they walked. Within seconds, they trekked farther than any of them had dared to go in the months since the apocalypse.

The moon flooded the night with much-needed light, allowing the men, fast friends, to deftly steer clear of twigs and litter their shoes could have snapped and crinkled. They'd noticed it from inside their home, but outside and exposed, it struck a deeper terror: No animal howled. No animal hooted. As they do when a monster storm looms, the wildest among them had given up the ghost.

About halfway down the drive, Winston pointed to an opening in the wooded lot next door and raised his palms and shoulders in a question.

Kevin shook his head, and they stepped carefully—heel to toe, heel to toe—on the drive toward the state route. Too noisy, he suspected. He wanted to avoid the bodies on the road, too, but not at the peril of becoming a corpse himself.

Moments later, there they were, at the juncture of the drive and the road. Three in total: a woman, man, and child. In this moment, Kevin regretted that the moon and snow illuminated so much. Their faces and limbs were frozen in inhuman and contorted shapes. Their intestines glistened, protruding from gaping holes in their centers.

Winston stood, his fingers across his mouth. Kevin tapped him and pointed down the road.

They'd never seen lights on at the Andersons' farmstead, and Winston and Marcel insisted they would have, even with the woods between their neighbor's place and their own. The structure proved dark tonight as well, but as old wood does, the porch groaned beneath their weight. Kevin paused, grimacing, and motioned for Winston to wait. He tiptoed forward and wrapped his good hand around the knob. He willed it to relent. It turned, but the door wouldn't budge.

Can we get a win, please?

He sidestepped to the front window on the left, cupped his hands around his eyes, and peered in, his breath fogging his view. He couldn't make out a thing. He carefully lifted the duffel bag strap off his shoulder and set it down slowly, set the aluminum bat steady on top of it, put his bad hand and his good hand at the bottom of the window, and pulled. The window wouldn't budge.

No.

They spent so long tiptoeing around the home's perimeter, trying windows and a back sliding glass door, that Kevin worried they were flirting with dawn. The side door was their last chance. He gritted his teeth as the screen door's metal hardware squealed like a rat in the night.

Winston leaned in to try the knob, and his shoulders slumped immediately.

Kevin shook his head. *It's not happening tonight.*

Winston backed up and gestured to the bat Kevin carried. He pointed to a window.

Kevin shook his head and pointed a thumb behind him. He didn't know if the monsters could hear, and he didn't want to learn because they impatiently smashed glass in their first attempt to find food.

They'd have to try someplace new tomorrow night.

Every face—even Ears's—beamed as the crew ushered the two men back inside and locked everyone back together, but dejection hung heavy when the room realized it: the duffel bag and the bookbag and every plastic grocery bag stuffed inside carried home nothing.

A WET, forked tongue burst forward, and Kevin awoke with a start. He lay awake, rubbing his eyes. It was no wonder his subconscious resurrected that woman as some serpent siren.

How long has it been? he wondered to himself. He'd called Graylock Mansion right before the world ended, worried he couldn't keep up this charade, and while Audrey knew him to be "at work," he'd reported there. He'd sat in a private room off the front study, waiting, palms sweating enough he'd wiped them a few times on his slim-fit jeans, when the woman intruded.

His first clue had been the way she licked her lips. His second was the way she locked the door behind her. His third was the condom she pulled from a purse and dropped on the desk.

"Hey," the woman purred, stepping over his seated body and hiking up what started as a knee-length skirt. "I haven't had sex in months. Help a girl out."

Kevin put his palms up. "I can't."

"You can." Her mouth felt warm on his neck. Part of him responded, though he willed it not to.

Kevin placed his palms on the woman's bare shoulders, the farthest point from the place she wanted him to touch, and pushed her back gently. "I won't."

The woman tipped her head, her curtain of hair falling forward, and met his stare. She raised an eyebrow and exhaled loudly. "For real? Have a little fun."

"No, thanks." He clenched his jaw.

Her eyes flashed. She dismounted and smoothed the skirt's black and red pinstripes. "Try as *you* might to forget it," she began, throwing the condom in her purse and the strap over her shoulder, "Audrey never would. Call me when you rediscover the urge to feel something genuine."

A week or two later, he lost Audrey to an apocalypse none of them saw coming. He sat up, frustrated, in the dark.

"You awake?" came Winston's voice, low and hushed in the attic where everyone not keeping watch slept.

Kevin craned his neck and found his friend crouched near the windows. "Had a dream—well, a nightmare."

"As if we fucking need more of those."

"You all right?" It wasn't Winston on watch tonight. They'd returned from their failed trek to the Anderson farm only hours before.

"Yeah." Winston's voice sounded distant, like he remained facing outside. The brave one didn't sound like himself.

Kevin sat up and crawled around the crew's sleeping bags and couch cushions toward the windows, pausing only to admire Amelia, who cuddled as she did with her worn, silver unicorn. He peeled back a corner of shiny candy cane wrapping paper from the window opposite Winston and peered down. Nothing moved, save the naked trees in winter's wind.

"What I wouldn't do to stand outside, unafraid," Winston

murmured. “Used to cover them bushes with Granny’s blankets. Shield ’em from freezes.”

“Didn’t do much gardening before,” Kevin said.

“I miss caring about those things, man. Used to pick roses and let ’em bloom in vases inside. Could count on heat, so I wasted blankets on bushes. Now? *Shit.* We shiver even with every blanket in this house. Can’t waste blankets on bushes.”

“Same grandma who inspired the stockpile?”

Winston nodded, face at the window. “Granny Julia.”

None of the seven would be alive were it not for Winston and Marcel and the cellar they’d stocked near the furnace, Kevin was sure of it. He remembered tearing up when that basement plank door opened, revealing rows of boxes and cans and jars and bottles and pouches of Lipton rice sides and, wow, even cream cheese frosting and sprinkles, the Christmas holly and berries kind. At the time, he thought they’d use them to bake festive cookies for the winter. In truth, they’d eaten the cookies long ago, a memorably bright choice in that rather dark second month of this mess. The crew was alive, and they’d barely known hunger. “We’ve had more than enough, thanks to you guys. We wouldn’t be alive if it weren’t for your rain barrels and those tablets.”

Kevin had learned so much from Winston and Marcel. Winston had explained one time as they’d scooped water from the barrels connected to the home’s gutters that that water was safer than water from the stream. No one wanted to end up with “beaver fever,” Winston had said—the giardia he’d contracted as a boy because he’d drank from a stream. Winston, he’d explained, had pooped himself raw and taken an antibiotic to rout the parasite. No such medicine was available now. Oh, Kevin often thought, how much they took for granted corner pharmacies with twenty-four seven availability. How much they’d taken *everything* for granted.

“We don’t have more than enough. Not anymore.”

“Hey.” Kevin pulled his face from the window and touched his friend’s elbow.

Winston met his gaze.

"We're going to find food. People left their doors unlocked. People left food at home. People left meds at home. We're going out every night until we bring back what we need. *More* than what we need."

Winston returned his attention outdoors. "Think this'll pass? That life will go back to normal?"

Kevin wanted to tell his friend yes but stared outside instead. It had been half a year. If a return to normal were possible, wouldn't someone have secured it by now?

20

November

Six months after

Audrey didn't speak to Mitch the entire next week.

Mitch lied brazenly to the elders to keep her safe. Yes, he and Audrey were speaking. No, he didn't have much to report. Yes, she appeared stable.

The lies he told them had purpose. He had to appear to do what they expected him to do, for reasons he could not disclose to the elders. It was agonizing.

~

Between the nauseating anxiety and avoiding the cafeteria every time she thought she spotted Mitch or Bram, Audrey lost another five pounds that week. She'd taken to stocking up on whatever she could as soon as the dining hall opened, until Bram caught her and started waiting for her at the crack of dawn.

"Audrey, I don't know what I did, but I'll make it right," he said the morning he found her hugging a half dozen muffins to her chest.

She shook her head and fled. *What, Bram?* she sneered as she scampered back to her suite. *Have to make it right to make payroll?*

Inside her suite, she dropped the muffins to the ground and sank to the floor. She was blisteringly angry. She was a bottomless kind of sad, too. She grieved. She no longer knew who she was. No. She'd never really known who she was. How much of her life had been *hers?* She was frightened by the ability of Mitch and Bram to seamlessly infiltrate her life and prove utterly convincing at doing so. She shuddered to think that if she'd been more open to it, more vulnerable, she might have fallen for Bram.

File this under reason number 842 why—she paused. *File.* All those months ago, during her snooping, she'd found that room with dozens, possibly hundreds, of file folders containing notes about people: their affairs, their medications. Audrey raised her eyes to the wall, mulling over the memory. Another piece of her life now fit: the woman in that room had looked straight at her, and Audrey had thought the woman pretended not to see her. *She couldn't see me,* she realized. *I was cloaked.*

Audrey wouldn't eat breakfast today either. She closed her eyes as Mitch had instructed and improvised: "Disappear," she whispered. Her face peered back at her from the mirror. "Disappear." No change. She straightened and shifted her tone. *I am not asking.* Instantly her body tingled all over.

Harness your power, he'd told her.

"I own you. Disappear."

She checked the mirror and inhaled, stunned. She was invisible. She raised her hands to her face, mesmerized, before springing into action. She didn't know how long it would last. Carefully, she peeked out her door. It was risky. To determine if it was clear the other way, the door to her suite would have to swing open without a body appearing to make it do so. The coast was clear to the left. She slunk back into her room but decided to do it quickly and it'd be fine. As she left her suite, she nearly ran into a couple of Descendant children she recognized. They peered around the door as it closed without a trace of a person, shrugged, and left. Audrey figured Descendant children would have been trained to pay closer attention to the unexplained, but she wasn't sorry they ignored it.

Invisible, she departed to find the files. This time, she'd hunt for one labeled Audrey Kelly.

21

Mercifully, the coast was clear. Cloaked—Audrey could tell because her body felt like every limb had fallen asleep and because her reflection was absent in the glass door—she stepped inside the filing room, the "vault" Mitch had called it. Slowly, she closed the door and tried a drawer, but it was locked. So were the second and third and fourth ones. *No, damnit.* It was no use trying for keys: the filing cabinets were secured with combinations. She sure as shit wasn't asking Mitch.

Discouraged, Audrey turned the doorknob to leave.

"Stop," a woman said on the other side, turning the knob at the same time.

Heart racing, Audrey flattened herself against the wall as a man pushed the woman through the door and pressed her against a cabinet. Audrey stood still, bewildered. She kept forgetting that people couldn't see her.

The couple kissed, hands roaming all over, for several minutes before the woman came up for air, breathing, "Okay, okay, I do owe this file to them."

"We'll be quick," the man insisted, kneeling before her and lifting her skirt.

"Tsk," the woman began. "I don't want to be quick." She sidestepped him to a filing cabinet.

Audrey crept behind the woman as she entered a four-digit code. *Gotcha*, she thought, satisfied with herself.

The man to the woman's right stiffened. "Did you hear that?" he asked, furrowing his brows and canvassing the room.

"Hear what?" the woman replied, paging through files.

"I swear I heard someone. A woman." His piercing eyes paused somewhere past Audrey.

Audrey's eyes widened. In a hurry, she envisioned the light blue door, slammed it shut, and locked both locks. She thought she'd closed her door more recently; she had a lot to remember and a lot to learn.

The man kept his eyes trained on something nearby.

"Here we are," the woman said, drawing a file and kissing the man. "Let's go."

They left, but not without the man taking one last look around.

Audrey stayed still long after they left, biting her fingernail. Once she dared, she entered the code into the top drawer of the first cabinet lining the wall. Its light blinked green, and she was in. Coincidentally, that top drawer was full of file folders labeled with names beginning with J. Audrey hoped few enough Js existed that she'd find the start of the Ks, a folder labeled Kelly. She was in luck. Kelly, Audrey. She paused, holding the crimson folder in her hands, unsure if she wanted to know its innards. She sat and opened it.

Interestingly, its contents didn't begin with a birth certificate or baby picture Kodaks. They began with the police report about the fatal car accident she'd survived on senior prom night. Audrey covered her mouth, instantly queasy. Her dad had worked hard to help her avoid the coverage and all its gory pictures: the car on its roof, the emergency responders in the river, the coroner's van. She inhaled sharply; tipped her head, confused; and flipped the page over.

To investigate reports of Audrey Kelly's disappearance on the night of this crash only to reappear days later, we commissioned a follow of the girl and the family. Audrey Kelly, we believe, is unaware she possesses the power to cloak. She is unassigned and needs to be managed immediately. More disturbing, it appears Charles Kelly and his daughter Audrey Kelly somehow escaped detection for decades.

Audrey's mouth fell ajar. *Dad? What does Dad have to do with this?* She flipped ahead to the final pages, curious what the Descendants and their Handlers had written about her before the world devolved.

H23 called to report a problem. Is unsure if he can continue to serve. Said "my lines are blurring." We've instructed him to report to Graylock Mansion. May need to reassign.

Audrey paused. *Who's that? Bram? Can't be,* she thought, locating the date. *This was months before I met the asshole.* She paged backward.

H23 reports no signs of Audrey's powers. Medication appears to be a viable long-term option. If it ever comes up, she needs the meds for anxiety and depression.

The words made Audrey swallow and blink, and she was glad she'd stopped taking those meds. She paged backward through dozens of reports, catching words here and there on what appeared to be routine reports about her. She saw a handful of photographs and flipped forward to them. She gasped.

She'd feared she would forget his face, but there was Kevin, his green eyes stoic, his square jaw as handsome as it ever was, his curls. She traced his lips with her finger and exhaled. She cocked her head and moved her finger. A label's edge wrapped around the front of the image from its backside, compelling her to turn it over. Scrawled on the label were the terms *H23, Kevin Williams, first assignment.*

"No," Audrey whispered, pushing the folder and pictures away and standing up. "No, no, no." She paced, cloaked, the tingling in her body at full tilt. "Not you. Not you." She sat back down, pulled the folder and its scattered pages to her lap, and kept browsing. Each time she spotted his name or another photograph, she stopped and scanned. It sharpened, the stabbing realization she'd rather never have made.

Kevin Williams, the man she'd cried over, spending countless nights missing, was H23. And she—Audrey Kelly—was his assignment. An assignment.

She'd entered the vault, her trust broken. Now her heart was, too. She never would have guessed, with everyone she loved above ground with those monsters, that anything could break her further. She was wrong.

~

AUDREY SPENT the next week puffy-eyed and unkempt, exhausted from rewinding the scenes of her life and attempting to dissect what had been genuine and what had been lies. The times she considered steadying herself with the five Ws, she couldn't. The questions started with *who?*, and she didn't feel she knew that answer anymore.

She remained bitterly angry at Mitch, but the truth was, she was stuck in the Underground, and now more than ever, Mitch was the only one she could trust. Despite Mitch's insistence she reengage, she'd continued avoiding Bram without telling him why, and that had been nearly impossible. Thankfully, they didn't have cell phones and Facebook Messenger down here, where her receipt of messages would have been obvious. She felt afraid and betrayed, but she knew Mitch was sacrificing a lot: he told her truths she could use to destroy his family and the society they'd spent decades preserving. *If they let me out of here. If anyone cares after what's happened.*

It was super late the night Audrey mustered up the courage to approach him.

Fuck me, she thought upon encountering the locked door to his corridor. *Can I get a break around here?* She opened her blue door and hoped he'd hear her.

Within moments, Mitch opened the door, shirtless and in soft sweatpants.

"Hey," she said to him.

"Hey," he replied, peering past her and ushering her inside.

Her curls were tangled. Her eyes were bloodshot. She dropped her gaze and let him pull her close.

"I'm so sorry, Audrey," he whispered in her ear.

She pulled his door shut behind them. It was only the second time she'd been inside his suite. It was dark inside, apart from the glow of a lava lamp.

"Kevin was a Handler," she began, pulling her curls to one side of her head. "Is a Handler. I have so many questions."

Mitch lowered his gaze. "I'll answer what I can," he said softly.

Ever a man of his word, from two in the morning until people milled about the Underground at dawn, Mitch answered most of her questions. Kevin and Handlers were recruited by the Descendants and trained to care for people like Audrey. Occasionally, people discovered their abilities, and additional suppression tactics were employed. Milligrams were increased. She winced at this revelation. She should have paid more attention to medication Kevin helped her get, but her anxiety and depression had been debilitating, and she'd trusted him implicitly. Loved him implicitly.

If additional suppression tactics failed, memories were erased, Mitch concluded.

"How?" Audrey asked.

"It's a power few of us have, but it can be done," Mitch replied.

"So, Kevin, because he was assigned to handle me, he would've married me? He would've had kids with me?"

Mitch shook his head. "We would have prohibited him from having children with you. The aim is to reduce the number of people who have powers and aren't raised by us," he said. "Any child you have, we'd expect to have your abilities."

Audrey flashed back to Jenny's Diner, when Kevin had immediately clammed up about the prospect of having babies. *Had he fallen for her and wanted to but wasn't permitted to? Had he never loved her?* Audrey shifted away from Mitch on his couch. "Mitch, it's really messed up. Truly. You're altering people's lives, their *lineages*. All so you can control who's powerful."

"It's not that, Audrey," he said. Rarely and dangerously, people discovered their abilities and used them to hurt others. Those people, unbound by the Descendants' expectations, had created chaos—

massacred innocents, levelled whole towns—several times throughout human history. When they couldn't be contained, he explained, they were eliminated.

"Eliminated?" she said.

"Either housed someplace where they can be managed or ..." He trailed off.

Audrey didn't ask him to elaborate. She laid her head on the back of the couch.

"What are we doing, Mitch?"

"Unsure."

"Why are you telling me all this? What do you want with me?"

"Try to trust me," he replied.

"Do you want me?" It was a daring question, but what more did she have to lose? Besides, wasn't desire why most men give women what they wanted?

"Want you?"

"Yes, Mitch. Do you want me?"

"Yes."

"Why let the whole Bram charade happen then?" she asked, turning her gaze to his face.

"I have responsibilities, not choices. If I interfered, you could have been in danger."

"Am I in danger now?"

He paused and lowered his eyes. "It depends on what we do now."

"Can I ask you a question?"

"Yes."

"Who *are* you? You're the only person people call 'sir' down here. Why?"

He half-smiled; this was a more available Mitch than she'd spent the last months trying to get to know. "I'm the oldest, living descendant of Puck and Raven Gray."

"Why do those names sound familiar?"

"Their faces are on composites all around this place. They are the patriarch and matriarch of the Descendants."

"So, wait, does that make you some sort of royalty?"

He pitched his head to the side. "No. When the elders meet, I'm there as a vote from the people who came before. I have the right of veto."

"You can veto the elders I've heard about?"

"Yes, Audrey."

"Even if they all vote one way, you can tell them no?"

"Yes, Audrey."

"Why?" She felt one part curious and, she admitted to herself only with her light blue door closed tightly, another part even more attracted. *God. Could I want you more?*

"I've been reared to take the helm since I was young. The elders are our board. I'm like a CEO."

That made some sense to her. She'd worked for a newsroom whose publisher called the shots but answered to the board of directors.

"And it's because of your age and blood line?"

"Yes. The closer you are to Puck and Raven, the stronger your abilities."

"Wait. Do you do more than read minds?"

"I do," he replied.

"What can you do?"

"Let's be careful. The more you know, the more you have to hide."

"Why tell me anything?" she repeated.

Mitch regarded her silently. "I told you. I need you to trust me, Audrey. I need you to feel safe here. I need you to stay."

Thirty-five years before

Within hours of their cleaning and wrapping him, naked, in the customary red wool, the newborn twice surprised the Descendants, even though they sensed he'd be different.

Samantha carried and birthed Mitch in the same way Descendant women had carried and birthed their babies for generations. Her own power intensified as the baby's power grew within her, and that wasn't unusual. But the clip at which she controlled new, astonishing forces piqued the families' interest in the baby they all expected. Samantha, the dark-eyed and dark-haired near-twin of her grandmother Raven, had long been among the most powerful of the Descendants. A matcher, she could create fire from nothing. A harnesser, she could direct the weather. With child, though, the only feats she couldn't do were cloak and prophesize. She could now read minds, and she discovered in an afternoon accident that she possessed another strength.

A young child had run onto the lawn of Graylock Mansion, crying hysterically. "The log, the log—he's caught, there's a log," the child had said breathlessly to Samantha, who'd just opened the mailbox to check inside.

Sam knelt down and placed her hands on the child's shoulders. "What's happened, Estelle?"

The girl pointed to the east. "Elio, he was crossing, he's caught. There's a log."

The river. Samantha, though nine months pregnant, burst into a sprint. When she reached the bank, she gasped. Elio, Estelle's twin brother, was flailing in the river, gasping for air and coughing water. She ran into the river toward him and tried to rip him up by his underarms, but he was lodged. He fell beneath the murky water, and Sam panicked.

Since her powers throughout pregnancy were already unheard of, she tried invoking him. "Baby, help me," Sam demanded, unsure what would happen. Sam screamed, "Stop!" and raised her palm. The river's frothy, forceful current froze. The tangled riverbed, ripe with fish and moss, drained, and Elio's feet were visible beneath the log. Holding back the river made Sam shake. The earth was strong, but *they* were stronger. Sam wasn't positive, though, how long they could keep it dammed.

The log was so big, and Sam had only one arm free. She leaned down, hugged what she could of it, and tried to lift it off of Elio. Her first attempt failed. "Baby," she hollered at the forest and the river and the sky and Mitch in utero. "Save him."

The baby kicked and squirmed within her, and all sound became muffled. Others gathered at the riverbank, but Sam heard none of their desperate cries. Wind gusted, and they witnessed her do it. She lifted the log, which was probably hundreds of pounds heavier than her, many feet wider than her, and many feet taller than her. Elio, though limping, was free.

Samantha doubled over as Elio sprinted away, his shoes squishing on the soggy riverbed. Contractions squeezed her abdomen and back. The Descendants at the riverbank moved swiftly to remove her as the water careened back the way it had before she and her baby had stopped it.

Though many of Samantha's laboring peers packed a bag and raced off to the hospital, she could not. It risked detection. Babies born to Descendants were often immediately powerful and did not know to hide it, so only when a mother's life was in mortal danger did the Descendants turn to Western medicine. A private hallway of bedrooms in Graylock Mansion was the family's birthing ward, and a trained doctor of the family attended to them.

Puck Gray and others gathered that late morning wearing the customary garb, their heavy, blood red cloaks whispering upon the floor as they walked. They burned sage as Samantha labored. The soul of an infant born with powers, especially presumably unparalleled powers, was a vessel coveted by creatures dark and sinister.

Mitch would be her firstborn, and her labor proved foreign and long. She groaned and winced for more than forty hours, and when it came time, she pushed for three more. Finally, he was here, all eight pounds, two ounces of him. Samantha and Warren cried upon meeting him. She'd wondered for nine months how he would look. He had green-gray eyes and barely visible blonde hair and a tiny button mouth.

An hour later, frustrated and hungry, the baby ripped her from her bed so he could nurse, literally lifting her adult body to hover above his bassinet, pulling off her shirt, scattering buttons, and leaning up to suckle her milk. To move a mother within hours of birth was unheard of. And so, too, was his next move: baby Mitch put his grandfather in the chair nearby, set the chair rocking, and levitated to his arms.

"We'll need to protect him," an elder in a red cloak said quietly, witnessing it. "This child possesses a strength we've never observed, and he's hours old. He could be a danger to himself—and to us—until he's properly trained."

Puck Gray snuggled his cheek to his infant great-grandson's face, felt his warm breath upon him, and nodded. The elder bowed with deference and left; best not to wake a sleeping baby. The baby's lips were parted with sweet baby snores, placing Puck in a bit of a trance. He'd not known love this fast since he'd met his daughter.

The next day, the Descendants cast the Cradle Incantation to suspend Mitch's powers until he was old enough to understand. For the first time, the elders, the baby's powerful mother, and Puck Gray himself were unsure whether the spell could contain the power of a little one.

Thirty-three years before

The boy was two, younger than most children were when the testing commenced. A man with wispy white hair stood to greet him. A small table; a bright red, yellow, and blue plastic chair; and a folding chair sparsely outfitted the room. Along a far wall stood a long table, covered in items. "Hello, dear boy," the man said, leading him to his seat. Like at every child's testing, only one adult sat in the room, and another adult sat behind two-way glass. Unlike every child's testing, the seated council of elders assembled to watch through cameras. Today's test carried immense weight for the Descendants' future. This boy would usher in a new era, one even the prophet couldn't see. He had tried.

"I'm going to ask you to do some things today, okay?" the man began.

The boy, dressed in short overalls and a bright blue turtleneck, nodded earnestly.

"And this is important," he continued, kneeling beside the boy. "I want you to believe you can do each task. Remember the Little Blue Engine?"

The boy smiled.

"I need you to 'think I can, think I can, think I can.'"

The boy in blue smiled more.

The man walked to the far table and began selecting feathers. Trying to avoid detection, he softly tapped the two-way glass. But there wasn't much the boy missed.

Stand and walk to the door, the woman behind the glass instructed without speaking.

The boy's eyes scanned the room. He looked behind him. He turned back to look at the man gathering quills.

Stand and walk to the door, Mitch.

The boy's blonde, barely there brows furrowed, but he stood and walked to the door.

The man with the feathers turned. "Very good, young man. You may sit." He held up an index finger and paused to jot down a word on a clipboard. He joined the boy at the table and laid three smoke-colored turkey feathers on its surface. "Now, I want you to move these feathers."

The boy stared briefly and reached his short fingers toward one.

"No, Mitch. Move them without touching them."

The boy raised his eyes and tilted his head. "How, Elder?"

"With your mind. Remember, Son. 'I think I can, I think I can.'"

The man, the woman, and the elders watching knew he'd pass this second test. He'd moved adult bodies with his mind within an hour of his birth.

The boy fixated on the feathers and concentrated. He squinted hard, but he was two. The boy shrugged. "Sorry, Elder."

"Try harder, dear boy. Don't just stare at the feathers. Envision them doing what you will them to do."

Compliant, the boy rested his chin on the table, near the feathers, and his eyes turned the color of oil. A rumbling sound began. All of a sudden, he whipped his face away. The feathers didn't float; the table *and* the feathers did. They rumbled for a short while before the ground itself began to rumble. Items on the far table quaked and cascaded to the ground.

The elder in the room shot a look at one of the cameras mounted inside the room. "Very good, dear boy." The man peered again at the cameras, this time staring longer than made sense to the boy.

22

December

Seven months after

The world above ground proved gorier on Tuesday than Mitch had expected.

"Sir?" a guard said in the dark before dawn, stepping forward as Mitch staggered to the mountain door. Mitch waved him off, a finger to his lips, and pointed ahead.

"H29, clear the red," the first spoke to the second by radio.

Mitch hustled through the red door past H29 and into the bathroom to the left. He pulled the seat up and gushed out sour insides. It burned and kept coming. Her face, pale and sunken. Her hollowed-out belly. A baby, its mother, gone.

We're failing them, he thought. I'm *failing them.*

When his heaving stopped, he laid his cheek on the toilet. Exhaustion didn't begin to describe it. He gave and his teams gave, and he knew others from other shelters were trying. Still the lurchers advanced, and they all—humans and Descendants—suffered for it, only humans didn't have sprawling cellars to weather the storm. Humans like Audrey.

Even on the days when he and the runners littered the earth with corpses, Mitch felt the weight. Around the Underground, he saw *dependents.* Every last one—the grandmother who patted his shoulder in the mornings and reliably dropped a chocolate chip cookie in his hand; the children who squealed, blissfully unaware of the lucky hand they'd been dealt; the three pregnant couples—they wouldn't survive if he didn't find a way to make it so.

The nausea didn't rise again like it had before dawn, but all day his heart and stomach stayed unsettled, and he didn't eat. Sometime after dinnertime, Mitch knocked on Audrey's door. The elders expected him to check on her daily, and he hadn't seen her today.

She opened the door, yawning.

"You okay?" he said.

"Livin' the dream," she replied. Her tone changed upon noticing Mitch's hunched shoulders and the hand gripping the door frame. "Hey," she began. "Are *you*?"

People didn't ask Mitch Gray that question. Since his birth, when the elders discovered how unlike them he was, he'd been their leader. Their protector. People didn't ask him questions that relegated him to their level, to their vulnerability.

Mitch swallowed and nodded, but Audrey quietly pulled him inside. She moved her pillows and patted the bed.

Just for a minute, he told himself. *I've got tomorrow to plan.* He laid down and closed his eyes. He felt her pull the comforter to his shoulders and pet his forehead and stubbled jaw. He didn't shave like he used to.

A minute in, Audrey whispered, "Hey."

Mitch's eyes blinked briefly, but he didn't respond. Didn't want to respond. He felt Audrey lay beside him.

He would sleep for eight hours.

HE AWOKE, but the nightmare woke with him. The same desperation he'd laid down with bubbled up, and he stared at a room. An unfamiliar room. He'd slept deeply, and he'd done so in the room of the woman he was not supposed to bring here. He sprang up and felt so disoriented, he felt drunk.

He was afraid. What if the elders were aware he hadn't keyed into his suite last night? He wondered how much longer he'd feel this way. He didn't have much use for fear—and certainly not now.

For most of his life, Mitch couldn't remember feeling afraid. He knew more, could do more, could tolerate more than everyone. But in the here and now, he felt afraid, and worse, he couldn't show his fear. He had to stand tall, chest out, at meetings where their ability to survive was gauged meticulously in the mitigation of disease, the food that remained and the water source they fastidiously monitored, the limited and violent progress of fighters led by him and others across the world. He had to assure his team they were safe fighting the lurchers alongside him, even when he collapsed while protecting them (it was happening more frequently lately). He had to laugh at jokes told by passers-by in the Underground, feigning he knew with resolute certainty that this life they all endured would come to an eventual end, so much so that Mitch Gray would entertain levity. Showing his fear would mean everyone would become more afraid. He could not do that to them.

His eyes adjusted now to the dark, and he surveyed his surroundings. Audrey lay snoring loudly, her face in the pillow. *How is that comfortable?* Mitch stood awkwardly, afraid she'd wake and be put off by him watching. He wouldn't do it for long, but she was only the second woman he'd spent the night with. The other time had been the exploration ordained by the elders. They most certainly had ordained nothing about this, or when he and Audrey had—. Mitch couldn't even admit in his own head what they'd done. He tilted his head, eyeing her body. She'd all but begged him to take her, and who would blame him if he had?

Vera. Vera would birth a cow.

His life had turned out so differently than their Descendant etiquette classes had prepared him to live. They taught him to be powerful in a different sort of world. They taught him that in order to preserve that world, they needed to suppress the abilities of others, including this snoring, curly-haired woman. But thoughts crept in, no matter how much he flailed to still believe what he'd been taught, to push alien, blasphemous thoughts to the periphery. What if their protocol had actually doomed the world? What if, by suppressing humans who could wield power, they'd made it impossible to defeat the threat outside?

Audrey shifted and snored louder than he'd ever heard anyone snore, but she didn't wake. She flopped this way and that, then cuddled the pillow he'd abandoned. It disarmed him. It was cute. Harmless. She was cute. Was she harmless?

What would they do now if people like her were dead because they'd chosen this path? What if? He rubbed his forehead. What if?

Mitch stole one last glimpse at the woman he wanted and could never have and left.

~

AUDREY HAD SPENT her newsroom career digging up answers, and she'd used that education to her advantage. When she wanted to know if the ex of her neighbor who'd made quite the scene, throwing his belongings on the lawn, had a rap sheet, she searched county criminal records (she had). She knew to search SEC filings to help her friends decide whether companies were worth investing in. And when the neighbors across the street wondered what the rundown house on their street sold for, she reminded them public deeds would tell them down to the cent.

But Audrey did not know where to start to figure out what powers were possible and whether she possessed them. Mitch wasn't forthcoming about his, but she knew cloaking was possible. He could read minds, so that—wasn't it called telepathy?—was possible. And Mitch had said erasing another's memory was possible. What else?

Audrey was no stranger to the truth that often a person is the only source of certain information. Mitch seemed conciliatory the last time she saw him—the night he spent in her room. She had watched him for the longest time, noticing little things she hadn't, couldn't have, before. The freckles spattered on his nose. A small cut beneath his lip. The way he balled his fists in his sleep, as though even then, he couldn't relax. She had woken the next morning, mortified by the puddle of drool on her pillow and instantly relieved when she realized he had left at some point.

Mitch possessed the answer to probably every question raging within her, and maybe she should try Betty Jane, but he had more to lose than Betty Jane: he'd told her things he shouldn't have. It was leverage, though she didn't plan on making any threats. Yet. When he knocked in his telltale way the night after he stayed, she opened her door and nodded him in.

"I can't," he said. "Sorry." He sounded more reticent than usual. Had he gotten in trouble?

"I'm not asking you to stay, Mitch. I need you to tell me something. It'd be best if I asked it in private."

Mitch looked left and right and stepped inside. The door swung closed behind him. Ever since he'd pressed his body against hers, leaving so little to the imagination, she felt somewhat intoxicated by his presence. There was something to be said about wanting someone and knowing he wanted you, too.

"Tell me another power that's possible."

"Audrey, I've got to go, and it's best you know less than more."

"I don't want to know less."

Mitch scratched the side of his face.

"I'll tell you something, you tell me something. Cool?" She was desperate to make it worthwhile to him—not that she had truths on nearly the same level to offer. But sometimes a reporter had to give a piece of information to get one. The reveal she considered sharing could get her in trouble with the man who held *the* power down here, she knew, but he had kissed her, and it was the card she had to play. "The first few days I was here, I saw Bram with his leg torn off."

Mitch jerked his head to stare at her.

"I didn't know it at the time, but I was probably invisible. Cloaked. Whatever you all call it. But I saw his leg separate from his body. And when I met him, he was *walking*. No limp, just walking. Is that some sort of power? Healing oneself?"

Mitch eyed her. "Are you speaking again with him?"

Audrey wrinkled her nose; being so close to the fraud had made her skin crawl. "I told him the talk of babies really triggered me. And I apologized for ghosting him."

"Solid redirect," Mitch said.

"So? He healed his leg? His leg was *off*, Mitch. Not wounded. Off. His. Body."

"I know what happened. He didn't heal himself."

"So...?"

"An elder did."

Audrey's eyes widened. "So healing is a power."

"It is."

She stared, and he stared back. "Mitch, do you really think, after all I know, I'm going to tell them anything? I keep my door closed, and I keep my trap shut."

Mitch pitched his head to the ceiling. "Healing is a rare power."

"Are you a healer?"

Mitch paused. "No."

"What's with the pause?"

"There's a rarer power: resurrection. They know of only two people who've possessed it: me and ... my dad. My dad," Mitch began, trailing off. "My dad died using it."

"I'm sorry, Mitch," Audrey murmured. She realized now he did know the kind of loss that shackled a person, that drew a line in the sand of before and after. A loss that steeped you in regret so unimaginable that you might just succumb but you knew, you knew, that your person would have wanted you to survive. You don't want to. But they demand it.

"Yeah."

"How? How did he die? I'm so sorry."

"I'd rather not."

Audrey understood. She wished she didn't know how it felt to have devastating scenes seared into her memory. The night her dad left. Prom night. She thought now, too, of her mom grinning with a mouthful of cupcake at the wedding. It was painfully possible that would be the last time she'd ever see her, and how incredibly unfair. She'd already lost her dad. Audrey hatched another plan now: she would discover more about the powers that were possible, unlock another, go to one of the two doors Bram had divulged, force her hand with a Handler or two, go above ground, use her power to survive those things, and bring her mom down here. So now she would push.

"What's a more common power?"

"What do you mean?"

"What can most of you do?"

Mitch exhaled. "I am telling you, the less you know, the—"

"Mitch, please. I'm working with you. Work with me."

"Most can harness the elements."

"Meaning?"

"Harnessers can create and control fire, wind, water, and land. The weather. They harness the elements."

"How does one know if they're a harnesser?"

"Audrey. I do have to go."

"Mitch, please?"

He checked his watch. "If we test you, there's only one place to do it down here."

She nodded, but a deep pit cratered within her belly. The only tests she knew of left Betty Jane with burn scars. Maybe she didn't want to know more after all.

"It'll have to be after I do what I need to do, and it has to be super late, when most are asleep. Be ready around two."

The man with the spattering of freckles left. He would return in the worst mood and covered in dried blood.

23

"Oh my God, are you hurt?" Audrey whispered when she opened her door. His freckles were hidden by a bright spatter of blood. His hands were stained, too.

He hushed her, shut her door, and made a beeline for the bathroom.

She followed. He must have washed and rinsed ten times before the water ran clear. He spoke not a word while he did it, and when he turned the water off, he leaned forward on his palms and stared wordlessly at his reflection.

"I sincerely hate my life."

Audrey bit her lip. She felt he appreciated her witnessing this, his having the space to hate it.

"This is human blood," Mitch continued, turning toward her.

Audrey recoiled and instantly felt badly that she did, but he was covered in *people's* blood.

"They died," Mitch said, too matter-of-factly for her taste. "Every last one. I can't count the number of times I've washed blood off or whatever fluid those things expel. I'm tired, but I'm not allowed to be tired. I don't get to feel tired or scared or sad. I never have."

Mitch also never talked this much, and it rendered Audrey silent. She opened her mouth to speak, then shut it. What could she say?

"I'm done. You ready?"

She hesitated. In the hours while she'd waited for 2 a.m., she'd wrestled with telling him never mind. Knowing whether she could wield different powers didn't mean she possessed the guts to leave this safehouse, and Betty Jane's inferno-of-a-house test was not something she felt confident she could weather. Still, she nodded from the door. The plan was in motion, and she would move with it. Mitch stepped toward her and paused, their bodies close. She didn't break eye contact, and it felt electrifying. He was so strong. She couldn't imagine being that strong.

"Cloak, please."

She did—impressed at how quickly her body tingled and cooperated—and followed his lead out the suite and up several walkways. They passed signs for the spring, the one she'd set out to find before but never located. He keyed in a code and pushed open an enormous red door.

She couldn't make out the end of the cavernous, stone room before them, and she gasped at the sight of an underground lake. Lights in the stone walls reflected in the water, and she peered this way and that. Stalactites dripped from the ceiling; she only knew their name because she'd toured a cave on a Lake Erie island as a child. Her heart pounded, and she began to sweat. Though she'd been a sucker for nature documentaries about mountain climbers and cave divers, bodies of water terrified her. Prom. Sequins. The river churning all that time. Dead teenagers. She backed up, shaking her head.

"Come," Mitch whispered.

"I can't," she insisted in a hushed tone.

"Come."

She peered at him, exasperated. She knew better than to argue in words, but she tried to argue with her face.

He ignored her, nodded with a silent guarantee, and started walking. He led her along the water's edge, which didn't extend far because most of the room was a gaping body of water. This fueled her anxiety, but she followed.

"Look." Mitch pointed toward the lake's left-most side. "The spring is twenty feet down. It's the reason we built here. We knew we would need water."

Audrey walked like a scarecrow, arms extended. She felt a bit ridiculous because she could see the craggy rock under the shallow water nearest them, could see she wouldn't easily drown in the still water, but her fear wouldn't relent.

"Move the water."

Audrey furrowed her brow. "What? How?"

"Move it, Audrey. You can."

Audrey stared at him, bewildered. *I can?* She concentrated on the water's edge and frowned. "How do I move it?"

"You tell it to move. Like you tell your body to cloak."

So she tried. She stood and willed the water, still as glass, to recede. She crouched and touched it, and it was surprisingly warm. She willed it to move. She stood, her palms up in defeat.

"Any power I have ever uncovered required me to believe. You must believe."

He said I can. Audrey sat down on the rocks and felt their cool sharpness beneath her. She shut her eyes. She envisioned the black water as her servant, required to do as she commanded. She imagined it moving.

It didn't. "Are you sure I can?"

"No."

"So why'd you say I could?"

"It's a common power, so I assumed you could. Let's go. If we're caught here, I—" He paused and shook his head. "Let's not be caught here."

She began to stand and recalled scenes that didn't make sense. A whirling cyclone of leaves. Her parents. *Mom. Dad.* She rubbed her eyes and shook her head. An intense fear gripped her.

"You okay?"

Audrey stared at Mitch. "I think so," she lied. A memory crept in from the periphery of her mind right now, and it didn't feel right, but it felt necessary.

"Oh my God, my dad."

Back inside his suite, Mitch paused mid-pour. He rarely drank, he explained, but tonight he wanted, no, needed, to take the edge off. "What?" he asked.

"Oh my God," she repeated, exhaling and drawing her knees to her chest. "He told us, and we didn't believe him. We didn't know *to* believe him."

"Told you what?" Mitch asked, topping off the drinks with vermouth. He handed her one, and she threw it back. "Careful. They're stiff."

She met his eyes. Could she tell him? Should she? *I can trust him. Maybe he can make this right.*

"Remember how I told you about prom night?"

Mitch nodded.

"Months later, on October 26, my dad and I were having dinner when—" She paused, unsure how to describe it. "He came off the hinges—I don't know."

Her dad had peered several times outside, paced around and wrung his hands, and then the phone rang. After a brief and uncharacteristically hushed conversation, he'd quietly burst into action. He'd hurried Audrey to the car, shushing her questions, and threw in a bag he appeared to have ready. The wipers could barely keep up with the rain that night. She sat in the passenger side for some time, eyeing the road, trying to recognize where they were headed. An hour in, she no longer recognized the names on the green highway signs. An hour and a half in, they exited the interstate to a road without streetlights. It was rural, and she became anxious. Country roads made her nervous; lose a tire, suffer a medical emergency, need gasoline, and you were screwed in parts like these.

"Dad, where are we going?" she tried.

"Audrey," he began, face forward. "Just trust me."

She turned her head and could make out cornfields.

Eventually, he turned left onto a gravel road and drove the rumbly surface. He put the car in park and without a word turned off its lights, grabbed the bag from the back, and ushered her out. Barely discernible in the rural darkness sat a small log cabin, covered in shriveled vines.

"What the—" Audrey began.

Her dad waved her off and put a finger to his lips. She obliged him, and they stepped over an overgrown path, up a leaning, rickety set of stairs and porch, and inside.

To her surprise, her mom sat on a couch in the dark main room, lit only by a few candles. "Mom?" Audrey said.

"Hey, baby," her mom said, standing and hugging her. "Go upstairs. I'll be up shortly."

Her parents were meeting up in a remote cabin? Alone? "What's going on?"

"Go upstairs, Dree," her dad demanded.

She never disputed that tone. She walked up the creaky stairs. Up on the landing, she walked in place so it would sound as though she kept walking. She turned, hands on the railing.

It was hard to make out what her parents were saying in the nearly pitch-black space. Her mother sounded curt and her father pleading. The longer she listened, the more she could decipher. Her father was insistent: ever since the car accident, someone had been following him. "These people, they showed up right after the police, but I don't think they were police," he said.

Audrey knew what he meant: the officials who'd shown up, asking more questions after the crash. They'd returned the week after she answered their initial questions, and it had struck her how they'd asked less about the crash and more about why Audrey hadn't been found. At the time, her dad theorized they were detectives from some other jurisdiction, seeking to right the local police officers' negligence.

"They've been following me—*us*," he said, his voice rising. "I think it's because I—maybe we—have powers, like supernatural powers, and they know it."

"What on earth do you mean, supernatural powers?" Ana Marlena asked.

"I know how it sounds," Charles began. "I mean I know exactly what you're thinking."

"Have you been drinking?" Ana Marlena hissed.

This, Audrey knew, was not the case. Her father had drank since she was a child, and she knew the smell. In recent months, he'd sounded and appeared more lucid than ever.

"I'll show you," he told her mother. "I'll show you I'm not crazy."

From the top of the staircase, Audrey heard her mother zip a jacket. The door clicked closed. She waited and crept downstairs, pausing and wincing at every creak. Upon reaching the floor, she stopped and crept to a window, moving the curtain ever so slightly to get a glimpse.

Her mom and dad stood out front, near a tire swing, and they were speaking, but Audrey couldn't hear them. She touched the heavy old window and pushed up. No dice. She reached above, careful to move slowly so as not to catch their eye, and swiveled the lock. She pushed up again, and the window moved but loudly. *Be quiet!*

Her mom and dad kept talking. She was in the clear, so she opened it more, enough to hear.

"—I don't know, Ana, I don't know," he was saying. "I don't know if I just developed these or if I had them all along. You know me, Ana, you know—"

"Charles, I can't do this. Dree's eighteen. Couldn't you have left her home? I don't want to fight in front of her. Let's leave and talk tomorrow. You told me you were in danger, and I drove all the way out—"

"We *are* in danger," her dad insisted. "They'll be here shortly. You'll see; I'm not crazy. I need you to see this. We don't have time."

Audrey's mother rubbed both eyebrows, exasperated. Audrey stayed kneeling near the window. Her dad raised his palms to the sky and murmured unintelligible words. Lightning crackled, but it could have been coincidence; it had rained all night. Then lightning crackled *through* him, and his skeleton illuminated impossibly when two fires erupted in each of his palms. Audrey almost cried out but stifled herself.

He didn't flinch. He held the fire and tossed it to the wind, and a slow, fiery vortex wrapped around her parents. They say it sounds like a freight train when the wind does this, but this private tornado was silent, save the slapping of wet leaves sucked in. Her mother's jaw dropped, and she turned in a circle, drinking in the sparkling spectacle. Satisfied, her dad closed his palms. The sparks disappeared, the wind died down, and the leaves squelched to the ground. Her mother's hand was now on her forehead. She moved toward him and took his hand, rubbing the top of it with her other. It had been years since Audrey had witnessed a gentle touch between them.

The moment was short-lived. Gravel rumbled and dust rose as four SUVs sped up to the left of her parents. Her dad stood, quiet, rubbing her hand. When possibly a dozen people exited the dark SUVs, he ran. Several people gave chase, and Audrey screamed when they pulled guns. Her mother looked aghast at the realization that her only daughter had witnessed it all through a window, but she didn't have the time to rush inside and comfort Audrey. More people descended upon her mother, asking where Charles had gone.

"Eventually," Audrey told Mitch in his suite, "they came inside and asked me whether I knew of a place where my dad might be heading. They sounded...suspicious?"

Mitch nodded knowingly, and it bothered Audrey.

How unsurprised you are by the night that was the *surprise of my life.*

Mitch heard her think it. "Sorry," he replied. "By this point, when your dad revealed his powers, they knew you both had powers, and the elders assuredly suspected that you and Charles could have conspired together to not be detected."

"Except I had no idea who he was or who I was. I feel like I blocked the night from my mind."

The night had ended in tears. *Who are you? Are you going to hurt my dad?* she'd asked. She remembered an embroidered patch on the woman's jacket: an infant, wrapped in red, its head eyeless, noseless, and mouthless. Instead of a face, the baby's head was the planet earth.

Audrey had gone on to live only with her mother, and though Ana Marlena tried to spare her daughter, her mother's anguish over her father was palpable. *If only he'd told me sooner he needed help,* she used to say. Without memory of the cabin's events, Audrey had assumed her mother meant he was an alcoholic. But Audrey knew he hadn't been drinking. Confusion was from then forth her reality.

Truth be told, Audrey had never felt angry. She felt hurt.

She remembered now, though, in Mitch's suite, her father's face when those SUVs rolled up. She hoped wherever her dad had gone, he never, ever felt that kind of fear again.

"So crazy I'm remembering parts of this only now," she murmured to herself.

"They likely erased you."

Audrey shook her head, stunned at the thought. "He was a harnesser, right? What you tried to test in me?"

"Yes."

Audrey started to speak and stopped, swallowing. She blinked back tears. "Nothing was ever the same. No one was ever the same. And as much as I appreciate what you did for me—I do—now I'm here, stuck with the people who took it all away."

24

The cafeteria smelled sweet, and on a carefree morning, Audrey would have relished the nostalgia it whipped up: her most-requested dish of her dad was his honey biscuits and slightly spicy gravy, but *his* favorite was warm syrup-slathered anything. Sausage. Cinnamon French toast. Soft pretzels.

Mitch pulled two cartons from a fridge and handed her one. They grabbed the morning's breakfast and headed to an empty corner.

It was the morning hour when Kevin used to run because it was a one-up. When every house he jogged by was dark, he proudly bounded to a five-mile finish before the neighbors brewed the day's coffee.

Mitch and Audrey had stayed up late, barely speaking but restless. Now they were in the cafeteria, alone. The void bothered Audrey. *Do they all sleep so soundly? Am I the only one down here who's plagued by nightmares about the people I love? About the truths I only now know?*

"I don't want it," Audrey said, pushing the orange juice at him once they sat.

"Oh," Mitch replied, cutting the bread before him.

"I don't like pulp." Usually, she'd say sorry. *They* should be sorry.

"I can get you one without," he began, setting down his knife.

"No."

Mitch raised his eyes to her, but she refused to meet him. "Maybe I can get you apple juice?"

She bit her lip, then met his glance with a blistering anger. "Can you get me a life not orchestrated by you people?"

Mitch lowered his gaze. "Audrey. Talk to me."

She glared incredulously. "We talked last night. What more do you need to pretend you didn't already know?" She touched her index fingers together, ticking off items. "Kevin was my life, I wanted to have his children, but he was a lie." She moved her right index finger to another finger. "You're the reason I've spent half my life without my dad." She touched a final finger. "Oh, and PS, Audrey, you felt all of your life you didn't really know who the fuck you were? Ding, ding, ding—you didn't. Thanks."

She paused, lowered her eyes, and met his. Her bottom lip quivered. She shut her eyes and tried to stay angry. She didn't want to cry, but she had so much to cry about.

Mitch chewed his lip, his food seemingly forgotten.

"You've stripped all control from my life for no fault of my own, and I—" She stopped and inhaled. "I'd rather be out there with the lurchers. At least I *know* they're out to get me."

Mitch inhaled sharply.

He looked defeated, but the man before her was powerful. All powerful. *You could have said no. You could have said this isn't right. You could have stopped this "Handler" shit. You didn't. You sat safe in your power, safe in your family, and so long as people like me didn't complicate your day, you were satisfied trapping us in lies you weaved.*

"Why do you have the right?" she asked. "Are you telling me none of your people have used power in ways they shouldn't have?"

"We've made mistakes."

"So how is it right that only us, I don't know, *half-breeds* get controlled when the reality is *anyone* with a power to their finger, to their *thoughts*, can be a danger?" Audrey exhaled. "You all could have built this safe place for more than yourselves. You could have warned us."

"Oh, really?" His tone was uncharacteristically sarcastic. "So people would have readied the troops and fortified their homes because our prophet said so? Because some man saw the future?" Mitch's eyes were dark.

"Prophet?" She reciprocated his terseness with annoyed skepticism.

Mitch shook his head. "Exactly, Audrey."

Audrey stood and picked up her plate. "I'm not hungry. Be safe, Mitch."

He stood and touched her arm. "You can't leave."

"Mitch," she said, turning back around. "No. No more. Don't tell me what I can and cannot do."

WHAT SHE WOULD DO to rewind time and sneak that crimson folder into her clothes so she could devour its pages right now. But she hadn't. Hands shaking, she'd put the folder, the secret reconnaissance of her life, back together that day as best she could and nestled it into alphabetical order the way she'd found it.

Audrey could sneak back into the vault, but she couldn't count on someone unknowingly fingering in the four numerals she'd need to gain access. She'd tried to remember the code, and she was sure she didn't.

Did she dare ask Betty Jane?

No. She trusted Betty Jane, but not enough to reveal that she knew the family's century-old secret. If she revealed that, she might reveal her source, and no matter how blistering her anger, she couldn't envision a time when exposing Mitch would be safe for her. She told him she'd rather be above ground with the lurchers, but it was a bluff.

Could she count on Mitch?

She eyed the clock. Nothing about Mitch's calendar was a given, but maybe she'd catch him. Sometimes he retreated to the steam room after dinner.

When she opened the door, enough steam escaped for her to see sure enough that there he sat, a towel around his waist. She sat opposite him and realized only after the door closed and the flow of steam turned off that another lay within. A woman.

Oof. She couldn't request his help aloud. She envisioned and undid the locks on the blue door but stopped, immediately flipping the locks back. She didn't know the woman. She could be a reader, too.

She could feel his eyes on her. She lay down, draping a towel over her own body, and met his gaze. "I need a favor," she said, hyperaware of her tone.

"What's that?" he replied.

"Remember that, um, book I found? With that crazy twist?"

He shifted and stood, pushing damp hair from his eye. His stare was knowing. "I do."

"Can you help me find it? I want to reread it."

The unfamiliar woman sat up, wrapped her hair in a towel, and left, tipping a slight wave to them both.

Mitch tightened his towel as the door fell closed. "Sure. When?"

"When works for you?" she asked, her tone more familiar.

"I have work soon, but I'll get dressed. Meet you in your room in an hour?"

Audrey sat up. "It's red, Mitch."

"I'll find it."

SHE SLIPPED fingers through the door to extract the folder, thanked him, and tried to shut the door quickly. He wedged the door open with a foot. *Imposing.* Not like the Mitch Gray she'd come to know. He wore a brown military jacket with two broad pockets across the chest. She'd noticed others in uniforms but none like his. A duty belt heavy with weapons spanned his waist. His foot in the door wore a combat boot.

Audrey met his green gray eyes.

"Three things," he started in a low tone.

She stared.

"We've made mistakes. I'm learning. You are a door I've not opened before. It's selfish, but please keep the door open while I figure some shit out."

A cuss word. Not like the Mitch Gray she'd come to know. She softened slightly at his show of self-awareness but didn't respond. She wouldn't make promises here, to him, holding what she held.

"That," he said, his eyes on the folder she clutched, "will be missed." His tone was grave. "I trust you. I have to return at dawn for it."

She nodded.

"Audrey." He looked left and right, confirming—she imagined—they had no audience. "If and when it's safe, I'll take you. So we can see what you can do. Earth is," he paused, inhaling deeply. "We're try—" His voice cracked, and he cleared his throat. "We're trying."

Emotional. Not like the Mitch Gray she'd come to know. Maybe not like the Mitch Gray anyone knew. She nodded.

"Be safe, Mitch." A big feeling crept in now, and she wasn't a fan. She worried for him. No. She cared for him.

He nodded, swallowed, and removed his foot. Now it was Audrey who held open the door, literally anyway, watching and wondering. What kind of work required all of that armor? She could guess, and it made her mouth dry.

She sat down, crimson folder opened fast, and flipped, scanning dates. She needed it back, the day the people who'd filled this folder had stripped from her memory. Mitch had explained that a person recovers an erased memory like one does a drunken one: with help or triggers. But she needed to know *precisely* what happened on October 26 all those years ago, on the day the phone rang and her dad drove them to a cabin and fled, never to see his family again.

She pinched Kevin-related items with the tops of her fingers, reluctant to touch them and more reticent to dive into more evidence of how he'd infiltrated her life. Maybe she'd read them later. It was going to be a long night.

She stopped when she found a pile of documents similar in appearance. *Transcripts*. They began in October. She paged forward. They ended on the date she sought.

FILE NAME: Charles Kelly Call No. 23

Audio length: 10:32

Date of transcription: October 26

SPEAKER 1: Charlie, where have you been? I've been trying to get a hold of you.

SPEAKER 2: Hey, you alone?

SPEAKER 1: Yes, why?

SPEAKER 2: Windows closed? You're inside, right? Can you go to your bedroom? Maybe the closet?

SPEAKER 1: Charlie, I'm inside. Everything all right?

SPEAKER 2: I was convinced I'd gone crazy, but I'm not. I'm fucking not. I need you to listen, okay?

SPEAKER 1: Okay, Charlie.

SPEAKER 2: So, I go to the diner last, I don't know, Thursday or something. Picking up soup for Dree. And I see this black SUV outside, and it's memorable because you know the area—not too many expensive-ass SUVs with blacked-out windows, right?

SPEAKER 1: Right.

SPEAKER 2: And I realize, I swear to you on everything, I've seen this SUV everywhere I've gone the past week. Heinen's, I went for some fresh fish. The office. And now this diner. And I mean, Rachel, I know how this sounds, so I test it. I order the soup, but I don't pick it up. I go to the bathroom window, and I climb through a window and run to the woods there, you know the Metroparks behind Lucky's?

SPEAKER 1: You climbed through the diner's bathroom window?

SPEAKER 2: Yeah, and get this: I stayed in the woods, and after a while, these people came. With flashlights. I hide, right?, and I follow them when they stop searching, and these people get into that SUV, and they drive away.

SPEAKER 1: Could be coincidence.

SPEAKER 2: Could be. So I go home that night, and the SUV is out in front of the house. And I start packing.

SPEAKER 1: Packing for what?

SPEAKER 2: And the next day, the police come back. Said they needed to ask more questions about Dree's car accident. And I was tired and frustrated and, I'll admit to you, scared, so I asked them why again so soon. Because they'd just been here, you know? I mean, I remember it verbatim. I said, "Why all these visits months later? Why two in the same week?" And get this, the one cop says, "We haven't been here since May."

SPEAKER 1: And the others were there—

SPEAKER 2: Last week, what the fuck. I assumed they were cops. Apparently they weren't. And I think whoever they are, they've been following us.

SPEAKER 1: Charlie—

SPEAKER 2: Just hear me out. I know how it sounds. Just listen.

SPEAKER 1: Okay, Charlie.

SPEAKER 2: So the whole police thing, it's got me, I don't know, ready to scream. And I make sure Dree is in bed, and I go outside, and I just, I don't know, I grit my teeth and I'm scared and confused, and I go to scream but of course you can't scream or the cops—the real cops—will be called, so I just, I don't know, I open my mouth and pretend, right?

SPEAKER 1: I guess? Charlie, I can come over tonight.

SPEAKER 2: Wait.

SPEAKER 1: You can tell me more when I get there.

SPEAKER 2: I'm not going to be here long. Anyway, I pretend to scream, and then I hear the weirdest sound. It's like nothing I've ever heard before. It's like a whoosh and then silence. And I open my eyes, and I step to the rocks, and the lake floor, Rachel, it's bare. It's naked. I can see shells and rocks where there's only ever been the lake.

SPEAKER 1: Weird. It's probably some lake thing. The lake can be weird, Charlie.

SPEAKER 2: And I realized, I did it. I pushed and held the waves of Lake Erie back with my, I don't know, my mind.

SPEAKER 1: Charlie, are you drinking?

SPEAKER 2: Rachel. You know I'm not.

SPEAKER 1: This is just—

SPEAKER 2: Just listen. So I experiment. Over the next few days, I try and succeed at the craziest feats. I make the wind blow the swings out back on a still day. I control the lake. And I sit with these, I don't know, thoughts, and it occurs to me: maybe I'm being followed because I have powers?

SPEAKER 1: Why'd you say you're not going to be there long? Charlie, I'm worried.

SPEAKER 2: And I get to thinking, I need to tell Ana Marlena. Maybe I'm a danger to my family, you know? Maybe if I leave—

SPEAKER 1: Charlie, did I lose you?

SPEAKER 2: No.

SPEAKER 1: Charlie, are you okay?

SPEAKER 2: No.

SPEAKER 1: Charlie, are you crying?

SPEAKER 2: Maybe if I leave, these people will leave my family alone. My family will be safe.

SPEAKER 1: Charlie, let me come sit with you.

SPEAKER 2: I have to go. She's on her way.

SPEAKER 1: Who's on her way?

SPEAKER 2: Ana Marlena. She'll never believe me if she can't see it. She's not like you.

SPEAKER 1: Charlie, come on. Let me come over.

SPEAKER 2: No. I have to have her see.

SPEAKER 1: Going to the cabin isn't going to help.

SPEAKER 2: It will. Showing her will help.

SPEAKER 1: Let me come with you.

SPEAKER 2: Wait. What'd you say?

SPEAKER 1: Let me come with you.

SPEAKER 2: No. Before.

SPEAKER 1: Let's stick together. I'm sure there's an explanation.

SPEAKER 2: No. You mentioned the cabin. You don't know the cabin.

SPEAKER 1: You've mentioned it before, Charlie. Don't you remember?

SPEAKER 2: No. I've intentionally never mentioned it.

SPEAKER 1: Charlie, you have.

SPEAKER 2: No.

SPEAKER 1: Charlie, you have, my love. Listen to yourself right now.

SPEAKER 2: How could you know about—oh my God. You're fucking one of them.

END OF AUDIO

AUDREY STARED at the wall as it sank in. Her dad's girlfriend, the woman who'd nearly become a stepmother to her, the woman who'd helped her pick out her black sequined gown for prom and cried when she tried it on, was a Handler.

She placed the last page of the transcript face down, the shake back in her hands. After it were handwritten notes.

We continue to monitor Charles Kelly's accounts. No log-ins to email or social media. No pings on his cell phone. His debit and credit cards remain open but unused. If Charles Kelly is alive, we don't know where.

She read dozens of scribbled-out dates and sets of initials indicating that she wasn't the only one wondering where her father was. Some of the notes were as recent as last year. A society of people, some of whom could read minds, had been hunting him and had found neither hide nor hair.

Oh, Daddy, she thought. *You must feel so alone.*

25

January

Eight months after

Twice a week or more, depending on the latest reports and elder requests (er, demands), Mitch would lead a team above ground. The elders and Descendant leaders counted on their and others' armies to fight the creatures with the charcoal black eyes and ghoulish mouths. But they craved firsthand reports from Mitch himself. He knew to watch for signs that the armies didn't.

Mitch and the team rarely left the Underground after daybreak. Again, his alarm blared at 12:40 a.m., and he dressed and made his way to the blood-red door with the circular door pull. A Handler on duty nodded at him. "Sir."

"Morning," Mitch replied.

"The team awaits you."

"Thanks, H74."

On the other side of the door and up the hallway, he met with the five. He had the jitters, but he knew better than to show them. All carried weapons. One slugged down her coffee and tossed the paper cup in a nearby garbage can. They greeted Mitch with "good mornings," and he returned the greeting even though nothing about "run" mornings felt good. "Let's," he said, walking toward the door, which another Handler opened for them. Out the mountainside they emerged.

It was late winter now, and apparently it had snowed. "Don't miss this shit," a team member whispered.

Mitch turned and stared.

The team member shut up. They couldn't risk being heard. Mitch paused and created a circle with his hands, and the team followed his unspoken command and closed in together. He knew his green gray eyes were turning black, and the wind picked up. He touched each person's left shoulder and crossed his muscular arms before his chest. The air crackled. Mitch fumbled a bit in the dark to find a stone off the forest ground and threw it at one of the female assassins. It bounced off the force field. They were protected—for a while. Mitch was already sweating, despite the frigid air, because of the energy required.

The earth was mercifully quiet this morning—a welcome sign after eight months of fighting. Though the team stood in a forest, which one would assume *would* be still, there had been more mornings than they could count marked by guttural screams and gunshots.

Mitch and the team walked to the road and followed it for a while, observing and listening. He saw no evidence of new, dark, erratic scorch marks indicating landings—more reason to feel optimistic. Maybe the lurchers were getting the sense this place couldn't be theirs.

STOP, he suddenly urged them without speaking. No one moved. Many feet down the road, barely visible, was a figure. *Cloak yourselves.* Every team member disappeared, save Mitch. Invisibility was one of the only powers he didn't possess. The six stood quietly as the figure tripped off the road and headed slowly toward the forest. It would probably have stood half as tall as the trees if it didn't lurch so. *Stay here.* They did.

Eyes still black, Mitch quietly followed the figure. With one palm outstretched toward the figure, which bumbled away from the road and toward the woods, Mitch extended his fingers, then folded them into a tight ball. His fist shook, and the figure turned, shrieking. It stumbled into a sprint toward him, snarling, its long limbs reaching for Mitch, but he stood his ground, fist shaking, sweat dripping down his face. Mere body lengths away, the figure's sprint slowed, it whimpered, and it fell. Now it was Mitch who stumbled forward. His team knew not to intervene. He righted himself and looked at the thing. It lay, splayed out and lifeless.

The team walked for another hour and a half, but the dead creature was the only living organism they saw. It was still so oddly quiet. Drenched in sweat because he had to keep fierce guard on morning runs, Mitch bit his lip, worried the silence meant more dead people. *Earth will not be yours,* he thought. *You'll have to kill* me.

It took her breath away to watch him murder, even if what he mercilessly ended was one of those heinous monsters. This man had touched her gently and passionately, and Audrey stood behind him as he panted and strained, his resolve outright incredible. She would have burst into a terrified sprint if one of those monsters reached and stumbled for her, but Mitch *knew*. He knew he would kill the thing with his *hand*. His *mind*.

I want to sleep with a killer, she realized, shaking her head as she watched the others stand silently, apparently waiting for him to give them an all-clear. How many times had she been alone with this man, who could end you with a thought? Of all the things he *had* divulged, he definitely had not revealed he could slay with his mind.

She'd asked Mitch to run with her in the mornings a few times, but Mitch had declined because of "work" he had to do before dawn. What work? she'd asked three times since, wondering if in actuality, he didn't trust himself alone with her while so many slept. She'd thought better of that suspicion when he met her third inquiry with a stern, "Audrey, it's classified," and then she'd hatched a plan. Woken at midnight by her alarm clock, Audrey had stuffed her curls into a sloppy bun, rolled on some deodorant, and spent too much time deciding what to wear when she didn't intend to be seen. (She went with a couple hoodies because she didn't have a coat; the Underground was perfectly regulated and she wasn't supposed to go outside, so she hadn't been given a coat.) She had had enough of secrets, of these people deciding what she would know and what she could handle. She would return to her roots and investigate.

"Disappear," she'd told her reflection that morning. She definitely had the hang of this, because the all-over tingles had spread swiftly, and she'd disappeared. Audrey hadn't been able to see herself in the mirror, but she'd smiled. To learn she'd lived a half-life all of those years she'd spent so unsure of herself felt *better*—like *of course* she'd felt that way. Before this, she hadn't known herself. She hadn't been allowed to know or be herself. Discovering and mastering this innate part of her felt satisfying. Tingling and with a burgeoning confidence —along with a deep, stomach-twisting fear—Audrey followed Mitch carefully from the main corridor to the team, all of whom were carrying weapons.

When she stepped outside and cleared the group's vicinity, she allowed herself a moment. A moment in the air, biting as it was, to relish that it was outside air, not inside air. It felt so good. So natural. So big and free. That was before he killed and before *it* happened.

Mitch apparently gave a direction she couldn't hear because she couldn't read minds, apparent when the team quickened its pace. She hung back a bit because she didn't know whether a bump into others would reveal her cloaked status. Her eyes widened, and she hurried her steps, carefully breaking into a jog, when it became clear they headed for the red door. She fell in line behind Mitch, confident she'd pull off this incognito mission, until the door opened with a hustle of bodies she didn't dare close in on, then closed in her face.

Oh my God, it's closed, and she raised her palms to pound the door but remembered she wasn't supposed to be here. Her anxiety exploded, and she whimpered. She definitely hadn't anticipated this blunder.

What do I do? Audrey thought. She couldn't knock, could she? And she had no clue when the door would open again, affording her the opportunity to sneak back in. She feared his reaction, but he had a lot to lose, too. She unlocked the locks on her thoughts and opened the door. *Mitch, I followed you. I'm locked out. Please help me.*

The night sky was lightening, and her panic built with breakneck force. Dawn was imminent.

MITCH STOPPED IMMEDIATELY in the hallway.

His team member, not expecting it, bumped into him. "Oops, sorry. Something wrong?" she asked.

He shook his head and motioned for the team to keep going. *Seem calm*, he told himself. "No. I'll meet you in the cafeteria." They ate together after runs above ground. But he'd heard Audrey's cry for help, and daybreak was near.

He turned back up the hallway, his thoughts disordered. *What do I say?* Handlers supervised who came in and out, and those movements were recorded meticulously and monitored by the elders. *Better yet, what do I tell* them?

I'm coming, he replied to Audrey, then shook his head. She couldn't hear, he had to remember. She didn't read minds.

"Sir?" the Handler at the door greeted him, an eyebrow raised.

"I need to double-check something."

"Alone, sir? The elders would advise against this. You know the proto—"

"H28." Mitch pitched his head toward the door, and the man quieted. He keyed in a code on the touch screen to the left of the hefty door, and swung it open. "Thank you," Mitch said. "I'll be swift."

Mitch's exhale was visible in the wintry air. *Where are you?* he wondered.

"Hey," he hissed. She immediately uncloaked, and he located her, shivering on the low branches of a tree. She wasn't dressed for the landscape around them, but of course she wasn't. *You are not supposed to be outside. Ever.* Dawn's first light was spreading. Ohio winter, though unforgiving in her brutal cold and depressing darkness, had a softness about her, too. He could begin to make it out now, the snow blanketing the forest ground and lacing the trees. Audrey climbed down quietly. "You've got to cloak. My God, if they see you."

Audrey immediately disappeared before him.

They made it back into the Underground without question, Audrey invisible. Though Mitch had vast experience walking with cloaked beings, he didn't have much of that experience in the Underground, where people were forced into proximity, and worse, where people never failed to want to stop him. He deftly navigated a couple of attempts, assuring a cousin and a pregnant woman that he'd be by to see to them after he handled "something." Lucky for him, Audrey kept her cloaked body to the periphery, and the Descendants took "not now" for an answer.

HE LED them to her suite, thinking it less a fatal error were they to be caught there than in his. Her teeth chattered still from the cold.

"What were you thinking?" Mitch hissed, rubbing her arms to warm her. "You cannot be out there, Audrey. *I* cannot be out there alone."

"I'm sorry, I just—I had to know. Where you go. What you do."

Mitch exhaled, frustrated. "This is an apocalypse the earth has never endured, never survived, and you're following me into it because you're *curious*? Now I've got to figure out what I tell the elders about why I stepped outside 'alone.' Audrey, lying to them is next to impossible." He scratched his neck.

Audrey rubbed her hands together, eyes down. The way a single tendril bounced upon her head as she moved caught his eye, as did her trembling lips. Ohio's cold had reddened her cheeks, and it made her more beautiful.

"I followed you because I'm angry," she said, her gray eyes meeting his. "I feel *owned.* I need *some* control over me. I need to know all of who I am. I want to know what's happening and who you are. I can't begin to understand why I—" She drew in a shaky breath. "Why *I*, I don't know, even knowing all of this shit about what your people have done to my family, why *I* want *you*. What I do with those feelings. It feels treasonous. I'm such a fucking mess."

He touched his temple, quiet, and rubbed his face. He reached for and cupped her bright red, chilled cheek in his hand. *We've taken so much from you, and we cannot give any of it back*, he thought, thumbing her cheek. He sighed, resigned to it, to his own treason.

"I don't know what to do either," he said, moving his hands down the length of her torso. "I cannot feel this way, and even with all of this," he said, his palms now hugging her hips, "I do. I just do."

Mitch lifted her face and pressed his lips against hers. Audrey stiffened but quickly wrapped her arms around his torso, pressing into him. His hands stayed on her hips, and she pulled his hips forward. She tasted as good as she had the first time—no, even better—and they must have kissed for ten minutes. The way she melted into him made him desire her like nothing before. Like the last time, she begged for more, but he knew they were waiting for him.

Mitch pulled away. "I don't know what we will do, but I have to return to my team."

She pouted, but with self-awareness, and he smiled.

"Right now, I want you to be safe," he said softly, tracing her lip with his index finger. "I know you need more. I know you're restless. But I need you to trust me. None of this works if you don't."

Audrey nodded him gone.

Mitch situated himself and left for the cafeteria. He didn't have time to predict where Audrey and he would go from here. The elders would interrogate him next time he stood before them about what he'd needed to "double-check," and right now, he needed to check in with his team. They were sure to be wondering where he went. Mitch wasn't a good liar, but he'd have to be one this morning.

26

Ears wagged an index finger, and Amelia pouted and flipped back over the small cardboard square, a sheepish grin carving deep dimples into her face. The two took competition to a new level when they played the Sesame Street memory game, and he did not tolerate her cheating, even if she was six. Kevin liked to watch them, Ears a silent enforcer of the rules, Amelia squealing with each victory she seized. Today, though, he didn't have time to watch.

None of them had time. He passed them bowls of elbow macaroni and tomato sauce and everyone dug in with spoons. These were their smallest portions to date.

The cellar had dwindled so much that they were more strictly rationing. Tonight's attempt—the fourth—felt heavier to him. Winston and he would not likely return until they found food, even if it kept them out, exposed, past sunrise.

"My rock," Winston told Kevin the third time they locked up after carefully navigating a return home. "I couldn't do this without you."

"You could," Kevin assured.

"Ice in those veins," Winston admired, shaking his head.

Kevin chewed his lip when praised for his cool demeanor in the face of stress. He'd come to possess that fortitude in the worst of ways: years of bitter abuse, ended only when his abuser died. But he could respect the ways he'd kept his cool.

"We have time, we'll find what we need," Kevin had assured Winston, who'd bloodied a fist punching a tree when they'd realized Run No. 2 had failed. Winston had pumped those same fists silently when they'd gained access inside the last home they tried, but his celebration was premature. They'd found perishable food all perished, the stench of it lingering long after they'd closed the fridge. It was a lesson to them both: with electricity most assuredly off in most structures, checking refrigerators was a futile, foul waste. The home's cabinets had proven bare, but the wrappers and cans and boxes littered in and around them led the two to agree later, sealed safely back inside their home, that the former inhabitants had eaten what they had long after the monsters had invaded. Had those people fled to some safe haven that they also could find?

Kevin and Winston did not speak of Run No. 3, not with others or each other. Kevin tried to not revisit it because the memory made his stomach turn and saliva flood his mouth. They'd heard a child, and they'd abandoned their hunt for food to find him. Their search had ended with Kevin giving hurried compressions and breaths near a creek, but it was futile. When the crew asked them how they'd come to be covered in mud, the men had met eyes across a dawn-lit room and shaken their heads. They couldn't shower: though Winston and Marcel had prepared better than most, their gasoline for the generator was depleted, so they couldn't pump well water to the bathroom. Kevin and Winston had bathed wordlessly and quickly the next day in the nearby creek. February waters ran the kind of cold that halted one's breath.

All but Marcel let it be. It was clear it bothered him that Winston wouldn't confide in him.

"I'm his husband," Marcel had lamented in confidence one day as he cooked for the crew.

"Marcel," Kevin had begun. "You have to trust him on this."

Run No. 4 would be their most grueling: they were trekking an hour to the one-pump gas station, stopping to check the doors of homes as they went. They felt safest under the night sky out in the open, not walking on the berm because walking there risked snapping twigs and shuffling grass. They exchanged a stiff, quiet high five when they tried the gas station door and it opened.

Kevin tapped Winston on the shoulder and raised a disfigured hand, a stop sign to his friend. He cupped the palm to his ear, an exaggerated show of listening. Inside, they'd be less able to hear what lurked outside. Best to pause and listen now.

Winston nodded.

Neither man heard a sound, and they stepped inside.

Jackpot, Kevin thought. The shelves were disorganized, and they had to step carefully over ransacked food on the tile floor, but they would leave with provisions. Kevin motioned to Winston to follow him to the back cooler and turned his back to him. Winston loaded up the Lightning McQueen backpack with as many water bottles as would fit and zipped it slowly.

They hit up the pasta and other processed dinners next, setting cans and packages inside the duffel bag as quietly as possible. Kevin had never salivated more over a can of dinosaurs and meatballs. When Winston pointed to another aisle, Kevin lifted the bag carefully. *Can't run with this now*, he realized. If he had to, he'd abandon it, he resolved. He wouldn't leave it without cause, however. The crew needed food more than it needed him.

Once Winston's backpack was heavy, too, and carefully closed, the friends began stepping back through the aisles, Kevin's eyes and hands intent on guiding the duffel bag to keep it from knocking against shelves.

Suddenly, Winston pushed down sharply on his shoulder, and Kevin's face snapped left. Winston shoved him down farther and dropped to his knees, stabbing an index finger multiple times forward. Kevin followed his stare, past shelves of charcoal bags and lighter fluid and through the glass wall.

A monster ripped a hose from the gas pump, spilling dark fluid on the pavement in the night. It threw the nozzle—a powerful launch ending in shattering glass—and craned its body. Winston and Kevin sank lower at the sound of its shriek. Kevin clenched the remainder of his hand. Were it up to him, they would stay hidden for hours, days if they had to, waiting for the thing to move on.

Kevin could hear his heartbeat in his ears, and his breaths disobeyed him, coming faster and louder than he preferred. The beast lurched only a few yards away. It swung a hooked tail. Its mouth, even when not shrieking, appeared twisted and gaping. A twisted crown—*horns*—grew from its top.

Then Kevin saw him. He rubbed an eye to confirm it. *What a nut.* Behind the thing, walking *toward* the thing—*what is he thinking?* —was a man, his palms up, his fingers curling in.

Kevin's and Winston's eyes were saucers upon one another. By the time Kevin returned his gaze to the scene out front, the creature looked different—stricken. It stumbled and fell, but Kevin's eyes didn't stay on the beast.

The man behind the creature appeared to snap his fingers, and the pavement ignited. A limb reached for the sky—*unfathomable claws*—and crashed back to the ground as flames consumed the creature. It screamed and stumbled forward. All fell silent, save the crackle of flames. The man circled it.

Talk about ice in veins, Kevin thought, an eyebrow raised. He never wanted to be so close to one of the creatures again, yet the man encircling the creature didn't look afraid.

Why do you look familiar? he asked of the assassin. *Why can't I place you?* He hadn't seen the man light or throw a match, and this was the first time he'd seen a person kill one of those haunting things. *How did you do that?* He squinted.

"Psst," Winston hissed. The friend placed his mouth on Kevin's ear, his breath hot. "We should approach. Join forces."

Kevin watched the man and shook his head, but he felt stricken with doubt. The man that had actually slayed one of those godforsaken things could just walk away. *Am I damning us all if we don't stop him and get his help? What if he has people, and they have more food, more water, more of an arsenal?* It occurred to him just as quickly: *What if they don't? What if* we *have more?* Which scared him more? Losing potential allies or having food stripped from the crew, his family, all they'd fought to piece together, or worse, their safety? He put his lips to Winston's ear. "We don't know who he is, what he is." He pointed to the means of survival they'd stuffed into bags. "He could steal."

Winston chewed his lip but ultimately nodded.

Kevin and Winston hurried to a back entrance and fled the gas station, sure it would explode. Flames licked its pavement and the blackened form collapsed upon it. Their walk home sounded as silent as the others, but it felt nothing like the others. Twice, Winston and Kevin stopped to hug, exhilarated by what they'd achieved. Kevin had to fight his urge to jump with gratitude and pride.

Every member of the family save Amelia wiped tears when they pulled the Honey Buns and Dinty Moore and Quaker Oats from the bags. Even Amelia listened quietly as Kevin and Winston described what they had witnessed. All cheered at the matches and lighter fluid the men had hastily stowed. Witnessing it, Kevin felt a peace he'd not known since he'd raced upstairs to spare Audrey. He didn't know if she'd survived, but in this moment, he finally felt like he could keep going. Like the universe had at long last given him, them, a win.

"It was crazy, I don't know how the man did it. Maybe he has a team. Maybe they're hunting. Maybe there are more. Maybe we *are* fighting back," Winston spilled excitedly.

Maggie for months had kept a journal she encouraged others to contribute to, though no one did. Kevin suspected no one shared her desire to preserve the memories of these unthinkable days. But a day after Run No. 4, he opened its garish, glitter gold front cover and paged through it. The book reminded him of how Audrey had meticulously stored reporter's notebooks in her home. When he'd asked her why, she'd explained that reporters had to keep and destroy notebooks in a way that protected their newsrooms and their sources. "You never know when a subpoena might come," she'd said. Oh, how Kevin missed her wicked intelligence. Her giggle. The way she maimed her fingernails when nervous. Hell, he missed her hatred of the sound of his chewing. He inhaled, overwhelmed by the cruel questions now accosting him. *Is she alive? If she is, where is she? Is she alone? How do I do this without knowing?* He was responsible for her in more ways than he was paid to be, and now he didn't know her whereabouts.

His fingers shaking now, Kevin paged to the last handwritten note in the gold notebook of his new household. His new family.

February? Maggie had written. She guessed at the months, as none had meticulously kept time. *W and K succeeded today. They brought home food and water.*

And hope, she'd scrawled on its own line. *There's evidence mankind is fighting back.*

WHEN SHE ASKED Betty Jane to work out on this day—early February, she figured—she floated in a cloud of confirmed mutual desire. She would try not to let it consume her, but.

Mitch. His lips had been soft and his body strong, and she felt guilty and wanted and still angry. She didn't want to want him. His family—no, *he* and his family, she wasn't absolving him of any of it—had orchestrated an unthinkable charade, and she couldn't sit long with how they'd irreversibly altered the trajectory of her life. It made a deep pit twist inside her if she let it. She would never get the years back with her dad. Possibly worse, she might never feel she could trust anyone else.

But. There was a part of her, and not an insignificant part, that knew he'd brought her here and not by chance, and she cared for him. She had had only him, really, to lean on for the better part of a year. She knew he protected her. She knew, after watching those creatures gape and shriek and thrash, she might be alive today only because he'd snatched her up that fateful day.

She decided to come out with it. "Hey," Audrey said breathlessly, slowing down her treadmill. "Why did you befriend me?"

Betty Jane raised an eyebrow and kept running, a wisp of hair matted to her face. "You know this, dude. I thought you were reading erotica." She guffawed at herself. Such a memorable laugh from that one.

"Ah," Audrey panted. *How is she a runner?* She knew it was judgmental, to think a woman with meat on her bones wasn't in shape. She certainly had been skinny (before) and not at all fit.

Betty Jane slowed her own treadmill and exhaled. "I was told to."

Audrey's eyes widened and she instantly felt dread. How had she not figured this out?

Betty Jane shook her head. "I'm not a—I'm not formally ... I'm not, ugh, I don't know how to say this." She took a swig of water. "I'm not an enemy. But I was asked to befriend you."

Audrey wanted to say, Jesus, can this family leave me alone? But she hadn't revealed all she knew, and she doubted she should. "Why?" she croaked.

Betty Jane touched her elbow, and Audrey fought the instinct to flinch.

"Seriously. I'm not a threat. Don't be alarmed. They needed you to have someone down here." Betty Jane gulped water.

"They? To what? Watch me?"

"Nah. If I'm honest," and now Betty Jane scanned the gym, confirming it was empty. "They have their ways for that."

Audrey parted her lips. She wasn't going to let on how much she knew.

"They wanted to be sure you had someone. And they know I'm a catch of a friend."

"Really?"

"What? You don't think I'm a catch?"

Audrey smirked. "They really just wanted me to have a friend." Her voice dripped of skepticism.

"The elders, they haven't been very friendly, huh?" Betty Jane was rolling her eyes, presupposing Audrey's answer. "They're not very friendly to anyone. Try not to take it personally. But they're not all bad, and you're here, alone. So yeah, a few asked me to reach out. I told them I would, but I also told them I wasn't going to bullshit you. If we didn't mesh, I wasn't going to force it. You know?"

Audrey's heart rate began to steady. This was plausible. Credible. But it wasn't only the "elders" who kept an arm's length. It was every single one—the men, the women, the grandparents. Last night, a couple had whipped their little one away from a conversation with Audrey about candy. *Candy.* Audrey had stood, stunned, turning so many shades of red and blinking back tears. Even nine months in and having not harmed a hair on a head down here, she remained the Underground's leper. "So why is everyone, I don't know, so unavailable down here? It's not just the people in, I guess, cloaks I've noticed. Everyone clams up around me. Some avoid me as though I've got scabies." Audrey paused. "It hurts my feelings."

Betty Jane shook her head, and Audrey worried she'd annoyed her. The world was ablaze, and Audrey had hurt feelings. But Betty Jane's smile relieved her of that concern, for now.

"People who moved here expected a certain level of comfort, the way you might expect to wear pajamas if you're visiting family."

Audrey nodded, hoping she'd continue.

"But you're here," the woman said, with a seriousness Audrey hadn't witnessed. "They can't be themselves. They don't know you, similarly to how you don't know them. They're not out to get you, Audrey, but they don't know you're not out to get them. Does that make sense?"

Yes, but. I'm not supposed to know. Audrey didn't know how to respond the "right" way. She suspected she could trust Betty Jane, but the woman had been asked to engage with her.

Betty Jane put a palm on Audrey's elbow, stopped walking, and leaned close, uncharacteristically earnest. "I told you things. Now you repay the favor, woman. Tell me what he's like," she whispered.

"Who?"

"Mitch."

Audrey tipped her face, intrigued. "You don't know? I thought every soul down here knew Mitch Gray."

"I know *of* Mitch Gray, but I've spoken maybe seven words to him," Betty Jane said. "My family didn't know the Grays. It's ironic: *you* are getting to know him better than a lot of us he leads."

"Leads how?" Audrey asked.

Betty Jane scoffed. "Come on. No bullshit, remember? Don't tell me you can't see he's the chosen one around here."

Audrey conceded she knew with a tip of her head. "But why Mitch? Why is he in charge?"

Mitch had given her his explanation, but she was curious how Betty Jane would explain it.

Betty Jane took another swig of water and toweled off, apparently done with the workout. "He survived something he shouldn't have. And that, that's not my business to tell. Now, dish."

MITCH SANK his head back into his pillow before throwing his legs over the side of the bed. He would see Audrey this morning. They wouldn't kiss, definitely never again. The last meeting with the elders had made abundantly clear they would have kicked her out if they thought she wasn't a security risk. "She goes outside, she very well may shriek and pound and draw those beasts to our door," one elder had told the others who'd voted unanimously to expel her. Their compromise didn't feel like much of one to Mitch, but it kept her safe. If she disobeyed their directives again, they would have no choice but to eliminate her. He wouldn't dare engage her in illicit behavior at the risk of her own untimely death. Still, he anticipated seeing her all the same.

She had kissed him, and she had tasted like maple oatmeal, and he hadn't forgotten the way she'd pressed her body into his. She monopolized his mind when he ate, when he showered, when he killed. He felt so increasingly attracted to her and ceaselessly guilty and so tired of feeling wrong about everything having to do with her. Mitch wanted to know Audrey in a different time and place, to unwrap what they could be absent an apocalypse and these countless watchful eyes. He shook his head, dismissing the wish, because their closeness wouldn't have materialized without the very reasons that made their intimacy impossible and dangerous. Before all this, he never would have dared touch

Audrey the way he had, and she wouldn't have entertained his advances. Mitch remembered the early days beneath ground, the way she'd talked about Kevin, the way his wellbeing equated to her wellbeing and how sick Kevin's probable death had made her. Pale. Enervated. Broken. If she ever discovered Mitch's involvement in her relationship—Mitch exhaled loudly. So much of what used to make sense, that seemed iron-clad, now made his insides twist with deep-seated, incurable regret.

He dressed in uniform for his duty later, and as he buttoned his coat, he stopped, turned, and opened his sock drawer. His fingers felt around, diving beneath rolled sock pairs, rummaging past nail clippers to the drawer's left-most corner. For a brief moment, his fingers' hunt accelerated with worry, but then his fingers closed in on it, a button. The brown, leaf-shaped button belonging to Samantha Gray. *Mom.*

What he wouldn't give to go back in time, before it happened, before he lost both Dad and Mom in the span of a couple weeks. He'd been told his mom died of a broken heart, and the thought perpetually pierced his own. Rationally, he knew there was nothing a child could have done to mend what his mother lost that night, but cruelly, he'd never stopped wondering if he could have—should have—saved her.

Mitch fingered the button. His mother had worn her forest green dress with the buttons so often. He could picture her wearing it in the mansion's kitchen, chopping root vegetables for hours for a Feast of Maturation. "I feel one with the earth," she'd say, kissing the veggies in a cartoonish way. "Of course I am one with the earth," she'd giggle. Samantha had retained her harnesser abilities after she'd birthed her only baby. Mitch used to feel those leaf-shaped buttons rub his face when she gave him hugs, almost always kissing his nose. Before they'd buried his mother in her favorite dress, Mitch had extracted the button he held now, the top-most one, and when the Descendants were told to store their most precious possessions in the Underground before *it* happened, the button was one of two treasures Mitch had tucked away. The other was his father's picture album.

What he wouldn't give, what he wouldn't give, what he wouldn't give.

Mitch peered at the button, then safeguarded it to the far left corner of his drawer and sat on his bed, his belt and weapons digging into his stomach. When the thought interrupted him—what kind of mother would Audrey be?—he stood and walked away from it. Were it left to the elders, the Descendants, and the Handler protocol, were it left to Mitch himself pre-this, she would never be a mother. "Untoward blood lines must be stopped at all costs," they used to teach them.

But Mitch wanted Audrey to have the children she so clearly desired. Mitch wanted her to sail on to so much more than they would have orchestrated. And, hypocritically, a part of Mitch wanted now for her to do it with him. It was lust, yes, as most early attraction is, but it was more than that.

He was walking the corridors now, coincidentally behind a couple. He envied the ease with which they showed affection, the man's hand on the small of the woman's back, her hand tucked into his back pocket.

What am I supposed to do with this? Bury it? Bury the one time it feels this way?

He followed the couple into the cafeteria and scanned the room. He didn't smile or wave or show his excitement, but when he spotted her, sipping from a mug, her round face framed by that lion's mane of curls, his heart beat faster and his breath caught, and then he approached.

THIS TIME when he offered the OJ, Mitch swiftly apologized. "I forgot about the pulp. Not sure how, given—"

She felt bad and waved him off, thankful for innocuous conversation. "I don't mind it that much."

Mitch set the juice down, an awkwardness about his behavior

dissipating. "Oh, this place," he said in a low tone, though it probably wasn't necessary, given the isolated diners in the cafeteria.

Audrey knew what he meant, this first time they were back together. Awkward, though not the Underground's fault entirely. "I feel you."

She watched him sit and felt at ease. She hoped it wouldn't put him off, but she'd been bold with Betty Jane, and it had worked out, so she decided to be bold with him.

"Who would you be if you weren't Mitch Gray?" she tried again.

"You journalists are a dog with a bone."

Audrey tilted her head unapologetically.

"Maybe a freer me, but who knows who that is. You?"

"I don't know. Better. So many above ground—they deserve another chance, too. They deserve all the chances we have to give. Hard to believe that for so many, this is the end." Audrey ducked her chin and eyes, thinking. *Mom. Dad.* "I would have forgiven my dad before all this. I spent too much time clutching my anger. Too much time desperate to find, to create family when I had family. I took a lot of things for granted and a lot of people, too."

Mitch dipped his meat into syrup, bit it, and chewed, his eyes on the room. "Been there. I have resented my lot in life more than is fair." He swallowed and met her eyes. "You can forgive him without hearing him ask for it."

She'd brought her dad up, but in truth, Audrey didn't care to talk about him. She propped her face in her hand. "Betty Jane said something so curious about you, that you survived something you shouldn't have."

Mitch stiffened. He turned his head briefly to the ceiling. "You know how you don't like talking about your dad?"

Audrey nodded.

"I don't talk about that."

Twenty-five years before

The press got it all wrong, but they always did where these matters were concerned, and when Mitch realized their errors many years later, he'd been ... frustrated. At every point, the Descendants' truth was not one the world could understand, *would* understand, and the Descendants knew demanding a correction would only draw unwanted attention.

Child, five, saved after fall from bridge. That was the headline. When police arrived, both adult men were in full arrest.

Samantha Gray was the police's only witness. She was also the Descendants' witness, and she was credible, but what she recounted was unheard of, even to the elders. The man had dove into the river after a child. The media reported it was his child. Warren Gray was driving Samantha down the road and saw it. He saw the child slip and the man dive, and he screeched their vehicle to the side, his seatbelt flung off and his door open before the car had stopped.

Samantha screamed, terrified, as Warren sprinted and flung himself off the bridge. "It felt like forever," she told both audiences, the police and the elders, of those moments she'd peered over the barrier, waiting to see or hear anything below. Warren surfaced with the child, who coughed and gagged, and the male, too, who didn't make a sound. Samantha couldn't see much until she stumbled down the embankment to where Warren swam them to shore and commenced CPR.

She held the child while the child sobbed, and she rocked and recited a protection spell as her husband breathed and pressed, breathed and pressed. (She said not a word about the spell to police.) When the man didn't move, Warren Gray stopped compressions, placed his hands on the man's body, mumbled words she wished in retrospect she'd been able to hear, and seized. His seizures continued until the man beneath him gasped and pushed away from the earth. Warren slumped before Samantha, who stumbled away from the child and screamed when she gathered her husband's limp head in her hands. A crowd now gathered, and the police lights bounced off the water's surface and the land, and some number of officers bounded down the grassy hill. They were able to save the child's dad, who later made headlines with descriptions of feeling resurrected from the dead. The man had seen an afterlife, he was quoted as saying, and "it felt benevolent."

Warren Gray was not saved. Mitch would never forget the way his mother's eyes swelled with tears, the way she bit her quivering lip, the way she stroked his hair when she told him Daddy was gone.

The papers the next day reported that police surmised Warren Gray had died of the stress. The Descendants didn't know why he'd died, but they knew what the media reported was unlikely. Warren Gray was the strongest among them. Giving CPR most certainly didn't take what should have been a longer-than-mortal life.

The Descendants held a deep derision for the media, given all they did not know and did not catch. The papers, in every follow-up story printed, pronounced Warren Gray a hero. This time, they acquiesced, the media got it right.

Twenty-three years before

Before Mitch, the Descendants hadn't known a child could do it. After Mitch, the Descendants taught children when they were learning to wield: You don't save a life. Even if you can, you do not. Saving a life extinguishes yours.

Mitch was a child when it happened.

The linens were pressed, the picture frames were plenty, and the casseroles scooped creamy. His aunt wore a black gown and navigated the home, thanking those there and tearfully absorbing their stories about her husband, but she wasn't present. She was miles away. *Grief* away. He knew how that could feel, having spent the last two years navigating his own grief journey as an orphan after his mother died so quickly after his father had. When Aunt Tiffany collapsed of her broken heart, a pie plate shattering, Mitch swiftly moved in.

"Move, move!" he said.

Those gathered did as he asked. Later, they'd tell the elders they were in shock. *We didn't know. That's why we didn't stop him. We couldn't have known.*

Mitch Gray did in that moment what no Descendant after him had dared to do. His was a power some had heard of before, in Warren Gray, but they'd not recognized entirely the correlation between death and giving life until the boy who should lead them gave life and died.

He came upon her in wind and fury, and the entire room fell silent, save the rustle of objects. His eyes flashed black, and he leaned into her, all of her. "No," Mitch said. Both palms placed upon her chest, he said nothing. The room had fallen dark, and no one spoke.

The door to the kitchen burst open and three elders, realizing what he might be doing, rushed inside, shrieking, "No, Mitch! No!"

Mitch didn't hear them. He stood, eyes black, the woman beneath him, her daughters kneeled before it all. He couldn't remember it, but they'd told him afterward. "Rise," he spoke. Light from somewhere blinded the room, and Mitch dropped to his knees.

"No, Mitch!" the elders shrieked in a swelling of fears. "No, no, no!" The Descendants in the room clutched themselves or each other.

He crumpled and laid still. She stayed still. The elders burst into action, swarming the boy. A man checked Mitch's pulse and grimly shook his head. They had to save him. They had to. The woman's daughters, Mitch's cousins, wailed. The light faded from the room, leaving it dark with lost potential.

A single minute passed.

Suddenly, Mitch gasped and gagged, clutching his throat, then his chest, unable to draw in breath. He turned over onto his stomach and kept trying. His nose bled. He seized, and each time he did, the room brightened from some alien source. His audience lived a second nightmare, watching their heir suffer.

He quieted, and he pushed his palms against the linoleum floor, slipping on his own blood. The child stood, wobbly, straightened his blue eyeglasses, and blinked rapidly. The room was lit now, and he turned in a circle, confused by the people staring at him.

Then she stood up. With a collective gasp and sudden action, her daughters became her crutches, holding her elbows.

The elders looked at no one but him. They didn't need each other's corroboration. Mitch Gray had willed a person back to life and survived. To their knowledge, and their knowledge had roots deeper than the spring that would lead them to construct the Ohio Underground where they did, no one had ever done it.

27

March

Ten months after

Some things never change, she thought, shaking her head at her reflection. Audrey had never mastered wrapping a towel around her body in whatever way people do where it actually stays up. She'd without fail resort to nudity or gathering part of the towel in an awkward knob to one side and securing it with a hair tie.

Towel tight, she brushed her teeth and let her hair down to detangle it.

You can forgive him without hearing him ask for it, he'd said. She wasn't ready to concede she'd never see them, her family, again.

She chewed the inside of her lip and set the brush down, eyes forward. The condensation had dripped down the mirror, revealing her reflection. She wiped more steam away and kept eye contact with herself: Audrey in the raw, no makeup, no hair cream, no clothing. She'd disliked this reflection of hers pretty consistently, for one reason or another, for all of her adulthood. She hadn't forgotten the emptiness she felt when she'd pulled the full-length mirror off the bedroom door at her mom's and stuck it, glass to wall, in the corner of her closet. She'd planned to use that mirror to apply makeup from the floor, but two realities solidified the night her dad disappeared: she found it difficult to care whether her eyeliner was even or her eyebrows were filled in, and she found it impossible to not see his gray eyes in her own. Long before the world had ended, she'd rediscovered the motivation most mornings to line her eyes and darken her brows, but she'd never stopped seeing his eyes.

Today, as she peered at herself, the cruel refrain crept in: *half the reason you exist left.*

This day, though, however stuck she felt in a world that started and stopped at a blood-red door she didn't have the power to open, Audrey had answers she had reason to believe. *He left because he was scared. He left to protect me, to protect us. He didn't know what he didn't know. I didn't know what I didn't know.*

She shook out her wet curls, closed her eyes, and willed it. When she reopened the cloud-colored eyes originating from Charles Kelly IV, she couldn't see them anymore. She could see no reflection, and her heart pounded from the exhilaration. *How ironic.* She knew herself better down here, invisible, than she did when free and in plain sight.

Unexpectedly, a memory crept in. Kevin had embraced her from behind, his large hands on her hips, his green eyes locked with hers in the mirror before them. "Couldn't have guessed how much I'd love you," he'd said plainly. "You beautiful, beautiful creature," he'd added, raising a hand to a curl near her eyebrow.

She'd blushed, but she'd believed him. *Really* believed him.

Audrey willed the cloak off and dropped her hands to the sink sides below. *Can I forgive you, too?* She scowled. *Do I want to? Do you deserve it? Do you have to deserve it?*

May

Two years before

When he read the news, Kevin immediately left work. A half hour later he stood staring at a wall of vegetables, his hands in his pockets and his eyes focused but fuzzy on its eggplant blacks and bell pepper yellows and reds and mushroom whites, until a woman reached in front of him to bag some leeks and broke his daze. He opted for cauliflower, a mushroom blend prepacked by the grocer, and radicchio.

Back home, he sauteed the ingredients in garlic and olive oil, layered them between sticky lasagna noodles, and baked his condolences at 350 for an hour. Coach and his family didn't eat meat—at least they hadn't twenty years earlier when Coach taught him to block and tackle and to look a man in the eyes when shaking hands—so he ditched his go-to recipe.

He dropped the lasagna at the family's house on his way to the funeral home, where he found the parking lot and street meters at full capacity. It suited him to walk in the brisk air, to gather his thoughts.

Kevin didn't take the family up on its invitation to share stories. If he had spoken, he would have wanted to tell them about how Coach had taught him so many basic life lessons he hadn't sniffed from his father. That story, he knew based on the ones others did tell, wouldn't surprise a soul in the dimly lit space. He might have told them all something they didn't expect had he explained the green JanSport backpack, the one Coach packed with food and casually threw him every Friday since Coach had unexpectedly visited the Williams house and figured out, among other unmentionables, what the teenager ate when free breakfast and lunch in the cafeteria weren't available. Kevin ate from the backpack for more than a year until he graduated high school. He didn't know if Coach ever told anyone about the thing, which he kept on a top shelf in his closet. Teenager Kevin sure hadn't. It had embarrassed him to need help.

The stories others told about the colleague, father, husband, coach, teacher, neighbor, friend, and competitor Coach had been alternated between making the crowd cry and laugh. It felt warm, yet unsettling. Kevin noticed a sinking feeling in his gut.

Trudging through the rain to his car after he departed, Kevin threw his wallet in the center console and sat in the dark car with the clink, clink, clink of the night's rain and the question that seeped in. *Who would have something of substance to say at yours?*

Within days, he'd submitted his two weeks' notice and later showed up frazzled, six minutes late to his exit interview, pitting out his blue button-down and apologizing. Ever the one hurt by his father's forgetfulness and tardiness, he hated being late, though this HR rep was a friend.

"You're fine, you're fine." She welcomed him in, standing to close the door.

He apologized no fewer than three times, lamenting the coffee stain down his front and the length of time it took to relinquish his badge. He loosened and removed his tie, which had borne the brunt of the spill.

Tatiana sat. "We're going to miss you, Kevin. Our loss is another's gain."

He chewed his lip and scratched his ear. "Maybe so, if I actually had other plans."

"Perfect segue," the woman said, her dark eyes now on the clipboard in her hands. "I know you don't have a new job lined up. What could we have done for you to remain employed here?"

Kevin shook his head and fidgeted with a Rubik's Cube from the edge of her desk. *The hell am I doing.* He had a cushion, but it would cover his bills for only a few months. Four, he'd deduced from a late-night budget review, if he dialed back all unnecessary spending. No beer, especially not craft ones. No cigarettes. No takeout, not even from the diner down the road that served those nostalgic $2.99 breakfast specials.

He doubted himself, too, the morning of the exit interview. *Can't make a difference if you're broke or starving or homeless.* But he remembered the experience, weeks before, as he'd buttoned a shirt and tied a tie and stopped. His hand had dropped, and he'd stared for enough time he'd been late to work. It didn't matter if the shirt was blue and the tie was yellow. *Every day the same,* he'd thought, eyeing himself. *Who's here to notice?* He had no life partner. No roommate. His colleagues, the only people he saw on the regular, had marriage and kids and marathons and you name it to fill their days. Even if he failed to touch people the way Coach did, he needed a change.

It wasn't the life he had imagined for himself decades ago from the only clean room of the house his father ruled. Countless nights in a twin bed nestled against a forest green wall lined with a shelf of football cards, Kevin had decided he'd make a difference for kids like him. Treat—no, cure—mothers like his. Change people for the better.

He woke up in the days after Coach's memorial service, thirty-six years old, tying colorful nooses around his neck on the daily to sell equipment for Evervont.

"Kevin?"

He shook off the memory and glanced at the wet tie in his lap. He put the Rubik's Cube back, his life enough of a puzzle.

"What can I tell leadership about your experience?" Tatiana persisted.

"This is all me." He chuckled. "I don't know, maybe I'm having one of those midlife crises. I need to serve more than a company's bottom line, leave behind more than an improved profit margin. I don't know," he repeated. "I don't know." He exhaled and met her eyes. "I'm being unrealistic. I mean, do most of us ever really make a difference?"

The woman shrugged and smiled patiently.

Kevin immediately leaned forward, palm up and waving, attempting to clear the air. "I didn't mean this work doesn't make a difference, I know the types of clients this firm serves, and I know the impact they make on the world, I—"

"Kevin, it's fine," Tatiana interrupted. She tipped her head to the side and nodded several times, slowly.

She gets it, he thought.

The woman pushed her hair behind her and leaned toward him, her palms flat on the desk, clipboard of questions to the side. "I've got a vocation that might appeal."

"With Evervont?"

She shook her head. "Not with Evervont, per se, no. It's classified."

Kevin folded up his tie and sat back in the chair, skeptical this was a well-intentioned but ill-fated attempt to retain him. "What would I need to do?"

A smile spread across the woman's face. "Let me make an introduction."

"You're local, so you get to meet him," Tatiana said as they stepped inside a deep stone alcove in the front of the most sprawling house Kevin had ever seen, a place shrouded in trees so tall and so thick they had to be centuries old. Carved above the front door were a family crest and a motto; Kevin didn't have enough time to tell what they were, and he couldn't read Latin anyway.

He hadn't a clue what she meant, but he did meet a man who looked to be Kevin's age. Tatiana didn't call the man by his name; she called him sir.

The man spent an hour explaining the opportunity; Kevin noticed the rough passage of time by the number of chimes from the tall grandfather clock near the mammoth stone fireplace.

Well before puberty, Kevin had developed a healthy reluctance to ask questions. His father resented even innocuous questions from his son, and Kevin had come to fear the clench of the man's jaw so much he would proactively tell him, "Sorry, Daddy, I'll shut my big mouth." Questions the man perceived as disputing his authority cost Kevin a tooth once and earned him bruises countless times.

Kevin's silence, then and now in this peculiar, gilded place with a man he presumed was some executive, didn't mean he *had* no questions. But he did not worry the way he suspected others might.

He earnestly did not want children, so he didn't worry the commitment to not have children required too much. In fact, when the man seated before him shared the unorthodox prohibition, he felt relief. It felt attractive to have such a decision not be his to make.

Kevin was nearing his forties without a wife, so whether he'd marry had been an unsettled matter for some time. His colleagues found it curious, but he shrugged it off. *Most women our age want children,* he'd explained it away more than once.

And he feared it only a little, giving his full self, his every day, to a cause. In many ways, the desire for a duty requiring more than the 8-to-5 and giving more in return was precisely why he'd quit Evervont. The older he got, the more he felt the need to create *some* legacy.

As much as he wanted a greater cause in this life, and as much as his friend in HR and the man in the military jacket said this would be it, what they described sounded implausible. *Who doesn't know they have powers? Why not bring them into the fold rather than orchestrate this elaborate sham? How has this been going on for more than a hundred years and no one knows?*

And, his eyes wandering the room, *what* is *this place?* It felt like a scene from the Titanic. Ornately carved wood walls and warmly lit sconces enveloped the trio. The few framed portraits of people fit right in. The buck antlers mounted to the wall spanned the length of a man.

"It's Graylock Mansion," the man said.

Kevin's eyes dropped from the arched, wood-panel ceiling and met the man's. "Yeah, I was wondering."

The man nodded. "Been in the family for a long time."

"What family?"

"The Grays."

"Your family?"

"My family. If you join us, it would become yours in many respects."

Kevin rubbed his eyebrows and crossed a leg over a knee. "I have some questions, if you don't mind."

The man regarded him. "Perhaps I'll start with the ones you thought to yourself?"

Tatiana's feathers were unruffled, but his were splayed. *Did he just insinuate he can read my mind?*

"I can."

Kevin's head snapped back toward the man.

"What was your first? Who doesn't know they have powers?"

The hairs on Kevin's body rose.

"Some things are confidential and some we can't definitively know, so I can't share numbers. We've learned from those we monitor, though, that it's easy to dismiss the infrequent surfacing or unintentional use of a power as some coincidence or illogical experience."

Kevin stared. This was wild.

"Think of the athletic greats and their children, many of whom grow up playing the sport their fathers did. If they grew up in a household where knitting was king, would those same children know their proclivity for that sport?" Mitch stood and pulled a drawer from a desk nearby. It sounded as old and looked as ornate as the room. "When you don't grow up learning you have an ability, it's actually natural to never realize you have it."

Sitting back down, Mitch extended a few photographs.

"You wondered why not bring these people into our world. The simple answer is, that's not how our ancestors set about handling matters, and the way we've been handling things has mitigated the risk we perceive." The man tipped his head. "You know the adage: if it ain't broke."

In the top black and white photograph, a man and a woman stood, holding hands. The man wore an overcoat with a short shoulder cape over top, his eyes on the woman. Beneath that image was another of the same man and woman near this sprawling estate, only its grounds were covered in snow and its trees weren't tall. Yet.

"My great-grandmother died because a woman discovered powers she didn't know to control."

"I'm sorry."

"This is the protocol the family laid forth so we could avoid it happening again."

"Has it happened again?"

"Yes, but no one died. Our mitigation protocol proved effective."

"And these people with powers they don't know they have, are they everywhere? I imagine they're not only in Ohio."

"They're not in Ohio only."

"So you have these people, people like me if I—if we—do this, elsewhere?"

"Oh, yes."

Kevin nodded. *So Northeast Ohio is the brains of a global supernatural power-controlling operation.* He shook his head slightly. *Who would have thought?*

"Everything starts somewhere," the man said.

"No, you're right," Kevin replied. He scratched the back of his neck. The man had told him what were most certainly closely guarded secrets. Didn't he *have* to accept the work now?

"We prefer you make the decision when the elders visit," the man began, again responding to words Kevin hadn't spoken. "Giving you time to think on this is wise. And you don't have to do this, no."

"When the who visit?"

"The elders."

"Visit me where? Will they know who I am? Will I know who they are?"

The man smiled, the skin crinkling at the corners of his eyes. "They'll know who you are, Mr. Williams."

August

One year, nine months before

The woman, young, plump, beautiful, and fidgeting with her fingers, stilled the room with her question. She opened her mouth, closed it, then grinned, embarrassed. "I know how this might sound, but what if he's abysmal at sex? Am I to sleep with only him for the rest of my life?"

The elders at the front of the room paused. The entire room of those training—people of all ethnicities and ages and motivations—waited.

"You signed up for this, yes?" a male elder replied.

"Well, yeah, but—"

"This is why we tell you your commitment must be steadfast," the man interrupted her. "This is not for the fickle or the faint. Your assignments may be arduous for more reasons than one. We ask you to accept the missions without stipulation. We also ask you to be honest with yourselves and us. If you feel incapable of serving, it's best we know before we place you. You are not a Descendant, but as a Handler, you become a branch of our family. We selected you scrupulously for your discretion and your dedication to service. We're fortunate for your service, but we also require these attributes of you."

Watching from the back of the room, Kevin had never even considered the problem.

The woman nodded. "I am committed. But this is the place where we can ask anything, yeah?"

The man and woman elders nodded.

"May we stray? If our situations warrant it?"

More than one in the room raised eyebrows, and none shook their heads: all were glad she had the gall.

The elders paused, stared at one another.

"If you are assigned to be someone's partner, it's best you be monogamous," one elder said softly. "These are people, H13. Just as you might sense when a partner is unfaithful, they could, too."

The attractive girl, dressed in an impossibly low-cut shirt, didn't argue. She didn't nod either.

The man spoke again. "It's paramount to remember, these people deserve *care*. It's not their fault we must intervene. In truth—" He paused. "It's our fault. The Handler mission is not one we began or continue lightly. Whether you're assigned to befriend or to partner or something else, we ask that you only accept with the best of intentions and assumptions. I'll remind you all: we pay competitive wages and bonuses on top of living expenses."

The girl nodded this time.

They proceeded. The group peppered the elders with more questions about medicating, keeping secrets from family, navigating situations when charges realized they had powers. The elders met those questions with suggestions and orders. *If an assignment realizes they have power, dismiss it. Suggest they imagined whatever it is. Call us immediately.*

"I have a question," raised a man in the back near Kevin. All eyes trained on the man, and the elders encouraged him to speak.

"Why hire humans? If the whole Handler protocol is meant to keep humans with powers unaware that powers exist, why make other humans aware they—*you*—exist?"

The elder nodded. She spoke in a protracted way, as though she knew every person in the room hung on her every word. (She was right.) "It's a fair question. We hire you because we committed errors. Descendants don't know what it is to be you, to be raised as you were. You do. If we mean what we say, and we do, we need your perspectives to do right by these people. You know best how to, well, be human. To live alongside them. To protect them."

"If we have to, do we stifle them with force?" the man persisted.

"Depends on the situation, H7," the male elder replied. "We'd prefer it not come to that, but it has, and it may."

H7 exhaled loudly and shook his head. "I'm going to control what I need to," he replied, and the room fell quieter.

"H7—*Bram*—you will do only what we ask," the elder replied pointedly, and the room took note of her cutting tone. "Acting out can be a tell, and we won't have that."

H7 cast his eyes low in deference. He didn't speak another word.

After about an hour of hearing from the small group, an elder asked, "H23, do you have any queries? You've been rather quiet."

"I do," Kevin—H23 here—replied. "What happens if we try to make our advance, and it doesn't work? I'm assigned to a woman. I'm to become her boyfriend. What if I'm not her type or if I turn her off accidentally?"

"We'll cross that bridge when we get to it," replied the elder. "But we coupled you with her for a reason. We have reason to believe she will respond well."

28

October

One year, seven months before

The Descendant elders reported to Kevin's home two months later, during his favorite of weather systems: thunder booming, lightning flashing, and the earthy smell of land drinking the rain. After he accepted the assignment and they left, he thumbed back through the photographs. A thirty-something-year-old Audrey Kelly wore a sweater against the backdrop of an Ohio orchard in one and raised a brown-sugar-rimmed ale in another. She looked *normal.* And in many ways, she apparently was. She was a reporter. Her parents were divorced, and she'd needed years of therapy to heal from that and other traumas she'd lived. She rode her bike daily, lived alone, and took cooking classes every month. Audrey Kelly also had been known to the Descendants for some time because she had the power to make herself invisible—they called it "cloaking"—though she didn't appear to know it. She was his assignment.

Though he had trained for this, Kevin felt anxious and unprepared: could he infiltrate a woman's life and monitor and manage her while making her feel loved? He hadn't chosen her, and no one really knew whether she would choose him. Handlers who'd done it before assured those in training it could be done. It still felt inconceivable to him.

The elders had left him with a calendar, *her* calendar, and encouraged him to find a natural in. He decided to follow their suggestion and make a move in late October.

The kitchen was large and commercial, and the staff had equipped each station with the ingredients necessary to whip up the meal. Kevin had arrived early and donned a blue apron. His heartbeat quickened when she entered the room. He met her eyes and grinned warmly. It worked.

"Hello," Audrey said, biting her lip and approaching his length of stainless steel counter.

"Hey," he replied. "I'm Kevin."

Her smile widened. "Audrey. You here alone?"

"I am," he replied.

"Want to cook together? We might have to," she began. "Most people come to these coupled up."

Kevin immediately nodded. "Fair warning—there's ample reason I'm taking lessons."

Audrey snickered. "Least you're trying."

That night, they rolled and cut dough together, crafted meatballs with allspice, then simmered them in a cream sauce. They toasted with wine as they ate the palatable puzzle they and others—all couples, Audrey had called it—made during the class. Kevin and Audrey were the only non-couple at the table, but he had an invitation he hoped would change that.

The moon was bright and high as they departed the kitchen. "Thank you," Audrey said as she stepped out the door he held open.

"You're welcome. Tonight was fun."

"I agree!" Her smile was really something.

"Can I walk you to your car?" he asked. They'd crafted Swedish recipes 4,100 miles away from Sweden in a safe suburb of Cleveland, but it felt right to him, walking a woman to her car.

Audrey nodded, and he placed his hand lightly on the small of her back, only for the first moments when she led the way.

"Well, thank you for being my intrepid partner," Audrey began, stopping at her sedan.

"Thank *you*," he replied. "Hey, um—" He paused, stuffing his hands in his pockets. "What about a cookoff, just us? I cook a three-course meal for you, you cook a meal for me?"

Audrey met his eyes and regarded him. "Winner gets?"

He couldn't be sure—they'd met hours ago—but it felt like she was flirting. Her eyes were the first gray eyes he'd seen, and he wasn't sure he'd seen curls so long. "You decide," he said.

"You do remember I've been taking classes for a year?"

He shrugged sheepishly.

"Your funeral," she chirped. She saved her number in his phone as "Top Chef."

They talked daily the entire next week. There was an ease between them. They talked about favorites—his favorite movie was *Stand by Me*, hers *Zero Dark Thirty*. They talked about intensely personal things, too, somehow—how he'd stayed single after his ex cheated, how she'd struggled with guilt after surviving a car crash that killed her high school classmates. None of it so far felt like a farce, and Kevin liked that.

It was his idea, so he offered to cook first, and they weren't skipping a beat: Audrey was available that Saturday, and so was he. Kevin had a menu to plan.

THE MOMENT he answered the door that Saturday night, Audrey surprised him. Dressed in an off-shoulder sundress, she reached and cupped his face and declared, "May I kiss you?"

The pages of background information he'd reviewed didn't come close to revealing the full woman before him or preparing him for her spontaneity. He grinned. "Oh, I suppose." After a week of beaming every time she texted him, touching her—and at her request—was decidedly on the menu. He was fulfilling a duty here, sure, but he'd begun telling himself: *Someone would have been assigned to her no matter what. The least I can do is be good to her. Great to her.*

The dinner he had working would not impress—he was definitely in over his head. Should have stuck to lasagna. His baked potatoes would be nothing special, though he had bought every topping on earth in case: gravy, green onions, sour cream, bacon bits, cheddar. He hoped the filet would salvage dinner.

It wouldn't. He'd stuck the broiler pan too close to the flame, and distracted by taste tests of newly-released pumpkin ales, they realized his mistake only when smoke filled the kitchen. "Oh, shit," he said, rushing from the couch to the room. The fire alarm began to blare. "Ah, shit, no, no," Kevin said, starting the fan. He opened the oven door to cuts of cow ablaze. He pulled them and, wiping his forehead, turned to find Audrey leaning on her elbows, stifling a smile. "Warned you I can't cook." He pushed open the kitchen windows.

"Not sure you told the full truth," she said.

He froze. If he carried out the mission he'd accepted, she would never know the full truth.

"Only kidding, handsome," she said, leaving her ale on the counter and pulling his waist into hers. She kissed his neck, and Kevin closed his eyes.

I didn't think I'd like you this much, he thought.

"Let's scrap this and order in," she suggested.

He felt drunker with her touch.

"First ..." she began, trailing her fingertips along his arm, walking into his living room, and lying down. "I can think of other things we can do."

Kevin scratched the back of his neck and laughed. "Yeah?" he replied, following her.

It didn't surprise nor disappoint him they didn't sleep together that night. He was not ready for it, intimacy with her, his "assignment." It did surprise him they ordered in lo mein and debated two Netflix originals before agreeing to a thriller only for her to fall asleep early, her head on his lap. She snored. She snored a lot.

Kevin liked that she trusted him, but he regretted it, too.

April

One month before

Kevin Williams and Audrey Kelly proved basically inseparable over the next year and a half. He'd expected some of what surfaced—her traumas, getting her medicated. He hadn't expected how he'd come to adore the way she snorted when she laughed, how true to himself he could be because she hid nothing, how fiercely protective of her he felt—only to remember his role wasn't only to protect. He had to suppress.

Kevin's insides twisted when the elders praised his seamless "meshing" and the evidence of their reliable match. "This will prove a long-term coupling," they'd say, figuratively patting themselves on the back.

After those monthly reports, he drank too much, and she would storm out, frustrated. He couldn't tell her he drank to forget the big, fat lie he lived. To forget the updates he delivered on how well the medication-induced suppression of Audrey's abilities was working. (Highly effective. He'd caught not a trace of her power.) To forget how much she'd probably hate him if she knew. How right she'd be to hate him.

The conversation inside Jenny's Diner was the last straw.

"After this, can we go make a baby?" She'd grinned and toyed with his knee suggestively.

He'd immediately lost his appetite and pushed the omelet away. *No, Audrey, we can't have babies because "we" are an elaborate lie, and because you aren't allowed to reproduce.*

"I've got a lot of growing up to do before a baby," he'd said instead.

His self-hatred deepened as she assured him how thoughtful and reliable and loving he was. The rationalizing he'd done for a year and a half began to crumble when he realized not only was he depriving her of the autonomy she deserved, but he was depriving himself of what he wanted. *So you care now, when* you *want different?*

The night he did it, she had plans with girlfriends and tapas. He felt stuck. Conflicted. And he knew better than to intentionally cross the Descendants. He figured some would know he'd cross them before he did merely because he thought it. He dialed the number.

"Graylock Mansion," a woman answered.

"Uh, hi, H23."

"H23, how can we help you?"

"I've got a problem."

"Does Mitch need to be notified?"

"No, ma'am."

"Please hold." The line fell silent until a male answered. "H23, what's the nature of the problem?"

"Sir, I'm unsure how to describe it."

"Detection? Med refusal? Use? Is anyone in danger?"

"No, sir."

"Please disclose, and I'll define."

"This is embarrassing, sir, but I have feelings for her. Unsure how to proceed."

"Have you broken protocol?"

"No, sir."

"Have you continued to use birth control?"

"Yes, sir."

"Are you capable of continuing to serve in your capacity?"

"I'm unsure, sir. My lines are blurring."

"When can you next come here?"

"During the day sometime this week." *Another day, another lie,* Kevin thought. Audrey wouldn't know; he'd be "at work." He hesitated and asked. "Sir, should I be concerned for my safety or hers?"

"No, H23," the male began. "We need to assess and advise. If you cannot continue to serve, we'll wipe your memory and assign another."

Kevin wordlessly hung up. He remembered the harsh tone some Handlers had when they spoke of their "assignments," and he shook his head to shake the memory. Maybe he shouldn't have said a word. He sat on the couch, his eyes boring into a wall they'd painted together, and wished he could take back the last five minutes. His choices were to continue loving Audrey and cheating her of whatever future she should have had, or forget she ever existed and leave her safety and happiness in the hands of another assigned to handle her. He couldn't do either one.

He wouldn't have a choice to make. A month later, the monsters crashed to earth.

29

Theodora's visits were strictly business, and there she was today, knocking at his door. "May I?" she asked.

Mitch immediately widened the door to his suite and stepped out of her way. "Of course."

Theodora stepped inside. "You know why I'm here," she began.

He suspected he did know. Beginning that night, when the aircraft first thundered to earth, the Bishop family had been responsible for monitoring and keeping order to Descendant-human relations above ground. There weren't supposed to be any such relations underground, of course, save the small number of human Handlers who'd been briefed and asked to report to the Underground.

"So, hey," Theodora said. "This sucks." She scratched her dark eyebrow but kept eye contact. "We know what you did."

Mitch shut his tall, heavy door for good measure, though he doubted she'd read him for fear of what she'd hear. Exes don't tend to want to know what the other is thinking.

"You cannot be engaging with humans on your runs, Mitch."

He exhaled carefully. *She's not here to talk about her.* That fear was unrelenting. Mitch blinked. "I don't plan to. Sometimes, it's impossible. I can't not act."

He'd felt the least sorry about the insubordination she was surely here to chastise him for, when he'd found the toddler on the sidewalk, a scruffy stuffed dog held tightly in the crook of his little arm. His team hadn't said a word because, knowing how much of himself Mitch expended to protect them and knowing the human suffering all around their Ohio corner of the earth, they felt loyal to him. Eyes black, Mitch built a force field around the child, lifted the boy into his arms, and stepped onto the front porch of the house the boy pointed to. When he tried the door and it squeaked open, the place appeared empty until a woman stepped into the moonlight permitted within.

"Oh, thank you, thank you," she'd whispered, scooping the boy up in her arms and stifling her sobs in his neck. She tried twice to speak before she could calm down enough to do it. "We were watching through the windows to see if the coast was clear because we need to—" She paused, shaking her head. "And we saw *him.*" Her voice caught. "We didn't know he'd left. I don't know how you got him back here without *them* catching you, but thank you."

Surprisingly, and luckily for the boy, Mitch hadn't crossed paths with a lurcher that night. Mitch touched her shoulder, told her to lock up, and said, "Stay put longer than you think you can stand it." Mitch turned to leave, but she pleaded.

"Please, can we come with you? Where are you headed? We can't keep doing this." Her eyes welled.

He paused. He didn't want to leave them. They deserved better—to sleep soundly, to eat well, to be protected. He met the woman's eyes and shook his thought away. "We will return. Stay—longer than you think you can stand it."

He never shook the scene from his mind: the child in dragon jammies and the woman, wrapped up in each other, closing the door on him. Mitch wasn't sure he would ever stop wondering if they lived.

Loyal as they were, his team members were required to report anomalies. Theodora's visit wasn't unexpected for this reason, and it wasn't her first.

"Mitch, you *can* not act," Theodora replied. "We can't have humans thinking salvation is coming their way because it isn't." She paused. "They must save themselves, as we must. Seems you need reminding again."

Mitch and she stood for a moment, awkward, just inside his suite. He fiddled with his watch.

She sighed. "You remember what preparations felt like? You remember what they said about our success, about you?"

Of course he did. It was nearly a decade ago when his twenty-five-year-old self had been summoned to Graylock and told the news: the Descendants had discovered an unprecedented threat from the mouth of the only one among them who could prophesize.

TEN YEARS *before*

"In here, Mitch," an elder urged him, hurrying him beneath the ivy and inside the mansion.

"What is this about?" Mitch asked, following the man. It was the first time the elders had demanded his presence in "less than an hour" at Graylock.

"We'll tell you more in a minute, Mitch." The man spoke not another word and led Mitch down the mansion's hallways, lit with lamps. They hurried beneath arched wood and by solemn family photographs. Radiators hissed.

Eventually, they stepped inside the place's brains, full of camera feeds and burning sage. Perpetually burning sage. Mitch sucked in his breath when he found every elder seated, save the one who'd met him at the east wing and let him in. This was a sight to behold. It made his stomach bottom out.

"Let us commence," a woman said, rising as he sat down. "Elders. Mitch. Evil nears."

She bowed her head, and the only Descendant known to prophesize stood. He didn't need a projector screen; their minds would do. Muttering beneath his breath and shuffling around the room, sprinkling salt in a circle around them as protection, the man held up his palms and spoke. "See."

The aromatic room before Mitch disappeared. He gasped. It was the first time his eyes were not his own, and figures with blood-red faces, charcoal-sized, black eyes, and mouths ghoulishly agape lurched into him, clawing. He startled backward in his seat and almost fell over. He righted himself, panting.

Much more aware that what they collectively witnessed was a prophesy, none of the others moved. It smelled of dead bodies.

How can it stink if it's not real? Mitch wondered.

"This comes for us," the prophet began, projecting into their minds the terrifying scenes of his vision. "In five or ten years' time, I'm sorry I cannot tell. It will kill humans. It will kill us. They want our earth. They believe nothing more powerful will meet them.

"We must defeat them." The prophet turned to Mitch, his eyes black, but staring him down. "*You* must."

The following months proved unforgettably miserable for Mitch. They didn't know when the threat would materialize, so they needed Mitch to be ready. He spent six days a week pushing and pulling weights and running the mansion's grounds until his lungs mercilessly burned. One time, and only one time, after a particularly strenuous five-mile run, he panted and sputtered, "Is this necessary? I'm not going to defeat them with my body."

"Mitch, it will take every power you have, mortal and otherwise, to survive," the beefy Descendant overseeing his training replied. "We need you to endure."

It was an unsettling but valuable lesson for him to learn. Power, he'd thought, was that which he wielded with his mind, but power stemmed from his humanness, too. (Seemed ironic that Descendants who crowed about how they weren't fully human now stressed to him the need to lean into his humanness.) He wondered, why not enlist mere humans to this fight? He didn't vocalize that thought.

Mitch wiped the sweat off his brow and doubled down on the

exercise that day. But he was tired. He was tired of the physical demands, and he was tired of the mental load.

The worst were the trainings specific to the dangers the lurchers presented. Lurchers, he learned in the years separating the prophesy and the apocalypse, were built for the carnage they intended to inflict. They stood impossibly tall, possibly ten feet, though the prophet couldn't say definitively. They wielded enormous, praying mantis-like arms. They would most certainly bite—the prophet spoke gravely of this particular fact, and Mitch did and didn't want to press him on the information—and they could hear terribly well. To ready him, Mitch had been catapulted with force and chased and bitten by dogs. In the fiercest of trainings, fifteen Descendants were to hunt Mitch after he took a two-minute head start. "Where can I hide in that time?" Mitch asked, readying to run.

"When they actually come for us, you'll have no warning," the elders replied.

They were right. No one had had a lick of warning.

He asked in the earliest months of training a litany of questions. "What are they? What do they want? Can we prevent their coming?"

Otherworldly monsters, he learned. They wanted to clear earth for reasons the prophet didn't disclose, and no, they would come as surely as the sun would rise. These were the responses he grappled with.

After hesitating and deciding not to ask it more times than he could count, Mitch ventured, "Who are we to save?" He was testing the waters with this one; he wanted to know if the Descendants, and the elders who governed them, knew what he'd been told.

"We save no one but our own, Mitch. You know this."

But he didn't know this. He had received instructions his people clearly had not. For the first time in his life, Mitch felt disingenuous toward them. Worse, he couldn't ask anyone for help. Mitch had felt alone for as long as he could remember, but this—this was on another level. He loved his people and wanted them to be safe, but he could vent to and confide in no one. The isolation made it hard to be the kind of strong they required.

He wondered what his parents would do, but he knew. His dad had died saving a human father. His mom and dad would be proud of him for saving a human, let alone working to preserve the planet for them. And for a long time, talking to them as though they could hear, and knowing in his core they supported him from wherever beings go after death, sustained Mitch.

30

The grandfather clock creeped her out, its crown a curious pair of intricately carved points. They made her think of devil horns. Maybe her inclination to see it negatively was rooted in the newness of this venture.

This clock, with its back against a towering wall in a long hallway in a house with a palpably guarded history, spooked and intrigued her. Audrey tilted her head, eyeing its moon dial, its minute hand, its hour hand, parts she'd learned on assignment in Reading, Pennsylvania. *What have you seen?*

Before she'd seen the clock, there'd come a knock on her door after midnight, and she'd opened it slightly. Mitch had held a finger to his lips. She'd thrown on a hoodie and followed him into the restricted corridor, past the enormous red door behind which the spring bubbled, creating the underground lake. Through another red door, she'd followed him on an incline, its dirt floor lit red by lights on the wall. She found the place's red doors and red lighting eerie, ominous, but Mitch had led and she'd followed until they'd reached an impossibly tall, spiral staircase. It didn't matter that she'd spent the last year working out to fill her days: she was out of breath before they'd climbed half its stairs. When he opened the door in this foreign place, the grandfather clock's face was the first to greet her.

Where are we? she thought, opting to ask him in the most silent way she knew how. All this time underground, and they could have come up here? *Some manor.*

"My family's home," he whispered. "We built the Underground beneath it." He looked down the corridor to the left. "Speaking in that way is just as loud around here."

So shut my door?

"Probably best."

Audrey closed and locked the pale blue door.

Mitch reached forward and around the devil clock, his eyes now on the corridor to the right.

She followed his gaze. The way the place sprawled reminded her of the dark mansion in *Beauty and the Beast*: every detail larger and more ornate than most architecture built now. The sound of a click made her turn her face toward him. Audrey's eyes widened as a piece of wall creaked open behind the clock.

Mitch placed a hand on the small of her back and encouraged her to slip through.

"Okay, but where are we going?" she asked. Their climb through underground tunnels, their emergence into a dark, endless corridor, and now their slipping inside this passageway felt forbidden. It wasn't like him to show her so much.

"The test requires the outdoors."

"We can go outside?"

"On these grounds, yes." True to form, he didn't elaborate.

If it's so safe here, why don't some stay here and not the Underground? Audrey wondered. It smelled old in the passageway, and she found the smell comforting, a reminder that this stretch inside this place had stood the test of many years and many scourges and would probably stand the test of this one, too. Unlike the other corridor, nothing hung on the walls in this dark and narrow vein through the house. It stood completely bare. She stopped looking around the passageway. Her heart rate accelerated. They were completely alone.

"No one's here, Mitch?"

"There are Keepers—" He stopped himself. "People take turns ensuring the conjuration holds. They're not here at this hour."

Conjuration. Theirs was a language she had yet to learn. He paused at a door they now met, his ear to it. He pushed, and it clicked open into a pantry. Mitch pressed a finger to his lips, and Audrey nodded, her eyes soaking in the narrow room. Old, built-in shelves rose from floor to ceiling. Along the bottom half of one wall were a dozen built-in drawers, above which were glass doors shutting in stacks of plates, rows of glasses, and teacups on saucers. Cobwebs moved as they disturbed the space, and Audrey touched her fingertips to a long table in the room, leaving behind a trail in the dust that had collected since those aircraft crashed to earth. The character and undisturbed nature of it all gave her the itch to explore, but Mitch kept moving.

She followed him out of the pantry and into an enormous kitchen, where they stayed for only a few minutes, listening. He approached and opened another door. She trailed him.

Holy shit. She inhaled, her eyes closed. In the dark of the home, she hadn't realized they were stepping outdoors. *Holy shit.* For only the second time since it all had happened, she stood beneath no ceiling. She stood free of walls. She had never spent ten months inside, and now she stood outside. Audrey lifted her face to the sky. *I missed you.* She didn't know the month, but she couldn't see her breath, and the stars were brighter than she remembered them, maybe because she hadn't seen them for so long, maybe because people—more specifically their pollution—were tucked away, maybe because this was rural Ohio. She couldn't be sure. Did it matter? She turned around, an entire 360 degrees, her arms to her side, but her eyes to the sky, drinking in its vast, glittering freedom.

She felt his warm breath on her ear before he spoke.

"I know."

She closed her eyes and turned her face to his. Completely alone with Mitch, back in the real world's deserted, ghostly version, she lived a fantasy she'd hatched, albeit at times guiltily, underground. She was with this man without another soul around.

"This way."

She couldn't see the grounds well in the dark, but the thick gargoyle perched on a dry fountain and a greenhouse implied the property was as sprawling as the mansion. Audrey followed Mitch toward the structure, her eyes scanning.

There came a noise, a sort of bang, and they stopped. Her eyes widened, and she attempted to quell her breaths. Neither made a sound. He tugged her to the left, inside the greenhouse and gingerly shut the glass door. Together they stepped over something overgrown and crouched and crawled beneath a shelf to listen.

Sitting, Audrey's eyes adjusted to the dark. Mother Nature had reclaimed the space. Dark, leafless vines covered so much. She couldn't see directly above them, but she could see pots hanging throughout the structure, their plants starved and brittle. A fog floated in the greenhouse, eerie yet welcome cover in the moment.

After about ten minutes, they turned to one another, their eyes up, down, and around. "An animal maybe," Mitch concluded quietly.

Audrey unclenched her jaw and leaned back.

He watched her.

She leaned back farther, lowering to rest on her forearms. Normally she would have worried about bugs. She didn't care about bugs right now.

Mitch crawled forward, his face above hers. He said nothing. She tipped her face and kissed him. He reciprocated with fervor, and she loved it. She wanted this to never end, but it did right away, and when he pulled away, he refused to meet her eyes.

"I have a question."

"Yes."

"Okay, I lied. I have so many questions. Why now? Why are we here now, 'testing' me? What happened to you?" She sat up as much as she could beneath the shelf. "I can't help but want to know."

Mitch ripped down a vine and crumpled it in his fist. "Not today. We have to go. But I will warn you."

Audrey peered up, hopeful.

"I have more to protect than you." It seemed he told himself more than he told her. She couldn't be sure. She never felt sure with him.

KEVIN STARTLED awake and at first, he wasn't sure what the reason was, but his heart raced immediately. Someone, possibly Maggie, sat up, too, rigid and silent, so he knew the sound wasn't isolated to him, wasn't some dream. He sprang up, ducking beneath the attic rafters, and scurried to the window, peeling wrapping paper back from the glass and squinting to scan the front yard. Nothing as far as he could see, but it was early dawn and he'd never had the best eyesight, least of all ten months into an apocalypse. Pearle Vision was closed.

Then he heard it. "AMELIA!" The scream came from the rear of the house.

Kevin froze momentarily, his eyes registering that everybody now sat upright in the attic room where they all slept. It wasn't a female voice, so the screamer wasn't Maggie or Stephanie. It wasn't Marcel or Winston because they'd been in the attic just moments ago, and he could hear them now, bounding downstairs. Kevin scrambled up and ran after them; the sisters followed suit. The sleeping bag where Amelia normally slept lay empty.

Jesus Christ. It's Ears. The man who for the better part of a year had never spoken was screaming. Kevin's heart pounded, his breath short. He followed the sound of hurried footsteps and found Marcel and Winston at the rear lookout station, attempting to restrain Ears. The back door was open, the boards normally spanning it on the ground. The back door was *never* open.

"—had to pee, and I came back and heard the silverware clanking, and I saw her. I saw her," Ears said, wrestling with the dads. "Let me go!" he roared. "She's out there. She's *alone.*" His last word sounded tortured. Kevin winced.

Maggie and Stephanie now stood behind Kevin. He needed to defuse the situation and quickly. "You have to be quiet," he began.

"She's out there, and they may not hear her, but if you keep this up, they may hear *you*."

Ears blinked, tears falling down his creased face, and collapsed to the ground, clutching his chest. "I stepped away for a minute. I swear. I promise. She must have crawled through that." He gestured toward the dog door.

The air was frosty outside. Kevin stepped to the door and watched and listened. He heard sniffles and a caught sob and turned only briefly to realize every adult behind him now cried, though they tried to do it quietly. Toward the property's edge, where overgrown grass met forest preserve, it lay. His heart dropped.

The rising sunlight glinted off a silver unicorn. Normally their six-year-old didn't leave a room without "Corn Cob."

"Fuck." Kevin raked his curls into a bun and turned to the sisters, the fathers, and the man with the white ear hair who never spoke, save tonight. "Maggie and Steph, load the guns. Marcel and Winston, get your weapons and the emergency bags." He pulled Ears up to sit in the lookout chair. "You stay here in case she shows up." Ears slumped and nodded.

They'd agreed months ago never to risk using the ammunition they had unless things turned dire. Here they were.

The sisters silently bounded away. The crew kept guns and ammunition upstairs, closest to where the family spent most of its time. It sounded, based on the creaks of stairs, like Marcel and Winston split up to grab some weapons from the upstairs closet and from the basement corner. They never used to keep weapons in easily accessible places throughout the home for fear Amelia would hurt herself or someone else. After they'd witnessed the danger that lurked and lurched and screeched outside, they'd moved weapons into more than one place and added to the collective arsenal the cast iron skillets they used to use for cooking and knives they used to wield when they had fresh fruits and vegetables to dice and slice.

Kevin kneeled near Ears and placed a hand on his shoulder.

The old man flinched.

Kevin doubled down on the gesture, squeezing his arm. "We need you here in case she shows up."

The old man shook his head. "It's my fault, and now you all have to clean up the mess."

With the family pounding around for supplies, he had time to comfort the man. "This could have happened while any of us kept watch. She is six. You left to *pee*. We all have to pee. She'll be relieved to see you if she comes back on her own. And we need someone here watching for *them*, too."

Ears kept a palm on his chest and his eyes down.

Kevin squeezed his shoulder again. "Look at me."

The old man obliged him.

"Tell me your name."

"Eugene."

"Eugene." Kevin sat with the revelation for a moment. "Eugene, do you trust me?"

The old man nodded.

"I will stop breathing before I stop searching for her."

Eugene's eyes welled with tears and his bottom lip trembled.

"I will stop breathing before I stop fighting for them. And for you. We'll be back, and we need you to keep watch. I'll get the walkies. Report any danger you see as soon as you see it. Keep to our code."

The family had a short list of one-syllable words for communicating via walkie. "Check" was to be used sparingly by those at home to ask if family outside was okay. "Home" meant anyone not home was headed back and would need those at the house to be ready to let them in. "Guard" warned that someone had spotted a creature near the house and all should get to the attic, barricade it, and stay quiet and unseen. The family had spoken all three of those codes at one time or another in their months together.

Returning to the kitchen from a downstairs room, Kevin stuffed one walkie into his bag and handed the other to Ears—*Eugene*. Maggie and Stephanie shouldered arm-length guns; Marcel, Winston, and Kevin tucked away handguns. Daddy and Papa also wore the bags of medical supplies and water the family kept stocked in case they needed to flee. Kevin peered outside, then turned to the people who'd become family. "Quiet. Eyes up. Keep in pairs. We go nowhere alone."

He patted Ears one last time on the shoulder and stepped outside. Each did the same and as Ears—*Eugene*—stood, walkie in his hand, he closed the back door. The old man reappeared, resolute, at the open window.

"I think I know why she left," the man whispered. His voice was gruff. Gravelly. Pretty much how Kevin suspected it would sound.

Kevin paused.

"You know Amelia and skunks."

The girl thought they were bushy-tailed cats. In the before, Marcel and Winston had caught her once, carrying a baby inside. She'd had plans to stuff the critter into a baby doll onesie, but her parents had intercepted her, peeling her fingers from the thing as though she carried a grenade. Somehow, the creature hadn't sprayed the child. The grimace Marcel made and the way he recounted the incident in granular detail—its series of moments graphically seared in his mind—had reduced the crew to crying laughter, a kind Kevin found particularly uplifting following the apocalypse. Too often in the aftermath, laughter remained impossible.

"She said she saw one. Worried it was outside all alone." Ears shook his head. "I shouldn't have left her." The man looked off into the distance.

Kevin pointed toward the silver unicorn. "There," he told the family. They would start there and comb the woods first.

He turned the knob on the walkie he held and nodded at Ears, who spoke into his own on the other side of the glass window. Batteries worked.

Kevin started walking, and Maggie, Stephanie, Winston, and Marcel followed. Kevin would stop at nothing to press the walkie to his lips and say, "Home," to bring them all back together.

~

Kevin lifted "Corn Cob" from the wet, tall grass and handed the worn thing to Marcel, and the man stopped walking and the family stopped with him. Marcel drew in a shaky breath and inhaled the stuffed animal's scent. Slowly he unzipped the bag he carried and pushed the unicorn inside. The crew stepped to the makeshift alarm system they'd built almost a year ago. Tied to yarn and stretched along every inch of the property's perimeter were forks, spoons, knives, and empty tin cans, which the crew hoped would clang and sound the alarm should someone or something stumble into their web. One by one, the five helped each other step over the line and into the woods.

We should have talked about how we'd track her, Kevin thought. There wasn't snow on the ground, and he had hunted zero times in his life. He knew no approaches.

More intimidating than that, they knew so little about the creatures. They didn't know how well they could see, how well they could hear, what mortally wounded them, though the one had died as flames consumed it at the gas station. Kevin reflected how glad he felt now that they'd packed those matches and lighter fluid into their emergency bags.

He turned to the crew. "One of you lead. I'll keep an eye from behind," he whispered.

Maggie raised a hand, shifting the gun on her shoulder. "I got it."

He figured she would. He stepped to her, placing a palm on a nearby trunk to ensure his balance as he stepped over tree roots, and further lowered his voice. "Let's walk the line here. I don't want to lose the houses."

It felt like they walked for an hour, but it was probably half that. Kevin split his time eyeing the forest to their left and the backyards and the houses to their right. The forest presented as it had before—no one trimmed and maintained a forest—but the houses were haunting. He and Winston had ventured out only when it was dark, so they'd never seen the full scope. So many windows were broken, grass knee-high, hedges overgrown. He sensed the scene landed differently for Marcel and Winston, who pointed often and clutched each other's arms from time to time. They knew the souls who used to make each house a home.

His eyes on one home in particular, Kevin bumped into the dads and realized the family had stopped. Maggie crowded them in together and whispered, "You smell that?"

Kevin's eyes bulged. *Skunk.* Amelia could be close.

"Let's split up here; some of us search the forest, some of us a house or two," he began. "Marcel, Winston, the chalk."

Marcel pulled a box from his bag and slowly, so as to be quiet, pulled out a piece for each of them.

"Draw arrows pointing back here so you don't lose your way," Kevin reminded. "Maggie and Stephanie, one of you to the houses with me." Kevin checked his watch.

Marcel and Winston did the same.

"Back at eight."

The men nodded.

The others stepped carefully away, stopping often to mark an arrow on a stone or a tree. It felt so exposed, being outside during the day. None had dared do it intentionally since they'd come together at 3224 Baldwin Road.

Kevin met Maggie's gaze and nodded toward the house closest to them.

She stepped forward.

"I'll take right and behind us; you take left and in front," Kevin whispered.

Together they advanced from the forest line toward a house that appeared empty.

31

The last time he'd been here, on the grounds where they'd reared him, the place where the trees were old enough to have borne witness to the inception of the Handler protocols, Mitch would never have done what he just did. He'd brought a woman, a woman with unschooled and unbridled powers, within, and he wanted to do things with her he almost refused to acknowledge, even to himself, even after having done those things. In the before, he wouldn't have *wanted* to do them. He would have been in a position to punish any man or woman who dared do it. He was *still* in a position to punish it, a Descendant's betrayal of the Descendants.

What did that make him?

Mitch shook his head, dismissing himself, his eyes on dead, crispy plants in the greenhouse. He had his reasons, and they would have to be enough. He shook his head.

"Did I do something wrong?"

He met her eyes, those striking, abnormally gray eyes. She gripped her own hands. She looked small. Uncertain. He suspected she was reacting to his ending their kiss and pulling away. This could trigger her, Mitch realized, and he needed to do that for this to work.

He had to hurt her for this to work, and the thought of hurting her—he dropped his eyes.

"Follow me," he said in a low voice. He wanted to extend a hand to her, as it remained impossibly dark outside, but he needed to isolate her to test her. *Make this quick*, he resolved. They hadn't come this far not to test if she could do it. But he couldn't risk being gone for much longer. If anything happened, if nothing happened, they'd need him, and they wouldn't think to find him up here. No one was supposed to leave the shelter's safety alone.

And what if something happened here? Mitch shook his head to dispel the thought.

Dark as they were, the grounds were familiar as ever to him. He could have found his way blindfolded from the greenhouse down the moss-covered stairs to the worn path in the forest that ended at the river.

Audrey followed him silently, her thoughts locked up tight.

Harnesser powers were a different breed to test, and he suspected the first test, underground, where the elements weren't really wild and free, had failed more because of the shelter's limitations than hers. Harnesser powers more often than not required emotion to surface: there was more than mere intent involved to influence earth, air, fire, and water. It was *hard* to do. After they'd tested Mitch for harnesser capabilities, he'd remained disturbed, afflicted by nightmares, for weeks. The elders had lied mercilessly through his tears and failed attempts, insisting Theodora would suffocate, was suffocating, within a collapsed cave because he couldn't harness an element to make it untrue. It hadn't occurred to them that Mitch Gray's powers had limitations, that he was not a harnesser.

He was five when they'd ascertained that. At no age had they shown him mercy.

Over the years, Mitch had witnessed harnessers pull off intense feats. He couldn't be sure if Audrey could harness, but they knew her dad could. Her awareness of her one power made it more likely she could surface another if it existed.

"Here," he said, stopping. "Sit here." He gestured to a boulder near the river.

"Can we talk before we do this?"

"We don't have time."

"I can't sit there, Mitch. I'm terrified of rivers."

"Audrey, we don't have time. I'm here. I'll keep you safe. Just sit."

She went to sit on the boulder but must have slipped or misjudged its location. Mitch heard the splash and her shriek, and he stepped in after her but couldn't reach her in time. The current was as swift as it had ever been, but luckily he proved faster, and he grabbed her arm and stopped her trajectory downriver.

Audrey burst into tears.

"I'm so sorry, I'm so sorry," Mitch said, pulling her into him. "You're okay, you're safe," he assured her, pushing her out of the water.

"Mitch?" She sounded alarmed. "Mitch, I cannot fucking see. Mitch?"

He stepped toward her, shushing her. "We have to be quiet, Audrey."

"Mitch, I cannot fucking see." Her palms were up, and her breaths were shaky. "Mitch, what's happening?" She began to cry.

Mitch peered at her eyes, squinting hard in dawn's first light. Confusion coursed through him. Their abnormal gray color appeared to have disappeared. Her eyes appeared black. "You can't see at all?" He touched her cheek.

Her palms still up and now touching his chest, Audrey let out a gasp. "Daddy?" she croaked.

She could see again, but what she saw was an impossibility. Extending an arm toward her, also to touch her cheek, was a different man. His face wrinkled in places it didn't used to, and his hair was unrecognizably long and white, but Charles Kelly IV had given her one thing most people didn't have, and she'd know those flint gray eyes anywhere, even framed by skin and hair rendered unfamiliar by two decades. "Daddy?"

The man tilted his face and moved his thumb over her cheek. "Dree." He smiled, and the lines on his face deepened. "Not a day has gone by that I didn't hope for this." His bottom lip began to tremble, and he pinched at the corners of his eyes. He used to do that when Simba nudged at Mufasa, trying to wake the dead lion after the wildebeest stampede.

The few times she'd watched *The Lion King* as an adult, Audrey had fast-forwarded through that part.

She'd yearned for half her life to see him, if only one more time, so when she broke eye contact, buried in conflicting anger and relief, she thought better of it and met his eyes, afraid he'd disappear. "How are you here?" she asked.

"I've not moved. You came to me."

Audrey furrowed her brow. That made no sense. But when she focused on what she could see, it was no longer the mansion's dark grounds. Her dad appeared to sit in a basement with glass block windows, in the flickering light of melted, misshapen candles, food and assorted items on one side of him and—it was dark—but it looked like papers and photographs on a bulletin board to the other side.

Audrey leaned in closer. Headshots. Headlines. All familiar. The three-year-old who'd beat that scary prognosis. The time the police hunkered down in a house with a murderer because a tornado tore through the city. The fiddle festival quite unworthy of coverage to everyone but the metro editors who needed inches to fill the pages of the small daily.

Audrey's breath caught. Tacked to a bulletin board hung so much of her bylined work, yellowed and crinkly, that it hung in layers, like shingles on a house. He'd kept a collection. Of her.

"I don't know how much time we have." Strange how a person can look so unfamiliar but sound so much like home.

"Wait. What do you mean? Where are you going?" *We just found each other.*

"I don't know how much time we have here, to talk, I mean."

"How are we talking?"

"I don't know. Where are you?"

"I'm at a house, a mansion. It's owned by these people who—"

Charles lifted a palm and cowered. He kept his head down for a couple seconds. He resumed eye contact. "Those creatures, have you seen them? With the horns? The black mouths?"

Audrey nodded.

"They're close," he whispered. He blinked rapidly. "To me."

"Where are you?"

He didn't answer. He ducked his head, his eyes on her, and lifted a finger to his lips. She couldn't decipher all the sounds, but she could tell from the way his eyes darted up that sounds came from above him.

Charles leaned forward and cupped her cheek.

Audrey's lip quivered, and she placed a hand over his. It felt dry and bony, and this felt like another unwelcome goodbye. She had questions, a half lifetime of questions, and she needed answers.

"I'm proud of you," Charles whispered. "That never changed." He sank lower, his eyes up, his teeth clenched. "You are more powerful than you think," he continued, his voice lower.

"Daddy, I know we have abilities," she began.

He nodded. "We do. Use them. Stay safe. I'll find you. Go now. They hear well."

The bulletin board and pantry items and his face faded from view. The rush of water returned, and there stood Mitch.

"Were you here the entire time?" she asked.

"Yes."

"I, I spoke with my dad."

Mitch blinked.

"I could see where he's been hiding, but I don't know where that is. It seemed like a basement. But I could see it so clearly. From here?" Her voice lifted in a question she didn't know could be answered.

"Audrey—" Mitch paused, scratching an eye. "I brought you to the river to see if you could harness, like your dad. But I—" He stopped.

She could feel and hear her heart race. Her hands felt cold and sweaty. "Spit it out, Mitch."

"I've met only one prophet in my life." He broke eye contact, his eyes scanning the grounds, which were coming increasingly into focus as the sun rose. "I think you may be the second."

What does that mean? Audrey could see gargoyles, the greenhouse, and gardens behind them. The river before them was wider and frothier than she'd ever imagined it could be. She shuddered. *I was just in that.* "Prophet?"

"Mmmm," he muttered to himself. "If you can *see*, that's—fuck. That could change so much."

MAGGIE'S EYES were bright when she emerged from the room. It had become second nature to check all cabinets and drawers inside any foreign place, and she held it up between her fingers: toothpaste, and a full tube. They probably would have celebrated were it not for Amelia's being unaccounted for.

Kevin nodded, his back flat against the hallway wall, relaxing in this moment, his gun falling to his right side. This was the last room to check on the first floor. Up they'd go.

He waited while she unzipped the bag on her back and tucked it away. Eyes scanning, they stepped toward the staircase. Kevin exhaled when the first few steps up revealed that these stairs didn't creak the way his childhood home's had. They didn't know if someone was inside, and they didn't want to inadvertently announce their presence.

At the landing, Maggie and Kevin split up to clear the rooms. The one he stepped into was that of a child—no, children: there were two beds. The walls were blue, one a darker accent wall, and hanging on that darker wall were framed pictures of toothy, grinning dinosaurs with affirmations including "You are brave" and "You are powerful."

Kevin reread the one. *You are brave.* He didn't feel brave. He felt compelled.

In the corner, near another door he monitored keenly for movement, stood a tall, stuffed T. rex. Not nearly as worn as Corn Cob.

Kevin had never loved a child until Amelia. Forced into close quarters with the girl and her stuffed unicorn, he'd learned to detangle her hair from its ends to its roots to minimize tugs, the way she fell asleep only with her forehead to an adult's forehead, usually one of her dads. The closer he'd become to her, the harder his own past had become to reconcile. He recognized in her innocence, his own; in her need for protection, his own. Before he knew it, he'd wordlessly accepted a shared responsibility to do for her the very thing he'd been convinced he'd fail at miserably: safeguard a child's mind, heart, and body. And ironically, he found himself doing it at arguably the hardest time *to* do it, when protecting a child meant following the scent of skunk into unfamiliar, abandoned houses while hulking, violent creatures were God knows where and liable to do God knows what. Not that he believed in God.

His gun up but not pointed in front of him, he held his breath and opened the closet door. Nothing. No one. This house may be empty indeed.

He found Maggie in another bathroom, placing a few bars of soap in her bag. They'd been out of soap for months, and they missed it even more with their hot water tank out of commission. Stocking up on personal hygiene items was a relief, but Kevin furrowed his eyebrows. Maggie caught his look and paused. He stepped toward her and placed his mouth near her ear.

"Most places are picked over," he whispered. "Someone's been living here and replenishing supplies. Recently."

She pulled the zipper slowly. Her fingers froze and her eyes met his when someone screamed. A wild, desperate set of screams. Outside, probably, though in a new place, could one be sure?

"Get down," Kevin hissed immediately. Ducking, he raced across the second-floor hallway toward the sound. He met a closed door and turned the knob until it clicked open. A deep voice came from behind.

"Don't."

Kevin looked to the right, his palms up instinctively. He turned.

"Drop the guns."

That, he had not done instinctively. He met the speaker's eyes and saw the barrel of a gun. His anxiety couldn't rachet up higher. They needed to find Amelia, not entangle with this threat. He slowly lowered his gun to the carpet, and Maggie did the same.

Outside, someone screamed for her life. Inside, the man leaned forward and dragged Kevin's and Maggie's guns toward and behind him. Eyes on them, he set the weapons on stairs to an attic they'd not yet vetted.

"We can be friendly, yes?" the stranger asked.

Kevin and Maggie nodded obediently.

"Come."

Kevin nodded at Maggie. The room the stranger gestured for them to enter was dark until he pulled material—foil?—from a window corner and peered out. The stranger pushed the material back into place and rubbed his eyes.

"Jessica." The man, unshaven like most in these times but hairier than anyone Kevin had encountered, scratched his head and his beard. "At first, the attacks seemed random. They heard you, they came for you. Right?"

Kevin's thoughts returned to the way he'd run up the stairs of that house Audrey and he had hidden in, the way the creatures had hunted him. He glanced at his mauled hand and met the man's eyes.

"It's not random anymore, dude," the man said.

Outside, no one screamed anymore. Inside, all three ducked their heads at the sound of a roar.

"It's house by house. They're burning what they clear. Killing who they find." Kevin couldn't see his lips, he was so hairy. "That was Jessica. She was the only one who remained, I think. Everyone else got out of dodge. Five more houses, it's me. Well." The man met Kevin's eyes, then Maggie's. "Us. Five more houses, it's us."

"We're trying to find a child. Have you seen a girl, this high—" Kevin's hand was flat in the air when the stranger interrupted him.

"Uh uh. I ain't heard nothin' but them things and my neighbor dyin'. You ain't never going to find a little one out there alive. Sorry. See for yourself. Don't let them fuckers spot you, though."

Kevin crawled forward and peeked. Beyond a certain point, every house appeared burnt to a crisp, their front window frames dead, hollow eyes. The lurchers hadn't burned the latest, it appeared, but the neighbor the hairy man had named—Jessica—lay motionless, splayed down her front stairs. Blood stained what fire hadn't yet. What a horror they all lived.

Kevin exhaled. What he wouldn't do to rewind and prevent that sweet baby from leaving. *Goddamnit, Amelia.*

"We can't stay. We have to keep looking. She's six."

"Seven soon," Maggie said softly. "Can we get our guns?" Maggie asked, haltingly.

The hairy man shook his head and raised his eyebrows. "You got balls," he began. "Suit yourself. But I need something."

Kevin clenched his jaw at the insinuation of a condition. They didn't have time. They hadn't had time even before they knew about this systematic annihilation rising like a tsunami through the neighborhood.

"I'ma need my toothpaste and soap."

MAGGIE'S IDEA HAD MERIT: the houses to the one end of the neighborhood, the burned ones, might be safer. They were already cleared.

"Those things think they're empty," she whispered.

"If they think," Kevin replied.

But weren't those houses also likely not where Amelia hid, if she hid? She could be anywhere: the woods, back at 3224 Baldwin Road, though Ears, no, Eugene, would certainly have radioed. Kevin's cruelest worry stretched its gnarled, loveless fingers, reaching from the periphery, trying to penetrate the options playing in his mind, but he pushed it away by forcing detailed consideration of the last idea. *What if we're out of range? She could be with Ears. We should check before too long. We—oh wait.* He quickly flipped his wrist. 7:43.

"I said eight?"

Maggie nodded.

They had time.

Kevin didn't understand why the hairy man stayed. Kevin wouldn't have stayed inside the place, knowing what the man said was imminent. But the man struck him as scrappy. He must have had a plan.

With the toothpaste and soap returned to the stranger, Kevin followed Maggie down the first few steps.

"Dude."

Kevin turned.

The man stepped gingerly down several stairs, an unsettling caution from someone so gritty, and whispered. "They hear *well*, dude. Be quiet out there."

Kevin turned to Maggie, an index finger on his lips. "Let's head back. You were right: their hearing is good. We'll tell the others and decide what to do."

They returned to the house's back door, and Kevin opened it stiffly. He leaned forward, and when all he could hear was his heart racing, he stepped outside. Guns poised, the pair walked briskly but carefully, crouching once, teeth clenched, at the sound of a strange pounding. A roar kept them still for longer.

Kevin exhaled when he found Marcel and Winston and Stephanie awaiting their return.

"Those things are everywhere," Winston hissed.

Kevin pulled the crew into a tight circle. "We met a man," he began in the lowest whisper he could muster. The family nodded him on. "Those monsters hear well. And they're now killing and burning house by house. Maggie and I think—"

"What's that sound?" Marcel asked, waving a palm frantically, clutching the machete with his massive hands.

Before anyone else registered that it was her high-pitched voice,

Kevin had broken into a furious sprint between two houses. He knew the five followed him only because he could hear their panting and the pounding of their feet. Kevin nearly fell as he cut a turn on the gravel drive, his eyes tearing across the neighborhood.

It was her. There, several houses down in cotton candy pink pajamas, Amelia stood. "Daddy? Papa?" Her back was to them, but her voice carried.

Kevin's feet now tore across the neighborhood. He wanted desperately to tell her to be quiet, but he knew adding his voice to her noise wouldn't help.

"Daddy? Papa?"

Kevin's legs burned.

"KEVIN!"

Kevin stumbled to a stop, flying forward as he twisted to peer behind him. His eyes couldn't decide where to look. Winston fired a shot, and a creature roared, falling back and releasing Marcel, who fell to the pavement. Maggie and Stephanie chugged forward with a spray of bullets from their automatic weapons, and the impossibly tall creature chittered and shrieked and slammed to the ground, still moving. Kevin turned back to Amelia and squinted. *What?* His blood turned colder. Some person had hands on her, their baby, drawing her into a house.

"KEVIN!"

He could feel a low rumble build under his feet and heard a roar followed by a second followed by so many he couldn't distinguish individual sounds anymore. They rose in a terrifying crescendo. He turned back and saw Winston and Stephanie dragging Marcel up off the ground, and then the wave came: creatures, so many creatures, ripping forward, crashing and crunching through mailboxes and cars and hedges to meet them, his family, where they stood. He ripped his face back toward Amelia and caught her face actually turned his way, her body halfway inside what appeared to be a basement window, a pair of arms pulling her down. Human arms.

They had risked all of this for her, and she was in the arms of a stranger, but it was a human. Behind him, creatures pursued the rest of his family—creatures with horns and hauntingly black mouths and appendages like sharp scissors.

Sweating, Kevin turned his back on the girl he loved, aimed his gun, and ran. They could rescue Amelia only if they saved themselves.

32

It reminded Audrey a lot of the night it all began: Mitch leading the way through a landscape familiar to him but unfamiliar to her, Audrey stumbling to follow while kept in the miserable and trepidatious dark.

She snatched his hand and yanked him backward.

He was strong, though, and merely turned around near the gargoyle. "It's this way. They need to know you can see. They need to know *what* you can see."

"Mitch, no. Not before *I* know what you're talking about. Explain."

Mitch's eyes flashed with frustration.

"Explain," Audrey repeated.

"Audrey, it's day. We agreed we'd get back by—"

"What did you mean by prophet?" She would not relent. He *owed* her this.

Mitch ducked his head and scanned the grounds. "It's rare. Prophets can peer into places and times not their own."

"And you've known only one?"

He scratched his neck. "He predicted the apocalypse. He's the reason we built the Underground."

"Where is he now?"

"He died."

Audrey raised her eyebrow.

"Natural causes," Mitch said.

"How do I do it—this prophesying?" she asked.

"Let's see if we can trigger it once we're back."

"No. Mitch. My dad's in danger. I—" Her eyes filled, but she choked back the sob. "Teach me to do it so I can figure out where he is." She paused and swallowed. "I haven't seen him in seventeen years. What if this is my only chance to determine where he went to, where he is?"

Mitch rubbed his forehead silently for a solid minute. When he looked at her, his eyes possessed a softness.

He pities me.

"You're afraid of water?"

"Very. You know this now. What does that have to do with this?" She couldn't help her terse tone. *He's wasting time.*

He turned around and began walking. "Come."

She followed, and though it was the response she wanted, she felt reluctant. "Why?" she persisted.

"Using a power at times requires more than knowing you can," he said. He paused. "As well you know."

Audrey raised an eyebrow.

"It requires emotion. Some can only cast under duress."

"What kind of duress?" She followed him, stepping over tall grass and stones. Her heart rate picked up as the sound of rushing water grew louder. *Not again.* She inhaled deeply and put foot in front of foot; she was afraid, but this was what she'd asked for. She wouldn't bitch now.

The river raced and poured, but she could see now in daylight how it split around an enormous tree in a stunning way. Sunlight made it a touch less scary, but only a touch. At least she could see what stormed past.

"You have to get back in."

"What? No. No way."

"Audrey, you must."

She grabbed her face, nauseated now. She'd avoided so many bodies of water throughout her life after the accident, but especially rivers. And this one had attempted to kill her mere minutes before.

"Is a vision coming right now?"

"No." She wrung her hands and scratched her head.

"You have to get in."

Mitch pulled off his shirt and his pants. His body looked like he'd spent the last year hunting and killing: sinewy and scarred. He stepped into the waters and kept going until only his shoulders were visible. "You're going to have to trust me."

Audrey exhaled, her hands shaking, and struggled to undress; her limbs did not cooperate, and wet clothes were a bitch to shed. She stuttered and stopped more than she wanted to, not confident at all she could bear this again. Prom. Death. Abandonment. Terror coursed through her. Her eyes on Mitch, she closed her eyes and stepped in. Her breath caught. The water ran stabbing cold and fast. It rushed and it pulled indiscriminately, onward along its journey. It didn't care she was there. It wouldn't care if she ceased to be.

Her breathing quickened. Her sight failed her. "Mitch, it's happening." She felt his hand on her elbow.

"Tell me what you see."

But Mitch wasn't there. Charles cried before her. "You shouldn't be here." He used his big paws to palm away the tears on his cheeks.

"Daddy, what's happening? Where are you?"

"They're going to find me—" A deafening crashing sound interrupted him. She'd never seen him so scared—no, she had, and her stomach roiled. The night he'd fled, his face had contorted in this way. He left her now, peering out some window, pacing the floor, peering out again. "I have to. I can't leave her out there. I have to." Charles opened the window.

"Daddy, what's happening?" Audrey croaked. "Tell me where you are."

"She needs help. If I don't save her, she'll die."

"Who?"

"I have to save her."

"Where are you?"

"I don't want you anywhere near here," Charles whispered emphatically, his focus entirely on her before it wasn't.

Charles scaled the cinderblock wall and stuffed himself through the window toward sunlight, and somehow Audrey's line of sight followed. Outside, a girl, dressed in pink, her fists in her mouth, cried for Daddy. Selfishly, Audrey waved her arms, unsure if he could see her, willing him not to go. But he was gone, sprinting, snagging, limp-running back with the girl in the crook of his arm, stuffing the girl into the window he'd exited. An unearthly roar rose, and Audrey was back inside where he was. He slammed the window shut and covered the girl and shushed her, but she wailed. Charles rubbed her shoulders before hugging her.

"Daddy?" Audrey whispered, when the commotion began to die down. Her view of him shimmered on the edges, melting away. She could feel her panicked breathing on the other side of the prophesy. "You must tell me where you are. Time is running out."

"Audrey," he replied. "It's house by house now. Stay away."

The vision was translucent now; she could see her father and the child and the river's current beyond them. She sharpened her tone. "I'm coming. Tell me where you are, and I'll be outside, looking, for less time."

Charles inhaled and shook his head. When he spoke, his voice was a whisper. "Only because of her," he began, petting the head of the one now hiccupping tears. "We can't let them get her."

Gray eyes met gray eyes. "1574 Baldwin Road."

And he disappeared.

THEY DIDN'T HAVE TOWELS, so they walked back to the mansion half naked, shivering and carrying their clothes. They didn't speak until back inside, and they didn't look at each other either. Mitch refused to look out of respect. He didn't want Audrey to feel uncomfortable, though seeing each other naked was the least of their concerns.

She followed Mitch up a carved staircase to a linen closet the size of a bedroom and thanked him for the towel.

"We have to go back. It's possible they haven't noticed."

"Mitch, where is Baldwin Road?"

He thought immediately of the forest's edge. "Thirty-minute walk. Fifteen-minute run."

"Which direction?" She was dressed; he wasn't far behind.

How could he make her see returning for her dad *after* they returned to the Underground was the right thing to do? "It's through the forest. That neighborhood, all the street signs start with B. Baldwin. Beech. Blue Jay. Let's go after we check in below."

Audrey started walking, leading him now through his family estate. "I'm going now."

"You will die. Wait and I will go with you."

"Mitch, there's a child. A girl. She's with my dad. I can't waste time. I can't wait."

Mitch bit his lip. He knew what Theodora would say, and he knew why. But he remembered the boy with the scruffy dog. The baby in the red, white, and blue footed pajamas. He'd never regretted saving the one. He would always regret he'd arrived far too late to save the other.

"I don't know what to do," Mitch said. "Let me think."

"Is it possible when they learn I can see, they'll understand why you brought me here and give us, I don't know, a pass? Become distracted by that and not our disappearance?"

Who knew. Mitch had earnestly assumed that when the prophecy came true, he'd stay dutiful. Do what had to be done. And he had, though the elders didn't know it. But he'd also ended up doing so many things he shouldn't have. He was the messiest version of himself when the Descendants needed him to be the tidiest. *Or do they? What if this is the version of me they need?* He locked eyes with Audrey. *Seems this is the version of me you need.* What she needed meant a ton. He *loved* her.

"How little?"

"What?"

"How little is the girl?"

"She's wearing pink pajamas."

Mitch scratched his face, frustrated and uncomfortable. He opened his mouth and closed it, shaking his head. He couldn't be sure he could save Audrey, and they needed her. None of this ended right if she ceased to breathe. But he bent down and rapidly tied his shoes. "Let's go, and let's run."

AT FIRST THE run wasn't treacherous, and though her lungs couldn't expand enough and her legs were dragging weights, Audrey dared not complain. Adrenaline surged within her. Gratitude, too. She had never wanted to go it alone.

They neared a forest, and that's where things became sticky. Mitch didn't let up. He hurdled thick tree roots and brush. She followed his lead, confused and panting as he ran in a sort of diagonal until they met a worn path through the mansion's forest. This was much easier to traverse. The sun was bright and high in the sky, and she was glad what lay before them was visible—until they cleared the forest.

He lifted a hand, a signal to stop. He listened. She didn't listen, really. Her eyes darted from one place to the next, her heart sinking.

They had emerged into a neighborhood, if one could call it that. Directly ahead was a white house with pale blue shutters, its grass high, its front door open, its windows broken. All over the brick house next door crawled immense ivy. Its front gutters had caved in the middle from the weight of vegetation that never should have sprouted from them. Vehicles sat, abandoned in the street, their doors ajar. A red tassel hung from the rearview mirror in one. Her stomach twisted at the thought of a recent graduate, facing it all, and she found herself, briefly, reliving the night they had abandoned Kevin's car. Kevin. *Is he alive?*

Audrey wondered if any of these cars' drivers survived, if any hid in the houses before them, now eyeing this couple who'd emerged from the adjacent woods. She searched for movement but detected only the fluttering of shredded curtains through a couple windows. American flags dotted the landscape, tattered, wrapped up in something, or crumpled on porch steps. In another life, they would have been utterly disrespectful. The flags weren't meant to fly in the elements and the chaos they had. They were supposed to have been returned to attic and basement storage spaces for the next year's Memorial Day festivities.

Audrey let a ragged sob escape. She covered her mouth, instantly sorry, but she hadn't seen how far the world, how her Ohio, had sank, and it made any return to life as they all knew it feel so impossible. *How do we even rebuild?*

At the sound, Mitch met her eyes. He touched her elbow and leaned in, his breath hot on her ear. "I know. Follow me."

Did he know, though? Were any of the people who'd raised families here, who'd ridden bikes here, who'd counted on safety here, his people? Didn't he have a mansion connected to an underground where only his kind could retreat?

Audrey forced a nod, not that he waited for it. He wove in and out of bushes and dead flower beds and brick walkways more green than they were brick, and she pursued him because he knew where Baldwin Road was and she didn't. This was not her corner of Ohio.

Suddenly his hands were on her, shoving her against the siding of a house. His finger was perpendicular to his mouth, and he pushed her forward into prickly bushes. She winced as their unimpeded growth caught her skin, but she forged forward until it simply wasn't possible. She couldn't catch her breath. The roar that came was so inhuman it took her breath away further, and she didn't turn her face to his until he tapped her shoulder.

"We need a code," he whispered. "If I double tap you, hide. If I single tap you, run."

She had nothing to do but nod. Another roar reverberated through the morning air, and she shrank down. It was so unlike anything she'd ever heard, though it was possible she and Kevin had heard something like it the night of the wedding. That felt a lifetime ago, for her. If she had had the time, that truth would have made her feel guilty—she was certain others had lived with this terror, day in and night out. Mitch was moving, and she followed.

She didn't know it was Baldwin Road until he told her. They weren't out in the open, of course, because that would be suicide. The roar had risen to a deafening pitch, and a crescendo of other unwelcome sounds met them as they slid against the side of some trellis. Glass broke. Something tore. Worse yet, a human screamed. But things clicked for Audrey: the street her father had sprinted down was before her. The black street lamps confirmed it.

Mitch leaned in and began to whisper but stopped. A monster tore right by them, howling. They shrank into each other, shrouded in rose overgrowth, full of soft petals and sharp thorns, and Audrey closed her eyes.

A terrible screech rang out, met with human screams and an explosion. Through the brush, she saw a rail-thin man, his clothing torn, but his gait familiar. *Impossible.* But true. Kevin. *Kevin?*

He was shooting a stream of bullets from a gun, screaming, "Go, go, go!" There was a flash, and some number of humans, she couldn't tell how many, retreated in all directions, without pursuers. A number of creatures advanced on Kevin, and he was unloading now, reloading now, shooting again now. It had been the better part of a year since she'd seen him and months since she'd discovered who he really was, but fear skewered the very core of her. She very much wanted him to survive these monsters.

"Mitch, that's—"

But Mitch was gone.

"Kevin!" Mitch screamed. "MOVE."

Audrey paused, dumbfounded. *He knows him.*

Mitch had his hands up, and he was in the center of the street now, facing monsters, crumpling one, two, three, but not fast enough. He nearly toppled over but righted himself somewhat, his palms crutches on the pavement before they were again weapons in the air. But the lurchers surged in another tidal wave. She stepped forward, then retreated, wringing her hands. She had to act.

The edges of her vision blurred, and she felt glad. She shut her eyes and forced the vision. She saw her dad, but he was running. "Dad? Dad!" He didn't stop. He bounded ahead to a figure in pink, screaming emphatically. The vision faded, and the figure in pink, in the flesh, actually bounded toward Mitch, bounded toward Kevin, screaming. Charles pursued the girl.

Audrey shook her head, petrified. The girl was outside, no longer safe with Audrey's dad who also was outside, running, running, running. *Daddy, no!* He was seventy years old and moved like it. Desperately slow amid creatures who were desperately large and desperately fast. Couldn't he see there were others to save her? *Go back inside. Go back inside right now.* Audrey stepped forward, showing herself, then thought better of it. None of them needed another person to save right now.

The child, though, didn't know what she didn't know. She collided with and clutched Kevin's arm, and lurchers descended upon them.

33

With Amelia clutching his arm, Kevin could no longer fire, so he scooped her up and looked toward Mitch. *Mitch. That's who I recognized at the gas station.*

"GO!" Mitch screamed, his palms up. This time, he wasn't attacking.

Kevin paused, entranced. Creatures swiped, but their giant claws crashed into something unseen around Mitch. A force field.

"GO!" Mitch repeated, stumbling on the pavement.

Kevin waited no more and ran, gulping for air. Her six-year-old body was heavy and unwieldy, and he had to zig-zag between abandoned cars while searching for the right place to hide. Impossible.

"Quiet," he exhaled, tripping, his feet splashing in puddles.

"I'm scared!"

He shushed Amelia, stumbling to a sprint. He veered right, down a private alleyway, nearly tripping in mud, and cut a sharp right up a wooden deck consumed by vines. He tried the back door, but it was locked. He didn't dare break the glass. He remembered the gritty man's words: "They hear *well*, dude."

He held her tightly to his chest, sweaty and afraid, and looked left and right. Nothing moved, though unearthly shrieks pierced the air. He lowered Amelia to the ground and smoothed her arms.

"You okay?" he whispered.

The girl nodded.

"We have to be quiet like a skunk," he whispered. "Can you do that for me?"

A tear fell from her eye, and he wiped it away, but she didn't speak. He peered around them and noticed a gas grill on the deck, covered against the elements. He pulled its cover up and opened the doors below. She could fit. He ushered her inside. Two giant eyes implored him to explain.

"I am not going far—" he began before another shriek sounded. Amelia cowered. "Stay here until you hear nothing or until I come back."

Amelia stared.

"Promise me."

"I promise," she said.

Kevin closed the doors, then drew the cover back down. The silence was promising. Could it be? Had Mitch, that all-powerful man he'd met at the mansion all that time ago, defeated the wave? Should they be fleeing now that all was quiet? Where were Marcel and Winston and Maggie and Stephanie? He stepped softly down the wooden stairs and edged to the left wall of the house. He inhaled and peered around the side.

The proximity of another person scared him so much he tripped backward.

"Holy hell, Mitch," he said breathlessly from the ground.

"Where is she?" Mitch replied. His eyes looked strangely black as he scanned the yard, the deck, the woods.

"I hid her in the grill."

Mitch cocked his head and looked incredulous before he murmured, "Oh. No, no, where is Audrey?"

Kevin froze, his mouth ajar, his palms pushing his body off the tall, itchy grass. "Audrey?"

"We were there," Mitch said, pointing somewhere left. "I have to find her."

"Do you mean my Audrey? Audrey Kelly?"

Mitch snapped his face toward Kevin's. "I mean that Audrey, yes."

"She's ali—"

"Mitch?" came a voice.

Kevin's eyes darted toward it, and she emerged from some brush. His body flooded with surprise and relief: he recognized her voice after all this time. Audrey was alive.

Kevin silently absorbed the sight. Her hair was wild, her face bore scratches, but it was Audrey. He inhaled sharply. She startled. He scampered up.

She backed away, her eyes on him fleetingly, then on Mitch. Back to him. Back to Mitch.

"Audrey," he said, his palms on his chest. "My God, Audrey. You're alive." He kept his voice low, but his heart rammed inside. He opened and shut his mouth; he looked like an idiot, but he didn't care. That she had survived was a dream. *His* dream.

Audrey stepped forward. "Mitch, are they gone?"

Mitch shook his head.

"I killed several," Mitch whispered. "But they have a hive mind. They may all know we're here."

Kevin stepped forward, dying to hug her. Audrey moved in. He knew she was relieved, too, that they were both alive. "I didn't know what to think, but I hoped so hard," he breathed.

"Kevin. I know."

He nodded, smiling.

She didn't return the smile. "No. I *know*."

Kevin stopped advancing toward her, and every part of him felt colder. She couldn't mean *that*, could she? He peered at Mitch, but Mitch didn't meet his eyes. The picture sharpened for him. She knew Mitch. Mitch, whose family had orchestrated the Handler protocol. He stared into her eyes, and it dawned on him. *She knows.* Grief waved through his body. *She thinks that's all she was to me.*

She was so much more than the woman assigned to him that

rainy night. She'd cried the first time he made a loss lasagna in her presence. It had surprised him, and he'd rinsed the sticky mozzarella shreds from his hands to hug her. She'd made him realize it was okay to cry, even if at reality TV, and to do that after a childhood of repressed emotions had freed some caged part of him. Over time, he'd come to wish he'd never met her rather than having met her under their circumstances and knowing what his involvement, however well intentioned, had stolen. He had told the Descendants he couldn't do the job any longer: he couldn't not love her.

But Audrey knew none of that. He was afraid now. The lurchers didn't scream in this moment, but his mind did. *I truly love you. I love you.*

The sky opened up with a crack of thunder and pouring rain, and Audrey and Mitch moved in, and the three ran to the sliding glass doors near the grill where Amelia was stashed. Mitch tried the door, and when it wouldn't budge, his eyes darkened and his palms forced the issue with some ability he had. Kevin leaned down, raised the cover, and ushered Amelia inside. There they stood, in some very modern house, drowned and familiar yet unfamiliar, a man with power, the human Handler he'd hired, a girl, and a woman with power.

Kevin rubbed Amelia's damp arms and assured her.

"Who are these people?" Amelia asked, her eyes as round as buttons.

"This is Mitch," Kevin whispered. "And this—" He peered up from his kneel near the girl. "This is Audrey."

"You know them?"

Kevin nodded. "I do."

"How?"

Kevin stood and smoothed his hair from his face, somewhat glad she persisted. "I worked for Mitch. And Audrey and I ... we're friends."

Audrey didn't break eye contact with him, and he felt his heart jump.

Mitch broke off from them all, opening cabinets in the kitchen, searching.

"What are you doing?" Audrey asked.

Mitch didn't answer, opening higher cabinets now.

"Mitch?"

"We hit the lottery," Mitch said, pulling down a box, ripping it open, and extracting something rectangular and shiny. He used his teeth to open a package and turned around, chewing what appeared to be a granola bar. "We need to eat. We don't know when we'll find more food."

THEY ALL DEVOURED chocolate chip bars, with Audrey and Amelia splitting the last one in the box, and in a different time and place, Kevin and Amelia would have danced their wiggly-worm dance. It had been some time since they'd tasted sweet. But this was awkward, and even the six-year-old detected it. Eyes down, she played with her fingers. She never played with her fingers.

Kevin fumbled to extract his walkie. They hadn't anticipated the need to communicate this one, and he didn't know where the others were, so he kept it short. "Amelia safe." He overthought it to death before he broke the ice. "Audrey, can we talk?"

Audrey met his eyes, and it made his heart sink. Her gaze looked apathetic. She opened her mouth, closed it, and opened it: "Mitch, we need to find my dad."

Kevin stared, confused.

Mitch regarded Audrey solemnly. "We will," Mitch replied.

"How?" Audrey replied.

"Let me think for a few."

Audrey stared silently at Mitch.

Kevin motioned to some room beyond. She obliged him, her eyes on Mitch, and Kevin followed.

"We have to be quiet," she began.

Kevin nodded, and palms up, *I'm not a threat,* his message, he approached to whisper in her ear.

She allowed it.

"I have so much I'm sorry for," he began, unsure she could hear him with how low he spoke.

She exhaled, and he paused, but she didn't move away, and he felt comforted by her willingness to allow him this close.

"Kevin, what happened to your hand?"

Kevin winced and cradled the disfigured thing. He had been happy to have not lost all his fingers, but her question reminded him of its ugliness. "The night it happened, one got me."

Audrey didn't touch him, but she did peer at his hand for an eternity before meeting his gaze. She looked sorry they had taken it from him.

"I signed up for this, I did, but things ended up so differently than I expected," Kevin resumed. "Audrey, I've worried every night for you."

Audrey faced away and shook her head. "You know my whole life, all I wanted was to be loved. You've ruined so much for me."

He swallowed. "I'm so sorry. It wasn't my intention. I wanted to do important work, and they told us horror stories, and I, I believed them. It was only after we were, well, *us*, Audrey, that I realized what I had done. What I had taken from you. How unfair it was. Is."

She exhaled with a hand through her hair. Those curls. He used to touch those curls.

"You hate me. You have every right to. I didn't, I—"

"You know what I fucking hate the most?"

He stared at her. He wouldn't presume to know.

"I worried for you. I yearned for you. Even after I discovered who you actually were—*are*—a part of me couldn't let go. It's like," she continued, becoming more irate but whispering, "what the fuck did I ever do to deserve this sort of existence? My dad was gone, and I found you. You." She sounded incredulous.

"Your dad *was* gone? What do you mean?"

"He's here."

"Your dad? You've seen him?" *How? Where? What was it like?*

Kevin didn't have time to ask more questions. Audrey whipped her hair up into a ponytail and left Kevin and the room. She spilled hushed words to Mitch in the kitchen. Mitch, the reason he'd met Audrey. How did Mitch and Audrey meet? Kevin wondered, standing in the dining room where he'd offered an apology he hadn't expected to have the chance to give. How much did she know?

A hurried knock at the window shook him from his relentless questions. Kevin instantly ducked, clenching his teeth. Who—what—could see him right now?

Another knock came, and he lifted his face. Through the home's overgrowth of vines and ivy beyond the paned window, four familiar sets of eyes met his.

KEVIN BURST INTO THE ROOM, interrupting her conversation with Mitch. She'd been insisting they go now, come what might, and she felt frustrated. She didn't have time for Kevin. She wouldn't make time for him.

"Marcel and Winston and Maggie and Stephanie, they're out there, over there, we have to let them in," Kevin insisted breathlessly, pointing to the dining room. "They're my crew." Kevin shook his head. "My family."

Audrey met his stare, and the fire she found in those green eyes felt so familiar. Kevin was a passionate man. Her dad was out there. If it were her dad, there, outside the dining room window, they'd let him in, no questions asked. She nodded to Mitch, and Mitch nodded to her.

When they opened the sliding glass door, two men and two women hurried inside, dripping wet from the rain, wordlessly accepting and sharing the patriotic hand towel Mitch snagged from the kitchen to wipe their faces dry. Amelia didn't care about their drenched state; she was all over them all, giving exuberant and earnest hugs and kisses. She called one man Daddy and the other man Papa, the latter of whom bled from his abdomen, evident from the stain on his cream-colored shirt. The wounded man put up a finger, unzipped the backpack he slung off his shoulders, and pulled out a worn unicorn. Amelia squealed.

"Uh uh," the man tsked, withdrawing the stuffed animal from the girl, and she pouted. "I need you to promise me something."

"Anything!"

"No more chasing skunks."

Audrey furrowed her brow. *Skunks?*

The girl lamented the ask—something about how the skunks need more friends—and the others in the group chuckled knowingly.

The other man was the first to speak, and Audrey watched, curious about these people who knew her former lover. She clutched her hands awkwardly and bit a fingernail.

"I thought I'd never see you again," the smaller man whispered to Kevin, clobbering him with a hug.

"I know," Kevin replied, rubbing the man's back. "This is Winston."

The big man cried now, quietly, holding his side, and the other man stood nearby, wiping his eyes. They were so thankful to reunite with a man she wasn't sure she was happy to see. Kevin hugged the other man tightly. "So happy you all are okay," he murmured. "Marcel, you okay?"

The big man nodded but grimaced.

The two women—Audrey couldn't remember their names—embraced Kevin next before all four stood silent, peering at Mitch, at Audrey, at Kevin.

"This is Audrey," Kevin began.

"Audrey? *The* Audrey?" one of the women whispered. Her head snapped toward Audrey, and the woman blushed.

Kevin chuckled. "Yes, the one and only." He smiled.

He'd told them about her. She felt her reticence to accept him, despite what he'd done, thaw a tad.

"Nice to meet you, though these circumstances sure suck. I'm

Stephanie," one of the women said. She looked a lot like the other woman.

"Audrey," Audrey said, shaking Stephanie's hand. "You two—are you sisters?"

Stephanie peered at the other woman. "We've been told we look alike. Yes, Maggie's my sister."

Maggie. Audrey knew she wouldn't remember their names.

"Hey, is there food here by chance?" the other man asked. He looked sheepish but earnest. "We haven't eaten since the skunk."

Audrey still didn't know why they spoke of skunks.

Mitch moved to the kitchen, extracting cans and jars, and the four moved with him, hungrily feasting on tuna fish and canned corn with their fingers.

"Man, we got lucky with this house," Kevin murmured. "We've hunted for food, and trust us, it's not easy to find."

"I need to see if my dad is still there," Audrey said to no one in particular.

Kevin gave her a curious look. "Where? We should be careful. They could be out there."

"I can do it without leaving," Audrey replied. "Mitch, how? Here?"

Kevin glanced from Audrey to Mitch and back to Audrey, but she didn't explain.

Mitch, taking a can opener to some more food, met her gaze. "Go run a bath."

Upstairs, in a bathroom the size of many bedrooms she'd rented, she inhaled and turned the spigot. Water gurgled forth, and with it gushed her relieved breath. They were fortunate to be in well country and in a home with a generator. She imagined running water had ceased to be a thing in the cities. The thought of not having water to drink and to use—she paused, her fingers beneath the cold flow, consumed with the thought of people dying of dehydration.

Though she was alone, she couldn't help but think being naked wasn't wise—they didn't know what danger lurked outside and whether it would burst at any moment indoors—so she laid down in the water fully clothed. She gasped at the frigid temp, inhaled, and shut her eyes. *Daddy?* she called without speaking. As had proven the case with cloaking, she was able to force visions because she knew she could, and that was a comfort. She didn't want to be afraid every time she needed to see. She was exhausted by fear.

The tub and its steel faucet and its colorful shower curtain faded, and she leaned forward. She could see him. Her dad lay in a pool of blood in the place she'd seen him before, his arms crossed around his chest.

"Daddy?" she exclaimed.

"Dree." He attempted to sit up but failed, falling back and sputtering. "One of those things got me. I tried to save the baby, but she ran upstairs and out the door. I followed, of course, but—"

"Daddy, she's safe. The girl is with us. We're coming, just hang on."

Audrey flew out of the tub, water flinging off her body, snatched a towel from the door, and bounded downstairs. "We gotta go. I have to go," she said, her eyes on Mitch. She shivered from the water, and she shivered at the idea of braving those things.

Kevin approached. "What's wrong?"

Mitch flanked Kevin now. "I'll go with you."

"I will, too," Kevin said.

Audrey didn't care who did what. She would go alone if necessary. The other adults crowded round, and they probably didn't mean to, but they suffocated her. "I have to go," she repeated. "My dad. Mitch, where do I go?"

Mitch held up his palm. "I need to check the address. Stay here."

Audrey, the sisters, and Winston walked to the home's front door with Mitch. The other man—Michael? Was it? Some M name—stayed with the girl. Mitch placed his hand on the doorknob and turned. "Stay." He turned it slowly, and they all cringed when it creaked. He inched the door forward excruciatingly slowly and tiptoed outside.

Audrey crouched near Winston. She wanted a distraction. "How do you know each other?" she asked Kevin.

Kevin peered at Winston. "He saved my life."

Winston somehow found the strength to smile in the moment. "He's repaid it. You saved our baby," he said, his eyes on Kevin.

Kevin touched the man's shoulder. "I would have died trying."

The front door moved, and everyone stilled. Mitch stepped back inside and leaned down. "It's 1700 Baldwin Road. Audrey, he's at 1574, yes?"

"Yes," she whispered.

"We're on the right side. We're not far. I don't hear them, and I didn't see them, but we don't know. We can't."

34

It was daytime, but so dark. From the moment they descended the porch steps, the rain made Mitch and Kevin as wet as Audrey was from the bath. The sky thundered the same way it had before the earth came under siege. In a way, that was a comfort. Maybe Earth could be her former self again someday.

This also was a comfort: the pelting drops drowned out the sound of their walking. It would have drowned out their voices, too, not that they dared whisper. The storm was their shield.

They walked, Mitch on the left, Audrey on the right, Kevin to the rear, their eyes watchful. When they found the plain black mailbox with the numbers 1574, her heart leapt. *My God, we're going to do it. Hang on, Daddy.*

Mitch tried the front door, and it gave way, and the three silently scoped the place out. Audrey snapped her fingers when she found it, a door opening to a staircase below.

She hadn't seen him in the flesh for years, decades, but there he lay, her dad, his eyes wide. He tried to sit up, but she waved away his attempt.

"Daddy," she said, "where did they get you?"

Her father grimaced and pointed to his right side, and Mitch leaned in.

"May I?"

Her dad nodded and lay back down.

Mitch pulled up his shirt, and they found a deep gash. Charles winced and inhaled deeply. Fear coursed through Audrey's body when more blood oozed from the wound.

Kevin knelt beside her, and she met his gaze. She felt comforted he was here, though it struck her as wrong to feel comfort. There was a familiarity to him, though. In the year and a half they'd been together, he'd watched her grapple with her dad's absence more than she'd ever let her mom witness. Her mom had her own wounds with regard to her dad, and she hadn't wanted Mom to bear her hurt, too.

"We need to stop the bleeding," Kevin whispered, peering around the basement.

Mitch met Audrey's eyes, then Kevin's.

She wished Mitch had lied and that he could heal him, but he'd told her he wasn't a healer, and his next words cemented that truth.

"When we return to the Underground, the healers will render it gone. But he has to survive until then."

Two thoughts bombarded her. The first: *Mitch said he can bring people back to life. If Daddy dies—* Audrey couldn't stomach the thought, so she stopped thinking it. The second: "Can *I* heal, Mitch?"

Mitch stopped moving. "I don't know."

"How do I try?"

"Place your palms above his wound, and imagine it gone. I'm not a healer, but that's what the healers do."

Audrey kneeled beside her dad and placed her palms above his gaping wound. It terrified her, how every breath he took let more of his life source seep. She imagined them emerging from this terror, his abdomen solid, his bleeding gone. She wanted to cry but refused. She didn't want him to worry.

Nothing changed, and now the sobs really threatened. Audrey stood and walked away, afraid that her fear would influence her dad's recovery. It *had* to be recovery. She couldn't lose him again.

Kevin reappeared with a bag of cotton spiderweb décor, and they wrapped it tightly around and around and around. Blood seeped through immediately, but the stopgap would have to do.

KEVIN WATCHED Audrey plead for them to head straight for the mansion and its Underground healers, and he commiserated with the desperation of her plea. But her dad insisted they first retrieve the little girl.

"She's the only reason I told you where I was," Charles reminded his daughter gently.

She seemed comforted he was conscious and speaking.

They almost made it. As they climbed the porch of the home where Kevin's family hid, Audrey's dad bolstered by Mitch and Audrey, all desperate to not make a sound, there arose a commotion. A wail from someone new. A human scream. When the gun shots rang out, Audrey, Mitch, and Kevin ducked behind the gingerbread railing, pulling Charles with them. Kevin peered out and inhaled, stood, and bounded away. He had to find these people, whoever they were. They must have worked hard to stay out of sight and safe all these months, and now monsters chased them from a house. He could not leave them.

"Kevin, don't," Mitch said, but Kevin was already down the steps. His legs burned with the effort, and he met the woman and the children in the road and shushed them so hard he spit. It surprised him their cries were audible over the storm. It also scared him.

He leaned down and grabbed one kid and turned to the woman and the other. "You have to shut up. They—"

A shrieking interrupted him, and he motioned for them to follow him behind a car. "You have to be quiet," he hissed. "Come this way."

The woman and the older child understood, and they followed swiftly and silently, but the wave came faster. Before he could lead them inside, the ungodly creatures thrashed and shrieked and crushed an SUV adjacent to their hiding spot. The younger child screamed bloody murder, and that was it. The creatures bounded grotesquely their way. They were known, and they were probably dead.

He wouldn't not try.

Holding the one child, Kevin scooped up the other and sprinted, his lungs bursting, his arms burning. If he'd had time to ponder it, he would have figured he was leading death straight to his family. He didn't have the time. He pushed the children up the porch stairs of 1700 Baldwin Road and grabbed the woman, then thrust her forward. "Go!" he screamed.

The creatures' foul, sour stink permeated the air. They lurched many feet taller than the vehicles abandoned on the street, and they crashed and tumbled to get to him. *Can I outrun them?* Kevin jumped from the porch and ran, his arms pumping, his legs pushing, his eyes forward until he turned to ensure it worked. He screamed a sound he hadn't known he could make for good measure. Bloody fucking murder.

It worked. The creatures, God, it might have been ten of them, pursued him relentlessly, their mantis-like pinchers thrashing the space separating them. Kevin didn't have time to register much, but his body was jacked up with adrenaline. He weaved in front of and behind houses, and the demons crashed in and out with him.

He sprinted and the land appeared open before him until he fell, caught by searing pain in his torso. He peered down. An enormous claw skewered the right side of his abdomen. He turned his face and found it penetrated him through the left side, too. A sob escaped him.

He would have screamed but couldn't. The demon punctured him another time, this time through his leg, and bared its mouth to the sky, screaming. Kevin lay wishful but unable to rise and run away, stilled by the strikes, his eyes on the dark, stormy sky. *This is it. This is it.*

In the moment, he saw nothing but the rain. It pelted his face so much, he turned and focused on a porch, overgrown, deserted. No one would come for him. No one should come for him. Kevin lay, thrashing a few more times, but resigned himself to death.

The monsters stopped running and crowded round, and he turned his face the other way, refusing to face untimely and violent death. What he found made him blink rapidly. Audrey stood, eyes unseeing, hands to the sky, and the fire began.

MITCH RAN to the road and screamed so loudly, Audrey couldn't believe his bravery; she knew he did it to distract them, to divert them from Kevin, but it wasn't working. Tall figures with their grotesque scissor arms chased Kevin across the road and behind a house, and she couldn't stop herself.

"NO!" Audrey screamed, bursting forth from the porch. "NO." She thrust Mitch back with a "Get my dad to safety" and fled, and as the lurchers kept pursuit, she pursued *them*. She sprinted down the street lined with black streetlights, despite Mitch's screams, and beat one with her fists. She fought the desire to retract her hands from its sharp, reptilian scales. "NO!"

The creatures turned and menaced her, tall and reaching. Their mouths leaked, and they shrieked, and she knew fear but also a resolute courage. NO. Before she registered his reemergence, Mitch pushed her from them, his eyes black, his arms up and visibly shaking. Whatever he expected to happen didn't, and a creature punctured his leg. He screamed with anguish. She had never heard the man scream like that. What unfolded was among the most surreal moments of her life: Mitch crumpling to the concrete, his bloody hands trying to protect himself after saving so many others. He diverted his gaze from the creature closest to him and met Audrey's eyes. She had never seen the man afraid.

One of the creatures lunged for his neck, and he dodged it, but he was powerless and crawling, a blood trail behind him despite the rain. The same creature raised its pinchers on both sides of Mitch's body, intending, it seemed, to cut him in half. Kevin lay nearby, already in a skewered state, watching. He mouthed something at her, but she couldn't see what through the rain.

"NO!" Audrey screamed again, spittle flying, and she thrust her fists down toward the earth.

The creatures around Kevin and Mitch stilled. Audrey felt the most intense tingling in her body, and she felt drawn to put her palms out to the sky, and she felt pulled to scream again, "DIE! Today, you die!" It was again so surreal. Who did she think she was? How could she be so ready to risk her life, having reunited with Dad?

The sky burst with thunder, and in a frightening and unreal display, lightning bolts descended, skewering every creature around them, igniting their skeletons in the most unnatural show and muting their screeches. Audrey felt electrocuted herself, her limbs numb and her scream gone. Somehow, though she couldn't feel her legs or her arms, her palms stayed up as the creatures shook to the ground. Something burned. She stayed, strangely confident in this position, palms forward. An intense heat coursed through her, and the lurchers seized before her and Kevin and Mitch, not one, not two, but every last one. She could and couldn't be sure and peered at her burning fingers. They were dark. Tinged with soot.

Did I do that? She collapsed.

She lay on the concrete sidewalk, gasping, praying for air. The rain was relentless; it didn't care that earth was besieged, that it could use a break. She lay as Winston and the sisters met them in this part of the suburban street, gathering around a body nearby. Not her body. His.

Nothing screeched. Nothing lurched. Audrey blinked and sputtered, "No, no," before she passed out.

When Audrey came to, her hands flew to her face, wiping frantically. *Why is my face wet?* She panicked, inhaling and coughing. She rolled, shaking liquid from her face. Thunder cracked, lightning flickered, and she turned to the sky. Rain. It was rain. She tried to kneel but fell forward when her palms struck the ground and gave way.

Audrey yelped. Her hands were fire-hot, and the water intensified the burn.

"Audrey, Audrey," a female voice said.

Audrey tore to the right and threw her palms up, her fingers curled, in a protective stance.

The woman waved her own palms and backed away. "Audrey," the woman said, "it's Stephanie. Kevin's friend."

It didn't take long for the scene to return to her. The storm. The fried skeletons. Kevin. Audrey quickly came to and lowered her hands.

"Audrey!" Mitch's voice was a comfort right now.

Audrey sat up, cradling her palms.

Mitch limped to her, a flannel shirt tied around where he'd been injured, and knelt beside her, his hand on her back. "We've got people coming. They're going to take us underground."

"My dad?" Audrey croaked. Her throat seared. Every bit of her, actually, burned.

"He's managing. We'll be safe soon."

"Kevin?"

"They're taking all of us underground."

Audrey leaned forward, dropped her face in her hands, and bawled so hard she couldn't breathe. When men in uniforms with long guns cupped her elbows and softly urged her to stand, she stopped crying, wiping the snot away. Her eyes met Mitch's, imploring him for the next step.

"We need to go, Audrey."

She would never forget the scene at the door as long as she lived.

They followed a corridor in the mansion, a devastatingly vast place when every step exhausted her, though she didn't walk on her own. Two uniformed men pushed open a heavy door that groaned open, and they descended down an intense spiral staircase, the one Mitch and she had climbed to come above ground. Audrey staggered, uncertain in her abilities, and the men on either side of her walked her down, one in front, one in back, determined to get her there. When their feet met an earthen floor descending farther, Audrey dared to look around. Red sconces lit their path and illuminated the faces of the men whose big hands gripped both her arms. They were black and white, both H something, both stalwart. She stumbled, and they gripped her more carefully. She desperately leaned on their strength.

When they met a red door, Audrey's heart rate quickened. Mitch limped forward and knocked in a particular way, softly and four times, and the door opened immediately. A man, hefty and silent, lifted his chin.

"Mitch," H16 said. Here stood the same damn man who'd reluctantly let her in all those months ago. She recognized him, though he'd grown a mustache.

"H16." Mitch let on no emotion.

The hefty man looked now to Audrey. He bowed his head, and Audrey's breath caught. The man met her eyes again, and he reached up to finger a touch screen at the door. He punched in a few numbers, and the screen blared white.

"For The Descended, ma'am," the man said, stepping aside. "For the world."

Down Audrey's face trailed a single, hot tear. "For the world," she choked, held up by men in a familiar uniform.

Audrey stopped and turned, and the Handlers paused, their direction apparently hers to give. Others, numbered as well, carried in two stretchers, and behind them walked Kevin's crew and another woman and her children. The whole procession paused on her stall and only proceeded when she exhaled and gripped the arms of the men flanking her.

They were all inside. They were all inside.

AUDREY'S MUSCLES ached incredibly the first night she spent back underground. She groaned, turning over. It had been a long time since she'd run for her life. She hoped she never would again, but she knew that was wishful thinking. There was no way the scourge was entirely over, she just knew it. She lay, staring at the dark room, closed her eyes, and exhaled. She'd been so moved last night when the Descendants had let them in. They'd rushed her dad to the medical wing, but she had been turned away from his bedside. After an excruciating hour spent chewing her fingernails and pacing her suite though her body hurt, there'd come a single knock on her door. An elder surprised her with her presence. She was worried about Mitch, because no elder had seen fit to see to her before. "Your father is stable." They were a mere four words, and they'd caused Audrey to slide to the floor and cover her face in her hands. "We'll notify you when you can visit. May we attend to your injuries?"

Audrey had wiped her face. She'd dismissed medical care last night, worried it would distract from her father's care. She'd figured she would survive her gashes and bruises and burns. "Mitch?" she'd croaked.

"Mitch is expected to have a full recovery."

"Thank you so much."

"It appears, dear girl, we have much to thank *you* for. Rest now."

The elder had left, and that's when Audrey had finally lain down. But she couldn't stay in bed for long. If she was going to do this, it probably had to be now. Rest would have to wait.

The clock told her the sun wouldn't be up for another few hours, not that they'd enjoy its light back down here. She walked to the cafeteria. No one walked the halls, a welcome solace, and no one worked the steel commercial appliances. It was exactly the scene she'd hoped for.

The kitchen sprawled—she bet it was larger than any apartment she'd called home—and that made sense. It fed hundreds. Audrey willed herself visible. The Descendants understood more about her than she did right now, so cloaking seemed an unnecessary cover when no one was present.

She never had liked cooking in another's kitchen, even Kevin's. She searched low and high for a skillet, tried probably eight drawers before locating the spatula and spoon she needed, and pressed more buttons than necessary before the oven roared to preheat. She moved like a thief, scrounging the minimum fistfuls of beef she needed from an outsized package dethawing in one of six refrigerators and scooping up an onion and a pepper from the vegetable pantry she discovered.

Audrey used to hate peppers, before she'd tasted the lasagna Kevin had made for a colleague who suffered from preeclampsia. *They do add a brightness,* she'd conceded to him after he'd convinced her to try a bite of the bubbling pan he'd baked on the side for the two of them. He baked an extra lasagna on these occasions, and he never failed to grin when she asked for more.

Audrey paused, her hands on either door of a food pantry. *Impressively so full even now,* she reflected. She browsed the shelves and found an Alfredo sauce. Not what she sought, but it would have to do. It reminded her of a lasagna Kevin had crafted for the Dennisons down the street after their dog, Bandit, was hit by a car. The fluffy gold creature had lived, though on three legs following that. The Dennisons threw a clam bake annually, so Kevin had devised for them a lasagna of seafood, creamy Alfredo sauce, spinach, and bacon.

Audrey shook her head. She'd felt actual hatred for him, Kevin. And that felt fair. He'd deceived her in the worst of ways, under the guise of respect and honesty and vulnerability and love.

But she didn't hate him. She didn't know what to feel. Numbness? Regret? Empathy? Love? All of it?

When she couldn't find the right knife, she butchered the onion and pepper with a butter knife, stopping twice to give her singed fingers the rest they demanded, and threw the vegetables into the skillet. She cried, and not just because of the onion. She added the beef but a door opened, and she felt caught. *Hide*, she told herself, and she began to will her body invisible—but then she stopped. No. She was done hiding. She had done nothing wrong. She would stand her ground. She straightened, wiping tears from her cheeks, and turned back up the heat. Only then did she face whomever had just entered.

Betty Jane stepped forward. "Hey. I heard."

Audrey met Betty Jane's eyes, and her bottom lip quaked.

Betty Jane closed the distance between them, and Audrey dropped her head into her hands and leaned into this woman, a friend. When the tears stopped, she pulled away and seized the spatula.

"The fuck you cooking?"

Oh, Betty Jane. She could be counted on to bring a gritty comfort to most any scenario. "Condolences," Audrey replied.

Betty Jane nodded, though she couldn't have understood. Betty Jane pulled up a stool and placed her palms in her lap, and that meant a lot to Audrey. She didn't want to cook this alone. She didn't want to marinate in these thoughts alone. All those years she'd spent, this past year she'd spent, seemingly alone, wishing so fervently for family, and now she'd found her dad, and she'd come to care for people here, and she'd ... learned to forgive herself, too. Audrey bent over and rolled her neck, and it cracked. She dug her hands into the frigid cheese mixture and dropped it here and there before spreading it with a spatula over the hot beef veggie layer. She carefully extracted more cooked, fragile noodles and started anew: three fat ribbons, lined up precisely, beef veggie sauce scooped over top, all of it topped with copious cheese. She was hopeful even the kiddo—Amelia was her name, she was almost sure of it—would eat it.

Kevin. She forgave him, she truly did. She was learning ever so slowly and ever so quickly that family loved hard *and* disappointed hard. Family was as imperfect as every person was, and that was every person's experience—human and otherwise. Audrey swallowed a sob and grabbed the pan. She cast a glance at Betty Jane, who nodded her forward. She paused, the oven door open and its heat warming her face, while Betty Jane, usually a woman of so many words, wordlessly watched.

This lasagna, slid in to bake under aluminum foil for the next hour before most would awaken, would be for those who'd loved Kevin Williams.

35

When the Handler stepped into the kitchen, Betty Jane barely reacted, but Audrey recoiled. "No reason for all that," Betty Jane mused. "It's a new reckoning."

Audrey had no idea what she meant, but the lasagna bubbled, and the timer counted down—presently seven minutes and fourteen seconds, squarely the window when the parmesan on top would brown and crisp. Before them was the same man who'd allowed Audrey in with gravitas yesterday. *The one who wanted to keep me out all those months ago.*

"H19?" Audrey guessed, awkwardly waving because she didn't know what else to do. To her right, Betty Jane chuckled. She seemed so knowing in a moment that felt otherworldly to Audrey.

"H16 actually," the hefty man replied, pointing to his uniform. He smiled.

Audrey raised an eyebrow.

"Ma'am, I am now your security detail. I've been asked to take you to him."

"My what? To whom?"

"I'm your protection, and Mitch has asked to see you." She noticed he carried a gun the length of an arm.

Audrey peered at Betty Jane, who nodded her forward. "It's time," the woman, her friend, said, and it deepened Audrey's confusion.

"Can you pull the lasagna, when the timer goes?"

Betty Jane nodded again, shooing her gone.

Audrey stepped to the Handler and tilted her head. The irony. *It used to be your job to stall my entry, and now you protect me. From what?* the thought nudged in. She followed him through quiet halls, down a locked corridor, to a ward labeled the medical quarters. When they stepped where Mitch was, Audrey's heart rate picked up. He was connected to wires and machines with screens whose numbers vacillated and whose lines jumped constantly, and it scared her. *I really don't want to do life without you.*

"Audrey," Mitch said, and his voice soothed her nerves.

"Mitch." She put her hand on his. "Are you okay?"

"I hurt," he replied, grimacing to sit up before she insisted he stop. "But we've got a form of medicine down here the Cleveland Clinic never sniffed."

She smiled.

"H16, give us the room."

The Handler left, and Audrey peered intently at Mitch.

"When they got me," Mitch began, "I had more time than I expected to think on things."

Audrey sat at his bedside.

"I thought only of you and my mom and dad."

This was different. Mitch had steered every conversation away from his parents. He didn't do that now.

"Every moment I've lived in their absence, I've fought to make them proud of me," Mitch said, his voice faltering. "My very being draws on what they would do, how they would behave if they were told the things I was told, in a society that would not have them commit the crimes I have, least of all during some apocalypse. *This* apocalypse. I wouldn't have had the strength I did were it not for my conviction that they would have done not a lick different. My dad died saving a human."

"What were you told?"

"Do me a favor. Light a match and toss it in that bowl."

Audrey looked where he motioned: a small iron cauldron stuffed with dried herbs. "Pretty sure we shouldn't light matches in a hospital," she began.

"This isn't a hospital. I need you to see. *We* need you to see. The elders say it should work, given you are a prophet."

A prophet. These past few days were nothing short of surreal.

Tentatively, but persuaded by his nods, Audrey struck a match, lit herbs she didn't recognize, and turned back to Mitch.

"Breathe that in three times," he instructed.

She did as she was told.

"Now, see me in Graylock on the day they gave me the prophesy."

She doubted this would work, and she had no idea what he was talking about. Barely a moment into the doubt, however, Audrey's vision faltered, and she now laid eyes on a much younger Mitch. She sat back down, dizzy inside the hour he once lived.

TEN YEARS *before*

Older men and women filed out in grievous silence, but Mitch didn't move at first. When he did rise and stepped to the ring of white matter drawn around the table, he paused and stepped over it, heading for the door.

"Mitch," a remaining man said.

Mitch stopped immediately and turned. The man gestured to the chair he'd left, and he obliged him.

"There's more," began the older man. He raised his palms, summoning a vision. Audrey knew it because it crowded her sight, too. "Close your eyes."

When Mitch did, the man laid fingers on his eyelids. "See," he commanded.

"Prophet, please, what do you need me to see?" young Mitch asked, and in the moment he raised the question, Audrey saw it: a woman, no, her very self, dressed in a bright apron and standing in a small group of people, slicing a leek. Braising a leek.

The woman cooked, and young Mitch looked confused.

She wasn't confused in the least. She remembered the cooking class.

The prophet removed his fingers from Mitch's eyelids. "Her name is Audrey. Audrey Kelly."

"Elder?"

"The night it happens, you will find her in a neighborhood not far from here, in a gown of sequins. You must not return to the Underground without her. She is the key to our survival."

This felt downright trippy to Audrey. They spoke of *her*.

Mitch furrowed his brows. "Who is she? A Descendant? You said we will build a sanctuary for Descendants."

"In part, she is."

His eyes widened. "She's one of them?"

The elder man tilted his head and rubbed his beard. "She is. I didn't see the end, but I saw enough. From her erupts a power unlike that which you or I or any Descendant can effect. She kills so many of those *things*, she gives us a chance. You must bring her through the red door."

"The red door?"

"You'll know what I mean when you live it."

"Elder. I'm confused."

Audrey knew the door. She couldn't believe what she now knew.

The man turned his back to Mitch, his rich, velvety cloak waving from his shoulders as he walked to a mammoth mirror. The room's grandfather clock chimed several times, ringing in a new hour.

"Mitch, when it happens, you and the others will flee, leaving behind so much. The world you return to won't be the same." The old man grunted and braced himself on the table. "I know you will flee, but follow your gut. Follow your heart." He turned, his eyes burning and serious. "When it makes sense, follow her."

Young Mitch nodded, stepped over the salt, and made his way to the door. He turned and met the man's eyes. "Why wait until the others left to reveal this? Won't they need to know why I've brought her within?"

"They will know—eventually. Dear Mitch, I was five the first time I had a prophesy. Not one of my nine has been untrue. But you don't need my gift to know this: people sometimes don't see the truth until they, themselves, are outsiders, you included. Keep your truth until *she* makes them see what they don't yet see. Assuredly you will suffer, but that's important to the process, to your seeing the fuller picture. It's important to the young woman's journey, too."

Mitch turned to leave.

The elder spoke once more. "Mitch."

Mitch stopped walking.

"You cannot resurrect yourself. Be very careful when the fight moves to the lake."

AUDREY SHOOK her head when the vision ended. "Mitch," she said. "You knew? You knew all along you'd bring me here?"

Mitch grunted, and the machines above him made a more urgent beeping sound than before. "Listen to me, Audrey."

Audrey reclasped his hand. His grasp made her feel rooted.

"I didn't know a thing past that. The elders made out like I should have just told them." Mitch laughed uncharacteristically at the governors of his life. "As though they would have believed it, absent what you just did. *You* enable us to save the world. *You.* I don't know how, and I don't know when because I'm not a prophet like you or him, but I knew going in, yes, that you make it possible that all of us—me, you, the Descendants, and so many humans like Kevin—survive because there's something innate in you that just, I don't know, works."

Audrey furrowed her eyebrows. "Kevin?"

Mitch nodded. "He's in the room next to mine."

Audrey stood, reeling. No one had told her he survived, so she'd presumed they tried to protect her from more pain by not telling her he was gone. Her stomach couldn't drop lower or roil more. She steadied herself on the wires above Mitch before she thought better of it. *I thought you were gone.* She stifled a sob, relieved.

She'd thought so many things, but never ever that she was the key to everyone's survival.

"Your door is open," Mitch said.

Audrey considered closing her thoughts to him, but she needed the connection, to let him in.

"I didn't know more than what he told me," repeated Mitch, the most powerful of the Descendants, laid up in a hospital bed. The man she couldn't fathom losing. "I'm glad I can finally tell you everything. No more secrets. No more omissions. No more lies. Just you and me and the beginning of life as we know it. As we make it."

Audrey walked the room, touching the wall because it felt real when nothing else did. *Who on God's green earth thought it wise to appoint me the savior anyone needs?*

Mitch heard her. "Does it matter, Audrey? You're it."

ACKNOWLEDGMENTS

To those with expertise in bees, architecture (Gibson Taylor Thompson Architecture & Design), and wastewater treatment (Northeast Ohio Regional Sewer District), thank you for graciously giving your time so the fiction I've written could be accurate in the ways it should be. Authors, don't hesitate to reach out to folks who possess the knowledge your books need. People's generosity will surprise you, I promise.

To Kate Broad, thank you for being such a thorough, detailed, generous, talented, and kind editor. To Xavier and the Coverkitchen team, your cover truly captured the spirit of this book. Kate Randolph of Ripped Pages LLC, you marketed this book creatively and thoughtfully to find its audience, and I thank you.

To Mark McElroy, I bet mentoring me on this journey wasn't on your 2025 bingo card, huh? I have leaned on and learned from you more than I knew I would. Your generosity is your legacy, and I'm better for knowing you, and that's been true since the Toledo documentary project.

To my alpha and beta readers who spent hours reading this work (some of you, during both feedback rounds!), I couldn't have done this without you. You helped me nix what felt boring, anticipate readers' questions and hopefully answer them to satisfaction, and cheered me on along this long, sometimes discouraging, journey. Thank you doesn't do it justice, really. But it'll have to, so thank you Lisa Bolstad, Maggie Bowles (my best friend in the world), Josh Brubaker, Sam Dolgin-Gardner, Amanda Dunn, Khaz Finley, Jan Leach, Darci Leffingwell, Deana Letterle, Stephanie Mills, Ben H. Rome, Abby Slutsky, Lisa Speckman, and Erin Zifcheck.

To Katie, Marie, and Judy, I couldn't have guessed that my closest author allies would live on the opposite coast among the palm trees, hahaha. Thank you so much for your encouragement, the accountability our author calls continue to inspire, and the many hours you've spent reading my work.

To Jenny, I'll never forget learning Russ sent you the working draft and the words you said to me—that I had a talent for this. Thank you and Randy and the entire clan for every bit of support and also that salty, scrumptious stuffing you make at Thanksgiving.

To Steph and Tiffany, thanks for the sad emojis and encouragement every time I messaged you a screen grab of yet another rejection. I did it anyway!

To Mom, who inspired parts of this story, I love you. Thanks for letting me run with it, for always reading my work, and for stoking my love of storytelling, even if at times we both wondered how I'd make a living doing it. Love, your baby girl.

To Steven, "my co-author" and wannabe cover designer (you all should see some of the ridiculous illustrations he's proposed), they say whom you marry is the most important decision you make in your life. They're right. I'm ever grateful for every last writing webinar and conference you made it possible for me to attend; for every brainstorm session you tolerated, even when I was shooting down your ideas, sorry; and for your listening to the godawful audio versions to give me your feedback at every stretch of the way. We did it. That legacy you wanted for our babies? It *exists*. Forever. I love you.

To Lawson, Micah, and Casey, I love you forever and a day. May you remember every time Mommy was "writing her novel" with some positivity even if it took me away from you; I appreciate the sacrificed time together to chase this dream of mine. Please never let someone gatekeep you from your dreams. This is for you, even if no, you're not old enough to read it. Yet.

ABOUT THE AUTHOR

Michelle Park Lazette has written professionally for two decades, first in newsrooms around the country and for the last 11 years as a corporate storyteller and marketing strategist. She doesn't enjoy business-only author pages, so ...

She's a wife to a person who remembers what they did on a random weekend in 2012, and she loves and envies how effortlessly funny he is. She's a mother to three children she adores, even if their requests for food keep her busier than her full-time job. She's a daughter and daughter-in-law to the strongest women she knows, a sister to women she admires, and a cat-mom. She likes chicken paprikash, especially the super creamy kind. She doesn't particularly enjoy working out but does it because they say it's good for you. And she isn't an all-out prepper, but COVID taught her it's smart to have some essentials on hand in case you can't leave the house today or tomorrow. Or in case there's an apocalypse.

For more books and to subscribe for news: www.flyingsnakepress.com

Made in the USA
Coppell, TX
04 January 2026

68080758R00187

Park and Recreate

Fill Your Wellness Tank

Todd & Marsha Davis
"The Fun Coach"

ISBN: 979-8-89663-910-7

Dedication

To Marsha…

After years with the City of Scottsdale Parks and Recreation Division, I envisioned creating "Corporate Games," a pioneering business to meet corporate recreation and event needs. The concept had promise but only saw modest success until I met and married my soulmate, Marsha. With her by my side, my dreams took flight. Our achievements, both personal and professional, have been built on Marsha's incredible talent, unwavering loyalty, and partnership through the twists of economies, business highs and lows, and all my new ideas.

Together, we began teaching the Pike Place Fish Market Philosophy to company teams over 25 years ago. In those sessions, we found a pattern; nearly seven out of ten participants felt out of balance. People who nurtured their physical, spiritual, and social lives showed up to work happy and went home happy. With this insight, Marsha developed our "Life-Leisure Balance" workshop, which has become a resounding success.

This book is dedicated to Marsha, whose passion has fueled our Work-Life-Leisure sessions and seminars, benefiting professionals, college students, association members, and volunteers. She has championed wellness in our "Recreation Game Plan," adding depth and meaning to my 50 years in the field of recreation.

Thank you, Marsha, for being my partner in every sense.

Acknowledgment

Thank you to all the participants who shared their "balance" issues stemming from not having time or feeling guilty for making time. Your input has guided us to this book, which was created to help people fill their wellness tank, and Park and Recreate to improve their physical, spiritual, social and emotional well-being. From our interactive sessions and participant input, we realize that living life weekly and having an intentional game plan will fuel your energy cells to complete all of your obligations with the right attitude.

My career started 50 years ago (1975) with the City of Scottsdale, where I received the best program training and customer service values that anyone could ask for. Thank you to Bob Frost, Bill Exham and all of those who guided me towards a lifetime professional career.

A special thanks to CFMA, Construction Financial Management Association, for allowing us to work with your leadership program, Spring Creek, for over 15 years and for taking the time to listen and learn. Your trust in us and the interactive sessions with professionals have made a difference in our lives! We treasure and look forward to working with your members and management team every year.

Finally, thank you to Maricopa Community College District for allowing us to be adjunct instructors educating and motivating future recreation and social work professionals through our class “Leisure and the Quality of Life.

About the Authors

Todd & Marsha Davis have been helping people and companies have FUN since 1988. Their ability to release people to the value of having "fun at and away from work" is a gift that just makes sense. Besides a long history with the concept of Home–Team Play USA, they founded Fun Coach USA in 2002 to focus on the wellness of teams and the individuals who bond within that team. Today, they offer a discovery program consisting of Fun At Work and Fun Away from Work, or Park and Recreate, Stop for Fun. Fun at Work provides managers with a process to engage teams, while Fun Away from Work is all about work-life recreation balance.

They have discovered that people who come to work happy usually leave happy. This value of happiness comes from making and taking time with your interests while being fit physically, spiritually, and emotionally to fill your wellness energy tank.

Together, Todd and Marsha have built a successful career in the field of corporate recreation and team building. They have two daughters, son-in-laws and grandchildren. Besides work, they support their community, volunteer and help people succeed in their endeavors.

Fun Coach 50 is Todd's theme for this book, as he is just beginning his 50th year in the profession. He loves what he does, volunteers throughout Scottsdale, and is passionate about Park and Recreate, making and taking time for your wellness.

The book was written from Todd's perspective, but consider it from both Todd and Marsha's years of professional expertise. Together, everyone (we) achieved more!

Contents

Introduction

Everything we do is influenced by the energy we bring to our activities, whether work-related or not. Work can take many forms: a job, parenting, caretaking, or any other responsibility. Essentially, work is any period where we have duties we must fulfill.

For a full-time parent, raising children is a form of work that demands a lot of time and effort. However, this book primarily targets those who earn an income through their job, whether they work for themselves or someone else. These individuals invest a significant amount of time in earning money and fulfilling specific responsibilities.

Over the years, I've observed that people who make time for fun and recreation tend to be happier and more balanced. Leisure activities benefit us in four main areas: *spiritual*, *physical*, *mental*, and *social*. Although these aspects are interconnected, this book will focus on recreation.

Recreation includes activities that get us outdoors, such as hiking, biking, walking, sports, swimming, fitness, fishing, and camping. These activities allow us to engage with nature and enjoy ourselves. The essence of this book is to explore these physical activities that bring us joy, often in the company of others. Hobbies like crafting can also be deeply fulfilling.

For instance, gardening to grow food for your family is work, but gardening as a hobby can be pure enjoyment. It's a wonderful way to connect with nature and find peace. Similarly, bicycling can serve two purposes: commuting to work is a duty, but bicycling for recreation is a chance to have fun and enjoy the outdoors.

Finding time for fun away from work is crucial. It recharges us and keeps us energized for our responsibilities, whether through outdoor activities, hobbies, or simply taking a break.

Think of your life like a cell phone. We know what drains its battery and how to recharge it. Similarly, our daily routines and obligations can deplete our energy. Just as we recharge our phones, we must recharge ourselves.

You might wonder how to recharge. As mentioned, engaging in recreational activities is key. You need to participate in activities you enjoy and look forward to. This choice is yours to make and should be embraced. Over the years, I've found that helping teams incorporate more fun into their lives was a good start. True happiness comes from investing in personal enjoyment outside of work. I began encouraging people to see it as their individual responsibility to invest in their leisure time so they could come to work happier.

It's time to stop blaming your co-workers or boss for your unhappiness. Yes, there will always be challenges, but ultimately, you are responsible for your own joy. It's time to say, "I'm going to schedule time for my interests. I'm going to recreate with others and engage in activities on my own time. I'm going to claim my health and happiness." No one else can do it for you.

From my experience working with people, those who invest time in activities that enhance their well-being; spiritual, physical, mental, and social are generally happier. A Native American friend once shared a story that captures this well: "Todd, our spirit of happiness is with us wherever we go. When we're home, that spirit comes with us. When we go to work, the spirit comes with us." It's like carrying an endless supply of joy. Who we are follows us everywhere; you can't just flip a happiness switch when you start work or when you return home. Your involvement in spiritual practices, physical activities, hobbies, and social interactions creates this enduring spirit of happiness.

This holistic approach is key to a fulfilled life.

Statistics show that the number of people who report being happy at work has declined significantly. In the early 2000s, about seven out of ten people reported job satisfaction. Today, it's closer to three out of ten. The shift to remote work and increased isolation have made it even more crucial to find and make time for recreation and fun.

It's not just about finding time; it's about managing and integrating it into your life. The happiest people are those who deliberately set aside time for their interests. They avoid overscheduling and instead dedicate specific blocks of time, perhaps four hours a week, to different activities. This intentional planning allows them to invest in their well-being.

Those who master this balance tend to be happier and more vibrant. They find joy in both their work and leisure, making happiness a constant companion.

Moreover, people who schedule activities that enhance their wellness and well-being look forward to them. This anticipation adds excitement and joy to life beyond mere obligations. For instance, knowing you have volunteer work, bike rides, church outings, or hobby time scheduled gives you something to look forward to and enriches your life.

In our workshops and focus groups, we consistently found that the happiest people at work were those who made time for activities that brought them joy outside of work, whether volunteering, outdoor recreation, hobbies, or social gatherings.

In this book, I will focus on the recreational side of things, though we will also touch on spiritual, physical, mental, and social well-being. Each section will guide you in identifying and planning activities that support these areas. For example, after the chapter on spiritual well-being, you'll have the opportunity to list activities that support your spiritual growth and schedule time for them.

By organizing and planning your time, you'll be on your way to a balanced and fulfilling life. Keep reading for more insights and ideas!

Chapter 1: Park and Recreate

"If you drive by the park every day and don't stop to have fun, you've missed the chance to recreate and enjoy life."

The concept of "parks and recreation" has a deep-rooted history, especially in America, where it has grown into a vibrant industry. Since I began working in this field in 1975, I've witnessed its profound impact on people's lives.

A "park" is any outdoor space designed for public use, such as a city park for sports, a hiking trail, or a peaceful lakeside spot for fishing. To "recreate" means to engage in enjoyable activities like softball, volleyball, or golf. The core idea behind "park and recreate" is straightforward: you need to stop and make time for fun.

In today's fast-paced world, it's easy to become overwhelmed by daily responsibilities. We often rush from work to home, from one task to the next, neglecting the very places and activities that help us relax and rejuvenate. This book encourages you to "park" to pause your hectic schedule and "recreate" to engage in activities that renew and restore your spirit.

Recreation is crucial for avoiding the feeling of being "stuck in the mud." It helps you break free from routine and rediscover joy. Many people feel trapped by life's demands, losing touch with hobbies and interests they once enjoyed or have a desire to try. This book aims to help you reconnect with these activities and improve your overall well-being.

When we neglect recreation, we become more susceptible to stress, which can affect our mood, kindness, and ability to empathize with others. This imbalance can lead to burnout, depression, and a diminished sense of fulfillment. Intentional recreation helps alleviate stress, renew our energy, and revitalize our spirit. Without it, we risk becoming "informationally obese" from excessive media consumption or "spiritually fat" from absorbing spirituality without sharing it.

Often, we focus on how work affects our happiness and quality of life, but we overlook how the lack of recreation impacts our mental health, relationships, and overall well-being.

Failing to make time for fun can lead to:

- **Deteriorating Relationships:** Work stress can spill over into personal relationships, causing friction and misunderstandings and making you less appealing to others.
- **Mental Health Issues**: Without proper recreation, stress accumulates, potentially leading to anxiety and depression.
- **Workplace Problems:** A lack of recreation can result in burnout, decreased productivity, and job dissatisfaction.
- **Overall Happiness:** The absence of joy and relaxation can make life feel monotonous and unfulfilling.

- **Quality of Life (QoL):** QoL encompasses physical health, mental well-being, and emotional satisfaction. Without enjoyable activities, our QoL suffers, impacting all aspects of life.

Happiness vs. Contentment

Happiness is a state of joy from engaging in activities you love, while contentment is a sense of satisfaction with what you have. True happiness comes from pursuing activities that bring joy and fulfillment. Without recreation, you may be content but not truly happy, leading to a sense of emptiness. Our college class book states that happiness is 50% genetics, 10% circumstances and 40% being intentional and involved in activities.

As mentioned before, your energy levels are like a phone battery. Without regular recharging, it will run out, leaving you drained. Recreation acts as a similar recharge for your mental and emotional battery. Without it, you may find yourself less kind, energetic, and incapable of positively influencing others.

It's important to balance passive and active leisure activities. For example, if you spend excessive time on social media, try reducing it and using that time for more active recreation. Engaging in active recreation can significantly enhance your overall wellness tank.

Benefits of Active Recreation

- **Improved Mental Health:** Recreation helps reduce depression and stress.
- **Longevity:** Engaging in recreational activities often correlates with a longer life.
- **Enhanced Quality of Life:** Recreation boosts happiness and satisfaction.
- **Stronger Relationships:** Being active makes you more appealing and engaging to others.

Invest 16 hours a week in recreational activities, and you'll likely experience greater happiness and longevity. Recreation includes a wide range of pursuits, hobbies, fitness, community involvement, and volunteering, all contributing to your overall well-being by providing a break from routine and opportunities to connect with others.

The hardest part is often simply stopping. Imagine driving at full speed, so focused on your destination that you miss the nearby park. You need to pull over, step out, and immerse yourself in nature. Go for a bike ride, take a walk, or join a game of volleyball.

In our busy lives, making time for fun can feel like a luxury. Yet, it should be a vital part of our daily routine. Society's rush often makes us overlook activities that bring joy. "Park and Recreate" is a call to intentionally schedule time for activities that renew and restore us.

A song that resonates with this message is *"I'm in a Hurry*" by Alabama, which highlights the importance of slowing down and savoring life. Many people can recall moments of joy but struggle to explain why they aren't having fun more often. This disconnect often arises from an imbalance between obligated and recreational time.

Scheduling Fun: Start by tracking your time for a week. Take note of everything, from work and chores to meal times and screen time. This will reveal pockets of time you can repurpose for fun activities. Categorize your activities into essential tasks, necessary tasks, and discretionary time to uncover opportunities for recreation.

Intentional Recreation: We often dread unscheduled plans that lack enthusiasm. To overcome this, be intentional about how you spend your free time. Schedule activities you look forward to, which can enhance your overall outlook and mental well-being. Look at your next week's agenda and schedule some fun time.

Reclaiming Lost Time: There are 168 hours in a week, no more or no less. By understanding your obligations, you can identify free time (leisure) available for activities that benefit your well-being. Distinguish between obligations and time for recreation, obligations include necessary tasks, work time, caretaking, and sleep, while recreation encompasses activities that renew, restore, and rejuvenate us.

Active Recreation vs. Passive Leisure: Leisure may include relaxing activities like reading, quiet time, hobbies, and more. Active recreation involves engaging in activities that are enjoyable and socially enriching, such as sports, volunteering, or outdoor adventures. These activities are vital for restoring your body, physical health, and mind or mental and emotional wellness.

Overcoming the Convenience Trap: Digital entertainment is part of our lives but often discourages physical movement and outdoor activities. While passive activities have their place, it's important to balance them with active recreation for a healthier lifestyle.

Choosing Fun Activities: Reflect on activities you enjoyed in the past and reintegrate them into your life, or consider new activities that you have always wanted to explore. Dedicate time daily and weekly to activities you have an interest in, and these moments will accumulate into an active lifestyle, positively impacting your well-being.

Illusion of Fitness as Recreation: While fitness is important, it often becomes another obligation rather than a source of joy. Working out every day or intensely can become an obligation. When you can pair your physical workout routines with recreational activities to be more fit, for example to hike, then you have balance. True recreation involves activities you choose to participate in for your competitive side or activities that bring pleasure and relaxation. Invest into fit time to gain the energy and strength needed for your obligated and free time.

Importance of Social Connection: Recreation is not just about physical activity but also social interaction, or, as we say, shared time. Both structured (group activities) and unstructured (solo activities) forms of recreation are valuable. Don't isolate yourself; maintain social connections for emotional and mental health. We all need friends that focus on fun, not just the serious things in life.

Creating a Balanced Schedule: Once you identify your free time and preferred activities, create a balanced schedule that includes work, obligations, and leisure. This balance will enhance productivity and happiness. If you can invest 16 hours into your interests every week, including spiritual, physical, social and emotional interests, you will improve your overall mental well-being.

Power to Say "No": Overcommitting can prevent you from enjoying personal time. Learn to say no and prioritize activities that bring joy and fulfillment. By being selective about your commitments, you'll have more time for what you love. Be intentional and integrate your interests weekly, and make that a priority. And when you say 'NO' or 'YES,' have NO guilt.

Creating a Culture of Fun: Encourage friends, family, and colleagues to join in fun activities. Organize events like game nights or outdoor outings to foster a culture that values joy and recreation. This shared time will allow your free time to be inclusive of all your needs. Walk and talk with a friend, either in person or on the phone. Take the kids or friends to volunteer. Partner up and play, but also find your alone time for interests and hobbies.

By overcoming barriers to making time for recreation and focusing on what brings you joy, you can improve your overall well-being and enrich your life.

Now, take some time to reflect on the following:

What did I learn?

What do I want to do?

Chapter 2: Make and Take Time

"You have 168 hours in the week, and how you invest into your wellness determines who you are at and away from work."

As we explore the concept of balancing work and leisure, or simply taking time to have fun, it comes down to a fundamental value: *people need to make and take time for themselves.* No one can give more than 100% of your time, you just have to make your time count in all you do.

This involves two distinct tasks. First, we must identify where our obligated time goes each week. With 168 hours in a week, most people spend about 120 hours on obligations. These obligations could include work, sleeping, or helping family members like parents or kids. These are tasks we perform regularly, week after week.

However, amid these obligations, we must carve out our free time and the hours available for activities we genuinely enjoy. This is the essence of a balanced lifestyle and well-being: making and taking time for personal enjoyment. Often, people feel as though they lack time or are perpetually out of time. Yet, once they sit down and chart out their obligations and free time, many realize they do have available hours. The challenge then becomes understanding how that free time is spent. Is it invested in fulfilling activities or wasted on passive pastimes like excessive TV watching?

To find this free time, start by listing your workplace-related activities, including the hours from getting ready to leave for work, the commute, and the work itself. This could range from 40 to 60 hours a week, depending on your schedule. Next, consider your sleep routine. From the moment you start preparing for bed to the time you wake up, these are obligated hours. Some might read a book or watch TV before actually sleeping, which can affect the quality of rest positively and negatively.

Another intriguing aspect of time management is the shift that has occurred over the past 20 to 30 years. If we look back to the pre-2000s, people generally had more free time because their jobs were confined to specific working hours. They would work from 8 AM to 5 PM and then return home to relax with their families. There was a clear boundary between work and home life.

In recent times, however, this boundary has blurred significantly. The modern working environment and culture has changed, making people feel more occupied with their jobs. The rise of technology and constant connectivity means that work often follows us home. People frequently check their phones for work emails or messages, even during their supposed downtime. Modern problems like using electronics or watching TV in bed can disrupt sleep, preventing people from getting the rest they need. This shift has led many to feel as though they have no time for themselves.

Nowadays, time feels more like a continuum. Work, family, and personal obligations intermingle, creating a scenario where there's no clear distinction between professional and personal time. This continuous flow of obligations makes it challenging to find time to relax and recreate.

Back in the day, people knew their work hours were from 8 to 5. They could clock out and leave work behind. Today, with the advent of technology, information, and constant communication, people might read personal emails at night or respond to work-related queries outside office hours. For instance, we teach college courses online, which means receiving questions and messages at all hours, disrupting the traditional concept of office time.

So, when can we shut off and make time for ourselves?

This is a crucial question in today's world. To achieve a balanced life, we need to clearly define our work time, sleep time, and other obligated time, such as shopping, cleaning, or yard work.

Understanding where the majority of your time goes each week is the first step.

So, how much time are you actually spending on your various activities each week?

What's your free time really like?

As we delve deeper into this book, we're not here to dictate what you should or shouldn't do. Instead, we're here to help you figure out your goals and how to take time for the interests that matter to you.

We'll be exploring different categories of recreation, from fitness and physical activities to sports, hiking, biking, collecting, and volunteering. This book is designed to guide you in deciding where and how to allocate your time. I recommend starting with a block of 12 to 16 hours a week dedicated to integrating your interests. Think about where you can fit these hours into your schedule.

For a balanced and fulfilling life, consider activities that touch upon the four key areas of wellness: physical, spiritual, social, and emotional well-being.

Here's how you can approach this:

Physical Well-Being: Physical fitness is another cornerstone of a happy and healthy life. We recommend spending four to six hours a week on activities that condition your body. This includes taking care of your body through exercise and proper nutrition. Whether it's going for a jog, practicing yoga, or simply eating healthier, these activities help keep your body in top shape. A healthy body contributes to a more positive outlook on life and gives you the energy to engage in other fulfilling activities.

Spiritual Well-Being:

Spirituality plays a crucial role in mental well-being. Many people find that spending even 30 minutes a day on their spiritual practices can significantly reduce stress and improve mental clarity. However, spirituality is a broad concept and can mean different things to different people. For some, it's about religious practices, while for others, it might be connecting with nature, meditating, or simply reflecting on their day.

Whatever your spiritual practice may be, it's important to schedule it. If you live near natural surroundings, you could combine a spiritual walk with meditation or prayer, blending outdoor recreation with spiritual fulfillment. This dual approach not only enriches your spiritual life but also enhances your overall well-being.

Social Well-Being: Human connection is vital. Make time to interact with friends or join groups that share your interests. Social activities help you feel connected and reduce feelings of isolation.

Maintaining strong social connections is essential for a balanced life. If you're in a relationship, make sure to schedule regular activities together. Plan a hike followed by coffee or any other activity you both enjoy. Putting these activities on your calendar makes them intentional and ensures you don't overlook them.

When we stop scheduling recreational activities or special interests, we risk falling into a routine of inactivity. It becomes all too easy to just sit down and turn on the TV, which, while relaxing, doesn't contribute much to our overall happiness and well-being.

Emotional Well-Being:

Engage in hobbies or interests that stimulate your mind. This could involve pursuing continued education, reading, or even solving puzzles. Keeping your mind active is crucial for overall well-being.

Activities that nurture your soul and emotions are essential. This could be anything from meditation and mindfulness practices to spending time in nature or engaging in creative pursuits.

Interestingly, a statistic from 20 years ago showed that seven out of ten people were unhappy at work. Today, around 50-60% of people report being content with their jobs, yet many are still looking for better opportunities. This shift could be due to a variety of factors.

In the past, people had friends at work and less overall stress. Nowadays, post-COVID, there's a trend toward more isolated work environments. People might be happier with less stress and conflict, but this isolation could also be contributing to a sense of disconnection.

Moreover, many people spend around three hours a day watching television. While TV can be a source of entertainment, it's often a passive activity. Instead, consider how you can replace some of that screen time with more participatory activities that contribute to your wellness.

Volunteering is another vital activity that can improve emotional and mental health. Seven out of ten people express a desire to volunteer but often feel unsure about where to start. The key is to find a cause you believe in and enjoy. Volunteering should be a fulfilling experience, not just another obligation.

Whether you volunteer once a week, once a month, or once a quarter, scheduling this time can make a significant difference in your life. Volunteering not only helps others but also provides a sense of purpose and connection. Volunteering with friends can also boost your social well-being.

As we continue exploring how to carve out time for personal fulfillment, it's crucial to focus on integrating joy into your everyday or weekly routines. The key here is scheduling time weekly for the activities that make you happy. Waiting for a vacation to have fun isn't enough; you need to find joy every week.

Through years of experience, we've found that people who intentionally participate in weekly activities tend to have better overall well-being and come to work happier. It's fascinating how often people say, "I don't have any free time." In fact, about 70% of participants in most workshops express this sentiment. However, by the end of the session, they often realize that they do have time. They just need to choose how to spend it to improve their quality of life.

As we progress through the book, we discuss each category of interest, whether it's fitness, recreation, sports, hiking, biking, collecting, or volunteering, and we will invite you to consider how you can spend your time on these activities. Our focus isn't on traditional time management techniques but on how you can invest your time in ways that make you happier and healthier.

For example, when it comes to physical fitness, we recommend investing four to six hours a week in activities that condition your body. Whether it's walking, jogging, or working out, about 45 minutes a day, three to five days a week, can significantly enhance your physical well-being. A healthy body contributes to a more positive outlook on life, making you more enthusiastic about participating in various activities. We can't say this enough!

Don't wait for a special occasion or a holiday to enjoy life. By making intentional choices about how you spend your time, you'll enhance your well-being and bring more joy into your everyday life.

So, how do you invest time in the activities that make you happier?

Where do you schedule that time?

Well, that's up to you. Everyone's work schedule is different; only you know when you can make time for yourself.

The act of scheduling the activities we talked about above is crucial. When you put something on your calendar, it becomes a commitment. This intentional planning helps you manage your time better and ensures that you make room for activities that enhance your quality of life.

The goal is not to overwhelm yourself with too many commitments but to thoughtfully integrate activities that bring you joy and fulfillment. By making these intentional choices, you can lead a balanced, happy life.

So, start by identifying your obligated time and charting it out. Then, look at the free time you have left and decide how to use it in ways that make you happier and healthier. Whether it's through physical fitness, spiritual practices, volunteering, or social activities, the key is to be intentional and make time for what truly matters. Get yourself an accountability partner to help you stick to your goals as you set them.

Principle of LLW (Live Life Weekly)

I recently had a conversation with my back doctor, who emphasized the importance of getting off the couch and moving around. Sitting all day, whether on a couch or in an office chair, is detrimental to your health. It's astonishing to hear that sitting for prolonged periods can be as harmful as smoking. This emphasizes the need to incorporate movement into your daily routine.

One of the key principles in this chapter is "Live Life Weekly" (LLW). If you don't schedule time for activities that bring you joy and fulfillment on a weekly basis, you're likely to miss out on them. Consistently looking forward to specific nights or days for your hobbies and interests creates a sense of anticipation and happiness. If you don't integrate these activities into your schedule, you might find yourself saying, *"I used to do this,"* or *"I used to enjoy that."* Your time is still there. You've just reallocated it to activities that may not be as healthy or fulfilling.

Making and Taking Time

The goal of this book is to help you make and take time for your interests so that you can give 100% at work and 100% at home. It's not about the number of hours you spend at work or home but about the quality of time you invest in each area.

One of my clients once said, *"I give more time to my job than my home."*

I explained that it's not about the hours; it's about giving your best self to both. You can't give too much time and energy to work without depleting yourself. Many people feel so engrossed with their families that they forget to make time for their own interests. This is particularly true for parents who want to be good caregivers. They often sacrifice their hobbies and interests, such as volunteering or favorite recreation activities, because they believe it will make them better parents.

However, neglecting your own interests can lead to burnout and dissatisfaction. It's essential to strike a balance. For example, if you're in a relationship, make sure to schedule regular activities together. Plan a hike followed by coffee or any other activity you both enjoy. Putting these activities on your calendar makes them intentional and ensures you don't overlook them. Share your schedule with your accountability partner.

Sitting all day can have severe health implications comparable to the risks associated with smoking. This underscores the importance of integrating physical activities into your daily routine. Whether it's taking short breaks to walk around or scheduling regular exercise sessions, these activities are vital for your well-being.

In our busy lives, it's easy to let guilt creep in, even for good parents who are doing their best. Guilt is a powerful emotion, but as Marsha says, *"I can't make you feel guilty; only you can let yourself feel guilty."* This feeling often arises when people don't take time for the things they love. Over time, this neglect can lead to depression, anxiety, and, yes, more guilt. Our well-being must make and take time each week for activities we love.

Relationships are not just about spending time together; it's also essential to do things you love independently. I once heard on a radio show that the happiest couples are those who continue to pursue their interests, whether it's education, hobbies, or something else throughout their lives. The key to their happiness? Encouragement from their partners to keep following those passions. This mutual understanding and support are vital for the continuous pursuit of happiness.

But what about those who are single, older, and alone?

Many face depression and wonder who they can share their time with. Men and women often react differently to being older and alone. Research shows that older men tend to be more depressed than older women. This is partly because men generally have fewer social opportunities, while women often find more ways to socialize. Society tends to be more sympathetic and empathetic toward women and children, giving them more chances to connect with others. Today, more than ever, all people struggle with where and with whom to be friends and how to share time in recreating.

Whether you're in a relationship or single, young or old, the message is clear: make time for what you love. Encourage those around you to do the same. It's not just about filling your days with activities; it's about enriching your life with joy and meaning.

One of the things my wife and I experienced while raising our kids was the joy of shared activities. Early on, we did a lot of fun things together, and our social circles expanded through our children. Our friends were often from our church and our kids' school, forming a tight-knit community. For about 14 years, it felt like we had an abundance of friends. We socialized frequently with the parents of our kids' friends, and life was full of social gatherings and shared experiences.

Then, suddenly, the kids graduated and went off to college. Guess what? Those adult friendships began to fade away. This shift was tough on both of us. It's a common experience for many parents. The friendships you build around your children can dissolve, leaving a void that can be hard to fill.

Whether you're single or in a relationship, isolation and loneliness can affect anyone. These feelings often stem from a lack of friendships. I've noticed that one of the highest statistics of suicide among my national clients is within the construction industry, highlighting how crucial social connections are. In our 30s, we often have friends at work and engage in activities together. But as time passes, work environments change, or we change jobs, making it harder to maintain those friendships.

So, what's the solution?

The key is to make and take time to nurture friendships outside of work. But the question remains: *where do you find new friends?*

There are many solutions available. Activity clubs or groups, for instance, offer a variety of social opportunities. These groups aren't about finding a romantic partner; they're about recreation and shared interests. Adventure groups, activity groups, there's something for everyone.

If you're looking to find friends, consider the following steps:

Volunteer: Contact volunteer organizations and see how you can help. Volunteering not only gives back to the community but also introduces you to like-minded individuals.

Join Meetup Groups: Look for local meetup groups that align with your interests. Whether it's hiking, biking, or any other activity, these groups can be a great way to meet people.

Pursue Outdoor Activities: Find an individual outdoor activity you love, such as swimming or hiking. These activities not only keep you physically active but also provide opportunities to meet others with similar passions.

Find a Hobby: Engage in a hobby that you care about. Whether it's crafting, gardening, or playing an instrument, hobbies can be a gateway to new friendships.

Join Clubs: Look for clubs that align with your interests. A hiking club, a biking club, or a hobby club can introduce you to people who share your passions.

It's important to acknowledge that men often struggle more with loneliness, but women also face challenges. My own wife sometimes worries about maintaining friendships as life changes. For my partner and wife, Marsha, many active adults and women, staying involved in activities is crucial for finding and keeping friends.

Park and Recreate is about the importance of recreation and socialization. Engaging in recreational activities gives you a better chance of meeting people with common interests. These connections are vital for your emotional, spiritual, and mental well-being.

So, the challenge of this chapter is clear: You must find a way to make and take time for social outings. By intentionally planning and scheduling activities that bring you joy, you ensure that you don't miss out on the things that matter most. Whether it's physical fitness, spiritual practices, volunteering, or spending time with friends and family, the key is to be intentional. This approach helps you manage your time better and enhances your overall quality of life. Don't forget to get an accountability partner, two are better than one for having fun!

Socialization is not just a luxury; it's essential for a fulfilling life.

Now, take some time to reflect on the following:

What did I learn?

____

____

____

____

____

____

____

____

____

____

What do I want to do?

Chapter 3: Categories of Fun

"To recreate is to renew, restore, rejuvenate your life through activities, interests and service."

From a young age, I've always been drawn to the concept of "park and recreate," essentially, the idea of stopping to have fun. My journey with recreation began in my youth when I spent countless hours playing basketball. As I grew older, my interests expanded to volleyball, outdoor cycling, and numerous other enjoyable activities. These experiences have deeply influenced my teaching and my understanding of recreation categories.

One of the biggest pieces of advice I can give is to *'get a hobby.'* Hobbies are enjoyable activities that allow us to immerse ourselves and release stress. They boost our mood and provide a sense of accomplishment. Whether it's a physical activity, a creative pursuit, or a social event, having a hobby enriches our lives.

Picture a high school student hunched over a workbench, carefully crafting a wooden cabinet. Years ago, this was me, discovering the satisfaction of creating something tangible with my own hands. As I grew older, this passion for woodworking stayed with me, evolving into a source of pride and accomplishment. Each finished shelf or cabinet displayed hours of dedicated work, creativity, and skill.

However, woodworking is just one of the categories in the list of hobbies you can choose from. From the meticulous restoration of classic cars to the art of jewelry making, hobbies spread across a wide range of interests. They're not just pastimes; they're portals to personal growth and community connection.

In the early 1980s, I had the privilege of working as a special interest coordinator in Scottsdale. My role was to be a bridge between skilled instructors and eager citizens, facilitating a community-wide pursuit of passions. Whether it was painting, ceramics, cooking, or dancing, I coordinated all the special interest classes, which helped me see the broader picture of recreation. I witnessed firsthand how hobbies could transform lives and build connections.

One of the most magical aspects of hobbies is their ability to induce *'flow,'* a state of complete immersion and focus. When you're in flow, time seems to stand still. You start a project, and before you know it, hours have passed. This state of flow isn't just enjoyable; it releases stress and a sense of personal fulfillment.

Hobbies also offer a unique form of self-expression. They're deeply personal, often pursued alone or separate from partners or spouses. This nature of hobbies allows for true self-discovery and growth, uninfluenced by others' preferences or expectations.

Let's not forget the physical benefits, particularly when it comes to sports and active interests. As someone who once organized sports leagues, I've seen how physical activities not only improve health but also serve as excellent stress-busters. The simple act of hitting a softball can be cathartic, releasing pent-up frustrations and boosting mood through the release of endorphins. Did you know that a 10 minute walk can release much of the stress built up during the day. Depending on the day, 20 minutes may be just what you need.

In this generation, where social interactions often revolve around passive activities like going to bars or pubs, there's a growing need to rediscover active, engaging hobbies.

"Recreate first," a simple yet powerful mantra for stress relief and personal growth.

We often forget the simple joys of recreation. It's not just about socializing or hanging out; it's about actively engaging in activities that refresh our minds and bodies, earning our relaxation time.

Under the *sports* umbrella, we had activities like softball, volleyball, basketball, flag football, and soccer. Each of these activities falls under the sports category, a subset of recreation. This diversity in activities allows for a rich array of options for people to engage in.

Sports, in particular, offer a lifetime of benefits. Whether a sport you learned as youth or someone picking up a new activity later in life, the impact is profound. Take pickleball, for instance. This sport has taken the world by storm, attracting people who may have never considered themselves athletes before. It's a perfect example of how it's never too late to embrace a new physical challenge.

But sports are more than just fun and games. They're life lessons wrapped in sweat and determination. Every match, every game, teaches discipline, goal setting, and the art of gracefully handling both victory and defeat. These skills seamlessly transfer into our professional lives, creating a healthier work-life balance.

Fitness is another critical category that keeps us energized. Group activities like yoga and dance classes or individual pursuits like gym workouts all contribute to our physical health. A young man who works for me stays in shape through dance classes, where the movement and rhythm keep him fit and happy. Fitness activities relieve stress, improve health, and enhance overall well-being.

Perhaps the most accessible and rewarding form of recreation is simply stepping *outdoors*. It can include all types of recreation, including fitness, sports, and social and traditional forms. Nature isn't just a backdrop; it's a healing force. The simple act of soaking in vitamin D, breathing fresh air, and surrounding yourself with greenery can significantly lower stress levels. It's a form of spirituality connecting us to something larger than ourselves.

Yet, many of us have fallen into the trap of an indoor lifestyle. We commute from climate-controlled homes to offices, missing the natural world around us. This disconnection takes a toll on our mood and overall well-being. The solution? Rediscover what's in your own backyard.

Take a leaf out of Johnny Ringo's book, the Jeep Tour driver from Carefree, Arizona. His passion was introducing people to the hidden wonders right in their neighborhood, the mountains, hiking trails, and places they never knew existed. It's about opening your eyes to the adventure that awaits just beyond your doorstep.

Personal experience speaks volumes. There's an indescribable joy in riding a bike for 20-25 miles, feeling the wind on your face, observing people enjoying parks, and connecting with the environment. It's not just exercise; it's a mood elevator, a stress buster, and a way to rekindle our relationship with the world around us.

Outdoor recreation activities offer a fantastic way to enjoy our free time and connect with nature. Whether it's a leisurely walk in the park or an adventurous mountain climb, outdoor recreation has something for everyone.

Recreation plays a crucial role in our mental wellness. It helps us manage stress and provides a much-needed break from the pressures of daily life. Physical activities like sports, hiking, or even gardening can lower stress hormones like cortisol, which accumulate from our daily work routines. Engaging in leisure activities also boosts our mood by releasing endorphins and serotonin, chemicals that make us feel happy and relaxed.

In today's fast-paced world, many people neglect the physical activities that can enhance their mental well-being. Physical fitness often serves as the foundation for many recreational activities. While some people work out due to high energy levels or health concerns, others do so to enhance their performance in outdoor activities. Consider the hiker who strengthens their muscles at the gym to tackle more challenging trails or the kayaker who builds upper body strength to navigate turbulent rivers. Even golfers, often perceived as participating in a leisurely sport, engage in targeted workouts to improve their swing and overall performance.

This interconnection between fitness and recreation creates a positive cycle. The desire to excel in a beloved outdoor activity can fuel motivation for regular exercise, leading to improved overall health and well-being.

However, recreation isn't limited to the great outdoors. Indoor games, often overlooked, offer substantial benefits, particularly in cognitive development. These activities foster strategic thinking, problem-solving skills, and memory enhancement. For older adults, such games can be crucial in maintaining mental acuity.

Take, for instance, the interaction between a grandmother and her young granddaughter over table games. These sessions strengthen their bond and teach valuable life lessons about competition, winning, and losing gracefully. Such experiences contribute significantly to a child's emotional and social development.

In recent years, the definition of recreation has expanded to include activities once considered mere pastimes. Online gaming, for example, has evolved into a recognized form of recreation and even a competitive sport at the university level. This digital realm offers its own set of benefits, including community building and the development of quick decision-making skills.

The key to meaningful recreation, regardless of its form, lies in its ability to foster social connections, improve mood, and enhance focus. Whether it's a hike in the mountains, a board game with family, or an online multiplayer game, the most valuable recreational activities are those that engage us fully and leave us feeling refreshed and connected.

As we navigate the diverse world of recreation, we must remain open-minded. What might seem like an unproductive activity at first glance could offer unexpected benefits. The challenge lies in finding the right balance, incorporating a mix of physical, mental, and social activities that cater to our individual needs and interests.

Some may say, "Finding fun and finding friends isn't so easy in this era," but it's important to actively seek out and engage in recreational activities. They serve not just as pastimes but as vital components of a fulfilling life, offering pathways to physical health, mental stimulation, and meaningful human connections.

Participating in recreational activities is essential for maintaining a healthy mind. Recreation improves cognitive functions, such as problem-solving, mind games, and creative pursuits like arts and crafts. These activities stimulate the brain and keep our cognitive abilities sharp.

One of my favorite benefits of recreation is the *social interaction* it fosters. When we isolate ourselves and engage in activities alone, we might lose interest over time. However, when we participate in activities with others, we look forward to the social interaction. Group activities and hobbies create social connections and reduce feelings of isolation. Whether attending events, concerts, or just hanging out as a group, these experiences are enriched by the presence of others. These activities are particularly enjoyable with friends. However, meeting new people can make the event more enjoyable even when we go alone.

Nowadays, many people feel isolated despite having a content job. Going to work and coming home without engaging in social activities means missing out on friendships and the joy they bring. Recreation activities can significantly help you with this, improving your mental and emotional well-being, which is a core principle of this book.

How do you keep the three areas of your life energized: Personal, Professional, and Social?

Recreation is one of the key answers.

Let's explore some categories of recreational activities.

<u>*Outdoor sports*</u> like hiking, biking, swimming, and team sports such as soccer or basketball are fantastic ways to stay active and socialize. As adults, many people enjoy pickleball. When I served as a parks commissioner for the City of Scottsdale about eight years ago, residents frequently requested more pickleball facilities. I initially wondered,

"What's pickleball?" Today, it's one of the most popular participatory sports, often played outdoors, though indoor play is also common.

Traditional indoor activities also offer recreational benefits. Reading, cooking, playing board games, knitting, and painting are all hobbies that provide relaxation and mental stimulation. These activities touch us in different ways and contribute to our overall well-being.

But, in our increasingly digital age, the landscape of recreation has expanded far beyond traditional boundaries. Online gaming, once considered a niche hobby, has blossomed into a vibrant form of social interaction and skill development. These virtual environments foster teamwork, collaboration, and communication skills, even when players are physically distant.

In today's workplace, where remote interactions are commonplace, the ability to effectively communicate online is invaluable. Young people engaged in these games are inadvertently preparing for a future where digital collaboration is the norm.

Mobile gaming, too, has carved out its own niche in the recreational sphere. What might appear as mindless tapping on a screen actually serves multiple purposes:

- **Stress relief:** Offering a temporary escape from daily worries.
- **Relaxation:** Providing a calming effect before bedtime.

- **Achievement satisfaction:** Fulfilling competitive drives through level completion.
- **Social interaction:** Connecting players through multiplayer mobile games.
- **Cognitive engagement:** Keeping minds sharp is especially beneficial for aging populations.

However, the key to harnessing the benefits of these digital recreations lies in balance. We fill our "wellness bank," a metaphor for overall well-being by consciously integrating various forms of recreation. This means actively planning and allocating time for different aspects of personal wellness:

- **Physical activities:** Scheduling 4-5 times weekly for bodily health. Remember a body in motions, stays in motion, and a body at rest, tends to stay at rest.
- **Mental exercises:** Engaging in activities that challenge cognitive abilities.
- **Social interactions:** Dedicating time for in-person connections with friends and family.
- **Digital recreation:** Incorporating online gaming or mobile apps in moderation.

The goal is not to completely avoid digital activities but to ensure they complement rather than dominate our leisure time. By consciously balancing these elements, we can enjoy the benefits of modern technology while maintaining the essential aspects of physical health, mental acuity, and real-world social connections.

The beauty of recreation lies in its timelessness. As we wrap up our exploration of hobbies, sports, and leisure activities, let's focus on a crucial message: *it's never too late to start.*

Whether you're considering learning to play the guitar, diving back into swimming, or trying something entirely new, age is merely a number.

Take, for instance, the inspiring story of Todd and Marsha's Greenbelt Electric Bike and Tours in Scottsdale, Arizona. These tours have become a gateway for people in their 60s and 70s to reconnect with cycling. Many participants hadn't been on a bike in years, yet with the assistance of pedal-assist electric bikes, they found themselves able to enjoy the outdoors, get exercise, and experience the thrill of riding again.

This example illustrates how adaptive technologies can bridge the gap between desire and ability. Electric bikes offer a perfect balance, providing assistance when needed while still allowing for physical exertion and the enjoyment of fresh air.

The benefits of such activities extend beyond mere enjoyment. For the tour guide Todd, who had suffered a back injury years ago, riding an electric bike led to significant health improvements, including weight loss and better back health. This personal experience underscores the potential for recreational activities to have profound impacts on our physical well-being.

The key takeaway is that recreation is vital to our overall wellness. When we engage in activities we enjoy, we're not just passing time, and we're actively contributing to our physical health and emotional well-being. By scheduling time for recreation, we're consciously deciding to prioritize self-care.

It's important to recognize that taking care of yourself through recreation isn't selfish. Instead, it's a necessary part of maintaining a balanced, healthy life. By accepting and embracing the value of recreation, we open ourselves up to new experiences, improved health, and enhanced quality of life, at any age.

So, whether you're 25 or 75, remember that it's never too late to start a new hobby, revisit an old passion, or explore a new form of recreation. Your future self will thank you for the investment in your wellness and happiness.

Now, take some time to reflect on the following:

What did I learn?

____

____

____

____

____

What do I want to do?

Chapter 4: Physical Well-Being (Invest 4 Hours Per Week)

"Life is fun when you can be fit enough to enjoy those things you want to do."

In our relentless search for happiness, success, and the achievement of our goals, we often overlook the most important aspect of our lives: our health. It is the foundation of everything we aspire to accomplish. This chapter explores the connection between our physical well-being and our ability to pursue our dreams effectively.

Imagine trying to build a skyscraper on shaky ground. It's going to be a heck of a challenge, nearly impossible. Similarly, attempting to construct a fulfilling life without a solid foundation of health is a dangerous attempt. Our bodies are the vessels through which we experience the world, and neglecting them can lead to a constant struggle to keep everything together.

In today's world, it's easy to let our physical health take a backseat to our busy schedules. But what if I told you that investing in your physical fitness could be the key to unlocking a more energized, productive, and fulfilling life? Let's explore how making time for exercise can transform not just your body but your entire approach to life.

Envision waking up each day with boundless energy, ready to tackle your workday without feeling drained. This isn't an impossible dream to achieve; it is within your reach if you are willing to accomplish it.

When it comes to physical activity, people generally fall into two categories:

The Daily Devotees: These individuals approach fitness with an almost obsessive dedication, working out every day. While this commitment can sometimes feel like an obligation, it often correlates with success in other areas of life.

The Casual Movers: This group doesn't necessarily engage in active daily workouts but recognizes the importance of keeping their bodies in motion

For those who don't have a structured fitness routine, the key is to integrate movement into your weekly schedule. Ask yourself: *Where can I take time for physical activity? How can I make time for my fitness?* Then, actually, implement it within your week. The good news is that even little efforts can yield significant benefits:

- A 45-minute walk, 3-4 times a week, can keep your body healthy and energized.
- A brief 15-minute stroll after work can effectively dissipate the day's accumulated stress.

When it comes to scheduling your workouts, consider *morning workouts* because they can jumpstart your day, providing an energy boost that lasts for hours. You can also go for *evening walks,* as they offer a perfect opportunity to decompress and transition from work mode to relaxation.

Now, here's the challenge: *How can you invest at least four hours a week in getting your body in shape?* It might seem like a lot at first, but consider this: that's less than 35 minutes a day. By making this small investment in yourself, you're setting the stage for a dramatic improvement in your overall well-being.

It might be a little challenging to indulge in activities that don't interest you. So what's the secret? How do people stay consistent and fit? The secret is to find a physical activity you genuinely enjoy. Whether it's pickleball, running, golf, tennis, biking, swimming, or hiking, finding a physical activity can make fitness feel less like a chore and more like a pleasure. The goal isn't to become a fitness guru overnight. It's about making consistent, manageable changes that align with your lifestyle and interests.

One of the most effective ways to maintain fitness is by tying it to activities you genuinely love and making it convenient for you. Take these examples:

- Weekend warrior? Prepare for that bike ride or hike by incorporating complementary exercises during the week.
- Golf enthusiast? Focus on arm and back exercises to enhance your game and prevent injuries.
- Swimming aficionado? Take advantage of this full-body workout, accessible even in colder climates through indoor pools.

Perhaps you've always wanted to start running again. Before you lace up those shoes, get a thorough checkup on your heart, knees, and overall health. Once you're cleared, why not set a goal to participate in charity runs a few times a year? Not only will you improve your fitness, but you'll also contribute to worthy causes and potentially make new friends who share your passion.

If running isn't your thing, there are countless other options. Maybe you'd prefer cycling 10-20 miles on weekends, playing pickleball with friends without losing your breath, or even taking up bowling to work on your arm and shoulder strength. The key is to choose an activity that excites you.

It's about enabling yourself to live life to the fullest. Whether you dream of conquering mountain peaks or simply want to have enough energy for your loved ones at the end of a workday, fitness is the key that unlocks these possibilities.

Picture attempting to climb a mountain without preparation. You'd likely face two scenarios: potential injury or an exhausting, unfulfilling experience. This metaphor extends to our daily lives: Staying fit allows us to tackle our daily "mountains" with strength and enthusiasm.

We're all familiar with excuses: it's too hot, too cold, too windy. The key is to adapt. If outdoor activities are challenging due to weather, bring the workout indoors. Be bold: rearrange your living space to accommodate exercise equipment. Your health is worth more than the perfect feng shui.

Transform your home into a fitness-friendly environment:

- Move that couch or recliner to make room for a treadmill or exercise bike.
- Set up a space where you can exercise while watching TV or listening to music.

A well-designed home should support all aspects of well-being, including physical fitness. Here's a game-changing tip: invest in a walking machine or treadmill. Place it somewhere convenient: your living room, bedroom, or back patio. This eliminates the "it's too hot/cold outside" excuse. Put on your favorite tunes or podcasts, and just walk. You'll be amazed at how good you feel after a 45-minute session.

While physical activity is crucial, don't forget about nutrition. Balance indulgences like an afternoon espresso with energizing foods such as fruits. Your body needs proper fuel to support your fitness journey.

While you are doing this, ask yourself:

- What activities do I genuinely enjoy?
- How can I integrate fitness into my daily routine?
- What small changes can I make to my environment to support my fitness goals?

Start small, be consistent, and watch as fitness becomes not just a task but an important, enjoyable part of your life. You're not just working toward a better body by prioritizing your health; you're laying the groundwork for a happier, more successful life in all.

As your physical fitness improves, you'll notice a ripple effect in other areas of your life. Suddenly, you'll find yourself with more energy to pursue your goals, both at work and at home. You might even feel inspired to volunteer in your community or engage more deeply with your spiritual practices. Physical fitness doesn't just benefit your body, it energizes your entire life.

Now, let's address the elephant in the room: why don't more people prioritize fitness? Have you ever found yourself too tired to enjoy your favorite hobbies after work? Perhaps you used to love working on crafts outdoors, but now you're more likely to pour a glass of wine or have a dish of ice cream and sink into your chair for the evening.

It's easy to chalk it up to laziness, but the reality is often more complex. Many of us aren't lazy; we're just incredibly busy. We've become so caught up in the chaos of our daily lives that we've forgotten to make time for what truly matters: *our health.*

This isn't laziness; it's a symptom of a larger issue that we'll call "body neglect."

Many of us spend hours sitting at desks, unknowingly putting strain on our hearts and backs. The solution?

Movement. It's crucial to get up and move regularly throughout the day and to prioritize physical activity after work. Even a 15-minute walk or a quick session on a treadmill can make a world of difference. Remember the body in motion theory, keep moving and you stay energized.

Here's a tip I used to give my college students: Before diving into a late-night study session, take 20-25 minutes to do something physical. Go for a walk around the park or do some light exercise. When you return to your tasks, you'll find your mind clearer and more focused. This isn't just about physical fitness, it's about mental sharpness, too.

It's time to shift the perspective. Instead of viewing exercise as another task on our to-do list, let's see it as an investment in our energy, productivity, and happiness. By taking care of our bodies, we're giving ourselves the strength and vitality to excel in all areas of life.

A healthy body supports a healthy mind. When you're physically fit, you're more likely to have the energy to read that book you've been putting off, explore new hobbies, or engage in meaningful conversations instead of passively consuming content on a screen.

Physical activity acts as a mental "decluttering" process. It reduces stress and helps clear our minds, allowing us to be more present both at home and at work. In today's high-pressure work environment, where many professionals are putting in 50-70 hour weeks, making time for recreation can seem challenging. But it's precisely because of these demands that physical activity becomes even more crucial.

Interestingly, people who enjoy outdoor activities like hiking, biking, and camping are often healthier overall. Why? Because they prioritize making time for these activities, which naturally leads to better physical stamina.

For families, outdoor recreation offers an incredible opportunity to bond and create lasting memories. You and your children, hiking the same trails or cycling the same paths 20 years from now, sharing stories and laughter. These aren't just activities; they're traditions in the making.

But what if you don't have a family to recreate with? Don't worry! The outdoor community is huge and welcoming. Join a hiking club, a biking group, or a local outdoor meetup. You'll find friends who share your interests and passion for the outdoors.

The most common concern people face is that "I'm not fit enough to start." Remember, everyone starts somewhere. If you're struggling with weight or have physical limitations, consult your doctor first. Then, start small. You don't need to conquer a mountain on day one. Begin with a walk around your neighborhood or even in your home.

Moreover, regular exercise often leads to better nutritional choices. When you're active, your body craves water and nutritious foods rather than sugary drinks or unhealthy snacks.

Speaking of nutrition, let's touch on the importance of breakfast. Many people skip this meal, but it's often called the most important meal of the day for good reason. As you start prioritizing your physical health, you'll likely find yourself paying more attention to fueling your body properly.

In a world filled with countless diet fads and exercise trends, it's easy to feel overwhelmed when starting your fitness journey. But there's no one-size-fits-all approach to health and fitness. What works for one person might not work for another. That's why it's crucial to create a personalized action plan that suits your unique needs and interests.

Summing up, let's break down this action plan into simple, achievable steps:

1. **Choose Your Adventure:** First, pick a physical activity that excites you. It could be anything, biking, golf, walking, hiking, charity runs, kayaking, or even stand-up paddle-boarding. The key is to choose something you genuinely want to do. This activity will become your motivation, your driving force.
2. **Get a Health Check:** Before diving into your new activity, make sure to get a thorough health check-up. This step is crucial to ensure you're cleared for physical activity and to identify any potential health concerns.
3. **Prepare Your Body:** Once you've chosen your activity and gotten the all-clear from your doctor, it's time to prepare your body. Join a gym, invest in home exercise equipment, or find free resources

online. The goal is to condition your body for your chosen activity.

4. **Fuel Your Journey:** As you work on your physical fitness, research which foods best support your goals. Remember, nutrition is a crucial part of any fitness journey. If you're unsure, consider consulting with a nutritionist for personalized advice.

5. **Start Small, Dream Big:** For most people, a great starting point is walking. Aim for 2-3 miles, 3-4 times a week, at a pace of 15 minutes per mile. This isn't a leisurely stroll; you should be moving at a good clip and breathing a bit harder than usual.

6. **Make It Social:** Here's a pro tip, turn your fitness routine into a social activity. Call a friend or family member during your walk. Not only does this make the time fly by, but it also helps you maintain important relationships. It's a win-win! Challenge them to walk and talk with you.

By following these steps, you're not just improving your physical health. You're opening the door to new adventures, stronger relationships, and a deeper connection with the world around you.

The journey to better health isn't about drastic changes overnight. It's about small, consistent steps that lead to a more energized, focused, and fulfilling life. Remember, there's no "perfect" time to start. So, why not start today?

Take a short walk, try a new healthy recipe, or simply stand up and stretch. Your body and mind will thank you.

So, what are you waiting for? It's time to park, recreate, and rediscover the joy of movement. *Your outdoor adventure awaits!*

Now, take some time to reflect on the following:

What did I learn?

____

____

____

____

____

____

____

____

____

____

What do I want to do?

____

____

____

____

Chapter 5: Spiritual Well-Being (Invest 4 Hours Per Week)

"Your soul needs nourishment so invest into that which you desire or need."

Recreation isn't merely about filling idle time; it's a deliberate choice to refresh and renew our bodies and minds. We must also prioritize our own spiritual and mental rejuvenation. It encompasses a wide range of activities that serve to replenish our energy and uplift our spirits. Recreation also includes spiritual pursuits, which we'll explore in two distinct forms:

1. **Religious spirituality:** Traditional practices aligned with one's faith.
2. **Outdoor recreation:** Seeking spiritual connections through nature and outdoor experiences.

Before diving deeper into spiritual wellness, it's crucial to acknowledge the importance of physical health. Our previous chapter emphasized that physical wellness is the foundation upon which we build other aspects of our well-being. Without adequate physical energy, we may lack the vitality and focus needed to pursue spiritual growth and fill our "energy bank."

Nurturing the Spirit Through Nature and Self-Care

It's easy to lose touch with our spiritual side in this era. The interconnectedness of body, mind, and spirit forms the foundation of our well-being. When we care for our physical health and engage our minds in continuous learning, we inadvertently shape our spirit, the essence of who we are and how we interact with others. This approach to self-care has a ripple effect, influencing not just our own lives but those around us.

When we neglect our well-being, our spirit often darkens. We become less inclined to help others, finding excuses to avoid acts of kindness. On the other hand, when we prioritize self-care, we're more likely to extend compassion and assistance to those in need. It's a simple yet true fact, happy people spread happiness while misery begets misery.

However, in our busy lives, we often fall into the trap of constant activity. This "busyness" can impact our spirit negatively, leading to disconnection and discord in our relationships. The key to breaking this cycle lies in cultivating our spiritual well-being, which in turn enhances our sense of purpose and direction in life.

Spiritual wellness can be viewed as a personal pursuit of happiness. It's a highly individualized concept that may include various elements depending on one's beliefs and preferences. Regardless of the specific path chosen, dedicating time to spiritual pursuits offers numerous benefits.

The 4-Hour Goal

Aim for a minimum of four hours per week dedicated to self-reflection and spiritual activities to reap the benefits of spiritual practices. This can be broken down into manageable daily sessions:

Ideal scenario: 45 minutes to an hour daily.

Alternative: Four hours of self-reflection, complemented by additional time for outdoor recreation.

Self-reflection can give you the most results by simply reflecting on whatever progress you make. Self-reflection goes beyond simply pondering our actions or interactions. There's a scientific approach to this practice, as demonstrated by programs like *Heart Math*. This innovative program can measure energy levels based on one's ability to relax, meditate, and clear the mind.

Key aspects of effective self-reflection include:

Meditation: Taking time to stop, clear your mind, and look inward.

Listening to your heart: Tuning into your inner wisdom and emotions.

Studying and reflecting on personal beliefs: Deepening your understanding of your own values and principles.

Spirituality with Outdoor Recreation

One powerful way to nurture our spirit is through outdoor recreation and connecting with nature. There's something transformative about being immersed in the natural world, the rustling of leaves, the fresh mountain air, and the solitude among towering trees.

This connection with nature often translates into a deeper sense of empathy and consideration for others and the environment. Whether it's gardening, taking care of pets, or maintaining inanimate objects, these activities can have a great impact on our mental state. They teach us patience, responsibility, and the value of nurturing something outside ourselves.

This concept isn't new. Historical examples show how societies recognized the importance of balancing intense work with soul-nourishing activities. For instance, in the Ottoman Empire, even those with demanding and psychologically taxing jobs were mandated to spend time tending to gardens or livestock as a form of spiritual rejuvenation.

Now, outdoor recreation doesn't necessarily mean intense physical activity; sometimes, it's as simple as:

- Taking a leisurely walk in nature
- Sitting quietly in a park or garden
- Riding a bike through scenic routes

These moments allow us to pause, breathe, and marvel at the world around us. It's in these instances that we often feel a deep connection to something greater than ourselves.

Engaging in outdoor activities often involves a return to simplicity and minimalism. When we step outside and connect with the sun, plants, and earth, we strip away the complexities of modern life. This simplicity can be very refreshing, offering a much-needed respite from our often cluttered and chaotic lives.

Outdoor recreation offers a unique avenue for spiritual connection. It allows us to forge a bond with nature, find inner peace, and cultivate a spirit of kindness and consideration. Whether it's a serene walk in the woods, a challenging hike, or simply sitting by a lake, these experiences can deeply impact our spiritual well-being.

Those who regularly engage in outdoor activities often exhibit qualities that make them stand out in various aspects of life. They tend to be more mindful, self-aware, and considerate of others. This observation suggests that taking care of the outdoors might indeed correlate with taking care of people.

It's important to recognize that spirituality is deeply personal. Unlike organized religion, which often involves group activities, spiritual well-being is something you own. It's about your soul and your journey through life. The question then becomes: *How will you nurture and grow your spirit?*

As we spend more time outdoors, we often develop reverence for nature. This respect extends beyond the environment, influencing how we treat others and ourselves. It's a beautiful cycle, the more we connect with nature, the more we understand the importance of preserving it and the more attuned we become to the interconnectedness of all things.

Perhaps one of the most powerful aspects of outdoor activities is their ability to foster a sense of community. When we share these experiences with others, we create bonds and memories that strengthen our social connection. Consider the example of a community coming together to replant trees after a fire. This act of renewal not only benefits the environment but also creates a collective sense of purpose and accomplishment.

These shared experiences become even more crucial in today's globally divided world. They remind us of our common humanity and shared stewardship of the planet. We can make a tangible difference in the world by engaging in activities that benefit our local environment and community.

Single-Tasking

We often fall into the trap of multitasking. However, research, including studies from Heart Math, suggests that true relaxation and spiritual connection require our undivided attention.

When you try to meditate while watching TV or cook while practicing mindfulness, you're not fully engaged in either activity. The result? Instead of relaxation, you may actually be increasing your stress levels.

To truly calm your body and spirit, it's essential to unplug and focus on one thing at a time. This might mean:

- Dedicating time to sit quietly and visualize a peaceful scene, like a serene lake.

- Engaging in prayer or meditation without distractions.
- Immersing yourself in nature without the interruption of devices.

When we give our full attention to these practices, we allow ourselves to experience deep relaxation and spiritual connection.

Quality Over Quantity

It's tempting to squeeze spiritual practices into small pockets of time. However, rushing through these moments often leaves us feeling unfulfilled. Instead, aim for quality over quantity:

- Set aside 30-45 minutes for uninterrupted spiritual practice.
- Create a dedicated space for reflection, free from distractions.
- Allow yourself to fully immerse in the experience without watching the clock.

Benefits of Spiritual Well-being

Prioritizing our spiritual well-being can have far-reaching effects on our overall happiness and life satisfaction. Research and personal experiences highlight several key benefits:

- Increased overall happiness and life satisfaction.

- A stronger sense of purpose and meaning in life.
- Improved mental health and resilience against depression.
- Greater inner peace and contentment.
- Enhanced ability to cope with stress and life's challenges.

When we nurture our spiritual side, the positive effects extend beyond our personal lives. Those who prioritize their spiritual well-being often:

- Approach work with a more positive attitude.
- Maintain better relationships with family and friends.
- Contribute more meaningfully to their communities.

In essence, by taking care of our spiritual needs, we're better equipped to navigate life's challenges and spread positivity to those around us.

By consciously unplugging, reflecting, and connecting with something greater than ourselves, we open the door to a more fulfilling, balanced, and joyful life. It's not about perfection but about consistently nurturing your spiritual side. Your future self will thank you for the investment you make today.

Self-Awareness and Spirituality

We often find ourselves at the intersection of self-awareness and spirituality. Let's explore how these two fundamental aspects of human existence intertwine, shaping our choices, behaviors, and overall well-being.

At its core, self-awareness is about understanding our needs, recognizing what benefits us, and identifying what may cause harm. It's a powerful tool allowing us to navigate life's complexities more clearly. However, true self-awareness often requires a guiding principle or framework, as many of us struggle to discern what's genuinely good for us.

Interestingly, our journey toward self-awareness often leads us to spiritual or philosophical paths. These belief systems can serve as compasses, helping us align our actions with our deepest values and aspirations. Whether it's a formal religion, a philosophical school of thought, or a personal ideology, having a structured belief system can enhance our self-awareness and guide our decisions.

The relationship between spirituality and well-being has multiple layers. Those who actively pursue spiritual growth often find themselves making healthier lifestyle choices. They may gravitate toward better nutrition and increased physical fitness, recognizing the interconnectedness of mind, body, and spirit. This holistic approach to well-being underscores the extensive impact that spiritual practices can have on our overall quality of life.

However, the path to spiritual growth is not always straightforward. In some cases, individuals are born into religious traditions, while others make conscious choices later in life. The Mormon and Amish communities provide interesting examples of how different cultures approach this.

The Amish, for instance, encourage their youth to experience the outside world before committing to their way of life, while Mormon culture often involves mission trips as a rite of passage. These practices highlight the importance of personal choice in spiritual matters, allowing individuals to "own" their beliefs rather than feeling that they were imposed upon them.

It's important to remember that pursuing what we believe in and making a difference in people's lives is a universal right, not limited by nationality or circumstance. This individual spirit, the drive to be who we are meant to be while doing what we're meant to do is at the heart of personal fulfillment and societal progress.

Thus, self-awareness requires us to look inward, question our assumptions, and sometimes challenge societal norms. By embracing this journey, we open ourselves to a richer, more fulfilling life where our actions align with our beliefs and our choices reflect our true selves. The key is to remain open, curious, and committed to your personal growth. After all, the most deep discoveries often lie at the intersection of self-reflection and spiritual exploration.

These seemingly small actions have the power to heal our souls, strengthen our communities, and make a positive impact on the world around us.

Spirituality and Work

We often find ourselves caught in a whirlwind of responsibilities, juggling work, family, and personal commitments. But what if we could approach this with a renewed perspective?

Our spirit is the essence of who we are, guiding us through our daily activities. It's not just about what we do but how we do it. The energy we bring to work doesn't simply disappear when we clock out; it follows us home, influencing our interactions and experiences beyond the office walls.

Let's consider this for a second. If you're constantly drained at work, that negative energy will inevitably seep into your personal life. Conversely, if you're fulfilled and energized in your personal life, you're more likely to bring a positive attitude to your workplace. It's a cycle that can either uplift or deplete us, depending on how we manage it.

But what if you find yourself in a job you don't love? Before you hand in your resignation, take a step back. The issue might not be the job itself but rather a disconnection from your spiritual purpose.

Ask yourself: *What's the underlying purpose of your work? Is it to provide for your family, to make a difference in your community, or to fund your passions?*

Here's a framework to help realign your spirit and improve your overall satisfaction:

Physical Well-being: Ensure you have the energy to tackle your daily tasks.

Spiritual Alignment: Seek out your soul's purpose and let it guide your actions.

Volunteer: Giving back can provide a sense of purpose and perspective.

Reassess: After taking these steps, reevaluate your attitude toward your job.

Remember, you don't need to have your dream job to find fulfillment. If your current position allows you to pursue your passions outside of work, that's valuable, too. The key is to find your spirit first and bring that positive energy to everything you do.

By focusing on your spiritual well-being, you can transform your approach to work and life. Instead of pitting home against work, strive for a harmonious balance where your spirit shines through in all aspects of your life. This all-rounded approach can lead to greater satisfaction, both professionally and personally.

With a nurtured spirit, you'll find that work becomes more than just a paycheck, it becomes a part of your greater purpose.

It's about being true to yourself while navigating the complexities of modern life.

Now, take some time to reflect on the following:

What did I learn?

What do I want to do?

Chapter 6: Social Well-Being (Invest 4 Hours Per Week)

"People are a necessity for well-being, so find your friends to enjoy life with."

This quote encapsulates the essence of true friendship. In a world increasingly focused on material possessions, the experiences we share with others truly enrich our lives. In today's fast-paced world, the significance of friendship cannot be overstated.

This chapter delves into the crucial role that friends play in our lives, especially in the context of corporate America, where social connections seem to be declining.

Historically, the workplace was a fertile ground for friendships. In the past, up to 70% of colleagues considered themselves friends, engaging in activities like volunteering, sports, and sharing life stories. However, this landscape has dramatically shifted. By 2016, the response to after-work social invitations had changed to "Why would I go bowling with people I work with?" This shift reflects a growing disconnect in our professional relationships.

Several factors contribute to this friendship drought:

- Political divisions create social rifts.
- Lack of energy due to demanding lifestyles.
- The aftermath of COVID-19 and increased isolation.

- Time constraints and prioritizing family over work relationships.
- The diminishing benefits of workplace friendships.

The decline in workplace friendships has far-reaching consequences. In the construction industry, for instance, there's a concerning trend of high suicide rates, particularly among Caucasian men in their 50s and 60s. This raises questions about the link between diminishing workplace connections and mental health.

Studies show that building friendships in the workplace leads to increased job satisfaction. These connections provide support, enhance collaboration, and create a more positive work environment.

Your career path can be more than just a means to a paycheck. Professional association memberships offer a unique blend of personal growth and social connection. Engaging with these groups not only enhances your workspace skills but also provides a sense of purpose beyond the 9-to-5 grind. It's about finding your workplace friends, people who understand your challenges and celebrate your victories.

It's essential to recognize the value of workplace friendships. By investing time in these relationships, we not only improve our work life but also contribute to our overall well-being. The challenge lies in finding ways to nurture these connections in our busy, often fragmented, modern lives.

Over the past decade, there's been a notable shift in how we approach friendships. Instead of relying solely on workplace connections, the focus has turned inward. It's now up to each individual to take responsibility for their social life, seeking out opportunities for fun and connection. This proactive approach is key to achieving a balanced life.

Addressing the friendship deficit in our lives requires conscious effort and, sometimes, significant life changes. Whether it's joining a club, volunteering, or considering a move to a more socially conducive environment, the key is to be proactive.

It's not just about giving back; it's a powerful tool for building friendships and relationships. Regular volunteering enhances social skills, fosters teamwork, and creates a sense of belonging to something larger than oneself. It's a remedy for social isolation, strengthening community ties and providing a sense of purpose.

Sometimes, the most rewarding connections start with a simple invitation. Hosting a game night or organizing a group hike might feel difficult, but it's often the first step toward building a vibrant social circle. Many people are in the same boat, looking for a connection but unsure how to find it. These steps can combat isolation, enrich our lives with meaningful connections, and contribute to our overall well-being.

Creating new social connections requires effort and creativity. You can opt for the following:

- Join a club or take an art class.
- Participate in a book club.
- Get involved with small church groups.
- Find fitness programs that emphasize social interaction.
- Volunteer with like-minded individuals.
- For seniors, consider moving to an active lifestyle community.

As people age, the sources of their friendships often change or disappear due to the following:

- Loss of a spouse or partner, and by extension, their social circle.
- Children growing up and moving away.
- The erosion of workplace friendships.

There was a senior singles group I spoke to in Scottsdale, Arizona. Despite living in an area rich with parks, programs, and activities, these individuals struggled to form meaningful friendships. Their experience highlights a common issue: the desire for connection often clashes with the reality of isolation, especially among older adults.

One solution that's gaining traction is the concept of active adult lifestyle communities. These environments are designed to foster connections, providing numerous opportunities for social interaction. For many seniors, such communities can be life-changing, offering not just friendship but also increased activity levels and potentially longer, more fulfilling lives.

In our increasingly digital world, the importance of social connections has been underestimated. Recreation is crucial in fostering these connections, reducing stress, and improving overall quality of life. Let's explore how recreational activities contribute to social wellness and provide practical ways to engage in them.

Key Benefits of Recreational Activities

- **Building Relationships:** Participating in sports clubs or hobbies helps create friendships and a sense of community.
- **Enhancing Communication Skills:** Activities like book clubs or team sports encourage conversation and improve social interactions.
- **Creating a Sense of Belonging:** Whether it's camping, hiking, or crafting together, shared activities foster a feeling of inclusion.
- **Stress Relief and Emotional Balance:** Recreation with others provides a unique form of stress alleviation and emotional support.
- **Promoting Inclusivity:** Engaging with diverse groups helps break down barriers and fosters acceptance of differences.

- **Improving Mental Health:** Regular participation in social activities contributes significantly to mental well-being.

Despite these benefits, many people, especially youth, are not engaging in enough social and recreational activities. The prevalence of technology has led to a decrease in hands-on hobbies and face-to-face interactions. This trend underscores the vital need for intentional efforts to incorporate recreation into our lives.

For those wondering where to start, here are some practical suggestions:

- **Join Local Clubs:** Websites like Meetup.com offer platforms to find groups with common interests.
- **Attend Community Events:** Festivals, fairs, and sports events are great opportunities to connect with others.
- **Participate in Classes:** Local parks and recreation agencies often offer a variety of classes, from cooking to yoga, providing opportunities to learn and socialize.
- **Plan Group Activities:** Organize outings with friends, such as music concerts or outdoor adventures.

The key is to find activities that interest you and commit to them regularly.

Imagine a world where seven out of ten people want to make a difference but don't know where to start. That world is our reality. Volunteering stands as a beacon of hope, offering not just the chance to give back but to find your people. It's about aligning your passions with purpose, whether it's organizing a neighborhood clean-up or participating in a charity run. These activities not only benefit the community but also serve as a springboard for lasting friendships.

Public Places

Where traditional family structures are often dispersed, finding alternative social connections is important for mental health. Loneliness and isolation can lead to depression, highlighting the vital need for social engagement. Organizations, from churches to corporations, play a significant role in creating opportunities for fun, recreational activities that bring people together beyond their primary functions.

Such organizations also include your local gym, basically anywhere social with people. The local gym isn't just a place to sculpt your body; it's a social hub waiting to be tapped. It's as simple as walking into a fitness class, exchanging smiles with familiar faces, and suddenly feeling part of something bigger. This sense of belonging often extends beyond the gym walls, with members organizing hiking trips or biking outings. It's an example that physical and social well-being are deeply interconnected.

Social Media

In the Internet age, the community is no longer confined by geography. Online groups, from camping enthusiasts to professional networks, offer a platform to share experiences, learn new skills, and feel connected without the pressure of face-to-face interaction. These digital communities can be stepping stones to real-world connections or valuable in their own right.

Making friends is a skill, and like any skill, it can be learned and refined. It starts with a genuine interest in connecting with others. Contrary to popular belief, even introverts seek friendships, they just might be more selective in their approach.

Below, you can find some tips for connecting with people:

- Avoid common pitfalls like talking over people or constantly steering conversations back to yourself.
- Read Dale Carnegie's "How to Win Friends and Influence People" for time-tested techniques on social interaction.
- Focus on being an active listener rather than dominating conversations.
- Show genuine interest in others' experiences without making every story about yourself.

It's important to note that these strategies aren't just philosophical musings; they're grounded in research and practical application. Making friends and building connections is a skill that can be developed through practice and intentional effort.

We've explored various strategies for building connections. Now, let's delve into the subtler aspects of social interaction, the art of patience, self awareness, and genuine curiosity.

Patience

In a world that moves at breakneck speed, cultivating patience is a revolutionary act. It's not just about waiting; it's about accepting and embracing the diverse aspects of human interaction. Some people speak slowly, others quickly. Some take time to warm up, while others are instantly sociable. Recognizing and respecting these differences is the key to building lasting connections.

Self-Care and Awareness

Before we can comfortably fit into social situations, we must first be comfortable with ourselves. This involves self-care and self-awareness. Understanding our own social strengths and weaknesses allows us to navigate group dynamics more effectively. It's about finding that sweet spot between authenticity and adaptability.

As many have retreated into isolation, social awkwardness has become increasingly common. The key to overcoming this is to focus on shared interests. When we engage in activities we enjoy with like-minded individuals, conversations flow more naturally, and social anxiety often takes a backseat to genuine enthusiasm.

Listening

While the ability to carry a conversation is valuable, the art of listening lies at the top. True connection happens when we give others our undivided attention, showing genuine interest in their thoughts and experiences. It's not just about hearing words but understanding the emotions and intentions behind them.

One powerful tool for better communication is the *A to B listening technique*. When you ask someone about their interests, and they start sharing, resist the urge to interrupt. Let them finish their thought completely, from point A to point B. This shows respect and genuine interest, encouraging deeper sharing and connection.

Asking Questions

One of the most powerful tools in building connections is the ability to ask thoughtful questions. Sometimes, the path to connection begins with a straightforward question: "Does anybody have friends who like to go hiking?" This seemingly simple inquiry can open doors to new friendships and shared experiences. People generally enjoy talking about themselves and their experiences.

By asking questions, we not only learn about others but also show that we value their perspectives. It's about being proactive in your search for like-minded individuals, whether you're looking to join a hiking club or explore any other interest. While having common hobbies is a great starting point for connection, it's not the be-all and end-all. Even in seemingly quiet activities like fishing, there's potential for deep conversation and connection. The main thing is to use these shared experiences as a springboard for deeper understanding.

However, it's crucial to balance curiosity with respect for boundaries, knowing when to probe deeper and when to back off. Trust is built through consistent, empathetic interaction in professional and personal relationships. Whether you're supporting a client or nurturing a friendship, the principles remain the same: show genuine interest, respect boundaries, and be reliable in your interactions.

Layers of Human Complexity

Every person you meet is living a life as rich and complex as your own. As Jordan Peterson wisely noted, *'If you find people uninteresting, the problem lies not with them but with your perception.'* Each individual carries within them layers upon layers of experiences, thoughts, and emotions that make them infinitely fascinating. The key is to approach each interaction with genuine curiosity and openness.

Finding common ground with others can seem like a challenge. We live in an era of unprecedented social division. Political affiliations, cultural beliefs, and personal values often create seemingly unbridgeable gaps between individuals. Just recently, my wife lost a 20-year friendship simply because she refused to engage in political discussions, preferring instead to focus on shared experiences like raising children. Her friend said, “See ya!”

Today’s social landscape is marked by a reluctance to engage in open, honest discussions. Many people are quick to dismiss opposing viewpoints without giving them fair consideration. This trend has led to a breakdown in communication, where individuals often shut down conversations that challenge their beliefs.

Despite these challenges, there are effective ways to connect with others and nurture friendships through deeper conversations.

The key lies in identifying shared interests that transcend divisive topics, such as conversations about everyday activities like fishing and camping or discussing children’s education, which can reveal common ground and foster connection.

This approach aims not to change the other person’s mind but to create an environment where they feel heard and understood. The goal is to open channels of communication, especially with individuals who are typically reluctant to share their thoughts. By taking these steps, you’re investing in your own happiness and contributing to a more connected and compassionate world. Start today, and watch as your social landscape transforms, one interaction at a time.

Take the first step: volunteer.

Now, take some time to reflect on the following:

What did I learn?

What do I want to do?

Chapter 7: Emotional Well-Being (Invest 4 Hours Per Week)

"If you don't fill your mental wellness tank, you may run out of energy."

We often find ourselves caught up in the daily grind, neglecting one of the most crucial aspects of our lives: our emotional wellness.

But what exactly is emotional wellness, and why is it so important?

Emotional wellness goes beyond the mere absence of mental illness. It's about actively nurturing our psychological and emotional well-being. Think of it as tending to a garden, it requires consistent care, attention, and the right conditions to flourish.

Many of us struggle with emotional well-being not because of clinical issues but due to a lack of intentional investment in our emotional health. It's like trying to grow a plant without water or sunlight, it simply won't thrive.

Imagine your well-being as a web, with emotional wellness at its center. Three crucial strands support this web:

1. Physical Fitness
2. Spiritual Well-being
3. Social Connections

Each of these elements plays a vital role in supporting your emotional health.

Let's explore how they work together.

The Physical-Emotional Connection

The link between physical health and emotional well-being is more deep than you might think. It's not just about maintaining an attractive appearance; exercise acts as a natural mood enhancer for your brain. When you engage in physical activity, your body releases a cocktail of feel-good hormones, including endorphins (nature's painkillers and mood boosters), cortisol (which, in appropriate amounts, helps manage stress), and serotonin (often referred to as the "happiness hormone").

This chemical boost triggered by exercise can have multiple positive effects on your mental state. It can reduce stress and anxiety, improve your mood, enhance sleep quality, and even sharpen cognitive performance. The benefits create a positive cycle: better sleep leads to improved performance at work, which in turn elevates your mood and overall satisfaction with life.

This connection between physical activity and emotional well-being highlights the importance of incorporating regular exercise into your routine. It's not just about physical fitness; it's about nurturing your mental health to create a more balanced, satisfying life.

The Spiritual-Emotional Connection

Spiritual well-being is a key component of our overall health, but it doesn't necessarily mean religious practice. Instead, it's about finding meaning, purpose, and connection to something greater than oneself. This spiritual aspect of our lives is interconnected with our emotional well-being, each influencing and reinforcing the other in various and impactful ways.

When we have a clear sense of purpose, we're better equipped to handle life's challenges. This purpose-driven approach provides us with a unique perspective, making difficulties seem less overwhelming when viewed through the lens of a greater purpose. It also fuels our motivation, providing the drive to persevere through tough times. Moreover, understanding our place in a larger context can help moderate extreme emotional responses, leading to better emotional regulation. We teach that shared time with others in activities that helps connect friends with interests.

Feeling connected to something greater than ourselves can provide significant emotional comfort. Even in solitude, we can feel part of something larger, reducing feelings of isolation. Connecting with others who share our values or beliefs can provide emotional support through shared experiences. This sense of belonging to a larger whole can boost self-esteem and emotional security, creating a strong foundation for emotional well-being.

The search for inner peace is often associated with spiritual practices and directly impacts our emotional state.

Practices like meditation or reflection can lower stress levels, promoting a sense of calm and balance. Spiritual introspection often leads to a better understanding of our emotions, enhancing our emotional awareness. As a result, a calm inner state can lead to more measured emotional responses, fostering emotional stability in our daily lives.

Spiritual growth often involves deep self-exploration, which in turn enhances our emotional intelligence. Understanding our values and beliefs leads to better emotional self-awareness, allowing us to navigate our feelings more effectively. Recognizing our place in a larger context can increase our empathy for others, improving our relationships and social interactions. Finally, aligning our actions with our spiritual values can lead to more authentic emotional expressions, allowing us to live more genuinely and fully.

The Social-Emotional Connection

Investing time in social connections and recreation is very significant. Human beings are inherently social creatures, and meaningful relationships play a crucial role in our emotional health.

Let's go deeper into the connection between our social interactions and emotional well-being. Strong social connections offer emotional support that becomes a critical support system during challenging times, significantly helping to reduce stress and anxiety. These meaningful relationships foster a sense of belonging, which is crucial for self-esteem and overall happiness. Regular social interactions not only boost our mood but also provide opportunities for joy and laughter, contributing positively to our day-to-day experiences.

Furthermore, relationships often challenge us in ways that promote personal growth. They encourage us to learn, grow, and develop new perspectives, which are essential components of our emotional maturity. Additionally, our social connections act as a buffer against the stressors of life, helping to prevent or mitigate the effects of depression and other mental health issues.

By investing time in nurturing these social connections through various recreational activities, we can significantly enhance our emotional well-being. The efforts we put into building and maintaining these relationships pay off by enriching our lives with support, happiness, and opportunities for personal development.

We teach don't prioritize by ranking, but integrate all your interests to fulfill your life needs. So, how can you actively cultivate your emotional wellness?

Prioritize Physical Activity: Find an exercise routine you enjoy and stick to it. Remember, it's not just about physical fitness, it's an investment in your emotional well-being.

Practice Mindfulness: Take time each day to check in with yourself. How are you feeling? What do you need?

Nurture Social Connections: Make time for friends and family. Engage in social activities that bring you joy.

Seek Support When Needed: Don't hesitate to reach out for help, whether it's to a friend, family member, or professional.

Invest in Self-Care: This could be as simple as taking a relaxing bath, reading a book, or pursuing a hobby you love.

Ensure Quality Sleep: Prioritize getting enough restful sleep each night. It's crucial for emotional regulation and cognitive function.

A Holistic Approach

Remember, emotional wellness isn't about achieving perfection. It's about creating a balanced, fulfilling life that supports your psychological and emotional needs. By investing time and effort into physical fitness, spiritual well-being, and social connections, you're laying the groundwork for strong emotional health.

The Work-Life Connection

Most of us spend a significant portion of our lives at work. It's no surprise, then, that our job satisfaction plays a crucial role in our overall emotional well-being. But here's the twist: it's not just about what happens at work.

The 30-Point Scale: A Window into Our Emotional State

Imagine a simple exercise: rate yourself on a scale from 1 to 10 in three crucial areas of life:

1. Time spent on hobbies.
2. Spiritual pursuits.
3. Community service.

With a perfect score totaling 30 points, this activity offers a quick snapshot of our emotional landscape. Surprisingly, many people tend to be harsh critics of themselves, rarely scoring above a 5 or 7 in each category.

But here's where it gets interesting: those rare individuals who confidently rated themselves a perfect ten across the board showed an outstanding transformation. Not only were they emotionally content, but they also brought that happiness into their workplace.

This revelation paints a clear picture. People who invest time in self-awareness, self-esteem, and emotional growth don't just feel better, they perform better. They arrive at work with a positive mindset and leave with the same energy, creating a virtuous cycle of happiness and productivity.

The key takeaway is to navigate life's challenges, be it parenting, work stress, or difficult situations, we must prioritize our physical and mental well-being. It's not just about surviving; it's about thriving.

The Domino Effect

Imagine your life as a series of dominoes, where the fall of one influences all the others that follow. Poor physical health can lead to low energy at work, which often results in subpar performance. This underperformance can cause feelings of disconnection and dissatisfaction, and these negative feelings often follow us home, affecting our personal lives.

But here's the good news: this domino effect works in reverse, too! When we take care of our physical, spiritual, and social well-being, we're more likely to feel connected and perform well at work. This positive performance boosts our mood, creating a cycle of well-being that benefits all aspects of our lives.

The Power of Anticipation

Have you ever noticed how excited you feel when planning a vacation? That feeling of anticipation is a powerful mood booster. Now, imagine harnessing that power in your everyday life.

When you schedule activities you enjoy on your calendar, you're doing much more than just planning an event; you're actually crafting multiple moments of joy.

This process begins with the excitement you feel when you first schedule the activity. Following this initial thrill, there's a period of anticipation leading up to the event, which can be just as enjoyable. Then, of course, there's the pleasure of the activity itself.

After it concludes, you're left with positive memories to savor. This underscores why hobbies and interests are so vital for our emotional well-being. They provide something to look forward to, breaking the monotony of our daily routines and infusing our lives with excitement.

Expressing Yourself Through Hobbies

Imagine the satisfaction of preparing a delicious meal, the joy of strumming a guitar, or the pride in completing a painting. These are more than just pastimes, and they're vital outlets for our emotions and expressions of our inner selves. Hobbies aren't just fun; they're powerful tools for managing stress and improving emotional health.

Engaging in activities you enjoy helps reduce stress hormones in your body, while learning and improving a skill boosts self-esteem and confidence. Many hobbies provide opportunities to meet like-minded people, fostering new friendships and social connections. The focus required by hobbies offers a break from worries and promotes mindfulness while completing a project or reaching a goal, giving a sense of accomplishment.

Engaging in a hobby after work helps you switch hats and disconnect from job-related stress, providing a much-needed mental break. Doing something you love can rejuvenate you for the next workday, renewing your energy and enthusiasm. Perhaps most importantly, hobbies remind us that we're more than our job titles, contributing to a strong sense of identity beyond our professional lives.

Engaging Your Mind

While we often turn to our phones for quick mental stimulation, there's a world of brain-boosting activities waiting to be explored. Engaging in activities such as solving puzzles, reading books, or learning a new language comes with significant cognitive benefits. These activities are not only enjoyable but also serve to keep your mind active, thereby improving cognitive function overall. They are instrumental in enhancing mental agility, which is crucial for keeping the brain sharp and efficient.

Moreover, the process of learning new skills is associated with memory enhancement, helping to maintain and even improve memory over time. Additionally, such tasks have the added benefit of increasing focus and concentration, enabling you to concentrate for longer periods without succumbing to distractions.

However, it's crucial to find a balance. While digital puzzles and games can be beneficial and offer convenience, they shouldn't replace hands-on activities or social interactions entirely. It's important to ensure that digital entertainment does not monopolize your time or prevent you from engaging in activities that stimulate your senses in the real world.

Finding the Right Balance

To achieve a healthy balance, setting time limits on digital activities can be effective in preventing overuse. Allocating specific times for these activities ensures that they do not encroach on time that could be spent on more enriching experiences.

Additionally, diversifying your hobbies to include both digital and non-digital activities can lead to a more well-rounded approach to cognitive stimulation and personal enjoyment. Engaging your senses through hobbies that involve touch, movement, and real-world interaction can provide a more immersive and beneficial experience, contributing to both mental and physical well-being.

Recreation:

Recreation isn't just about having fun (although that's a big part of it!). It's about rejuvenation, personal growth, and community connection.

Exploring Special Interest Classes

Many communities offer a wealth of recreational opportunities through parks and recreation departments. When we talk about recreation, we often talk about "special interests," activities people pursue purely out of passion or curiosity. These can range from art classes and dance lessons to cooking workshops and beyond. These "special interest" classes can be a gateway to new passions and skills:

Music Lessons: Learn to play an instrument or improve your singing.

Art Classes: Try your hand at painting, sculpture, or photography.

Language Courses: Start learning a new language.

Sports and Fitness: Discover new ways to stay active and healthy.

Don't hesitate to reach out to your local parks and recreation department to explore what's available in your area.

There's something magical about being a beginner. When you start a new hobby, you just naturally open yourself to new experiences, challenge your brain, promote cognitive health, meet new people who share your interests, and discover your hidden talents and passions.

It's not about being the best. It's about the joy of the journey, the thrill of creating, and the satisfaction of progress.

Practical Steps to Incorporate Hobbies into Your Life

1. **Explore Your Interests**: Make a list of activities you've always wanted to try.
2. **Start Small**: Begin with short, manageable commitments.

3. **Schedule It**: Put your hobby time on your calendar, just like any other important appointment.
4. **Join a Group**: Look for local clubs or online communities related to your interests.
5. **Be Patient**: Remember, the goal is enjoyment, not perfection.

As you incorporate more enjoyable activities into your life, you'll likely notice positive changes. You may find yourself with increased energy and enthusiasm at work, experiencing an improved mood and a more optimistic outlook on life. Such changes can also lead to better resilience when facing stress, stronger social connections, and a more balanced and fulfilling life.

Shifting Focus: From Stress to Service

Remember the last election cycle that had you stressed? Here's an idea: channel that energy into community service instead of getting caught up in political arguments. By focusing on helping others, you can gain perspective on your own challenges, connect with people outside your usual social circle, make a tangible difference in your community and boost your emotional well-being.

Volunteering

It is a mutually beneficial activity that significantly impacts emotional well-being and fosters community connection. When you decide to volunteer, you're embarking on a journey that not only aids others but also enriches your life.

Volunteering imbues your life with a sense of purpose, offering a meaningful way to give back to society. It's an endeavor that can elevate your self-esteem, as knowing you're making a tangible difference enhances your sense of self-worth. Through volunteering, you're likely to encounter like-minded individuals, thereby expanding your social connections with those who share your values.

Additionally, many volunteering opportunities are avenues for learning and practicing new skills, contributing to your personal and professional growth. Beyond these benefits, volunteering helps in building emotional resilience. Engaging in acts of kindness and support can lend perspective to your own challenges, making them seem more manageable.

Creative Community Projects

Food Sculpture Competition: Imagine your neighborhood coming alive with creative food sculptures, knowing that all that food will be donated to charity. It's fun, it's creative, and it makes a real difference.

Corporate Clean-up Challenges: Turn community service into a team-building activity. Cleaning up a neighborhood becomes an exciting competition when done with colleagues.

Board Memberships: Joining a non-profit board can teach you about governance, event planning, and leadership.

Mentoring Programs: Guiding students through college not only helps them but also sharpens your coaching and communication skills.

Event Organization: Planning charity events can improve your project management and teamwork abilities.

These projects do more than just help the community; they create shared experiences, foster connections, and inject a sense of fun and purpose into our lives.

Emotional Intelligence (EQ)

While we've long recognized the importance of IQ, there's a growing awareness of its equally crucial counterpart: EQ, or emotional intelligence. EQ encompasses:

Self-awareness: Understanding your own emotions and triggers.

Social awareness: Recognizing and responding appropriately to others' feelings.

Self-management: Controlling your emotional reactions.

Relationship management: Using emotional understanding to build strong connections.

Developing your EQ isn't just about expressing yourself better, it's about cultivating a deep understanding of your inner emotional landscape and using that knowledge to navigate the world more effectively.

At its core, emotional well-being isn't about putting on a show for others. It's about finding contentment in your choices and actions, regardless of external opinions. When you're at peace with yourself, you become resilient to life's ups and downs.

This doesn't mean ignoring others' feelings or perspectives. Instead, it's about building a strong emotional foundation that allows you to engage with the world authentically and confidently.

The Communication Conundrum

In today's fast-paced work environments, a silent epidemic is brewing: emotional distress caused by poor communication. Many employees go through their workday unaware of the toll that unexpressed thoughts and feelings take on their well-being. They find themselves in a paradox:

Speak up and risk feeling awkward or facing repercussions,

Or,

Stay silent and suffer internal chaos.

Neither option seems ideal, yet the cost of silence often outweighs the discomfort of speaking up. True emotional fitness empowers you to bear the consequences of truth-telling, recognizing that the alternative, bottling up your thoughts and feelings can be far more detrimental in the long run. Check out our book "Fun At Work" for tips and strategies to improve communication and build engaging teams.

However, emotional fitness isn't about unleashing every thought that crosses your mind. It's about developing the wisdom to know when to speak up, how to express yourself effectively, and when it's better to hold your peace. This discernment is a crucial skill that can transform workplace dynamics and personal relationships alike.

Imagine this scenario: You're part of a team tasked with building a 7.5-foot-tall structure using Tinker Toys in just five minutes. The pressure is on, the clock is ticking, and emotions are running high. Some teams triumph, while others falter.

This exercise brilliantly illustrates the interplay of emotions in high-stress situations:

Success and Satisfaction: Teams that complete the challenge often report a sense of fun and accomplishment. Their emotional state is sustained by their success.

Frustration and Disappointment: Teams that fail to meet the deadline may experience negative emotions, feeling that the lack of time made the task unenjoyable.

But what's truly important is what happens during the challenge:

How do team members communicate under pressure?

Who takes the lead, and how do others respond?

How does the team handle setbacks or disagreements?

These micro-interactions are a microcosm of everyday workplace dynamics, offering valuable insights into emotional fitness and team cohesion.

As you reflect on your own emotional fitness, consider:

1. *How would you rate yourself on the 30-point scale?*
2. *What areas of your emotional intelligence could use some strengthening?*
3. *Are you making time for activities that truly recharge you emotionally?*

Putting It All Together: Your Action Plan

1. **Explore New Hobbies**: Try out different activities until you find ones that resonate with you.
2. **Check Local Resources**: Look into classes and programs offered by your local parks and recreation department.
3. **Set Aside "Me Time"**: Schedule regular time for your hobbies and interests.
4. **Find a Volunteer Opportunity**: Look for causes that align with your values and interests.
5. **Practice Self-Awareness**: Regularly check in with your emotions. How do you feel during different work situations?

6. **Develop Communication Skills**: Learn to express your thoughts and feelings clearly and respectfully.
7. **Cultivate Emotional Resilience**: Build your capacity to bounce back from setbacks and handle stress effectively.
8. **Foster a Supportive Environment**: Encourage open dialogue in your workplace. Be the change you wish to see.
9. **Seek Balance**: Recognize when to speak up and when to step back. Wisdom often lies in this balance.
10. **Reflect and Adjust**: Regularly assess how your activities contribute to your emotional well-being and make adjustments as needed.

Prioritize your emotional fitness and invest in yourself.

Now, take some time to reflect on the following:

What did I learn?

____

____

____

____

____

____

____

What do I want to do?

Chapter 8: Filling Your Wellness Tank "Game Plan"

"Energize all four areas of wellness, and your batteries will stay charged."

As we conclude the book, I want to share a story with you a story of recreation, connection, and the simple joys of human interaction .

It's the 1970s in Scottsdale, Arizona. The sun is setting, casting a warm glow over the parks where people gather to play. Softball bats crack, volleyballs soar, and the squeak of tennis shoes on basketball courts fills the air.

As a young coordinator for the Parks and Recreation Sports Leagues, I witnessed something beautiful at those places. People didn't just come to play; they came to connect. After the last point was scored or the final inning played, they'd gather at a local pub or grab ice cream with their families.

These weren't just games; they were the ways people used to interact and connect with the community they used to live in.

But as the years rolled by, things changed. The 90s brought a technological revolution and, with it, a new pace of life. Suddenly, everyone was in a hurry. The post-game celebrations became rarer. People would play, then rush off to their next appointment, their next screen, their next distraction. The emotion of making time to play, let alone celebrate, became a challenge in itself.

Curious about what we were losing, I hopped on a journey to Ireland. I wanted to explore the roots of pub culture and understand what made these gathering places so special. What I discovered was eye-opening.

In small Irish towns, pubs weren't just places to grab a pint. They were the beating heart of the community. News was shared, stories were told, and friendships were formed over pints of Guinness and hearty laughter. It was a total opposite of what I'd been seeing back home.

But it wasn't just about the pubs. Everywhere we went in Ireland, hotels, restaurants, shops, people treated each other with a kindness that had become rare in America. It was refreshing, a reminder of what we'd been missing.

As I reflect on my 50-year career in recreation and hospitality, I can't help but think we've lost something precious. We've sacrificed our emotional "tanks," our social connections, and even our physical fitness in our rush to keep up with the digital world.

So, here's my advice to you, dear reader: Stop. Take a breath. Make time for fun. Fill your emotional tank. Find your PUB, People Uniting Better, in recreation time together. Connect with people face-to-face, not just through a screen. Keep fit, not just for your body, but for your mind and spirit too.

The most important app you'll ever need is the one that connects you to the people around you. Nowadays, every moment seems accounted for, and the concept of "finding time" for yourself might seem like a luxury.

But what if it's not just a luxury but a necessity? What if those moments you carve out for yourself are the foundation of a well-lived life?

Your mission, should you choose to accept it, is to "Find Your Pub." But don't worry, we're not talking about drowning your sorrows in a dimly lit bar. We're talking about discovering a recreational experience that ignites your passion and connects you with like-minded individuals.

Imagine a group of people, flushed and sweaty, laughing as they cross the finish line. They've just completed an "earn your beer or ice cream" run.

The motto was to "Just go recreate." It's not about the reward at the end but the joy of movement, the thrill of challenge, and the warmth of shared experience. This is what finding your pub is all about.

In an increasingly divided society, where children wear shirts targeting political figures, it's crucial to find common ground. Your pub isn't about politics or differences; it's about unity, fun, and shared interests.

It's about volunteering, playing, and enjoying life together. It's about filling up your emotional tank, not with anger or hatred but with joy and connection.

So, how do we make this happen? Enter your game plan:

Find Time. Make Time. Invest in Yourself.

Just by carving out just 16 hours a week. That's less than 10% of your time to invest in yourself. It's easy to forget that you are your most valuable asset, but your well-being isn't a luxury; it's a necessity. It's the foundation upon which everything else in your life is built.

Let's break down this art of self-investment into three simple yet powerful steps:

Find Time

It's out there, hiding in plain sight. Maybe it's that hour you spend scrolling through social media or that TV show you watch out of habit rather than enjoyment. Your well-being is as crucial as any meeting or deadline. Treat it with the same respect. Cut through the noise of unnecessary obligations and distractions. Your time is precious, so allocate it wisely.

Make Time

This is where intention meets action. Don't wait for the perfect moment to focus on your well-being, create it. Block off those hours in your calendar. Treat them as non-negotiable appointments with yourself.

Invest in Yourself

Here's where the magic happens. When you dedicate 16 hours a week, just under 10% of your time to nurturing your body, mind, and soul, you're not just spending time. You're investing in a future version of yourself that's more resilient, focused, and connected. The dividends are healthier, more balanced, and energize you.

These 16 hours are your opportunity to nurture the four pillars of your well-being:

Physical

Let's zoom in on one aspect of this self-investment: Physical Well-being. Your body is your lifelong companion, the vessel that carries you through every experience. Here's how you can invest 4 hours a week in its care:

- **1 hour of Cardio:** Get that heart pumping! Whether it's a run in the park, a cycling session, or a swim, this is your time to boost endurance and heart health.
- **1 hour of Strength Training:** Build those muscles, strengthen those bones. Weights, resistance bands, or your own body weight. The choice is yours.
- **1 hour of Flexibility and Mobility:** Stretch it out. Yoga, Pilates, or a good old-fashioned stretching session will keep you limber and prevent injuries.

- **1 hour of Outdoor Activities:** Connect with nature while staying active. Hike a trail, join a sports team, or simply enjoy a recreational activity in the fresh air.

This isn't just about looking good; it's about feeling good, having the energy to pursue your passions, and building a strong foundation for everything else in your life.

Move your body. Join a sports league, take dance classes, or simply go for walks in nature.

Spiritual

Spiritual well-being isn't necessarily about religion, it's about finding meaning, purpose, and inner peace. Here's how you can invest 4 hours a week in your spiritual growth:

- **1 hour of meditation or mindfulness:** Calm your mind, center yourself, and cultivate inner peace.
- **1 hour of inspirational reading or reflection:** Gain wisdom and insight from spiritual texts or thought-provoking books.
- **1 hour in nature:** Take a walk, sit quietly in a park, and reconnect with the world around you.
- **1 hour of community connection:** Attend a service, join a group meditation, or participate in a spiritual event.

Feed your soul. Meditate, practice yoga, or engage in whatever activities bring you peace and purpose.

Social

As humans, we thrive on social connections. Here's how to invest 4 hours a week in your social well-being:

- **2 hours of group recreation:** Whether it's hiking, playing sports, or board games, shared activities strengthen bonds.
- **1 hour of social meals:** Share a meal with friends, colleagues, or loved ones. Nourish your relationships as you nourish your body.
- **1 hour of community involvement:** Volunteer or participate in community events to connect with others through shared purpose.

Connect with others. Join clubs, volunteer, or organize game nights with friends.

Emotional

Emotional health is the foundation of resilience and happiness. Invest 4 hours a week in your emotional well-being:

- **1 hour of journaling or emotional check-ins:** Reflect on your feelings and experiences.
- **1 hour of therapy, coaching, or self-care:** Seek professional help if needed or engage in activities that bring you peace.

- **1 hour of creative expression:** Use art, music, or writing to release emotions and foster personal growth.
- **1 hour of relaxation techniques:** Practice breathing exercises, take a soothing bath, or listen to calming music.

Nurture your feelings. Practice self-care, engage in creative activities, or seek therapy if needed.

The Power of 16

In a world that often seems designed to drain us, it's up to us to find ways to replenish ourselves. By dedicating just 16 hours a week, 4 hours each, to physical, spiritual, social, and emotional well-being, you're not just investing time. You're investing in a more balanced, energized, and fulfilled version of yourself.

This isn't about drastic lifestyle changes. It's about small, consistent steps. It's about finding time in the nooks and crannies of your week. It's about making that time sacred. And most importantly, it's about investing in the most important asset you have, yourself.

Be patient with yourself. Some weeks, you might hit all 16 hours. Other weeks, life might get in the way. That's okay. *The goal isn't perfection, it's progress.*

So, are you ready to find your special interest friends?

Are you ready to invest in yourself?

It's time to park your worries and recreate the art of human connection through fun.

Remember our key points:

- A Body in motion stays in motion, while a body at rest stays at rest. Energize your Physical Self.
- Shared time with others in activities completes your need for friendship and fun.
- Don't prioritize or rank your life, integrate and pursue your interests equally as you do your profession.
- Get an accountability partner or friends to share your successes.
- You have 168 hours in a week, invest 16 hours into the areas we have shared to fill up your wellness tank.

Todd & Marsha Davis

Fun Coach USA

Now, take some time to reflect on the following:

What did I learn?

____

____

____

____

____

What do I want to do?

Made in the USA
Coppell, TX
02 March 2026

72759732R00069